SERPENT IN PARADISE

Harry walked to the blood stain and the scorched wall. IT was something capable of illuminating a room and slicing into a wall. Anson must have backed up, retreated hastily from the doorway. IT fired. Blood. Scorchmarks. The end of Anson Young.

Harry had witnessed a murder. A murder wherein the murderer is unknown, the murder weapon is unknown, and the murder victim is not to be found.

Then, the doorknob began to rattle and Harry Porter froze . . .

THE PARADISE PLOT

ED NAHA

BANTAM BOOKS
TORONTO • NEW YORK • LONDON

THE PARADISE PLOT
A Bantam Book / November 1980

ISBN 0-553-13979-7

Published simultaneously in the United States and Canada

Bantam Books are published by Bantam Books, Inc. Its trademark, consisting of the words "Bantam Books" and the portrayal of a bantam, is Registered in U.S. Patent and Trademark
Office and in other countries. Marca Registrada. Bantam
Books, Inc., 666 Fifth Avenue, New York, New York 10103.

PRINTED IN THE UNITED STATES OF AMERICA

0 9 8 7 6 5 4 3 2 1

For the pep squad:
(*in order of appearance*)
Pat, Sydny, Joyce, and Robin

THE PARADISE PLOT

PART ONE

"Civilization begins at home."
—Henry James

1

The hotel room was small, hardly bigger than a closet. One soot-covered window allowed a slim trickle of light into the darkness before him. The sunbeams reflected off the gun muzzle across the room.

Within seconds, he could be a dead man.

Then again . . . A chain of dim memories began to flicker to life.

"Hope is the thing with feathers that perches in the soul . . . " Emily Dickinson.

Ethereal stuff.

"He that lives upon hope will die fasting."

Trust old Ben Franklin to put things in their proper perspective.

A strand of drab brown hair fell over one eye. Had he been more athletic in nature, he probably could have avoided all this. His body was stocky, but not hard, fluid without being muscular. Hell, he had always meant to start doing those push-ups and sit-ups in the morning. It was too late now.

Harry Porter gazed at the pistol aimed at his head. "There's no need to point that at me," he offered nervously. "I'm not going anywhere."

His back pushed against the wall of the vacant room,

Harry lapsed into one of his famous boyish grins, designed to dissipate any and all tension within a five-mile radius.

On some days, such as today, it proved less effective than on others. Harry stifled a sigh of anguish.

You do the best you can.

The disheveled figure across the room continued to clutch the plastic handle of the laser gun firmly. An ordinary man wielding extraordinary power. Eyes bulging, sparse hair matted with sweat, the diminutive man in the rumpled blue suit shifted his weight from one foot to another in an agitated, deliberate rhythm.

"No, you're not going anywhere," the pig-faced gunman wheezed. "Point of fact. But I'm not putting down the pistol, either. Another fact to consider. In the meantime, Mr. Porter, do be seated."

Not wishing to become a statistic at the age of thirty-four, Harry slowly slid down the side of the wall; squatting on the dusty floor in a semi-sitting position so as not to soil his only suit

If he survived, he wanted to survive neatly.

The gunman before him continued to sway gently, like a runted weed in the breeze. "It was nice of you to meet me here," he commented in a high, nasal tone.

Harry attempted a friendly attitude. "No trouble. You knew I couldn't resist."

"Ah yes, my note," the gunman laughed. "Quite a melo-dramatic touch, wasn't it?"

Harry grimaced, sending his mouth into an unexpected spasm. He could kick himself for falling for such a simple trick. Paying attention to a confession note penned by a madman. He caught himself mid-thought, rearranging his countenance into a state of calm. No need to aggravate this fellow any more than he had to . . .

The gunman, sensing Harry's mental plight, attemped to soothe his nerves with a charming giggle. What emerged from his lips was a thin, hyenalike whine. The tension was getting to both of them. "It *was* a rather primitive move, I admit. But I knew, being the emotional type you are, that you couldn't resist."

To hell with the suit. Harry slumped down onto the floor, shrugging his shoulders in acknowledgment of the gunman's superior logic. He could see the headlines now: REPORTER KILLED—MOTH GALLOPS TO FLAME.

The killer grew serious. "I've been reading what you've

2

been saying about me in print," he whispered reverently. "I've enjoyed your work immensely."

Harry wasn't sure he was hearing correctly. He had run across some real loons in his time, but this guy was a real prize. A 51-card special. Not quite a full deck. "Uh, thank you."

"No really," the gunman enthused. "Good writing is all but a lost art form these days. Everything is so video-oriented, geared toward larger-than-life imagery."

Harry's mouth began to twitch.

"Yet, using mere words, you managed to effectively portray a series of senseless, bloodthirsty crimes in a very realistic and incisive manner. Quite touching, really. You've described the victims' lives as well as their subsequent deaths. And, although it's very factually oriented, there's an almost permeating poetic sense of futility, of needless loss. It's made for spellbinding reading, I assure you. I admire your talent, Mr. Porter. My hat is off to you."

Harry ran a finger across the bridge of his nose, ensnaring a droplet of sweat. A lame grin affixed itself to his lips. One flick of that trigger and his entire head would resemble a leftover portion of rice pudding. "I'm flattered," he managed to say.

The gunman accelerated his pacing, raising and lowering his feet so rapidly he resembled a bear cub jogging in place. "The only element lacking in your stories, through no fault of your own I might add, is motive. Why?"

The stout little man stopped his pacing momentarily and gazed intensely into Harrys eyes. "Why did he do it?"

Harry watched the man begin his danse macabre once more. "I mean, why did *I* do it? What motivates a man to go around and fry the heads off so many innocent people? Am I crazy?"

The cherubic killer chuckled to himself, his features contorting into a jack-o'-lantern relief. "Well, that goes without saying, I suppose. However, I think you should know, Mr. Porter, that, up until the time of my first killing, I was considered quite normal. As typical a citizen as anyone. As typical as you, Mr. Porter, and just as bored . . ."

Harry flinched. "I don't understand."

The little man began to tremble, his voice quaking with pent-up emotion. "I said I was bored, Mr. Porter. That's all. I killed all those people because I was bored stiff. Period."

Harry watched the man become unhinged. He mentally

3

calculated the distance between his feet and the room's only door. It was about five yards. Five yards with a laser barrel in between. No good. The only fights Harry ever won were the kinds where he was holding a chair and the other guy wasn't. His mind sagged back into desperation; back to square one.

The killer noted Harry's silence. "Disappointed?" he asked with genuine regret.

"Uh, no. Just surprised," Harry hastily clarified.

"Well," the killer said sadly. "That's the *real* world for you. No sense of glamour whatsoever. No voices from beyond taunted me into committing the perfect crime. I wasn't angry at the world. There weren't even any bizarre sex angles. I love my wife and I don't fantasize about my parents. I was simply overcome by ennui."

The killer's already high-pitched whine suddenly leaped to air-raid siren status. Tears dribbled down his cheeks. "I wanted to experience passion! Fear! Rage! Exaltation!"

Harry watched the gun tremble with each new outburst. "I was tired of the proscribed amusements: the varieties, the holography emporiums, the tranx bars. Artificial annoyances. I wanted to taste life . . . real life. The way life used to be. I chose to do that by doling out death. Granted, this was an extreme solution to my problem, but not a totally irrational one."

The killer's eyes took on a glassy, far-away look. "To pick a living, breathing, subject. To stalk it. And then, to make it stop living, stop breathing . . . stop . . . period."

The little man ran his tongue along his lower lip. "Have you any idea of the *power* involved in that? I will freely admit that the killings excited me. But they excited you, too, didn't they, Mr. Porter?"

Harry regarded the pistol with the utmost respect. "I'm afraid you've lost me there, Mr . . ."

"Call me the Lasergun Killer," the man beamed proudly. "Everybody does these days. No, of course, you won't admit that my handiwork thrilled you. But I sensed it in your prose. My adventures brought out the best in you.

"They gave you a sense of kineticism, of movement, of purpose; a sense of life even in death. It was a change of pace from the usual garbage you people are forced to cover day after day. It was a glimpse of life's underside. Thrilling, was it not?"

Harry swallowed hard. He hated even to consider it, but there was some truth in what this maniac said. On the trail of

4

the killer, he had experienced a certain sense of adventure. He was the hound in search of the fox. Holmes on the trail of Moriarity. Harry squelched the thought. He was nauseated by the idea.

The gunman caught the puzzled expression on his captive audience and stroked his gun good-naturedly. "Aha. See? We *do* understand each other. Well, that's why I called you here. Your epic story needed a logical ending, a noteworthy denouement. And now that we have finally met and cleared up this turgid mystery, I bid you farewell, Mr. Porter . . ."

Harry's jaw dropped open with a crack as he watched the gunman slowly raise the pistol to his mouth. Harry scrambled to his feet, attempting to halt the inevitable. His body reacted sluggishly. His movement proved slow. The little man sighed and squeezed the trigger.

"No." Harry screamed.

The room was filled with a sudden, bright light. Harry threw his arms in front of his face instinctively.

"Wake up, Harry."

"NO."

Pieces of semisolid matter splattered against his shirt. The air around him grew putrid, ripe with decay.

"Harry, this is your second call. Wake up, Harry."

His knees began to buckle. He fell to the ground, twitching. Harry was surprised to find the floor so soft, so yielding. He pulled the sheet over his head, burying his face in the pillow. "No," he mumbled.

"I really must insist," the female voice droned. "You gave me precise instructions."

Harry's hand shot out from underneath the bedcovers and slammed the rectangular computer alarm "off." He opened his eyes and stared at the night table.

The gunman was gone.

Harry moved his head slowly from side to side. He was in a room. A yellow room. Surrounded by *things*. A small bureau with an oval electric mirror. Wall-sized TV unit. Quad speakers nestled in each corner. Circular closet. Microfilm viewer. Antique bookcase.

Jesus. He was home. His body gradually began to relax. Home. Harry reached out a hand to the other pillow. Time to wake up Anne. His fingers caressed a mound of rumpled blanket. Oops. A little bit of time distortion there. Anne was past tense. He'd get his history sorted out eventually.

He picked up his bedclothes and took stock of what was

sprawled underneath. A male body. Five ten or so. Normal build. A little flabby around the middle. Yeah, that was still Harry Porter underneath there.

Alive and well and at home.

And unable to think straight for more than ten seconds without some interruption. "Shutting down that terminal will not alter the situation," Harry's home computer system pointed out from an insidiously placed wall speaker above the headboard. "You left precise instructions . . ."

Harry cursed the day he had been talked into getting one of these units. Supposed to ease the pain of unexpected bachelorhood. Female voice and everything. He would rather have had a dog. He tumbled out of bed, the omnipresent voice nagging all the while. Harry faced the wall. "Fuck you, Machine."

The computer seemed to sputter for a millisecond. "A biologically impossible coupling, Mister Porter. As a journalist of some alleged merit, you should be fully aware of the shortcomings of the constant use of . . ."

"Please don't go into your 'colloquialism' song and dance this early in the morning," Harry pleaded.

"Garbage in equals garbage out," the unit replied somewhat smugly.

"I'm tired, Machine," Harry sighed. "Get the coffee ready while I take a shower, OK?" Porter traipsed into the bathroom. He'd start those push-ups and sit-ups tomorrow. God, how he hated that unit. It was like have an omniscient maiden aunt in your home. He called it "Machine" out of sheer malevolence. Let other dummies be tricked into giving their units human names and qualities.

The Machine wasn't a person.

It wasn't a pal.

It wasn't a wife.

It was a pain in the neck. An annoying assemblage of nuts and bolts. The latest bit of hardware foisted onto an unsuspecting public by those "better living through science" sadists. Artificial intelligence. Hah! Through the use of the moniker "Machine," Harry could effectively reduce the intricate computer to pencil sharpener status with the flick of his lip. Still, it *was* quite a device and it was amazing how fast the damned thing had been hooked into his household. The modifications hadn't taken more than a few weeks. It was all done while he was . . . away.

Harry stepped into the shower stall and shuddered, suddenly recalling the clammy sweat he had felt while facing the killer. He had hoped those dreams would have ended in the hospital. God knows they had ESPed him enough in there. Goddamn parapsychs, prying into every corner of his mind.

They had discharged him from the hospital two weeks ago. A new man. His mind, however, apparently wasn't aware of the trade-in. Same old dreams. He wondered how long he'd be seeing that little shmuck every time he closed his eyes.

Stepping from the shower, he paused for a moment at the bay window of his bedroom. Outside, life plodded onward. People jammed both the manual and automated sidewalks on their way to work. Subways, monotrams and crosstown shuttles sent them zipping off to various canyons of Manhattan.

Across the street, looming over a solitary, sickly tree, a titanic billboard advertised the latest advance in TVdom. A buxom blonde huddled next to the biggest wall unit yet... a twenty footer. "The bigger it is, the better I like it" was the catchy slogan that some advertising executive was paid $100,000 plus per year to come up with.

A real class act.

Harry stumbled into the kitchen where Machine had carefully brewed a cup of lethal coffee.

"Paper here?" Harry asked the wall.

"Not yet."

"What's today's big news?"

"Why don't you turn on the Newsat Ticker?"

"Because I *hate* the Newsat Ticker," Harry blurted, immediately feeling foolish at betraying his anger. What did Machine know? "It's a matter of principle," he explained.

"The Ticker has done you no harm."

"No," Harry answered. "But the fleet of lousy news satellites—which supplies your beloved Ticker with all of its headlines—nearly put yours truly out of a job. Without a job, yours truly cannot afford to keep an expensive Machine, such as yourself, wallowing in 3-in-1 oil."

Harry sat down at the breakfast bar and clutched his cup of coffee. He had a headache already. "Now, before I savage you with a screwdriver," he said sweetly, "will you please run down today's top news stories?"

Machine made a noise Harry would have sworn was a grunt of exasperation. "There was a fire at a Dallas tranx bar last night. Sixteen sedated patrons perished..."

"Cheerful."

"Scientists have discovered a cure for reefer lip..."

"Noble."

"The block-long microwave oven complex at Hamburgerland blew its doors today. The NRC says that none of the 50,000 patrons were effected by the radiation leakage."

"Did the hamburgers survive?"

"And the President is sending up an advisory Committee to *Island One* for its Tenth Anniversary Celebration."

Harry put his coffee down. "Jeez. It's been up there ten years already? Our all perfect *Island* ... the city in the sky. Titanic waste of ..."

"*Island One* is not a city per se," Machine interrupted. "It's the world's first and only space habitat and, as such ..."

"In your ear," Harry grunted.

"As I began to explain before," the unit dutifully informed him, "your continuous use of colloquial ..."

"Up your gears!" Harry shouted, not to be intimidated by a bodiless voice. "And another thing ... your coffee stinks! Who programmed you, Lucrezia Borgia? This is swill!" Harry held up the cup for the wall to "see."

"Fabricator," the computer replied. "As you continue your senseless monologue, please take note of the package that arrived for you while you were asleep. Had you awakened at the correct time ..."

Harry ran his fingers through his mop of thinning hair. A few strands came loose in his fingers. Goddamn it. On top of everything else now he had to worry about going bald! It was going to be one of those days. Maybe even one of those months ... or years! "Where's the package, dear heart," he cooed, attempting to calm himself.

"Two and a half feet to the right of your coffee cup and saucer."

For the first time since sitting at the counter, Harry noticed a small parcel covered with brown paper and sealed with old-fashioned nylon twine. "I thought it was your idea of a biscuit," he mumbled.

Taking the bundle in his hand, Harry promptly shredded the wrapper and ripped apart the twine. "Nuts," he blurted, viewing the contents with obvious disdain.

"Bad news?" Machine inquired.

"What else?" Harry sighed. He let the package's contents drop back down onto the counter and returned to his coffee. Atop the torn wrapping rested a small pamphlet with a note taped to the outside front flap.

"May I see it?" Machine inquired.

8

"Sure," Harry said, holding the book up for Machine's kitchen video eye.

The camera lens focused on the object, Machine reading its title aloud: "WEL-COME TO IS-LAND ONE."

"Now why would anyone send me this stupid thing?" Harry complained, already knowing the answer and attempting to ignore the enclosed note.

2

WELCOME TO *ISLAND* ONE

Dear Visitor,

Welcome to *Island One,* humanity's first habitat in space. Currently celebrating its tenth anniversary, *Island* represents humankind's boldest reach into the heavens to date. We hope you will enjoy your stay and we hope this pamphlet answers any and all questions you may have about our habitat.

WHAT SHOULD I KNOW ABOUT *ISLAND'S* HISTORY?

The space colony (or space habitat as Islanders prefer to call it) of *Island One* has a long and interesting history. Originally planned in the late 1980s, *Island* took some fifteen years to become a reality. Initially, NASA, on Earth, was allotted funds for the construction of the first attempted Moon-mining base; a base essential to *Island*'s eventual existence. After a short period of time, a Moon operation was successfully established and minerals were dug up that would soon serve as the groundwork for *Island* construction.

Once the Moon-mining camp and two small construction "shacks" (space factories) near the actual future site of the habitat were in working order, the minerals were shipped out from the Moon. The Moon rocks were actually catapulted from the Moon's surface via an electromagnetic track-launcher (or slingshot, if you prefer) called a "mass driver." The material was sent hurtling to a point in space called "Lagrange 2" or "L2" (dubbed after the eighteenth-century mathematician/astronomer Joseph Lewis Lagrange ... known as just "L" to his present-day spacefaring friends) where it was caught by a large space net or "catcher's mitt." The Moon rocks were then towed by space tug to a sector called "L5" and the colony was constructed via the use of the already established shacks.

HOW DOES ISLAND WORK?

Island is a complex, yet simple structure to understand. Located in the L5 area of space, it gravitationally "orbits" at æ point the same distance from the Earth as from the Moon. The habitat itself is composed of two large cylinders; each 1,000 meters long and 200 meters wide. These cylinders are constructed parallel to each other and always face the sun (our most precious supplier of energy). At one end, the two cylinders are connected by a cable under tension and, at the other, a tower under compression. Viewed from a distance, *Island* resembles two very long sunflowers. At the far end of the *Island*, cylinders sprout the "flowers'" petals ... a series of elongated mirrors.

Sunlight for our habitat's interior comes from the three flat "petal" mirrors hinged from the base of each cylinder. Controlled by our power station, these mirrors reflect the sun into our paradise in space for fifteen hours a day ("daylight"), allowing us nine hours of darkness ("nighttime"). In addition, located at the base of each cylinder are large, dishlike mirrors which catch the sun's rays and transform them into heat and energy.

The *Island* lifestyle is a natural lifestyle. Nonpolluted air is supplied by lunar rocks (giving us "oxygen") as well as hydrogen, carbon, and nitrogen brought up from Earth. As *Island* becomes more and more self-sufficient, these elements will be "mined" from nearby asteroids.

Water is produced by combining oxygen with our imported hydrogen. All water is recycled and reused in its purest form.

The rotation of our cylinders (about one "revolution"

or "turn" every two minutes) supplies us with an exhilarating sense of gravity, slightly less taxing than Earth's. On *Island*, the higher you climb, the lighter you get. Ask your guide about our light gravity health spas, pedal plane flights, and zero g basketball games.

For a delightful day in the "country," may we suggest you visit our agricultural cylinder where farm products as well as rabbits and chickens are tended.

The main thing to remember about *Island* life is that, as upside down as everything may seem, it is even more naturalistic than Earth living. As you have noticed, when standing on any one of our strips of land (called "townships"), if you gaze directly skyward you will see, not the sky, but two more communities suspended above your head, held firmly in place on the far side of the cylinder by our artificial gravity. Never fear, however; on *Island*, the sky will never fall.

WHAT ARE THE ADVANTAGES OF *ISLAND* LIFE?

Aside from pure air and water, the colony boasts a number of lifestyle pluses. Its citizens need never experience the crush of overpopulation, since there is more than ample living space for our population of 10,000. Unlike Earth, *Island* residents are not subjected to the constant worry of unexpected disasters such as earthquakes, hurricanes, and tidal waves. *Island*'s weather is controlled from within and, hence, is always mild and agreeable. Safety standards aboard the habitat are quite remarkable, well above those of Earth, and serious illness is practically unheard of due to our supervised exercise, preventive medicine, and diet plans. Crime is also effectively nonexistent since all Islanders work for common, altruistic goals.

3

From out of nowhere . . . a barely audible "click." A briefcase being snapped shut. A camera shutter springing back into position. It could have been anything, really. It was certainly nothing to worry about.

Swathed in carefully designed darkness, the tunnellike spacecraft stood serene. Sergeant Jeff Harden strained his ears against the nightfall for one hesitant second before coutinuing his rounds on *Island One*. Strolling on an alabaster walkway some 240,000 miles from his home planet, the muscular young policeman whistled softly, contentedly to himself. He loved nights like these.

The feeling of unreality was positively all-encompassing. He adjusted the short sleeves of his police tunic and tried to catch the melody the public address system was crooning. Was it Bach? He wasn't sure. No matter. It was soothing and fit this evening perfectly.

Harden scanned the vast stretch of manufactured terrain before him. Tiny, fairy tale buildings nestled in clusters, surrounded by clumps of strategically placed shrubbery. The structures were boxish and almost quaint in appearance. Above the officer's head, where the sky would normally be, more buildings and trees clung miraculously upside down to the opposite side of the tubular vessel. Harden shivered involuntarily. Even after three months aboard the habitat, he still found himself awestruck by the sight of its unworldly design.

He squinted at the colorfully lit constructions. It was almost like visiting one of those Hansel and Gretel villages he used to see on TV when he was a kid. After dark, when the electric cars and space tugs stopped running, *Island* lost much of its scientific luster, assuming a slightly surrealistic shine. This was the way Jeff had always dreamed it would be in space. It was perfect.

All his life, he had longed for serenity such as this. As a

boy growing up in Kansas during the '90s, he had envisioned himself being able to soar through the heavens, being able to live among the stars. It was the era of the space shuttle and he had thought for sure that he could hop aboard the first ship leaving Earth after his eighteenth birthday and simply take in the sights that were nestled securely beyond Earth's aura.

The task proved more difficult than he had imagined. There were tests to be taken, qualifying exams. Physical exams. More tests. The upcoming era of space colonization was obviously intended for an elite cadre of the best all-around examples of humanity. Only the best, the very best were chosen. During the course of his examinations, it became very clear that Jeff had no interest in mathematics or scientific speculation. In his eyes, space was poetry. Space was an everexisting image to be revered, respected, glorified.

At that point in time, the United States government did not seem overly interested in spacefaring romanticists and so, Jeff was left behind.

His dreams shelved indefinitely, he decided to carry on in a family tradition and become a cop. He was a damned good one, too, awarded citation after citation for an approach to law enforcement which mixed justice with compassion. He was considered an outstanding member of his community.

As luck would have it, he later found himself able to combine both boyhood dreams and adult realities, getting himself posted to *Island*'s small, but efficient, security force. They had kept him on file for nearly a decade. He was chosen to replace a cop who simply went to pieces one night while making the rounds.

Harden paused for a moment, listening to the night sounds generated by the habitat. It hummed like a contented motor. Like a telephone powerbox basking in the moonlight along a deserted country road. And what else was there wafting in the background? *Duet in F Major for Two Flutes?* Maybe.

Jeff still couldn't fully understand how anyone could actually crack up aboard this paradise in space. It had everything anyone could want. The climate was man-made and, therefore, totally controllable. For Harden, used to the sometimes harsh mid-west seasons, the colony was an endless summer. There were low-gravity swimming pools, man-made hills to pedal glide from. Even his job was fairly idyllic.

13

There wasn't much crime to speak of. No unrest. An occasional drunken binge or a fistfight now and then to break up the monotony, but it was sheer heaven compared to Kansas City. Hell, he'd almost had his guts blown apart a couple of times down there.

For the child still in Harden, working on *Island* was comparable to living in Oz. For the adult, it was the closest thing to Utopia he'd ever imagined. Yet, despite the wonder, the advantages, people still occasionally broke down ... badly. He couldn't comprehend the psychological reasoning behind it all but, apparently, some people, when isolated from Earth, experienced an intense sort of claustrophobic melancholia in space.

They felt trapped.

These cases, however, were getting rarer and rarer. Caught in their earliest stages, they were treated with mood altering drugs. Those unfortunates who were beyond medical help were sent back to Earth.

For Jeff, the isolation afforded by *Island* life suited him fine. As a result, he occasionally found himself stymied by some of the older officers' cynicism regarding the habitat. Harden figured that such attitudes came with the uniform. He dismissed it most of the time. Besides, right now, he was thrilled to be aboard during the tenth anniversary celebration. With a little luck, he'd be assigned to the governor's entourage.

A few delegates from Earth had arrived already. By week's end, *Island* would be hosting nearly a dozen VIPs.

Harden slowed his gate slightly, interrupting his own daydreaming. The hair on the back of his neck began to bristle. Something was wrong. A chill wormed its way through his body, causing his legs to wobble. A force in the pit of his stomach sensed danger.

Pausing beside a tree, Harden began his yoga breathing exercises, fighting the growing tension building in his limbs. He was letting those older cops get to him. "This whole joint is unnatural," Andrews had complained only this afternoon, "in a whole lotta ways."

All talk.

"And if you try to do anything about it," Andrews insisted, "they find you and shut you up." Andrews had stared meaningfully at Jeff at that point. Jeff always told his superiors what he thought about things, both in a positive and negative

14

manner. Had he been too outspoken? Nah. Everybody was tense these days. That was it.

Lately there had been some strained moments between some of the construction foremen and the research scientists, but that was mainly because of the president's committee coming up here. Rumor had it that those Earth delegates could shut down the entire complex on a day's notice if they wanted to. Who could live with that kind of insecurity without letting off a little steam? Jeff rested against the tree. There was no reason to suddenly let that sort of nonsense get to him now.

He raised a hand to his forehead. It felt pretty warm. That was probably the explanation. He was running a slight fever. He had caught a cold. He laughed to himself. Getting paranoid in his old age. Almost thirty. All he needed was some rest.

His stomach twitched.

The cop in him could not rest. An almost sixth sense was busily at work now, trying to shake the rest of Jeff's faculties into a state of alert.

Click.

That sound again.

Footsteps?

No, not at this late hour. Like a spacefaring dormitory, *Island* simply closed down around midnight. It wasn't so much an enforced curfew as an unwritten rule. Work began early each morning and everyone worked on the habitat, so . . .

Click.

Jeff pushed himself away from the tree, peering into the blackness before him. Folds of darkness seemed to undulate in the shadows. There! Not ten feet ahead of him! Something was moving in the bushes. He would swear to it. He eased the laser pistol out of his holster. Set it for short-range bursts. Using his free hand, he reached down for his videopack. Should he alert communications and ask for a quick scan?

No.

Suppose he was wrong?

He'd look like a fool. Worse yet, a coward. He was still a greenie up here on the habitat. He couldn't go running to his electronic mother every time he got a little spooked.

Click.

The sound was strange, yet familiar.

15

Metallic?

His jaw tensed. He'd handle it himself. Standing poised at the entranceway to a small commuter park, he thought he could make out an outline in the near distance. He walked slowly toward it.

"Hold it right there," he ordered half-heartedly.

With surprising agility, the shadow darted further into the underbrush. Startled, Harden fired a short laser burst into the greenery. Racked with both fear and embarrassment, he watched two small bushes smolder and wilt as the result of his nervous reaction. Anger began to well within him. So that sonofabitch out there thought he could put a fright into him, eh?

He marched into the park.

Click.

Up there on the right. He was sure of it. He charged into the foreboding, tree-lined area.

"I said, hold it," he cried, increasing his momentum. Diving through the flowerbeds, Jeff reached out and wrestled a drinking fountain to the ground. Sprawled next to the dribbling piece of plumbing, he was tempted to laugh. Sheer fright, however, prevented it.

Click.

He was sweating now, moisture running freely down his chest, clinging to his lightweight tunic. Damn it. What was going on here? Was he cracking up, too? No. He was sure that there was someone out there. Someone playing a pretty dangerous game of cat and mouse. Harden got to his feet and stumbled through the carefully arranged rows of flowers. He had to find this nut now. If he didn't, he'd catch hell tomorrow for trampling these plants.

Clickclickclick.

He froze in the middle of the flowerbeds. The sound seemed nearer. It seemed to be all around him. No, that was Bach. Gentle, soothing Bach. The bushes seemed to possess a life of their own, surrounding him. His mind attempted to untangle the confusing imagery at hand. Run. Get out now. He was helpless. Outmatched. Without warning, something sliced down in front of him.

He had seen just about everything a cop could have seen back on Earth . . . but this? He had to be hallucinating. It just wasn't possible. Overcome by fear, he ran back toward the walkway. He'd have to call communications. He'd have to let them know. But let them know what? Coward. Fool. Reach-

16

ing the outskirts of the park, he yanked his videopack from his side holster.

Clickclickclick.

Jeff stared at the videopack with disdain. No. He wouldn't use it. He'd handle whatever it was out there himself. He spun around and dropped down into firing position. Both hands on his pistol, he watched the outline approach him. As it grew nearer, something very vital within him broke, crumbled under the pressure.

He couldn't move.

He couldn't fire.

This couldn't be happening.

He began to whimper. Forehead burning, eyes tearing, his body began to shake. No. Please, God. No. Not here. Not here in Oz. He recognized the face of his visitor as that of Death itself.

"Oh no," he cried softly, feeling the pain shoot through the side of his neck with lightning speed. The air around him seemed to burst into flame. Every part of his body awakened, vibrated, exploded. A deafening roar drowned out the classical lullabyes being piped through the P.A. Nerves pulsating one last time, Harden surrendered to the inevitable.

Within sixty seconds, the only sound to be heard in the park was the gentle sighing of two flutes, languidly weaving their way through a masterfully composed duet.

In the soft glow of a nearby streetlight, a bleeding mass of flesh lay twitching on the pavement of the greatest scientific achievement in the history of humankind.

4

WHAT ARE THE DANGERS OF *ISLAND* LIFE?

Life on *Island One* is practically hazard free. Unpolluted and untarnished by heavy industrialization (our industry is conducted in the nearby construction shacks), the cylindrical habitat is nearly totally safe.

As on Earth, fire is a real hazard on our habitat, but

17

in our ten-year history, there have been no serious blazes; a tribute to both our conscientious citizens and our top flight fire brigade.

Meteroids are considered a minor threat. However, since these meteor chunks are rarely bigger than a baseball and since our twenty-four-hour on-duty repair crews are always ready for any emergency, there is no real danger to Islanders from stray space rocks breaking through our tough skin. (Any crack in our protective shielding can be repaired within six-hours time with no great loss in air pressure to the habitat.)

Cosmic radiation? Our heavy shielding (a six-foot-thick layer of pulverized moon minerals piled onto the outer surface of the colony) and atmosphere provide more than ample protection. During times of solar flares, underground shelters and special suits are used to protect our well-being. These flares, however, are few and far between and appear to be somewhat cyclical in nature.

5

Feeling conspicuous because of his unstylish apparel, Harry Porter sat at the crescent-shaped bar, trying desperately not to look conspicuous. After approximately two minutes of intense grinning and throat clearing, he abandoned all attempts at ersatz ease and lapsed into a comfortable state of abject misery.

In the dimly lit room, a horde of young people, nearly all dressed in tunics of one type or another, sat, crouched, or collapsed to the deafening strains of pop music. Harry hated tranx bars. He avoided them like the plague even before he was married. And that was too many years ago ... when the bars first started coming into their own.

Another sociological breakthrough of the late '90s, tranx bars owed their existence to the Federal Mental Health programs of a decade earlier. With the Mental Rehabilitation

18

Act of '86, nearly all federally supported mental institutions were scaled down to skeletal status. Patients were placed into local communities with greater frequency, living in specially owned and operated "hotels." The theory was: keep a patient in a mental institution for a long enough time and recovery would be impossible. Put a patient back into the "real world" and soon, reality would seep back into his or her life.

Patients thus "communalized" were given medicinal therapy in the hotel dining room and bar area. It was thus not uncommon for local residents to see hundreds of sedated citizens blunder out of these establishments en masse after a particularly potent round at the "bar." Citizens' fear of the tranquilized patients gradually gave way to anger and, eventually, envy.

With the Drug Decriminalization Act of '97, the youth culture was given the go-ahead to begin adapting the pill dispensary motif to their own needs. And so, tranx bars were born. Now, they flourished nationwide.

Harry thought they were damned unnatural. For one thing, a guy couldn't buy a drink in one and Harry appreciated a good drink. He liked to feel it burn on the way down, purge his system of the scars of the day. He felt more comfortable with a glass in his hand than a pill in his palm. Somehow, liquor seemed more organic.

"What'll it be?"

Shaken from his gloomy concentration by a particularly ugly albino bartender, Harry shrugged. "Uh, just a glass of grapefruit juice . . ."

The bartender could not hide his disbelief. "Grapefruit juice?"

"Yes, grapefruit juice," Harry replied, angry at his mounting embarrassment. "And two aspirin . . ."

"Aspirin."

"Yeah, aspirin. I have a headache from this music. And my stomach isn't feeling to hot, either."

"You sure you don't want milk instead of juice?" the bartender smirked. "For your stomach, I mean."

"Juice is fine." Harry glared

"You want your aspirin buffered?"

Harry shook his head "no," clenched his fists and carefully examined his knuckles; now white with strain. He knew if he stared at his fists long enough, the bartender would simply go away.

You do the best you can.

The bartender returned with a glass. Harry attempted a first sip.

"Hey, high flyer, want to really leave your orbit?"

Harry tightened his jaw, attempting to avoid the circus around him; most notably the teenaged clown now standing at his side. Dressed in sort of a silver space shuttle uniform bastardization (no respect), the youth, a pimply faced collection of badly angled bones with a shaved head and a patchy beard ignored Harry's intense antipathy and sidled up even closer.

"I mean it. I've got stuff you can't get in here. It'll take you to another dimension . . . farther even, I bet."

"No thanks. I'm sort of a homebody." Asshole.

"Really. I've got gin, vodka, scotch. All kinds of wine, how about a shot of tequila?"

"Just piss off before I give you a shot of black and blue," Harry whispered.

"Negative karma," the space pirate pronounced, shaking his head sadly while moving back into the clouds of cigarette smoke. "It all comes back you know."

Harry simmered, watching the retreating figure disappear into the crowd. Pukeheads. He rested his juice on the swirling, multi-colored pinball bar. Beneath the glass surface, tiny, computerized dots ricocheted off equally diminutive space stations. Twenty years ago, this place would have been referred to by members of his trade as a "dive." Today, it was termed "norm." Ordering two more aspirin, he glanced at the wall-length mirror behind the bar and watched the patrons fall over each other to the vague beat of a top ten tune.

Under the sea or above the sky
Just tranx me, baby, and I'll fly high
They say money's tight (but that's all right)
I've got enough to soar higher than a shuttle flight.

Harry chewed on his aspirin (a nervous habit he'd picked up in the Sino-Israeli Wars) and lifted his glass toward the mirror.

"Here's to humanity." Or what's left of it.

He suddenly remembered his father, back in the '80s, worrying about the world making it through the year 2000. A rather drab but terrifyingly earnest man, Timothy (Big Tim) Porter wallowed in the old Christian religion. He constantly fretted about the coming of the anti-Christ, the Second Coming of the Redeemer, and the arrival of an all-out nuclear war . . . not necessarily in that order. As it turned out, what he really should have been wary of was the presence of his electric clock radio near the bathtub.

And it came to pass that, one fateful Saturday evening, Mr. Porter senior, in the midst of a prolonged bath, knocked his favorite radio into the tub. Being a devout Christian, he presumably saw God. All that Harry and his mother heard from an ajoining room was a truncated rendition of the popular song "You Make Me Laugh, I Think." Shortly thereafter, Harry's mother married an electrician.

Harry looked a lot like his father. He wasn't as heavy as Big Tim yet, or nearly as morose. But he was working on it.

Picking up his glass of juice, Harry waded through a sea of bodies to a deserted table. He felt a little out of place wearing a shirt and a loose-fitting pair of denim slacks amidst the sea of tunics. He couldn't understand why those outfits were so popular on the tranx scene. Men with hairy legs looked downright foolish in them. At night, they stumbled around like spastic Sherwood Forest residents and, in the morning, they donned their pants and stalwartly marched off into the bowels of the business world. Seemed a bit odd.

Harry squinted his eyes, rubbing his forehead with the thumb and forefinger of his left hand.

Sinus headache.

Yeah, the world had made it through the year 2000. Life careened ever onward. Cars were a little smaller than in his father's day. Pollution a little less talked about. People a little less intelligent. As the nations of the world continued their frantically aimless political and economic transactions, their citizens grew more and more detached. More and more bewildered.

There were no more heroes. No more world shaping events. Leisure was the biggest worry now.

How to get it.

What to do with it.

Three-day work weeks left plenty of time for the masses to play. And play they did . . . desperately. Everything was hunky-dory. Okee-dokee.

Boring.

Harry suddenly sensed the arrival of trouble. Turning slightly to his right, he noticed a female figure gyrating his way, squirming to the pulse of the music. Her face was alabaster, her hair the color of day-old catsup. As the girl bumped and ground closer, Harry noticed that her pulsating buttocks were barely covered by her loosely cut tunic. Something base stirred within him. He chalked it up to the unbuffered aspirin.

The girl made for Harry's table. God, how he hated chance encounters. He was out of practice. He despised chit-chat. He abhorred being a bachelor. The girl was now dancing wildly in front of Harry's nose. He judged her to be about twenty-five. Her wig was somewhat younger. The girl suddenly stopped dancing and collapsed in the chair opposite Harry.

"Mind if I sit down?" she asked.

"Go right ahead."

"Come here often?" the girl inquired.

"Never." Harry attempted to change a grimace into a smile. "Did you lose your partner out there?"

"I never had one."

"You always dance alone?"

The girl giggled, revealing a mouthful of irregular teeth. "I wasn't dancing, really."

"Oh," Harry replied. "I just assumed by the way you were ... moving that ... "

"Oh no. It's all part of my gyro-yoga lifestyle. I have to meditate like that at least an hour a day or I fall into a deep depression."

"That was meditation?"

"Oh, yes."

"And doing that gives you inner peace?"

"Sure."

Harry was confused. "I thought astro-oral-meditation was the big thing. You know, *you think like you eat.*"

"Where have you been?" the girl replied, eyes wide in amazement. "That was passé ages ago. Months. All that crap Dr. Verner preached about his astro-yogurt."

"The Food of the Gods ... "

"Right. Well, it turns out that it was all a fraud. Very unorganic. It was laced with PCP."

"How awful."

"Really. Lots of calories. Gave a good buzz, though."

Harry allowed the young girl to talk. He didn't really mind her prattle. She was wrecked on something and she needed to communicate. He knew the feeling. Everyone needed someone or something in their lives to cling to, and these days, that was a hard trick to pull off. Society stated that, frankly, it was everyone for themselves.

Yet, people needed security in their lives. Maybe that was why these pseudo-psychological-religious fads seemed to sweep the globe on an almost weekly basis. When trendies weren't busy being their own best buddies, they were worrying about their social standing in the afterlife.

As the girl droned on, Harry put one hand into his shirt pocket and casually fished out the folded pamphlet with the note still attached. *Island One.* Harry guessed that if there was anything capable of inspiring worldwide change at this point, it was *Island*—the 10,000-peopled space habitat constructed a decade ago to mine space minerals and assemble both news and power satellites for Earth. (Actually, ten years ago, it did more than that. Offering inspiration for a brief moment, it took people's eyes skyward along with their spirits. The perfect panacea . . . albeit a fleeting one.)

The news satellites had been the first ones completed, sent into geosynchronous orbits eight years ago. Small craft, no bigger than a family car, but with an effect more widespread than anyone had originally envisioned.

Subscribers to the News Satellite Network were actually able to get the news delivered into their homes twenty-four hours a day via handy cable hookups. In essence, each individual could have an ever-changing newspaper at his or her fingertips; a constantly droning telex-print-out which kept them abreast of world developments. It was great for the multitude of people who hated to read, too. Only the headlines were delivered.

Porter frowned, remembering the shock waves those little devils up in space had sent zipping through the already weakened world of print journalism. From the outset, newspapers (and, hence, newspaper reporters) were not overly infatuated with the great scientific achievement brought forth by the space colony.

In direct response to the public's total fascination with the popular new satellite system, the Earth's newspapers had promptly collapsed into a state of fiscal ruin. Today, in all of America, there existed only the *Herald-Times-News;* a communal newsprint service run out of twenty-one major cities with individual regional editions produced in each one. Despite its orbiting competition, the HTN got by.

And Harry got by, usually stuck covering gossipy human interest stories which bored him to tears but kept both his eccentric readership and his landlord happy.

Every so often, a good story came along and Harry was allowed to flex his literary muscles. Those occasions, however, were few and far between, not like his cub reporter days. Lots of newspapers then. Wars. Protests. Action. Reams of typewriter paper . . . to this day he refused to use those damned computer consoles to compose a story. Typewriter and paper, that was the stuff stories were made on.

All this action came grinding to a halt a few months ago when Harry suffered his illness.

And went away for a while.

Harry rested his chin on his hand and stared vacantly at a crowd of tranx patrons gathered around a titanic video unit. On the screen, a bosomy brunette in an almost-dress was apparently doing push-ups while experiencing a melodic asthmatic attack. The lyrics, as far as Harry could ascertain, concerned doing something with "bananas in the dark."

Harry doubted that Paul McCartney would have ever written a song like that.

Harry doubted that Paul McCartney ever existed.

He was just a figment of his father's imagination.

Carefully refolding his pamphlet and replacing it in his pocket, Harry reflected on the fact that he had never gone to bed with a woman with exceedingly large breasts. Pity.

He returned his gaze to the girl before him, the all powerful music echoing through the room.

> *When they made you,*
> *They musta cloned Heaven.*

Harry smiled at the girl, gazing down her tunic.

Damn.

The young lady finished whatever it was she had wanted to say and leaned against the table in Harry's direction. ". . . and because of this spiritual reawakening, this rebirth of karma, I took the name Eve."

Harry sputtered to life. "Pretty name. Because of my mother's brother, I took the name Harry."

"A pleasure to meet you, Harry," Eve smiled.

"And you," he said. "Well . . ."

"Well," she repeated.

24

Harry tapped his foot beneath the table. "Well."

The girl cocked her head to one side. "Harry?"

"Yeah?"

"Would you like to copulate?"

Harry motioned for a waiter and ordered another round of aspirin.

6

At 1:40 AM Island Standard Time, a small light on a large console in Island Communications Central Command flashed blood red. Its repeated bursts of crimson activity went ignored.

7

At 1:45 AM Island Standard Time, Communications Officer Harold W. Mullins walked back to his console unit at the habitat's Central Command center, a bright yellow, rectangular building with equally brightly colored rooms and hallways housed within. Viewed from the outside, the shoeboxish modular structure reflected the type of architecture that is deemed "serviceable" by practitioners of practicality and "vapid" by those plagued by aesthetics.

Entering the Monitor One office, the emaciated-looking Mullins took great care in opening the door so as not to spill the cup of coffee in his right hand. Mullins, an easygoing (but by the book) sort with a small nose but a large overbite, licked his equine teeth in disgust. "Now doggone it," he complained to his junior officer Seabruck, "why didn't you pick up on this red one in Sector Six?"

(The slimy little toad was probably out partying last night.)

Seabruck, the compact young man at the main console, rubbed his bloodshot eyes with two pudgy hands. He disliked Mullins intensely, always having the vague feeling that his superior constantly kept him in the dark on most matters of priority habitat policy, that Mullins didn't trust him. This was largely due to the fact that, indeed, Mullins kept Seabruck in the dark on most matters of priority habitat policy, did not trust him a bit, and felt him capable of carrying out only the most simplistic of orders. In Mullins's eyes, men like Seabruck were a threat to the existence of the habitat.

"Guess I didn't notice," Seabruck replied.

Mullins checked his anger, convinced that the flashing light was a routine malfunction of equipment . . . installed, no doubt, by men of Seabruck's mental stature. "Guess I didn't notice," Mullins mimicked. "Go out for a cup of coffee and . . . hey, wait just a minute." Mullins's eyes narrowed into attentive slits. "There's something wrong here."

The red light flashing on the video console would not shut down, no matter how many back-up switches Mullins flicked with a free finger. "This isn't a malfunction at our end."

Seabruck scratched his nearly crew-cut hairline and waddled up to a nearby wall unit. "What the hell is that?" he wondered aloud, pointing to a small TV screen.

Mullins walked up to the monitor and nearly put his face inside the screen. "I dunno. Something's very screwy here, my friend. Who's on duty tonight in Six? Isn't it that new kid, Hardy?"

"Harden," Seabruck corrected, consulting a clipboard filled with names and time schedules.

"Well, he's gone and done something to his video unit. I'm getting a definite alert signal and all I can see on his monitor is gray shit. Stupid greenies."

Seabruck casually walked the length of the room-long monitoring system, a closed circuit TV buff's dream come true, housing dozens of small television screens; each picking up a transmission relayed live from both a series of cameras placed strategically throughout the entire habitat and a host of smaller scanning cameras actually worn by patrolling habitat police.

Seabruck flexed a handful of sausage shaped fingers and, with surprising dexterity, punched a series of buttons control-

26

ling the quality of Harden's individualized transmission. "Maybe something's haywire with his unit."

"Uh-oh," Mullins muttered, still staring at the monitor. "Lemme at this for a minute."

He walked briskly to Seabruck's side, nudging the squat fellow out of the way. Mullins attacked the contrast buttons, whistling through his teeth. "Damn. It's not the unit. It's not the unit at all."

He glanced back at the screen. "It's on, all right. Transmitting fine. Look at that. Perfect focus."

Seabruck regarded the transmission dubiously. "All I see is fuzz. Voidoid."

"Wrong," Mullins corrected. "See that over there? That line? That's a crack. A very small crack. And that little lump over there? You can barely make it out but that's a bubble. An air bubble. The kind one finds in moon-macadam. What we're staring at, my friend, is an extreme close-up of the pavement of Sector Six."

"Why are we doing that?" Seabruck asked.

"Maybe Hardy dropped his unit. Pan camera four in Six."

Seabruck dashed to another level of knobs. "Harden," he said. A monitor adjacent to the screen in question began to transmit an eerie panorama of the habitat at night. Huge shadow shapes blocked out entire sections of the walkways.

"Goddamn trees," Mullins hissed. "They build this place to house a shitload of cameras and then they put lousy trees in front of them so you can't see a goddamn thing."

Moisture began to dot Mullins's forehead. He didn't like the feel of this at all. He waved one hand in the air, choreographing Seabruck's movements at the console from afar. His eyes never left the monitors. "OK. Wait a minute. Freeze it. Good. Now zoom. Slowly. Slower."

Seabruck's attention was riveted to the console before him. "Zooming."

"Little more. Little more. Freeze it. Stop right there." Mullins gaped at the screen, his face drained of all color. With very little sound, he eased himself into a chair.

"Goddamn. Bring that phone over here."

"Who are you going to call at this hour?"

"Never mind. Just bring me the phone. I found Hardy."

"Harden."

"The kid."

27

"So what?"

Mullins made a dry noise with his throat. "I can make out his head in the picture."

"Yeah, so?"

"So . . . it's not on his body. His head isn't on his body."

Seabruck grabbed the yellow phone and began punching buttons frantically. Mullins looked up, dazed. "Who are you calling?"

"The police."

Mullins arched his back. "Put the phone down."

Seabruck stared back incredulously at his superior. "But I thought . . ."

"Put the phone down."

Seabruck did as he was told. Mullins slowly arose from his chair and, walking over to his coworker, grabbed the phone himself. "We'll call the governor directly on this."

"Why the governor and not the police?"

Mullins frowned at his companion. The man had the savvy of a gnat. "A matter of policy," he informed the fellow coolly, beginning to pick out the governor's private number with his forefinger. "And Seabruck . . ."

"Yes, sir?"

"For the record, you didn't see anything unusual on the monitors tonight."

The stocky young man gasped, looking at his superior quizzically. "A matter of policy?"

"You've got it, friend."

8

WHAT CAN *ISLAND* DO FOR EARTH?

In its first decade of existence, *Island* has already proven its worth manifold. Aside from constructing a fleet of popular communications satellites, *Island* has built a host of power satellites, sent into orbit high above the Earth, thus far providing approximately 35% of the United States with a source of economical electrical energy; solar power relayed directly from space via microwaves. In years to come, we hope to supply the entire country with a similar service, thus bringing utility prices down even lower, before turning our attention to the needs of other countries throughout the world.

Island, eventually, will be able to work wonders for all of the Earth, eliminating such global woes as overpopulation and famine via the construction of bigger and better space habitats.

As more colonies are constructed, more Earth citizens will be needed to populate them, thus reducing the world's ever-increasing population and providing more global space for the raising of food. *Island* also hopes to be able to replenish much of the Earth's natural minerals with minerals retrieved from space via the mining of both the Moon and passing asteroids.

In addition, *Island* has high hopes of influencing the world with its very existence. Thus far, it has served as an inspiration to many of the members of Earth's younger generation who identify with our modern-day pioneer lifestyle and noble goals. Truly, *Island* is the key to the future; an ever-present cornucopia of plenty hovering hundreds of thousands of miles away from its beloved mothership . . . Earth.

9

Harry realized that he was on his own for the first time in quite a while, and if he was to survive in this strange society, indeed, if he was to continue to make a living at his trade, he would have to immerse himself in it. Years of marriage had made him too soft, sheltered him a bit too much. He had to plunge head-first into the real world once again. He had to toughen up. It wouldn't be too difficult. He was a survivor.

Impassively, he watched the young girl across the table begin to nod out. Chin sagging against her chest, Eve flashed a membership card at his face, bringing to a close her psycho-sexual-political tirade. The card was pale yellow with a bright blue globe in the center. Harry recognized it as a "One Worldist" ID.

"And the reason everyone is so hung up down here," she slurred, "is that people have it so easy up there." She pointed to the ceiling.

"People up there?" Harry repeated, looking above his head cautiously.

"Those space colonists," she said with sedated venom. "Elitists. If we look around us, we'll find that we have all the ingredients for a Utopia right here on Earth. Right here. Enough jobs, enough money, enough tranx to keep everybody happy. But nooo, we have to lose money and jobs to those people on that spaceship. Somebody ought to blow the thing right outta the sky."

Eve's eyes began to flutter. "Right here on Earth. Everybody could be happy."

"Uh-huh."

"Did I tell you I was a Virgo?"

"You did . . . several times as I recall."

He calmly watched the girl slide under the table. Tranxed out cold. Luckily the floors were heavily cushioned for just such occasions and the sweet young revolutionary would be able to sleep it off peacefully. The bar's team of resident paramedics ambled over and gave Eve a quick medical onceover. "Just a precaution," one winked at Harry. "The law."

"Pays to be safe," Harry agreed.

Surrounded by the blaring music and pulsating lights, Harry heaved a wistful sigh and allowed himself to tumble into a wave of melancholia. He didn't know who he felt sorry for more: Eve or himself. Eve was missing a part of life, intangible but necessary. Harry had possessed it once and, then, let it go. He was quite aware of its absence. The girl didn't know it existed. Soul. Out of the corner of his eye, Harry spotted an elderly figure shambling his way. A familiar voice cut through the din. "Looking good, Harry."

"Feeling lousy, Lenny," Harry replied as his editor, Leonard Golden pulled up a chair alongside his. "Why don't you sit down, Lenny," Harry offered, checking his watch. "You're late."

The tall, stoop-shouldered man lowered himself carefully into the seat, his legs meeting resistance beneath the table. "What the . . ."

"Her name is Eve," Harry informed him.

Golden raised his busy eyebrows and peered below. "She's going to be very sore when she wakes up."

He leaned back in his chair, kicked off his shoes and rested his feet on the girl's back. "Ahhh," he sighed. "I've been walking all day." The old man ordered two downers.

Harry should have been surprised that Golden would go in for this stuff, but somehow wasn't. Golden was a strange old bird. He and Harry were total opposites, yet, despite their differences, the two got along splendidly, playing off each other's distinctive strengths and energies. The slightly misanthropic Porter was the quintessential investigative journalist. The gray-haired Golden was the distinguished four-star general, the impressive leader of the troops . . . with equally prestigious ulcers.

Golden was unique in a number of ways. He possessed a visual quality, for instance, not commonly found in distinguished professionals. He always looked miserable. With his longish hair and drooping mustache, he resembled a shell-shocked walrus. Porter sometimes suspected that the only way his editor ever got his reporters to obey orders was by playing on their sympathy. "If you don't do this right," his hapless look seemed to say, "I'll *die*."

He could look pitiful in a brand new tuxedo. Maybe it was the way he let his shoulders hang or the bad posture he displayed when he sat down. Whatever. His clothes always seemed to be at war with his body. Once more, his clothes always emerged victorious from the skirmish. Despite his aura of pathos, however, Golden was a top newspaperman.

One of a dying breed.

Harry enjoyed being around him. It gave him a sense of history. He identified with the long-suffering editor. They were men of letters in a time of picture screens.

Golden painfully twisted his face into a parody of a normal smile. "Hey, that rest did you a lot of good."

Harry nodded sweetly. "Like hell."

"Well, at least you got out of the city for a while. Missed the sanitation riots. Shouldda seen it. Garbage flying everywhere, like an old slapstick movie. And fire bombings? Over a hundred people killed. Animals."

"I always miss the fun stuff."

"So," Golden said, shifting his body uneasily, sending one of his feet sliding under the girl's dress. "What have you been up to?"

"Nothing much."

31

"No, really."

"Well, let me see. I spent a lot of time drugged at the hospital. It was just chock-full of mental deficients so I was somewhat stifled in terms of conversation. Oh yeah, when I wasn't drugged, my brains were being peeped out of existence by an army of ESPers."

"Parapsychs?"

"Oh yeah. Delightful. Lenny, you can actually *feel* them entering your mind. You can sense that they're up there, stomping all over your thoughts."

"Sounds inhuman."

"I'll never forget that feeling. Never. Anyhow, things were just barreling along like that for a couple of months, loads of fun, when suddenly they let me out. I guess they thought I was cured."

"You didn't go there to be cured," Golden pointed out, popping his pills. "You went there for a rest."

Harry wagged a "naughty, naughty" finger at his boss. "Lenny, I had a breakdown."

"Overwork."

"I used to cry all the time."

"Merely a bout with depression. Very common."

"I lost control."

"Who wouldn't have in your shoes?"

"You . . . and about 20 million other normal people."

"That's what I like about you," Golden cackled, playing with a mug of fruit juice ("disgustingly healthy crap they serve here"), "you're always full of shit. You'd been through hell for six months, covering that laser gun loon . . . er, fellow. Finding all those victims the way you did. Well, that certainly couldn't have been a very pretty sight."

"It wasn't," Harry admitted. "They all looked like beefburgers."

"And then you meet the creep face to face, and what does he do?"

"He . . ."

"He tells you his life story and fries his face off."

Harry shuddered at the memory.

"And then," Lenny went on, after asking the waitress for a small hallucinogenic chaser, "Annie walks out on you. Blames it all on your work and runs off with a Mexican painter. So you break down. So what? People can just take so much. Then the brain tells the body, 'Hey, boss, it's time for a pit stop.' "

"The guy wasn't a painter. He painted houses."

"Whatever."

"There's a difference. One's common. One is not."

"Pigs is pigs."

"I hired him, too."

Golden nodded approvingly. "Classic."

"Thanks." Harry folded his arms across his chest. "Did you get me released from the laughing academy, Lenny?"

"Naaah." Golden spoke too quickly. "But I did tell that head doc that you were the best reporter I had ever run across. That you made sentences sing. That you were the creme de la creme and I needed you back as soon as possible."

"Who quit? Pitken or Kay."

"Both."

Harry whistled through his teeth.

Golden pointed an accusing finger at Harry's half-puckered lips. "You were better than they were anyhow. You know that."

"TV?"

"What else?"

Harry chuckled softly. "Well, they have pretty faces. They'll do OK. They'll have fun experimenting with all that new 3V equipment, too. Especially Pitken with those eyelashes of his."

Harry reached into his pocket and yanked out the mangled space habitat pamphlet. "Got your note and your present. Fascinating reading. I'm not going."

"You are."

"Nope." Harry dropped the pamphlet onto the table with distaste. It wasn't that he hated the habitat, exactly. It had contributed a lot to society. But, hell, Earth was for people and space was for planets.

Besides, to Harry, science was a total mystery and one that didn't warrant unraveling. He didn't even know how an ordinary battery worked. What's more, he didn't care. He reasoned that the battery would do its job with or without Harry's encouragement. In a larger sense, so would *Island One*.

"Send someone else," he advised his boss. "I get nosebleeds from heights."

"This is an historic event," Golden countered. "For the first time in its ten-year history, that colony is inviting the press to come aboard. Inviting. They've asked one newsprint

33

and one TV reporter from the country up for a sightseeing tour. Tenth anniversary celebration. The works. We're the biggest commune left, so we got it."

"You mean, *I* got it."

"Semantics. You'll be the first real citizen of the world to see what's going on up there . . . the first independent, apolitical visitor ever!"

"I'm overwhelmed."

"Think of the implications in that," Golden continued. "As well as the timing of your visit. Right about now, it seems, *Island*'s ass is on the line."

Harry had heard vague rumblings about that. The project's initial trial period was over and it was looking for another ten-year renewal. "They'll get by," he said.

"That's not what I hear."

Harry perked up. "What do you mean?"

"What I mean is this: President Walker's reelection movement isn't exactly chugging along smoothly. The people find him about as exhilarating as a used facecloth. Inflation is rampant. Morale is lower than a snake's midsection and no one seems to give a flying fig about it. The only interesting movement bubbling in this country right now is that One Worldist crap."

"Shhh," Harry said, pointing to Golden's feet. "You'll offend her."

Golden lowered his voice. "Goddamn cosmic conservatives. They're really after the habitat. It's an illogical movement but a fervent one. Almost religious. Walker is worried. He's sending his fact finders up there right now, while the latest Gallup poll is being taken down here. If his committee can't come up with enough popular reasons to keep the colony going, its doors are closed. Period. And if the people down here, through the poll, tell the pres that they think the habitat is a waste of time and money, Walker will deep six it publicly with a good deal of fanfare."

"Before *Island* can become a campaign issue."

"Exactly."

"Nasty set-up."

"You said it. Now, in order to survive, the habitat has to give itself an earthbound shot of publicity. They have to overshadow the One Worldist line of crap through positive news."

"Which is why they want the media onboard."

"Yup."

34

Harry's interest waned. Just another Sunday feature story. See the many splendored think tanks. "No thanks," he said. "If I ever get the urge for breathtaking excitement along those lines, I'll take my chances covering an upstate livestock pageant."

"Be reasonable," Golden fumed. "No one's ever documented habitat life before."

"Test-tube sterility I can do without, thank you."

"Think of the money involved."

Harry was interested again.

"Book rights. Movie rights. The works. And the story is yours."

Harry licked his lips. "Well . . ." He needed the cash. There were hospital bills, Machine maintenance, liquor.

"There's a flight leaving tomorrow at six. It will have you there in two days."

"I didn't say I was going yet."

"You will."

"How can you be sure?" Harry asked, waiting for the old man to play his trump card.

"I'm sure you'll be intrigued by the reports of . . ." Golden lapsed into contrived silence.

"Of what?"

"Of strange goings on," the old man winked mysteriously.

"Come on, Lenny. That one has whiskers on it. Give me specifics."

"Don't have specifics, just rumors. A lot of crack-up cases are being shipped down to Earth hospitals and then being forgotten about. No one is supposed to know about this but, well, word gets around. No one is really sure exactly what's going on up there on the Q.T. but the rumors . . . mind-bending research, psychological traumas, that sort of *House of Usher* crap."

"How is it that we haven't heard about any of that stuff on Earth?"

"That's for you to find out, Sherlock," Golden grinned.

Harry found himself laughing, watching the elderly man's eyes begin to sag. "You win, Lenny. You're insidious."

"Lithuanian."

"But I'm only doing this for the money."

"Sure you are."

Harry picked up the *Island* booklet and stuffed it back into his pocket. "Is this place as boring as they make it sound?"

Golden's head began sliding toward his tie, the pills taking their full effect. "Boring?" he muttered. "It's supposed to be paradise. Who could find paradise boring?"

Harry glanced at the dance floor absent-mindedly. "Lucifer most likely."

Golden's arms slipped off the table. "Eeep," he replied.

Harry sat placidly next to his half-filled glass of grapefruit juice as his gray-haired editor slipped off his chair and oozed under the table. Getting to his feet, Porter bowed slightly toward the table legs. "Eve, I'd like you to meet Mr. Leonard Golden. Lenny, may I introduce Eve."

Patting the pamphlet in his pocket, Harry turned and, leaving the two unconscious figures sprawled upon the padded floor, walked out of the bar.

How he enjoyed playing matchmaker.

PART TWO

1

One recurring fact never failed to amaze Porter. Despite all
the technological innovations unearthed seemingly on the
hour by Earth's scientific community, no one had yet to come
up with a way for a normal human being to rest comfortably
in outer space. You had to be a potential Olympic gold medal
winner in order to twist your muscles into some semblance of
relaxation on a "space bed."

Harry struggled out of his form-fitting sleeping unit and
lurched across one of the space station's guest cubicles, his
eyes still heavy with sleep and his head still throbbing from
an excess amount of alcohol consumed the night before.
Making matters even more horrid for his beleaguered phy-
sique was the fact that the flight to the waystation had taken
two entire days and drained him of quite a bit of reserve
stamina.

His bones creaked slightly as he walked across the room.
He hadn't been in space for nearly ten years; not since doing
a profile piece on the first Moon miners, in fact. Even back
then, he had considered space travel a sado-masochistic
exercise in aerodynamics. He had to admit, however, that the

state of the art had improved a great deal in the last decade. A passenger no longer had the feeling that he was being hurtled across space in a large trash can.

The new ships were a cross between oversized space shuttles and down-home passenger planes. A lot faster than the old models, too. Ten years ago, the trip probably would have lasted a week or so. Harry's back popped as he attempted a deep knee bend. God. He wished those space engineering aces would come up with an improved concept of seating/sleeping arrangements. Every bone in his body seemed to have a mind of its own as well as newfound nerve endings that refused to be placated by a promise of exercise.

Walking to the porthole of his cubicle, he gazed outside at *Island One*, seemingly only a few miles away. Later today, he'd be arriving on that titanic twin structure. Watching it now, floating in space, he was overcome by a mixture of both reverence and revulsion.

The sight in itself, he supposed, was impressive. Two massive cylinders with petallike mirrors sprouting from their bases, tethered together in a sea of blackness. Harry grimaced. And, on the inside, thousands of tiny human beings crawled around like contented insects in a junior high school student's ant farm.

He turned from the porthole. This was a hell of a way for a guy to make a living. Still, he might be able to make a few bucks out of the trip, even if he was reduced to reporting about the tulip gardens of outer space. And, on the off chance that there was a real story to be found up there, he'd make the score of his career. He could use the money. Take a vacation. Fix up the house. Get an exceedingly sexy voice installed in his computer system and program it to talk dirty. He stepped into the shower stall and silently blessed whoever it was that pioneered the concept of artificial gravity. He remembered the horror stories told of showering in zero g, with water droplets bouncing around uncontrollably and harried astronauts attempting to remove both the soap and the water from their bodies with small vacuum hoses.

Stepping from the stall, he dressed quickly. In a few moments, he'd be conducting the first in a series of interviews with *Island* personnel. He was starting with Lieutenant Governor Anson Young and not really looking forward to the chore at that. Young, a ruddy, prematurely gray giant was, in essence, the habitat's chief flack. A publicist. A hype merchant. Harry had done a bit of checking on the man and found that, indeed, prior to his arrival on the colony, Young's background consisted exclusively of high level corporate publicity work. Harry wondered exactly how a fellow with those credentials could suddenly, successfully, take the plunge into space politics.

He had chatted with Young briefly the night before. The man was disarmingly folksy but still a flack, plain and simple. According to Young, *Island* was so perfect that life in Eden paled in comparison. A veritable Disneyworld in space. Harry didn't expect one straight answer from the man.

After completing the interview, Harry was scheduled for a last minute physical check-up, which was actually what the waystation was designed for. According to a pamphlet shoved into his face while he was still aboard the ship, the waystation would, some day, evolve into a quarantine checkpoint out of necessity. All visitors on their way to the habitat would be housed here for approximately one week. In the future, such an extended medical exam would be mandatory in that, like anyone living apart from "civilization" proper for an extended period of time, the isolated Islanders would run the risk of losing their natural immunity toward foreign Earth-originated germs. A new Earth virus would have the potential of sending the entire population reeling.

In essence, Harry's one-day layover was a trial excursion for the prolonged aggravation to come. He earnestly pitied the poor stiffs who were destined to spend a week stuck up here. He was bored senseless after less than eighteen hours.

Harry took leave of his room, carefully noting the number on the door. 17H. All the rooms looked alike and he had enough on his mind without worrying about getting lost on this tub.

The waystation was, in essence, a terrifically drab place. A circular craft, less than a city block in circumference, it possessed all the exotic whallop of a bus depot. Run by NASA in conjunction with the USAF, the craft was designed with the usual amount of artistic flair displayed by military minds throughout the ages. The interiors were painted latrine green, the overhead lights were baleful yellow (giving off that unique type of illumination which transformed everyone walking below into a waxen image), and the carpeting was a tasteful mud brown.

Harry considered it the perfect aesthetic combination of hospital ward charm and army barracks chic.

Arriving the evening before, Harry found that the government at least made a *small* effort at keeping their passengers from tearing their hair out by the roots. They had actually taken the time to install a cocktail lounge on the station.

Unfortunately, since no bona fide entertainer in his or her right mind would take a steady job in such a torpid locale, the "live" entertainment consisted largely of fourth-string military personnel who persisted in crooning torch songs next to the bar. They took any and all requests from the patrons except for the most frequently uttered ones; those that alluded to biologically unfeasible acts. There were even token "B" girls designated for Earth ambassadors in good standing.

Last night, while in a state of total fatigue, Harry was approached by a bar bunny. After exchanging short spurts of heavy breathing, Harry realized that the girl would be hard to shake. "Why don't we go someplace where we can both be alone?" he offered.

His playmate left in a huff. Meanwhile, Harry's wit amused a few of the young enlisted men at the bar, who offered to take him on a grand tour of the station; a trek that consumed less than one-half of one hour.

"What do you do for fun around here?" he had asked the tallest of his three companions.

"You're doing it," the boy had replied.

Despite the drabness of his surroundings, Harry had gotten an almost perverse sense of pleasure out of the tour. He felt like a city slicker visiting a distant pioneer outpost which, in essence, was exactly the case. Out here even boredom was a new experience.

The three young men had ushered Harry into a small rec room which was, apparently, designed for the desperate. In the center of the room, resting on a small altar, was an experimental model of a 3V set, "the next great step in video." A common looking television receiver modified to project bleary three-dimensional imagery, 3V, at its current stage of development, succeeded only in taking its viewers into the land of migraine. To make matters worse, the only programming available for the station's unit was a few army training films and such vintage cinematic delights as *Bwana Devil* and *The Creature from the Black Lagoon*.

Harry and his companions had proceeded to get very drunk very quickly in front of the 3V. The last thing Harry remembered was watching a touching tableau involving two young NASA trainees discussing an unknown malady in front of a Florida launch site.

40

"I have a sore," one dew-skinned fellow confided to the her.

"Where?" replied his mystified friend.

"Down THERE," the first speaker emphasized, pointing to an area off-camera, his eyes taking on a meaningful glaze.

Sometime later that evening, the three youths had returned Harry to his room in a semiconscious state. Drinking in light gravity was a humbling experience, even for a veteran guzzler who prided himself in his endurance.

Closing the door to his room, Harry scanned the hall. Rather than wait for an official call from Young, he decided to stroll around the place on his own. He needed some time to think. Since landing on the waystation, he had been inundated with what seemed to be pounds of cheerful *Island* publicity sheets and now, he would fashion a plan wherein he would be able to verbally pin Anson Young against the wall using his own hype as weaponry. He was sure that Young was responsible for the handouts and equally sure that half of the facts stated were exaggerations.

Harry walked by an open doorway. Inside was a dining area where a group of his fellow passengers sat, eating a light breakfast. Harry almost collided with a wiry, fish-eyed steward who was hurrying a tray inside. The fellow's eyes struck Harry as being familiar. He grunted a "g'morning" as he walked by, glancing only briefly at the gaggle of guests. Although he had seen all the faces in various media events, he knew only one man personally: Tony Safian, legendary TV commentator and maxi-ego. The classic Adonis type: chin of granite, head of meat. The type that made Harry gag. He wondered what brand of shellac the man used to keep his hair so well trained. Such a *natural* shade of metallic blue, too.

Harry was about ten feet past the doorway when a bolt of pain shot through his forehead. Caught by surprise, he reeled from the impact, his knees almost buckling completely. He stumbled into a nearby doorway, clutching his eyelids with both hands. His face seemed to be afire. He grabbed his forehead desperately, attempting to keep its contents from exploding outward. He dug his teeth into his lower lip. Blood trickled onto his chin. He mustn't cry out for help. He mustn't double over from the pain. No one must see him like this. He couldn't be yanked off the assignment now. He needed the money.

The burning sensation left his skull as fast as it had materialized, lingering only a few seconds. In those few

41

seconds, however, Harry had absorbed an intense feeling of apprehension, perhaps even panic. He had become the unwitting vessel for a brief telepathic message. He had felt that sort of mental sting before. Someone unused to the experience would be frightened by it but would probably dismiss it as a flash of tension headache or a harmless wave of nausea. But Harry knew better. He had felt those exacting mental feelers while confined in the hospital. Someone had just probed his mind.

There was a peeper aboard the waystation.

"A parapsych," Harry whispered to himself.

That made no sense. Parapsychiatrists didn't travel to space much, if at all. They were a very select breed of therapists, small in number, highly valued, and very rare. They were generally employed by the very rich, the very famous, or the very sick. Their kind had only been in existence for a decade and a half, a unique hybrid of PSI skills and psycho-therapeutical art. Wherever they went, they attracted attention. So why would one be traveling through space incognito?

Straightening himself up, Harry retraced his steps, crossing back in front of the roomful of passengers from Earthside. This had to be the sourcepoint of the probe. Harry peered inside. No one bothered to look up as he sauntered slowly by. He quickly counted heads. There were ten people in that room. Nine of whom were strangers. And one of those nine had to be a peeper. He was sure of it.

Harry leaned against the hallway wall. Now what the hell would a telepath be doing on a waystation over 200,000 miles from home? More to the point, why would one be heading for *Island One,* where there were supposedly no problems at all?

2

"Come in," came a voice from within the room. Harry swung the door open slowly. Inside a cluttered cubicle sat a slightly ill-tempered Anson Young. Piles of paper, file folders, and pamphlets were strewn haphazardly around the floor, making walking a virtually impossible task. Harry imagined that, within the confines of *Island One*, the Madison Avenue-bred Young was truly a political force to be reckoned with. On the waystation, however, the portly publicist was just another uncomfortable guest. Somehow, this thought pleased Harry immensely.

Young was a titan of a man, a solidly built colossus with long, though neatly trimmed hair and a positively Biblical beard; a businessman gone pastoral. His wits, however, were still big city sharp; lethally so, Harry guessed.

"Have yourself a seat," Young said in an almost drawl. Harry detected a mid-western accent that had obviously been lost over the years and, probably, was reconstructed for use in soft-sell meetings such as this. Young shifted his massive body within the confines of his black jumpsuit. "Sit down anywhere you can make yourself comfortable."

Harry slid into an empty chair. "If that's humanly possible."

The room echoed with Young's exaggerated laughter. "Very good point, Mister Porter. You know, I've never ever really gotten used to this place. After ten years, I *still* dread coming up here to this fort." He attempted to rearrange his bulk into one of the station's small seats. "They must have designed this place for folks without any spines whatsoever," he explained. After several seconds of squirming into a second chair, he faced Harry. "Now, we're supposed to have a chat right about now, I guess."

Harry placed a finger-sized tape recorder on the desk adjacent to Young's chair. The lieutenant governor eyed the machine suspiciously. Harry wondered how Young's contrived cornpone routine would sound played back. The bearded man emitted a low chuckle and lunged at the machine, engulfing it in his massive left hand.

"Tell you what, Porter. Let's make this first chat totally off the record. I know you have questions that you would like answered. And I have answers that I would like you to be aware of. But I know that some of your questions would be best not repeated in public. Likewise, some of my answers."

Young tossed the recorder back at Harry, who caught it easily. "I admire your candor," Harry said.

"It doesn't surface often." Young shrugged.

"All righty," Harry said. "Let's establish some of the ground rules for this trip. For openers, let me say here and now that I consider a good many of the reasons I'm up here total bullshit."

Young didn't flinch, pondering that statement for a moment. "Well," he admitted, "to a degree, I'd have to agree with you. But let's backpedal a minute. This entire media junket was my idea. So, both my ass and my reputation are on the line. It's my job to keep you fellows happy. And I've been in the business long enough to know that I can't do that by spreading out total bullshit. I will admit that some of my pamphleteering is littered with somewhat yellow journalistic rhetoric but . . . I have to gear my prose for the masses."

Harry admired the giant's chatty style. He wasn't sure whether he was being taken into the man's confidence or merely being taken in. "Now," Young continued, "I realize that this type of story is not exactly your cup of tea. Basically, *Island* is a scientific experiment and you are used to covering stories of a more 'earthy' nature, no pun intended."

Young pulled out a small plastic file card from his tunic. "You first distinguished yourself as an inner city investigative reporter before moving on to war correspondent stature. You returned to the states and earned a reputation as one of the nation's top crime reporters."

He glanced at Harry meaningfully. "One of the last of your profession, it would seem."

"I majored in Endangered Species in college," Harry explained.

"Rest assured that your visit to *Island* will be a real vacation for you, Porter. A real treat." He returned his attention to the file card. "Amazing what computers can do in amassing information, isn't it. Oh dear, I see that you recently separated from your wife of six years. Sad affair, that. I also see that you took the blow badly. Well, old-fashioned morality and loyalty are things to be admired. You'll find plenty of that on *Island*."

"A regular Shangri-La, eh?" Harry said, slightly annoyed with Young's detailed personality profile.

Young crinkled his nose as if suddenly becoming aware of a week-old flounder in the room. "Do I detect a note of cynicism in your voice?"

"Maybe just a smidge," Harry replied, raising a thumb and a forefinger in a "wee bit" gesture. "In my chats with gossiping computers, I've been told that you're not really a politician, Mr. Young. You're not a scientist, either. You are,

44

what is known in my profession, as a hypester. Pure and simple. You sell things. You package things. That's fine with me, but please don't try to convince me otherwise."

"Mr. Porter," Young responded, shaking his head sadly. "Do you think that I'm trying to sell you anything less than the truth?"

"You're getting warm."

"I've already admitted that I've embellished the facts slightly in those pamphlets, added an extra sheen for the benefit of the layman. But, believe me, Porter, the habitat is everything I say it is . . . and more."

Harry was not convinced. "No unrest?"

"Virtually none."

"No crime?"

"Nothing major."

"No sickness?"

"Common colds."

"How about mental health?"

"What about it?"

"Anything serious?"

Young crossed his massive legs, furrowing his brow dramatically as he formulated his answer. "Nothing special. A few cases of depression, isolation sickness. We treat those we get to in time. The rest we ship Earthside. There's really not much of that anymore, though. We've come up with a series of psychological tests that we give to each potential Islander that manages to catch all prospective trauma cases before they can be nurtured up here."

"How idyllic."

"To a degree."

Harry was about to mention his encounter with the peeper but thought better of it. It wouldn't pay to have Young watching his every move just now. Harry was sure that Young wasn't intentionally misleading anyone. He was doing his job; a man who had simply forgotten the fine line between truth and utter bullshit. You do the best you can. Harry decided to play Young's toe-to-toe game. He crossed his legs, duplicating the lieutenant governor's movement and asked. "Alright. You have a regular Heaven at your disposal. Why tell me personally what you've already printed in those leaflets?"

Young managed to hide any surprise at Harry's lack of tact. "The point is this, Mr. Porter. I've read your stuff. I like it. It's good. It's great. But I know you have a tendency to

45

root for the underdog, to take potshots at the Establishment. Fine. Everyone, within their hearts, loves to joust windmills; to strike a mighty blow for the oppressed. But, on *Island* there *is* no oppressed class. We have neither top dog nor underdog. Everything is *Island*. Everyone is *Island*."

Young lightened his tone, offering a verbal handshake. "We will, of course, cooperate fully with you. Anything you want, anything you need, you just ask us. But we'd also appreciate it if you'd cooperate with us. We have nothing to hide. The habitat is at your disposal. And, let's face it, Mr. Porter, the days of hot shot journalism are over. No one is really interested in reading anything grim these days. In that respect, your career is rapidly drawing to a close. Perhaps your stay on the habitat will open a whole new area of journalistic insight to you. Revamp your career. Give you a second wind."

"Do you write matchbook covers, too?"

Young ignored Harry's input. "So, I would personally appreciate it if you would not fabricate any feelings of paranoia or suspicion about *Island*'s uniqueness and, then, translate them into your copy. We are going out of our way to make things comfortable for all of our guests, especially you . . . Whether you know it or not, you are something of a minor legend back on Earth."

"A regular American buffalo."

"Frankly, Mr. Porter, many people still respect your opinions, which is why we specifically asked for you on this trip, despite your recent mental problems."

Harry stifled a sudden flash of anger. He had underestimated the flack. Young was in search of a weak spot for further reference. Let him keep guessing. "I'm flattered," Harry smiled sweetly.

Young sounded almost disappointed when he resumed. "Yes, well, as I said, you will be treated royally on *Island*. Knowing that you are currently of the single status, we have assigned a female guide to cater to your needs on a twenty-four-hour-a-day basis. She'll show you anything and everything you wish to see on the habitat."

"In other words, no wandering around on my own."

"A matter of safety," Young replied. "You won't be used to our modes of transportation or the freedom of movement afforded by low gravity. We'd hate for you to injure yourself. It would make everyone involved look foolish."

"Some more so than others," Harry muttered.

"Also, as a precaution and in the interest of factual clarity, feel free to show me any and all communiqués you wish to transmit back to Earth. I can use my private hook-up to the main computer to verify all numbers, percentages, and technical points."

Harry shook his head and sighed. "Translation: you want to see all my copy before I send it off."

"Consider me an extra editor, a fact checker."

"Right."

"You'll be staying in one of our finest guest suites, twenty-four-hour bar service, the works. I think that covers about everything. After your arrival on *Island,* just contact me and I'll set up interviews for you with anyone you'd like to cover, from the Governor on down."

Harry straightened himself in his chair. "I really appreciate your efforts, Mr. Young."

"Call me Anson."

"Anson."

"May I call you Harry?"

"Call me Harry, call me Ishmael, call me whatever you want," Harry said, his temper fraying around the edges. "But never call me 'bought.' "

"I don't understand," Young said, his eyes narrowing to slits.

"Then, by all means, let me explain. While I am genuinely touched by your concern with my well-being, I am horrified to see how your publicity skills have atrophied in a mere decade. You can't pitch a buy-out to someone who obviously isn't catching. You should have checked out my old-fashioned morality a little more extensively on your file card dealer.

"I don't need an extra editor on my stories, least of all a flack. Flacks have this nasty tendency of making everything read like the best of *Grimm's Fairy Tales.* My copy, for the most part, just doesn't read like *Hansel and Gretel.* I have never allowed anyone to monkey with my stories without my permission. And you, Mr. Young, do not have my permission.

"Another thing. If I really want to get laid, I'll find someone on my own. You don't have to assign some poor turkey to administer to 'my needs.' Also, if I want to get drunk, I'll get drunk on my own. And, lastly, if I want to take a walk at four o'clock in the goddamn morning by myself,

47

sans escort, I sure as hell will. If I can't tell me now and I'll be on the next flight Earthside."

Young slowly got to his feet, his cheeks a fiery red, his lips trembling in what Harry took to be a combination of rage and total shock. "Y-you misunderstand me, Harry."

Harry leaped to his feet. "No, you misunderstand me, *Anson.*" At this point, Harry noted that, standing eye-to-eye with the towering Scot, he was really standing eye-to-Adam's apple. Instinctively, Harry reached around and placed a hand securely on the back of his chair. If this guy swung at him, it would be best to have something to deflect the blow. Harry would have preferred a wall, but the chair would suffice.

Young relaxed his stance. "Shall we call this one a draw, Harry," he suddenly grinned. "You see, it was a good idea to keep this conversation off the record after all."

"Off the record," Harry repeated, laughing. He removed the tape recorder from his pocket, holding it up before the lieutenant governor's face. The cassette machine read "ON." With the startled politician watching, he flicked it "OFF." "A good reporter always carries some sort of insurance policy while on a story," he said casually.

Young smiled enigmatically. "Not only have I misunderstood you, I seem to have underestimated you as well."

Harry dropped the recorder back into his pocket. "Happens all the time. I'm not much to look at, I guess."

Without warning, a sharp, high-pitched howling split Harry's consciousness in two. He grabbed the back of his chair with both hands behind him, holding himself steady. He was afraid he'd collapse backward into the seat. He was petrified that Young would notice his sudden dizziness. The shrieking seemed to stab continuously at his ears. The room blurred for a millisecond.

Young, however, was not aware of Harry's weakened state. As Harry fought for his balance, the burly politician clutched a wristwatch affixed to his right arm. A small light was flashing on the dial. It seemed to disturb the man. Young casually flicked the light off. "If you'll excuse me, Porter," he blurted, "I've forgotten an appointment. I'm late as it is."

He rushed for the door, adding. "Just wait here. I'll have my secretary take you back to your room." It wasn't so much a suggestion as an order.

"Right," Harry managed to rasp. His knees were still trembling. He had been hit twice that time. He had heard a siren of some sort. Probably the alarm feeding into Young's watch. But how had he heard it? He could only have picked that up via a message from a mental source.

The peeper.

Harry had been being casually´probed by the parapsych when an alarm had gone off somewhere else on the station. Somewhere near the peeper. The parapsych had heard the alarm, reacted to it instinctively and, unwittingly, transmitted the sound.

Jesus. It was getting so a man couldn't even harbor a thought without worrying about someone muscling in and blowing it up in his face.

Not knowing what to expect next, Harry flipped his pocket tape recorder back to "ON" and casually opened the door to Young's cubicle. The hallway outside was deserted. He wasn't about to wait for any secretary to show him safely back to his room and out of the line of fire. There was something decidedly odious going on out there... and Harry could smell it from here.

3

Harry trotted down a series of empty corridors. Whatever event was occurring had to be located in a section of the waystation he hadn't encountered as yet. He rounded countless corners, finding nothing but pale green walls and orbs of sickly, jaundiced light. Winded after a few moments of jogging, he decided to call it quits and head back to his room. No sense making an ass of yourself over something that might turn out to be routine. Pulling the key to 17H out of his wallet, he walked from doorway to doorway, scrutinizing each identifying number. Finally, he stumbled across his own door. The key slipped into the lock smoothly. A bit too smoothly. The door was unlocked.

Harry tensed his body and, saying a quick prayer to the patron saint of idiots, pushed the door open with a quick movement. Just as swiftly, a pair of hands reached out from the darkness and grabbed Harry's arm, yanking him inside. He found himself flying across the cubicle. Well versed in the dealings of maniacs, Harry decided to keep quiet about the affair while hurtling into the opposite wall. He hit the surface with a sickening thud and crumpled onto the floor.

He staggered to his knees immediately, half expecting another assault. He wasn't hurt, but what little wind he had left after the corridor sprinting had been thoroughly knocked out of him. He shook his head from side to side, attempting to unscramble his wits. It was at that point he became aware of the fact that he was staring at a pair of bare feet.

"Are you all right?" the feet's owner asked from above.

The pair of hands helped Harry to his feet. "I'm really sorry about that," the intruder babbled. "I panicked. Reflex action. I didn't know it was you, Mr. Porter."

Harry, feigning comprehension, stood face to face with a chubby wild-eyed youth. The kid was clad in a pair of white pajamas.

"Do I know you?" Harry asked.

"No-no," the youth stammered, backing away nervously. "Well, yes and no. You lectured once at my college. It was five years ago. Actually closer to six. I met you afterward. Got your autograph. Not really an autograph. I wasn't asking for a fan thing. You critiqued a paper of mine and signed your name. No, I guess you don't know me."

Harry had the impression that he was in the presence of a caged animal. He was not far from correct. The kid was distraught. His rounded body was swollen, bruised. His close-cropped hair unwashed for days, matted down in spots with oil. Hands raked with small cuts and scratches. Whatever trouble this boy was in, he had been putting up quite a struggle because of it lately.

"Just who is it you're running from, son?" Harry asked.

"Just about everyone," the visitor replied, "except you."

Harry undid the knot in his stomach. "Well, if that's the case, why don't you sit down and relax. We'll talk all about it."

The boy began to pace furiously. "I can't sit. I can't relax. But I can talk. I must talk."

Harry tried to slow down his movements. The boy was petrified beyond belief. He didn't want to send him into a panic. He eased himself down into a chair. The boy did likewise, keeping his back arched. "I'm not crazy!" the intruder suddenly yelled. "I'm not!"

"Of course you're not," Harry said softly.

The boy let his shoulders sag. "Do you know what it feels

50

like to have everyone tell you that you're crazy when you're perfectly normal, Mr. Porter? When you're perfectly sane? They all stand there, pointing fingers, shaking heads, clicking tongues, all inferring that you've lost it. It's enough to *really* drive you over the edge."

"Yeah, I've been there, Jim."

The pudgy visitor managed a sheepish grin. "Oh yeah. The name is Seabruck. Ernest Seabruck. Mr. Porter, you've got to help me clear my name. Ernie. My friends call me Ernie."

"I'll do what I can, Ernie." Harry slowly walked across the room and pulled a bottle out of a bureau, the last momento of his wild night at the station. "Want a taste?"

"No. I have to stay alert," Seabruck stated. "I can't have anything dulling my senses, putting me off guard."

Harry understood. "Is that peeper up here on your account?"

"So, you know already?" Seabruck said, amazed. "Well, yeah. They're sending me Earthside. A certified loon. They'll put me away, get the peeper to swear that I'm not too tightly wrapped. It will be veggie city for me after that . . . for good."

"You're being set up?"

"Am I ever!"

"By whom?"

"Everybody."

"Sounds a little . . ." Harry let the sentence start before his mind could effectively squelch it.

"Paranoid?!" the youth nearly screeched.

"I'm ambivalent myself," Harry smiled, "but who cares."

"Yeah, right," Seabruck said, relaxing slightly.

"What did you do?"

"Committed a sin of gross ignorance. I told the truth."

"About what?"

"About a murder I saw . . . sort of."

Harry sat down on his bed, whistling through his teeth. "I need a drink. Now, let's go through all this . . . slowly."

Seabruck left his chair and began to pace, recounting a tale of a certain evening's graveyard shift at the communications center, of a guard named Harden slain on duty, of his own superior's call to the governor and of a vow of enforced silence.

"And nobody ever raised a ruckuss about the killing?" Harry asked.

"No one ever mentioned it," Seabruck said, mid-step. "At

first, I thought, maybe someone on top is handling all this. I mean, I'm not really up on politics or anything like that, I majored in Communications Arts and Poli. Sci. wasn't required. It once was but by the time I got there it had been phased out. But I'm not really aware of politics so I figured, well, maybe they know best."

"They."

"The men on top."

"But you changed your mind about that?"

"Yeah. I began thinking about it after a few days. I mean, nobody ever mentioned that cop after that night. Nothing in the paper. No investigation. It was like he never existed. But he had given his life in defense of something he believed in, you know. He was killed for a reason. I kept on thinking that. I kept on seeing him lying there, without his . . ."

Seabruck began to cry. Watching a man cry always got to Harry. Something about the way the facial features contorted inward. Watching a chubby man cry, really shook him up. There were more features to contort. Pitiful, really. "I'm sorry," Seabruck said, tears dribbling from reddened eyes.

"It's OK," Harry said sympathetically. "Murder can be . . ."

Seabruck nodded, slowing his pace. "Well, I decided to try to find out what happened to the cop by contacting our police chief. I never made it. Mullins . . ."

"Your boss."

"Yeah. He got wind of it. I don't know how."

"Room bug maybe."

"I don't know. All I knew at that time was that I didn't want this cop's life just erased from memory, you know? So I made an appointment with the chief, and . . ."

"You were picked up before you ever had a chance to keep it."

Seabruck stared at Porter, his round face transformed into a mask of astonishment. "How'd you guess?"

"*Island* seems to have adopted some classic Earthisms along the road to paradise," Harry reflected.

"So now," Seabruck reemphasized, "you've got to help me. They've classified me psycho, said the habitat got to me. That'll keep me locked up for years. You're on your way to the hab and you're a crime reporter. You can prove everying."

"Prove what, exactly?"

"Prove that the cop existed, that he was killed, that there was a cover-up. Prove that I'm telling the truth."

"Slow down there, I'm a reporter not the D.A.'s office."

Seabruck's round body seemed to actually deflate. "Then you won't help?"

"I'll do what I can, Ernie, I mean that. But now listen to me, what you've seen can add up to practically anything. Really. Your 'murder' could have been a suicide. The lack of publicity might exist to protect the cop's reputation. Or the victim could have been a bad apple, a cop on the take double-crossed and eliminated. Or, it could mean that you ..."

"That I'm really crazy and imagined the whole thing."

Harry shrugged his shoulders and attempted to bolster the boy's sagging spirits. "Yeah, it could mean that, too. I don't think so, though."

"You believe me?"

Harry nodded, taking a swig from the bottle. "Yeah, I guess so. I've never met anyone who could lie *this* badly."

"Great," Seabruck lapsed into a grin before abruptly tensing up. He dashed across Harry's room and ripped a metal leg from a night table. Returning to the doorway, he held it poised aloft, like a club. Harry's head suddenly began to buzz. He knew that the kid felt it, too.

"That's not going to help," Harry advised.

Seabruck clenched his teeth.

"You're outnumbered," Harry said, rising. "The peepers can get you no matter where you hide. That baseball bat will only hurt your case more. It'll prove that you have violent tendencies, that you're a real nut case. Believe me, lay off the rough stuff and you'll be doing yourself a big favor."

Seabruck glanced first at the club and then at Harry, his expression remaining fixed. His grip on the club did not slacken. "Maybe."

"Listen," Harry confided. "You want to drive those ESPing sons-of-bitches nuts? I'll teach you a trick I learned at a hospital. Read it in an old novel, of all places. Quick. What's the dumbest jingle you can think of?"

"Jingle?"

"A song, a lullabye, a commercial. What's the shortest, catchiest and most asinine one you can think of?"

Seabruck thought for a moment. Both men felt the approaching presence of the peeper. The air in the room seemed to grow tight, claustrophobic.

"Goddamn it," Harry hissed. "Don't write one, think of one."

" 'Gimme it.' "

"Can't you think of one yourself?"

"It's a risco-roll song. It just repeats 'Gimme it, gimme it, I wannit, I wannit,' over and over again."

"Artistic."

"I didn't say I liked it, I said I remembered it."

"Right. Now, here's the deal." Harry clutched his head. Soon, the PSI possessor would be in mind-scanning range. A matter of seconds. "You want to protect your mind from these creeps? Save your memory? Just concentrate on that song. Sing it in your mind. Over and over again. Think of nothing else but that song. They'll peep you like crazy and not find anything but those crummy lyrics. Just keep it up as long as you can. Eventually, the peepers will get fed up and let you be."

"I don't think I can do it."

The parapsych began locking onto Harry's mind. Another trick from an old book. There's a brick wall in front of my mind. Not a chink in it. Isn't it beautiful? Strong. Red and solid. Brick. Red. Sturdy.

"Then sing the goddamn song out loud if it will help. Do IT! Brick wall. He's already onto me. Red."

Not a chink. Solid. Red. Sturdy.

"Gimme it, gimme it, I wannit, I wannit,

"Gimme it, gimme it, I wannit, I wannit."

Harry's mind burned as the telepathic tentacles wound their way around the brick wall of his defense.

The door burst open. A small, emaciated man in a steward's outfit stepped in. The parapsych! Not a guest aboard Harry's flight. Not an ambassador on the way to *Island One*. A flight attendant. A blue collar slob. Damn it. Brick wall. How did Harry always manage to miss the most obvious? Not a chink.

"Don't move," the ESPer said, smiling, a prim bird of prey cornering its next meal ahead of schedule.

"Brick wall," Harry answered.

The peeper's expression suddenly shifted to one of outright horror. Harry's did as well when he realized what was about to occur. Seabruck ran up to the parashrink, club waving high above his head. With a shriek of emancipation, the boy sent the table leg slicing into the small man's head. The psychic pressure in the room exploded before shriveling away. The ESPer, still dimly aware of his surroundings, backed out of the room, blood gushing from his split temple. He collapsed with a prolonged sigh against a corridor wall.

Harry faced Seabruck. "Now see what you've done!"

The peeper wasn't dead but Harry was sure that his brains would be sufficiently scrambled to prevent him from an intelligible thought for some time to come, let alone mentally ensnare someone else's. Harry stepped out into the hall, making a loud "tsk-tsk-ing" sound. "You've hurt the poor little guy."

Once in the corridor, Harry made a sharp turn, walking straight into the onrushing fist of Anson Young. Harry tried to duck with only partial success. The blow caught him on the side of the head, sending him tumbling back into a black void. This was not destined to be one of his better days.

Awareness ebbing, Harry heard his body hit the floor with a peal of endless thunder.

Before losing consciousness altogether, he took note of an echoing scuffle occurring somewhere nearby . . . a scuffle accompanied by a continuous chant.

"Gimme it, gimme it, I wannit, I wannit."

The kid would probably keep himself alive.

4

When Harry came to, he was lying comfortably on the bed of his room. A man in a white smock, whom Harry assumed to be either a doctor or St. Peter, stood next to Anson Young. Young was the first to notice Harry's fluttering eyelids. "He's coming around."

The doctor latched onto Harry's face with his hands and, after pushing and pulling at the skin a few times, announced almost contemptuously: "He'll be fine. He has a thick head. He'll be sore for a little while but that's all."

Harry smiled at the doctor. "You guys sure run an exciting station."

The doctor glared at him and left the room. Harry sat up in bed and, rubbing his head, addressed the lieutenant governor. "Do you always play 'The Anvil Chorus' on your guests' heads, or am I the lucky exception to the rule?"

Young reddened slightly, keeping his tone light. "I didn't realize it was you. I thought you might be the nut case."

"The kid in my room?"

"Yeah. We get a few of them on the habitat. I told you about them before. The isolation gets to them. Most of them don't get violent, though. This case fooled us."

"I should guess so. How's the other guy?"

"Who?"

"The steward."

Young shot a suspicious glance Harry's way. "Oh, he'll be all right, I guess. I don't know whether he'll be perfect in the head area after that blow, but he'll live." Young crossed his arms before him authoritatively. "You're damned lucky I came along when I did."

"Do you think that kid would have pounded me, too?"

"Probably."

Harry blew Young a kiss. "My hero."

Seated in a chair next to the bed, Young began speaking rapidly. Probably to calm himself, Harry theorized. "Yes, indeed, you're lucky I came along. Those cases are hard to get a handle on. They're capable of anything. When he was in here, did that kid say anything to you? Make any wild threats or accusations?"

"About what?"

"About anything."

Harry noted the mounting worry in Young's eyes. He shrugged his shoulders. "Not a word. After you left your office, I waited around for your secretary. When she didn't show after a few minutes, I decided to find my room all by myself. It took a little longer than I expected (all these hallways look alike). I had just walked into the room when I bumped into your space-aged samurai. Then the steward came running in before I really got a chance to chat with my guest. The kid decided to play a quick game of stick ball on the guy's head. That's all I can remember, thanks to your magic mitts."

Young's tone brightened appreciably. "Well, I am truly sorry about that. But if you promise to forget the whole incident, I promise to show you an extra good time once we get to *Island*."

"I get *two* female guides now, right?"

Young pumped Harry's hand enthusiastically and shambled out of the room. Sitting on the edge of his bed, Harry surveyed his cubicle. Everything was in place. Even the three-legged table had been replaced by a new, four-legged one. It was letter perfect.

As usual.

Harry touched the side of his head. Damn. That Young could punch. He walked into the bathroom and wet a face-cloth with cold water before flopping back down on his bed. He placed the facecloth across his forehead and wondered about exactly what went on in here after he had been knocked silly.

"Harry, you're a genius," he exclaimed, sitting up too quickly. He reached into the recesses of his shirt. The lining had gotten torn somehow during the fray. Where was that little sucker? Harry latched onto the object in question. He yanked out the mini-recorder. It was still running.

"ON."

Harry punched the rewind button with glee. "Better living through science, indeed."

After a few seconds, he pushed "PLAY." The room came alive with voices.

"Don't move."

"Brick wall."

"Aieee."

The sound of a body striking the wall outside.

"Now, see what you've done? You've hurt the poor little guy."

A thud followed by a low moan that was unmistakingly his own.

"Gimme it, gimme it."

Hell. The sound was muffled now. He must have fallen on his chest and remained there, face down.

"Shut up, you, before I push your goddamn face in."

That would be Young.

"Did you tell this guy anything?"

Young referring to Harry.

"Gimme it, gimme it."

"Did YOU?"

"I wannit, I wannit."

"Don't play crazy with me, sonny. You're as sane as I am."

The sound of a struggle.

"I can't have you ruining things now. You don't realize what's at stake."

Footsteps. New voice.

Garbled. ". . . what happened here?"

57

Garbled. "... escaped patient. Attacked one of the station's crew."

"Is he crazy?"

"They'll find that out Earthside, I guess."

"Why is he chanting like that?"

"Maybe shock."

At least four different voices mixed in.

"Just move him out of here. Both of them."

"What about the guy on the floor?"

"Dump him on the bed. Guard, get a doctor."

The rest of the tape was fairly routine, until seconds before Harry's reawakening. "I hope he's all right," Young said, sounding genuinely concerned. "I really didn't mean to hit him. I've never hurt anybody before in my life."

"You push yourself too hard, Anson."

"I have to. To all these Earthsiders, I represent the hab. It's up to me to be cheerful and up, twenty-four hours a day."

"That's not it and you know it."

Silence. The doctor's voice again. "Feel like talking about it."

"I don't know what you mean."

"Something's bothering you, Anson. A lot."

"Nonsense."

"Have it your way. Only take it easy or that heart of yours will act up again. I may not be able to patch you back together again next time."

"Yeah, you're probably right. Hey, look. He's coming around."

Harry flicked off the tape recorder with mixed emotions. Whatever was going on here, if something was going on at all, Young wasn't totally responsible for it. Yet, obviously, he knew a lot more than he was saying. Which wasn't too difficult, considering the fact that he wasn't saying anything at all.

Harry stood up and hunted for his bottle. The image of Seabruck's frightened face as the peeper closed in for the kill haunted him. Harry sifted through the various pieces of information tossed at him during his brief visit to the waystation. He had encountered an undercover peeper. He had been beaten up by a sane man who was branded insane ... or an insane man who insisted he was sane. He had heard of a murder that could have been a suicide, or an accident, or the fate of a foreign agent, or the elimination of a bad apple, or the product of an overripe imagination.

58

"Or, or, or, OR," Harry muttered, running his fingers through his hair. He stared at the strands caught under his nails. Maybe a hair transplant would help.

The only thing Harry was sure of was that he wasn't sure of anything that had happened.

The peeper could have been onboard to keep the insane Seabruck's presence very low keyed during the Earth delegation's brief stay.

The peeper could have been onboard to mess up the kid's mind.

Regardless, Harry had been lied to.

Peeped into.

Punched.

To Harry's way of thinking, that constituted foul play.

Seabruck's face flashed before Harry's eyes once again. Scared stiff. He recalled his own first encounter with a parapsych. He had worn that face as well, inside and out.

"Sons of bitches," Harry thought aloud. If they were going to play with him, he was going to play with them, too.

He didn't really care if the kid *was* insane, no one deserved to be treated like an animal. And if the kid's story turned out to be true? Harry would find out.

Now, to toss a well aimed monkey wrench into the wheels of "justice." Where was that slip of paper? Harry rushed to his bureau and fished through the same drawer that had contained his ill-gotten liquor. Those three kids had given him their names last night, just in case he felt like spotlighting them in a story. Where was that tall kid's name and station?

"Aha!" He located the gin-soaked wad of manilla paper. Anthony Rogers, Communications. Bingo.

Harry jotted down a few notes and made his way to the waystation's tiny communications center, a series of four small rooms connected by a single walkway. "Is Tony Rogers here?" he asked a stone-faced receptionist sitting behind a plastic desk.

"He's on duty," she replied flatly.

"Could you tell him that Harry Porter . . . from Earth . . . is here to see him?"

The girl got up irritably and disappeared behind a closed door. Within seconds, the door opened and she returned with an obviously pleased Rogers. "Well, howdy," the lanky technician beamed, looking very much like a yardstick with teeth. "How's your head feelin' this mornin'?"

"It's not," Harry replied, grinning. "But I did have a mighty fine time last night."

"Think you can get a story out of it?" the boy weasled.

"Story? I can get two stories at least."

"That's righteous," Rogers whooped.

"Tell you what, though," Harry said, pulling the youth over to the side. "I do need a favor in order to pull everything together on these features."

Harry addressed the boy in hushed, conspiratorial tones. Rogers, realizing that he had just been taken into some sort of top secret confidence, returned the gesture dramatically. "What's up," he hissed, glancing nervously at the receptionist nearby.

"I have to get a videophone message to my boss," Harry said.

"No problem," Rogers replied. "I can set that up in a minute. You won't even have to wait for an operator."

"Yeah," Harry added, "but nobody can know about the call."

Rogers swallowed hard. "An unmonitored call?"

Harry nodded gravely. "Top secret. Bell can't have a record of it."

"Gee," Rogers swallowed. "I dunno whether I can swing it. I mean, I have clout, like I told you last night. But getting something by those phone guys . . . I'd have to pull in some heavy markers."

"Three stories. Life aboard the wayfaring station . . ."

The technician's face began to lighten. "Well . . ."

Harry dangled a slip of paper with a phone number on it in front of the horse-faced worker. "Plus the number of one of *the* hottest addresses in all of the upper east side of Manhattan."

Rogers colored slightly. "Really. OK. You just hold on a second."

He disappeared behind the door, emerging a few moments later.

"It's all set. Now listen. I'll take you into one of our one-man monitoring rooms. You make the call on the push-dial console. It'll take a little bit of time to make contact. Just remember that you have a ten second or so delay for your videophone message to get to Earth and vice versa. The more conversation you get into, the longer the call. I'll be outside the door. Try to make it short 'cause if they catch me, they'll can me."

"It'll be a quick one."

"Can I have that number now?"

Harry carefully folded the paper and tucked it in his wallet. He put his wallet securely in his back pocket. "After my call."

The gangly technician shoved Harry through a short hallway and into a small, console-laden monitor room. He made straight for the viewphone and punched out Lenny's number. Nothing happened for what seemed like hours. A blank screen. Zilch.

"Be home, Lenny. Goddamn you," Harry swore.

The viewscreen abruptly came to life. A startled Leonard Golden stood before it, his mouth open in surprise. Harry saw someone in the background. Hazy. A half-dressed female. He burst out laughing when he recognized her as Eve from the tranx bar.

"Just call me Cupid," Harry began. "Don't talk, Lenny, just listen. Don't ever let on I made this call. I'm not sure but I think that something really smells up here. It may be big or it may be small, but I've gotten a good whiff. I'm going after it. Whatever you hear from me officially from up here will probably be horseshit. If I say everything is fine, then everything isn't. Got it?

"Also, comb every happy home you can find until you run across a kid named Ernie Seabruck. That's S-E-A-B-R-U-C-K, I think. Take care of him. Make sure he isn't mistreated. Spring him if you can." Harry winked at the viewphone. "Let's just say he's a first cousin of mine. Take care of that for me, willya."

He pointed to the girl behind Golden. "And you with the asthma yet. Watch yourself, will you? One shot too many and you'll be looking down on that space colony from the Pearly Gates."

Harry flicked off the screen and left the room, bumping immediately into a perspiring Rogers. The kid looked like he had hitchhiked to work on a submarine. "There now," Harry smiled. "That was short, wasn't it?"

"I don't know," Rogers stammered. "It seemed like a year to me. I almost pissed in my pants waiting for you to come out."

"A quaint habit," Harry commented, "but one to kick if you're into big wardrobes."

"Now where's my hot number?" the technician giggled.

Harry removed the paper, unfolded it and handed it to the

boy. "A hot one. You won't be disappointed," he said leaving the area.

"Gee, thanks, Mr. Porter," Rogers beamed.

Harry walked back to his room and began packing his suitcases. He hoped that Rogers was into *really* hot times because Harry had just given him the phone number of the 85th street crematorium.

Served him right.

Corrupt youth.

He snapped his suitcases shut and glanced at his wristwatch. Within an hour he'd be aboard a spacetug heading for *Island One*.

He had a real reason to go there now; a reason named Ernie Seabruck. Despite his drinking, emotional problems, and misanthropic streak, Harry still had some smatterings of honor, of responsibility. A promise was a promise. And Harry had promised a lot to Ernie Seabruck.

PART THREE

"The civilized man has built a coach,
but has lost the use of his feet."
—Christopher Morley

1

Aboard the spacetug, Harry stared vacantly into the shiny surface of the wall next to his seat, mulling over the day's events. The interior of the craft was sleek and white, devoid of any and all architectural and/or artistic distractions. The cabin had all the personality of a large, enclosed bathtub.

Harry rubbed his eyelids slowly. Sinus headache. Nothing that happened today seemed to add up, which didn't surprise him too much. He was almost used to everything in his life making no sense whatsoever. No matter. He did the best he could.

The tug was a small, cylindrical craft which could seat approximately forty-five short-term astronauts. Its engines, derived from the old mass-driver experiments, used no combustible fuel whatsoever and provided amazingly smooth lift-offs and dockings. This latter achievement pleased Harry greatly. His stomach was already homesick and any semblance of calm was appreciated.

The tug was only half filled, with various delegates from Earth scattered randomly among the rows of seats. Harry sat in a nearly deserted side section. Growing tired of gazing at his own reflection in the mirrorlike hull, he unstrapped his seatbelt and walked to the nearly deserted rear of the ship. He found a seat next to a small porthole. There weren't many windows on the craft; a concession to the unpredictable power of cosmic radiation. But Harry needed a window near him right now. He needed to feel some degree of communion with whatever it was outside.

He pressed his face to the thick glass.

He was greeted by a vision of star-studded blackness.

Space.

As much as he hated the inconvenience of this entire junket, there was no way he could deny the magnificence of the cosmos before him. The bleak panorama was a chilling, yet alluring, sight; beautiful beyond description. Next to his spacecraft stretched timelessness itself. Infinity layered upon infinity.

Why, it was enough to puncture one's ego if one wasn't exceedingly careful.

Peering into the heart of this vastness, he experienced an unexpected wave of melancholia, of isolation, of insignificance. Like most of his unheralded bursts of depression, this emotional low was laced with secret things of almost perverse pleasure. At times, loneliness itself was a comfort. Emptiness seemed heroic. Sadness invited exaltation.

It somehow relieved him to realize that those stars, seemingly within his grasp outside the window, had endured for millions of years and would continue for millions more. And here was ever-aging Harry Porter, wallowing in self-pity. Bad marriage. Bruised ego. Archaic job. In the eyes of those stars out there, he was nothing more than a gnat.

A cosmic gnat. Harry smiled.

The ship lurched slightly and the "no smoking" sign flashed above his head, more of a courtesy to the ground crew than a safety precaution. Simultaneously, the "heave ho" sign began flashing in Harry's stomach. Holding his breath, he dutifully strapped himself into his seat securely and watched the ship approach the docking section of *Island One*. He observed the space colony coming nearer and nearer. The thing was a lot bigger than he had imagined. It positively engulfed the tug with its sheer bulk. Harry cringed slightly. He felt like he was flying head first into the World Trade Center.

Panic mounting, he took his eyes off the window and stared straight ahead at the rows of seats. 250,000 miles from home because of his goddamn job. That was either dedication or dementia. If he was living for his job, what would happen to him if that job was ever phased out?

He could always open his own tranx bar.

The ship glided to a halt. After a few moments delay, the flashing lights reading "remain seated" faded away and Harry made his way through the forward compartment and the exit hatch of the ship.

He gawked at the docking station awaiting him.

He was overwhelmed at the sight.

Had he not known he was on *Island One*, he would have assumed he was deplaning at any Earthly airport. The station was windowless and lackluster. Walking down four carpeted steps, he got the impression he was stepping into a small abandoned warehouse. The roof of the docking port was rounded, its orange inner surface illuminated by soft, blue lighting. The size of a substantial office building's lobby, the place was devoid of furniture and personnel. Limbo.

Harry and his fellow passengers stood, bewildered, outside the tug. "Now what?" he asked no one in particular.

As if on cue, the hirsute lieutenant governor emerged from the craft, now slipping into his official huckster demeanor. "Now, ladies and gentlemen," he began, "if you will be so kind as to follow me. We will take the motorized runway to the main lobby of the spaceport. Your baggage will make the trip alongside of you, on the small conveyer belt system to your right. Step this way, please. Hold onto the railing, if you will. When you're not used to the low gravity here, these runways can give you a devil of a time."

Harry smirked. What low gravity. He felt perfectly normal, the same weight he did on Earth. Harry followed the herd of visitors to the runway, a moving section of floor which zigzagged out of the domed warehouse, around a corner, and into visual oblivion.

When it came his turn to board the moving walkway, he stepped on casually, hands draped at his side. Although he had given his first step a lot of thought prior to actually taking it, as soon as one shoe hit the moving pavement, he realized he had miscalculated his movement . . . badly. Before he took two steps, he found his feet beginning to slide several paces ahead of the rest of his body. In a last ditch effort to postpone the execution of an impromptu backflip, he quickly reached out and grabbed the nearby hand railing. He noticed a grinning Anson Young gazing back at him. Young nodded in his direction.

Harry nodded back.

The smug bastard.

Harry would teach that hairy wiseacre a lesson. He'd master this gravity routine within a few minutes and then challenge the fat old duffer to a foot race.

The runway rounded a corner and the visitors entered a chamber of warm, yellow light. The conveyor apparatus emptied into a large, domed, glass structure that served as the main entrance and exit to the spaceport. For one brief instant, Harry thought he had died and gone to Heaven . . . or at least Hawaii.

Island.

Alighting from the runway, he stood gawking at the habitat facing him, a totally unique tunnel-vision vista. Contrary to Harry's expectations, the place did not resemble a machine shop in the least. It was green. A rich, lush, tropical hue. Ahead of him rested an elongated stretch of man-made geography lined with flowers and trees and small lakes. Sunshine poured in from the reflecting mirrors at the sides of the cylinder, cascading over the roofs of the minute, bungalowlike dwellings. There were no clouds in the "sky." No smog in the air. Vision was crystal clear. On the small streets below, people strolled leisurely on walking paths, rode bicycles, or puttered along in sleek golf cartlike vehicles.

It was as if a slice of rural Earth had been severed from its host and placed into a gigantic test tube. Harry was both fascinated and appalled. There was something quite unnatural about all this. Then again, his feelings could have been tainted by standard Earthside prejudices.

He waited until his eyes were satiated before continuing on his way. Picking up his luggage, he made a stab at walking briskly toward the exit. Much to his dismay, he found that the habitat's gravity, while not drastically different from that of Earth's, was light enough to make his casual stroll resemble a petit mal seizure. Clutching his luggage to his chest, he watched with morbid fascination the faces of startled passersby as he jerked across the lobby. He attempted to slow down his gait by aiming himself at fairly large, stationary objects, such as sofas, support beams, and stunned children. After what seemed to be a roller-coaster eternity, he was brought to a halt by Anson Young who held out a powerful and much needed arm.

"Careful there, Porter," the bearded politician laughed, "or the hab police will give you a speeding ticket."

"Funny," Harry muttered, sputtering to a stop. "Do you people wear magnets on your shoes to walk a straight line?"

"Don't let it get to you," Young advised. "It takes a little time to get used to the g pressure here. But, once you master it, you'll be able to perform veritable wonders."

"Such as?"

"Such as low g swimming, pedal plane gliding, love making. You name it. Come here, I'll show you what I'm talking about." He pushed Harry forward. "Here by the window."

Harry grunted and allowed himself to be steered to the side of the see-through dome. The Lt. Governor pointed to the far side of the cylinder. "You see how the colony is tubular in shape?"

"Yeah . . ."

"Well, in order to generate gravity, the tube has to spin. Now, the Centrifugal force generated by that spin allows us to walk around on our land areas, on the surface of the tube."

"What is this, Elementary Science 101?"

"Patience, dear Harry. Our gravity becomes less taxing as you move toward the middle of the tube, the axis. In other words, on *Island*, the higher up you are, the lighter you are. Climb a hill and you're lighter at the top than you are at its base. I'd guess you shed four to ten pounds every story you travel upward. The spaceport is about two and a half stories off the ground. You'll feel a lot more at home on street level."

"Fine. In the meantime, am I supposed to just turn cartwheels?"

Young slapped Harry on the back. "Don't take it so personally. I don't think anyone in your group is having an easy time of it." Young pointed to the disembarking ramp. Harry watched his fellow travellers flail about the docking center helplessly, their luggage flying every which way. Seasoned Islanders laughed and ran for cover behind the safety of refreshment counters as the American crowd sliced through the spaceport like a group of whirling dervishes. Much to Harry's obvious delight, Tony Safian was at the head of the group. The first one off the spacetug. The first one to fall flat on his face in the lobby.

Anson noticed Harry's glee. "There. You see? You're liking it up here better with each passing moment."

Harry shook his head in amazement. "You know something, Anson? You're almost as sadistic as I am."

"I'm flattered."

"Don't be. I said 'almost.' You still have a lot of catching up to do."

"I'll cram." He handed Harry a numbered card.

"What's this?"

"In the waiting room outside, there's a gathering of guides hand picked especially for you all. They'll see you around the habitat for as long as you stay. Each guide has a numbered uniform. Those numbers match the ones on your cards."

"Is this my hubba-hubba girl?" Harry smirked.

"That's entirely up to you, Porter," Anson shrugged, walking off. "You have a filthy mind for a man of your age."

"I practice," Harry answered, taking hold of his luggage and stumbling toward the exit door. As he neared the portal, he found himself humming to himself. The muzak in the building was infectious. This place wasn't as horrid as it was made out to be; sort of relaxing, really.

He stopped humming.

He noticed a group of men carefully arranged in a casual manner in front of the door. They were dressed like the typical space voyager, in loose-fitting jumpsuits designed for leisure wear. But there was something about them that struck Harry as being very *un*leisurely. Maybe it was their stance. The active movement of their eyes. For Harry, they might just as well have been sporting blue uniforms.

Police.

Harry was fairly certain that the men were armed security forces. Just to make sure, he took a carefully angled trip, propelling himself forward at a breakneck pace. He hit one of the Islanders full force, jutting his elbow into the fellow's side. The pedestrian let out a punctured moan of anguish.

"I'm awfully sorry," Harry gasped.

"It's all right," the injured man wheezed. "My fault, really."

Harry straightened himself out and continued to apologize profusely. "I'm still new to all this low gravity business," he said, backing out the door. "Again, I'm really sorry."

"S'all right."

Harry turned his back on the fellow and continued on his way. Either that guy was wearing an external pacemaker or he was carrying a shoulder iron beneath his jumpsuit. Harry surmised, from the position of the other men's arms, that they

68

were all similarly equipped. Now why would half a dozen gun-toting guards be patrolling the spaceport incognito?

So much for Heaven.

The muzak droned on.

Harry didn't feel like humming anymore.

2

"Number 13."

Harry stared at his card. "13." He winced involuntarily. He was wrong about Anson Young. That guy was even more twisted than he had initially suspected. What a number to give to a guy.

He stood in the middle of the reception area and watched the group of Earth visitors hold up their guide number cards. The visitors then met their personal companions and made their way to a series of clear elevator tubes leading them down to street level.

He wandered around the bevy of guides, mostly female, most very attractive. A particularly comely redhead caught his eye immediately. Harry flashed his all-purpose smile and tried to catch a glimpse of the number stenciled on her pocket. Great pocket. Lousy number. 9. Oh well, he reasoned philosophically, she would probably have only hurt him in the end.

As more and more of the delegates paired with their companions, the population of the room dwindled to a mere handful of people, with equal amounts of tourists and guides wandering about aimlessly. Harry spotted a young lady staring out the side of the reception room wall window. Her back was toward him but he caught her "13" tag affixed to her shoulder bag. She was shapely, if a bit on the thin side. Shoulder-length black hair. Harry chuckled to himself. Imagine being superstitious about the number 13.

He walked up to the girl and tapped her on the shoulder. "Miss?"

The guide turned around slowly, an inquisitive expression

69

playing across her face. She was even more attractive than indicated by her back and bag, with piercing brown eyes and high cheekbones which accented a pair of thick, sensuous lips. Harry gazed deep into her eyes.

"Oh, shit!" he exclaimed.

"Nice to see you too."

He dropped his bags onto the floor. "Sylvie, what the hell are you doing up here?"

"The name is Sylvia. It has always been Sylvia. It has never been Sylvie."

"Sylvie is your nickname."

"Wrong, buster. Sylvie is *your* nickname. You coined it. You used it. I never did."

"Are you going to start that crap again after, what, seven years?"

"Eight and a half and who's counting?" The girl clenched her fists, her face tightening visibly. Harry half expected to be pummeled to the ground. "In answer to your question," she hissed, "I work up here. I have for six months. And you .... are you with this bus tour?"

"No, I walked here." Harry rolled his eyes heavenward in exasperation. "I don't believe this. I don't believe any of it. Young must have known, that son of a bitch. 'I'll cram,' he says. Cram? He's already way ahead of Fu Manchu. He must have known about us all along."

Sylvie narrowed her eyes to reptilian slits. "US? There's nothing to know about *us*. There hasn't been an us since you walked out on me eight and a half years ago."

Harry's face paled before taking on a bright red mask of rage. "I walked out? I never walked out! You walked out! That's who walked out. I just stopped calling."

"Same thing."

"It certainly is not. We argued. You took off. I never heard from you again. You could have called me. What are you ... a mute? You had a phone and a dialing finger."

"I didn't think you wanted me to."

"Well, you were WRONG, goddammit," Harry barked, glaring at Sylvie Dunbar angrily. The girl glared back.

He suddenly picked up his bags and marched toward the elevator at a near 45° angle. "I can't believe Young has done this to me. A twenty-four-hour guide to administer to my every need. Hah! Here I thought he was setting me up with a racy bedpartner."

"Bedpartner!!" the girl nearly screamed, following Harry at a distance. "I wouldn't sleep with you if my life depended on it."

"You never used to mind sharing my bed."

"How the hell would you know? You were pickled so often back then that everyone referred to you as 'The Cucumber.' "

"I was going through a professional crisis."

"You were going through a fifth of Scotch for breakfast."

"Well, you weren't exactly Suzy Homemaker yourself."

"I did my best."

"Yeah. You used to dress to kill . . . and cook the same way."

"Don't you ever get tired of having yourself around?"

Harry pushed the button on the elevator. Sylvie grabbed his arm. "Just where do you think you're going with those bags?"

"To find dear Mr. Young," Harry sneered. "I want a new guide."

The woman blanched. "You can't do that."

"Why not?"

Her lower lip began to quiver. "Because it will cost me my job."

He saw that her worry was genuine. Hell, he never could sustain a good rampage. He took her by the arm and stumbled back to the window. "Are you serious?"

"Yes, goddamn it," she blurted. "And this job is all I've got left. So far, I don't think the powers that be up here have been too impressed with my . . . outspoken nature, either."

"Are you still outspoken?"

"Go to hell."

"Guess so." Harry smiled slightly. "What happened to your film work? I thought you wanted to direct."

Sylvie sighed. "Oh, Harry. That was such a long time ago. I couldn't make a living making soap commercials for the rest of my life. I gave it up. I was going nowhere fast. I went into public relations for a while. I did OK, but it got to be pretty tedious. Then, there was a job opening on the habitat. I thought it would be interesting, look good on my resumé, too. I applied. They took me."

"Young been rough on you?"

Sylvie crinkled her nose in a sign of disdain. "A little bit.

71

It's still not easy for a woman to deal with a man in a professional situation. Some men just don't accept it nicely."

Harry frowned his brow. "Has he . . . you know . . . well."

Sylvie laughed; a light, airy sound that stirred too many memories for Porter. "You always were a numbskull in certain areas. No, I haven't slept with him, dear . . . not that he hasn't tried."

Harry grinned boyishly, obviously relieved. "Do you know what I'm thinking."

"Is it clean or filthy?"

"Clean on our part, filthy on Young's. I think Mr. Anson Young has paired us together as a double dose of revenge for two of his most prominent troublemakers."

"Could be."

The twosome leaned on the glass wall. "Well," Harry began, "you're probably pretty good at your job. You were always good at whatever you tried. I need a reliable partner. So . . . I guess we're stuck with each other."

"Guess so."

"One thing, though," Harry cautioned. "You have to promise to be honest with me about conditions up here. I'm not here for fun. I'm here for a story. I have to be told the truth about everything."

Sylvie gave a mock salute. "Yes, massuh."

"Don't be a smartass. Something stinks up here."

"From the looks of your luggage . . ."

"No, I mean it. When I got off the tug just now, for instance, I was greeted by a small army of plainclothes cops. Shoulder holsters and everything. Charming, eh?"

"Are you kidding?"

"I never kid."

"How could I have forgotten? You have a shitty sense of humor when it comes to your job." She patted him reassuringly on the arm. "You wait here. I'll have a look."

Harry watched her stroll to the door leading back into the disembarking area. She hadn't changed much in eight years. She looked good. Perfect. She even still had that funny walk he had loved so much back then. Sort of a petite lope. She paused at the glass door, peered inside, and then returned to Harry. "There's no one there now," she announced. "Are you sure you're not hung over?"

"I don't drink anymore . . . much."

The elevator door opened. Sylvie led him by the arm. "Be

careful in the elevator, now. You get heavier as we get nearer to the ground floor. Hey, maybe those guards were there to protect the rest of the passengers from your rapier wit."

"In your ear, Dunbar."

"The famous Porter wit. As I recall, you couldn't get a laugh out of a hyena."

"Go ahead. Insult me."

"You love it, you masochist." Harry broke free from Sylvie's grasp, allowing her to enter the elevator first. As she sauntered by him, she removed a long brown hair from his shoulder. "Been losing a lot of these lately, old timer?"

He pushed her toward the back of the car. "Can it."

"Don't think of it as having less hair to comb," she smiled sweetly. "Think of it as having more face to wash."

"You may be the first tour guide killed in action," Harry muttered.

"Did you really mean that?" she asked as the elevator door closed.

"About murdering you?"

"No. About you wanting me to call you back."

Harry swallowed uncomfortably. "Well, yeah."

Sylvie smiled. "That's nice."

"Do you still snore when you sleep on your left side?"

Sylvie stepped soundly on his foot.

Harry grimaced, feeling his stomach tense as the elevator neared ground level. His limbs sagged under the increasing gravitational pull. It was a totally unnerving experience, the sensation being the exact opposite of that encountered in a descending Earth elevator.

The door slid open and Harry, luggage still in hand, followed Sylvie into the street.

"We can get a car across here," she said, stepping from the spaceport grounds.

With Harry in tow, she walked briskly across one of the habitat's small thoroughfares. After a few steps, she noticed that Harry was no longer at her heels. She turned and spotted him at the curb, hesitating before placing a foot on the street. He glanced to the left and, then, to his right. No need to get killed on your first day on the habitat by an intergalactic hit and run driver.

Giggling to herself, Sylvie retraced her steps and dragged him along. "That's the perfect way to spot a new arrival," she explained. "There's no need to do that up here. There's no danger of cars sneaking up on you. On the hab, the streets are

73

walkways, the sidewalks. At the very worst, if you're not careful, you'll be mowed down by a myopic jogger."

"Well, I've been having this streak of luck . . ." he began. "Besides, if the 'streets' are for people, where do your cars . . ."

"There are no cars per se," she said, crossing to the far side of the footpath. "We have a series of small, electric shuttle-craft. Go carts, really. They run along monorail tracks alongside the walkway."

Harry scrutinized the ground and noticed that, indeed, there was a barely noticeable metal track running along the side of the street.

"On one side of the street we have the electric cart track," she said. "On the other side, we have a small paved route, designated for bike riders."

"That doesn't seem very futuristic to me."

"Maybe not, but it's very efficient. The habitat isn't all that huge so it doesn't require a very complex means of ground transportation. You can walk practically anywhere in the cylinder in five or ten minutes. If you're in more of a hurry, you can pedal or ride in style."

"Level with me," Harry said solemnly, gazing into her eyes. "You memorized that from one of those cheesy pamphlets, didn't you?"

Sylvie ignored Harry's remark, turning to her right. "Yonder comes our chariot."

A small monorail car, akin to an earthbound golf cart, glided along the track, empty. Sylvie pushed a small button on a parking meterlike stand next to the track. The car slid smoothly to a halt.

"Climb in, greenhorn."

Harry tossed his luggage in the back of the car and stepped into the passenger seat. "Don't you ever have any traffic accidents on these things? I mean, with just one rail and all. Suppose you slow down and the cart behind you doesn't?"

"It's all monitored by the computer section at C&C . . ."

"Come again?"

"Communications and Control. When one comes to a halt, the car directly behind it slows down accordingly."

"Isn't anyone ever in a hurry around here?"

Sylvie wriggled into the "driver's" seat. "Chin up, old man. You'll get used to the calm." She typed out Harry's hotel destination on the dashboard keyboard. The printed destination appeared on a small dash-screen and the cart slowly began to pick up speed, finally reaching a cruising limit of 20 mph.

Harry felt like an adult caught in a kiddie amusement park. "Can't these things go any faster?"

"Not unless someone at Control goes bonkers and begins to toy with the speed levels."

Irritating Harry even more than the molasses motor movement of the cart was the constant melody which kept buzzing through his head. Where would he have encountered such an insipid strain? Finally, he realized that it wasn't his memory that was torturing his auditory senses, it was the habitat itself.

"Doesn't that muzak ever shut off?" he complained.

Sylvie listened for a moment. "What? Oh, that. You don't even notice it after a while. It's on all the time. Soothing, isn't it?"

"I feel like I'm touring an outer space shopping mall."

"Don't you like our colony?" she asked innocently.

Harry slouched in his seat. Had he been wearing a hat, he would have pulled it over his eyes. "Sure. It's very exotic. Just drop me off when we get to the shoe department."

3

As far as hotel rooms went, this one was pretty decent. Who was he kidding? By Earth standards, it was positively opulent. Harry paced around the room before moving onto the small terrace outside. Pulling up a basket-chair, he sat and observed the colony. On the other side of the terrace railing stood the most kaleidoscopic spacecraft he had ever imagined. Houses below him. Houses above him. "Never thought I'd see a world more upside down than Earth."

Everything about the space cylinder seemed ultra-efficient. Even his hotel room was arranged to give a visitor from Earth the consoling illusion of open space. With over 10,000 people packed into the colony's two miles, the habitat's designers had taken great pains to reinforce the concept of vastness. Houses were layered delicately between large tracks of fertile land, giving the 1,000-meter swaths of landscape the look of a modern day Sherwood Forest boasting occasional clusters of communities. Most of the entertainment centers and shops were located discreetly one-half story beneath the greenery.

Harry glanced at the grass beneath his feet. Even here, the master design was in evidence. His lush terrace was, in reality, the roof of the suite below him. And that room's terrace, the roof of the room below it. And so on, and so on.

The phone in Harry's room razzed him. Leaving the terrace, he padded across the suite's soft carpeting and picked up the receiver. Sylvie's face appeared on the unit's small screen.

"Just checking up on you."

"Thanks, mom," Harry replied. "The room is very nice. I am very tired. Any words of wisdom before I lapse into coma?"

"Just remember we have a dinner engagement this evening. All the Earth delegates will be present along with *Island*'s VIPs."

"Oh, wonderful," he groaned. "What time does the torture begin?"

"Eight. It's semiformal."

"I'll wear clean socks."

"Très stylish. I'll meet you in your room."

"Sounds exciting."

"You wish." Sylvie ended her transmission. The screen went dark. Harry sighed and hung up the receiver. That woman would make some man a wonderful rash some day.

He was dead tired. This spacetravel routine required a constitution somewhat sturdier than his. As he sat down on the edge of the bed, a sudden thought struck him. While he was still lucid, barely, he might as well start a bit of investigative work.

Rummaging through the contents of his dresser ("The NEW New Testament," "Leave Us your Laundry," "What Did You Think of your Stay in the Happyday Inn?"), he located an *Island* phone directory. He unbuttoned his shirt with one hand and flipped through the book's pages with the other.

Haller . . . Halzer . . . Hamdon . . . Hannord . . . Haping . . . bingo: Harden, Jeffrey.

76

Phonebook in hand, he punched out Jeffrey Harden's phone number on the video unit. The screen remained blank. No answer. Well, no matter. At least he had proof that Harden was not a figment of Seabruck's imagination. Thumbing through the phonebook once more, he came up with Ernie Seabruck's number. OK. Now he had proof of residence for Seabruck as well. Harden and Seabruck, two of the key pieces of whatever puzzle Harry was about to work on.

The fact that the names existed in the phonebook comforted him. Contrary to Seabruck's description, Harden hadn't disappeared totally from the face of the colony. His name still existed. Where there was a name, there were records. He fell onto the bed, still clad in his trousers. He wrapped the brightly colored bedspread around his exhausted frame and pushed the computer alarm. "Wake me at six-thirty, dear heart."

The computer speaker grunted an "affirmative."

Harry fell into a deep sleep and once again, came face to face with the sweaty little man with the laser gun.

4

A firm hand picked up the stylus. Reflected sun streamed in through a small window and bathed the sheet of writing paper in a rich, yellow glow. The stylus pressed down on the paper, revealing a handwriting style that was quite florid in nature, teeming with squiggles and exaggerated loops.

Dear Mr. Porter,

This is both an invitation and a warning. You have come to *Island One* in search of a story. I am prepared to give you one ... perhaps the biggest in your career. You are primarily known for your dealings with the criminal element. May I suggest that you are now aboard the biggest criminal mire ever conceived by humanity. You are a journalist concerned with justice. I am a judge. This habitat and the government which has

77

perpetuated it has committed the gravest of sins against the human race. And, referring to the most ancient of all judicial codes, the wages of sin is death.

A warning, Mr. Porter.

Unless this habitat is abandoned and cleansed of its blasphemy, human blood will be spilled. The blood of those whose hearts have been found wanting. The blood of the guilty.

Those who make the rules.

Those who enforce them.

Those who support them.

They will perish, one by one, until a baker's dozen of corpses has been amassed. A loss equaled to that suffered by the children of light.

An invitation, Mr. Porter.

You alone can stop the carnage. Warn them all. Tell them that retribution is at hand. Tell them to save their souls before they are devoured. You will have your opportunity tomorrow when the unlucky number convenes. Use this time wisely, Mr. Porter, or else pay the price.

You are considered a man of letters, Mr. Porter, so please take heed:

> *Yet each man kills the thing he loves,*
> *By each let this be heard*
> *Some do it with a bitter look*
> *Some with a flatter word*
> *The coward does it with a kiss*
> *The brave man with a sword . . .*

Mind the sword, sir. Mind the sword.

I will be in contact after your meeting tomorrow.

The hand holding the pen executed a quick sketch of an animal; part crocodile, part hippopotamus, and part lion. Holding the paper carefully, the letter writer printed the word "a m m i t" under the caricature. Finishing, the writer replaced the stylus in the small desk drawer, folded the letter carefully, and allowed it to sit in the late afternoon sunlight pouring through the window. Soon the sun would be setting.

5

By the time Sylvie Dunbar knocked on Harry's door, he was already dressed. He opened the door with a mock flourish. Sylvie stood in the threshold, her raven hair cascading onto her bare shoulders. She was wearing a translucent sari that titilated the imagination to the point of exhaustion. Porter stood transfixed, flapping his jaw in a vain attempt at a greeting.

"You look..." Harry was tempted to utter the word "delicious" but feeling that he would sound like a hairdresser, opted for the safer exclamation "nice."

"And your shoes are untied," Sylvie said, walking by him.

Harry led her to the room's bar where he had a drink already prepared. "A mai tai for the lady?" he grinned.

Sylvie returned the smile. "You don't forget a thing, do you?"

"Nope. Curse of my occupation."

She took the drink and poured it down the sink. "Well, sorry, Cassanova, I dropped that drink just about the same time that you dropped..."

"Alright," he said, turning his back on her and walking to the sofa. "Just drop it. Make yourself whatever it is you're swilling down these days. The drinks are courtesy of your boss."

Sylvie located a bottle of Scotch and began pouring. "You don't have to be overly nice to me."

"So I see. Aah, hell."

"What's the matter."

"I broke a shoelace."

"That's what you get for wearing antiques on your feet."

Harry threw down the strand of string he was holding. "Is this going to be full-scale warfare this evening or can I get by with just a Bowie knife?"

Sylvie laughed into her drink, genuinely pleased at his irritation. "That depends on you."

Harry stared at the broken lace on the floor, half-expecting it to slither away. He snorted in anger and pulled his suitcases from a closet. He began rummaging through them for an extra lace. Sylvie picked up her drink and perched delicately on the edge of the bed.

"Is this a good time for small talk?" she asked.

"Sure. Let's discuss dwarfs."

"How's Anna?"

"Her name is Anne."

"Whatever. How is wifey these days?"

"Wifey is ex-wifey, thank you."

She pursed her lips into a parody of a pucker. "Oooh. Did Harry leave Wifey, too?"

Harry tossed the suitcases onto the floor and marched to the edge of the bed, staring down at her. "No," he declared, thrusting a finger in Sylvie's direction. "Wifey left Harry, OK? Now is Sylvie pleased with herself? Harry hopes so. Now Sylvie can make Harry happy, too, by shutting her goddamn yap!"

Sylvie's face remained passive. Harry knew she was baiting him. He also knew she had already had too much to drink. She had obviously started nursing her wounded ego at least a half hour ago. Sylvie attempted a smile. "Getting thin skinned in your old age, chum."

Harry sat down beside her. "What's the matter with you? I thought we were getting along just fine this afternoon. What happened between then and now?"

"I thought a lot."

"About what?"

"You."

"And?"

"I decided that I hate your guts."

Harry shook his head sadly and left the bed. "Fine. Now that we've established that as groundwork, let's just shut up and go."

Sylvie was not through. "You're not a human being, Harry. You never were. You have no concept of normalcy. You're always 'on.' You're always thinking in terms of your job. Like that story this afternoon about the armed guards. Tabloid stuff at best. Maybe you need another rest."

Harry winced. Yet another one who knew about his hospital stay. He might as well make up a sign and hang it around his neck. *Former mental case: I feel better now, thanks.* He glared at her. "I'm fine, thank you. And my story was true."

"All in your mind," she said, pointing to her forehead.

Harry tried to control his mounting anger. He wasn't just seething at her, he was bridling over his current state of existence in general. But, getting critiqued by a lush. "Look," he said firmly. "If I find what I think I might find up here, I'm going to make you and your precious colony look pretty damned hellish to the world at large. There's something rotten up here . . . and that something may include murder."

Harry regretted his outburst even before he had finished. The woman nearly dropped her drink, physically stunned by his last remark. A wave of sobriety hit her hard. "Are you serious?"

"Constantly."

"Then, prove it."

"I can't just yet," he admitted.

The woman relaxed. "Par-oh-noyyaa," she sang.

Harry ran to the phonebook. "Like hell. I'm on the right track. Look. This fellow Seabruck, a guy I met on the waystation told me about a missing cop. The cop's name was Harden. Now, look in this phonebook. I found the guy. Haller . . . Halzer . . . Hamdon . . . Hannord . . . Haping . . ."

Harry gazed at the book in disbelief.

Sylvie read over his shoulder. "There's no such name in the phonebook, hotshot."

Harry was astounded. "But there was before I went to sleep this afternoon. I looked it up."

"Right."

"I swear to God, Sylvie, that name was in this book. Seabruck was right. Seabruck. Hey, wait a minute." Harry flipped through the phonebook. "Seabruck is gone, too."

"Let me guess," Sylvie said, "Seabruck was also present and accounted for before you went sleepums."

Harry was flabbergasted. He held the phonebook in front of him at arm's length, as if it was a poisonous snake. "This has to be a different copy of the book. Someone must have come in here while I was sleeping and switched books."

"The work of the legendary phonebook fairy."

"I'm serious."

Sylvie began rumpling the bedclothes vigorously.

"What are you doing?" Harry asked.

"Seeing if he left a quarter under your pillow."

Harry grabbed the girl roughly, digging his fingers into her bare shoulders. "Goddamn it. Stop playing the smartass. Whatever happened between us in the past is over. Period. It didn't work out the way you wanted it to. It didn't work out any better for me, if it makes you feel any better. But now we're both stuck up here under different circumstances. And, if what I'm thinking is correct, quite a few lives might be in danger."

Sylvie broke free from his grasp, stumbling to a mirror. "You're crazy, Harry. Nuts. They never should have let you out of that hospital. You're violent. Look what you've done to my shoulders. You've bruised them."

Harry stepped behind her. "Come off it. I didn't grab you *that* hard."

"Well, look at me," she said, touching a dark mark on her shoulder.

Harry grabbed her finger and held it to her face. "Your bruise is smudging," he said. He held up her hand. Her fingertips were covered with black. He ran his own finger along her shoulder. The bruise smeared. "That's ink."

He pulled her over to the night table. "The phonebook. Go ahead. Slide your hand across that page."

Sylvie hesitated before sliding her finger across the book. She held her finger up to the light. It was covered with ink.

"When were these directories printed?" Harry asked.

"Three, maybe four months ago."

"Ink doesn't smear after four months. This book is new. Which means, my doubting Thomas Watson, that old Sherlock here is not the idiot you make him out to be."

Sylvie blushed, walking quickly over to the bar. "I didn't mean what I said . . . I . . ."

"Yeah, well," Harry shrugged. "Sometimes it's better to say it and get it over with." He took off his coat. "Just let me change. I have your fingerprints all over my lapels."

Sylvie poured herself a drink and pushed it aside. "Harry," she called into his bedroom, "if what you're saying is true and someone did switch phonebooks, why do you think they did it?"

"To keep me in the dark."

"About what?"

"I don't know."

"Then who switched the books?"

"I don't know that, either."

"You're a wealth of information."

Harry emerged from the bedroom wearing a new sports-coat. He was dressed in a casual, Earthly manner. Trousers. Jacket. Loose-fitting white shirt. He carried a necktie in his hand. He hated wearing one so he intended to put it off for as long as possible. "How do I look?"

"Old and tired."

Sylvie put her arm in Harry's and the two left the room. "Would it sound silly," she began, "if I told you that I was a little frightened by all this?"

"No," Harry said softly, giving her arm a gentle squeeze. "I'd say that was a very sensible reaction."

6

The clerk at the hotel desk attempted to get his papers in order. This had been the busiest day he had ever experienced on *Island*. For the first time in memory, the hotel was full. Confusion reigned. The clerk, a blond-haired man with bird-like features, pecked at the various scraps before him. Chaos. The phone on his desk buzzed. The clerk swooped up the receiver and put it to his ear. Thank goodness there were no videophones at his post. His hair was a mess. "Hello?"

"Yes, hello," said a throaty voice at the other end. "Is Harry Porter in residence?"

The clerk was sure he recognized the voice but just couldn't place it. It wasn't muffled . . . exactly. But there was something about the intonation that sounded distorted, almost neuter in gender. He scanned the room grid. "Why yes he is," he answered with the required amount of servility, "but he's out at the moment."

"Oh dear," the hoarse voice sighed. "That's just as well, I suppose. I seemed to have left an envelope for him on your counter. Could you make sure he gets it?"

The clerk was thoroughly puzzled. "I don't understand," he muttered. "When did . . . how . . ."

"Oh, I'm sorry," the voice on the phone explained. "I left it there quite by accident. I arrived in your lobby not one half hour ago with the intention of giving it to Mr. Porter in person. I met another one of your guests, got into a conversation, put down the envelope to shake his hand, and just forgot all about it."

The clerk scanned his counter top. "Ahh yes," he said, still very much amazed by this chain of events. How could he have failed to notice anyone near his station? "Here it is. Well, I will certainly pass it on. He'll be out for the evening, though. A reception of some sort for the Earth delegates."

"Fine," the voice rasped. "As long as he gets it by tomorrow morning."

"No problem," the clerk chirped happily, "I'll put it in his mailbox." Gee, would he be glad to get this weirdo off the phone.

"Oh no. On his door if you would be so kind."

"On his door?" Very unorthodox, the clerk thought. He wondered if he should ask the caller to identify himself . . . herself . . . itself? "Shall I give Mr. Porter a message? Tell him you called?"

"Oh decidedly not," the caller soothed. "I'm an old friend and I'd like to play sort of a practical joke on him. Haven't seen him in years."

The clerk chuckled knowingly. "Of course, sir. I understand completely. Consider it done."

"You are too kind."

"No trouble."

Both parties hung up, the clerk positively beaming. It was so rare to encounter a true gentleman aboard the colony. The caller turned out to be quite polite after all. Really appreciated the duties of a loyal employee, too. Took him into his confidence. Eccentric, though. Oh well. That goes with privilege. The clerk motioned for Sammy the (oh-my-god-is-he-dense) bellboy. "Place this at Mr. Porter's door, 3G, if you will."

A flat-nosed boy of about eighteen clumped up to the desk and took hold of the small envelope in the clerk's hand. "3B. Gotcha."

"G."

"ThatswottIsaid."

The bellboy took the envelope and ambled off. The clerk shook his head watching the simian youth head for the elevators. It was so hard to get good help these days. A sudden smile appeared on his face. He certainly hoped Mr. Porter enjoyed the joke.

84

7

Obligatory night fell. The mirrored panels outside the colony shifted and, within fifteen minutes, the reflection of the afternoon sun faded from view, sending the habitat into darkness. Streetlights flared cheerfully on all sides of *Island*.

The instant night experience frightened Harry out of his wits. Walking with Sylvie on the way to the banquet he was caught off guard by the fade-to-black action. It was like being trapped in a windowless room when the lights were unexpectedly snuffed out. Harry was used to gradual sunsets, not "on-off" periods of daylight.

After a short walk, Harry and Sylvie found themselves at their destination. The banquet room was part of a small entertainment complex located in the center of the populated cylinder. It was, essentially, a two-story structure, with one floor located beneath the "surface." Surrounded by dense greenery, the hall and its adjacent theater and video library resembled three alien bubbles arising from an Earthly meadowland.

They used the escalator to get to the main entrance. As the two stepped inside, Harry noted that, despite its ultra-modern exterior, the inside of the banquet room was fairly commonplace, even by terrestrial standards. A circular room with small tables scattered about and a dais located on a small platform on the far side. Around the dais were several chairs, no more than eight. It was hard to count them from the rear entrance.

"Who sits up there?" Harry inquired.

"Island's VIPs," she replied, moving from table to table in search of their namecards and assigned seats. "Well, well," she clucked. "Apparently you're considered hot stuff these days. We're in the vanguard of the guest tables."

"No autographs, please," Harry grunted, pulling out a chair for his escort. Damn. He was practically sitting on the dais. He truly abhorred functions such as these. They made him feel like he was attending his own funeral with hordes of people exchanging lackluster smiles and inane flattery while dressed as uncomfortably as the human anatomy would permit. Harry sat next to Sylvie. She motioned to his neck. He pulled out the tie from his pocket and half-heartedly looped it around his neck. Damned unnatural piece of apparel. He stared at the tablecloth. Namecards yet. He took note of the other namecards at the table, frowning as he did so. "Great," he grumbled, "we have Safian at our table."

"Who's that?" Sylvie asked.

"Imagine a set of teeth and a cleft chin on legs," Harry explained.

"Oh, the TV fellow," Sylvie nodded. "I think he's cute."

"You would. Pedestrian taste."

"You're just jealous."

He was. Harry tried to change the subject, watching the other guests file into the room. "Were you briefed on all the honchos attending this bash?"

"Yup. Part of my job."

"Well, why don't you do me a favor and give me a rundown on who I'm going to be stumbling over for the next few days."

"Why don't you do your own homework?"

"You're my guide," Harry pointed out. "So, guide me."

Harry spotted a gaunt, graceful figure glide into the hall. The man had high cheekbones and close-cropped sandy hair. His eyes were deep-set, blue; the almost transparent type of hue that gave the impression that they could see right through a person. A light yellow jumpsuit clung limply to his frame giving him an overall effect that was eerie, almost religious in nature. "Who's that?" Harry asked.

"Ryan Frantz," Sylvie said, nodding toward the door. "He's head of the NASA habitation team."

"Oh yeah," Harry replied. "The Moon man."

"Right. The leader of the first Moon-mining expedition. He's one of the key figures to watch up here; one of the few delegates present who has stuck to his guns concerning the topic of space colonization for *Island*'s entire existence."

"He looks spooky."

"Intense. Quiet, soft spoken. He doesn't say too much but when he does, it's pretty important. I don't know what his chances are up here, though. He seems pretty outnumbered."

"What do you mean?"

"See that fellow?" she pointed.

Harry turned his attention to a nervous blob of a man. Medium height, possessing a few treasured strands of blond hair plastered to his dome, the fellow was utterly devoid of personality. The kind of guy who could get lost in a crowd of two. His face was round, babyish, and made noteworthy only by a nose that looked like an overripe banana. He made a conscientious effort to pull in his blimpoid stomach while he waddled to his table. The effort bore little or no result.

"That's one of Frantz's chief opponents," Sylvie continued. "Archibald Curtis, the president's science advisor. He's a nonthinker's dream, having no point of view whatsoever. He's pretty much of a knee-jerk expert. If the president shouts, Curtis shouts. If the president smiles, Curtis smiles."

"And if the president runs scared from the One Worldists down below, Curtis is at his heels, right?" Harry concluded.

"Right."

"Jeezus," Harry exhaled. "These people look like imported character assassins." He gaped at the doorway. "Not Ferron! He can't be here."

"You shouldn't be surprised, Harry. With his reputation."

"I guess I shouldn't."

Harry and Sylvie watched Congressman Wayne Ferron scurry in. Once a handsome Massachusetts born and bred politic, Ferron was now a mere echo of his former self. The boyish grin now transformed into a buck-toothed travesty of a smile, longish hair now slicked back into a shimmering middle-aged wave, cheeks now jowls, muscles now random lumps, the former hero of the youth culture trotted past Curtis and took his place at a table near the dais.

"Congressman Wayne Ferron," Sylvie announced. "The last great champion of the American Eccentric. He somehow manages to latch onto every philosophical fad that sweeps the country and becomes their spokesman, faddists possessing the vote and all. A few years ago, he was the friend of the anti-Moon crowd, then he crusaded for the Pro-Polygamists. This year, of course, he's courting the One Worldists."

"I wouldn't exactly put the One Worldists in the same league as those other oddball movements," Harry said. "The One Worldists are a lot more vocal and have a lot more active members."

"Which makes Ferron an even more important figure to watch," she replied. "He's easy to dismiss when he's in cahoots with a vocal minority of kooks, but link him up with a genuine political stance . . ."

"It's like handing a laser gun to an eight year old," Harry concluded.

A silver-haired, distinguished-looking gentleman chose that moment to make his entrance. The suave Earth spokesman, in his mid-to-late fifties, walked into the hall as if he owned it . . . which he just might have. Clear eyed with a continental-cut mustache and a firm jaw, he somehow struck Harry as the kind of fellow who could make a fortune selling megaphones to mutes: regal in stance but possessing an inherent tenseness that could only be translated into terms of shiftiness. The knightly guest was shadowed by a wide-eyed, cadaverous young man in a well cut suit. The boy looked to Harry like a combination of a recent law school graduate and Dracula's favorite assistant.

"What's with Punch and Judy," Harry wondered aloud.

"The taller of the two is Howard Retson . . ."

"The billionaire?"

"You know of *two* Howard Retsons? Chairman of Kingdoms Inc. . . ."

"I thought Kingdoms, Inc. was an Earth monopoly."

"Watch your language there, old boy, or Retson will see you in court. He's very touchy about that monopoly business. Kingdoms has been involved in antitrust suits on and off for the last decade. Fortunately, for Retson and his associates, they've emerged unscathed from every one. Kingdoms is still the largest franchise operation in the world with fast food chains of every type: King Kone Ice Cream, King Kakes, King Kastle Burgers, and Kingdom Kola. He's up here to add his two cents to the discussions about the future of financial developments on *Island*, sort of a resident civilian with the Midas touch. He's also one of the president's biggest financial backers."

"Who's the hand puppet with him?"

"Ira Stramm. Legal eagle and resident gopher."

"Gopher coffee, gopher paperclips?"

"Exactly."

Harry began to chuckle. "About the class of lowlifes you allow on your colony."

Sylvie made a wry face at her companion. "Don't be so smug. We let you onboard, didn't we?"

Harry glanced at the dais. "Who's the guy on stage with no neck?"

A solidly built, middle-aged man strode onto the stage, obviously uncomfortable wearing a shirt and tie. His face was heavily lined, his eyes hard. A thick mustache perched on his upper lip. The figure looked like a character out of a vintage western, just itching to get out of the room and out of the scientific setting. "That's Joshua Hawkins, our police chief. He's a wonderful cop. Ex-Marine. He growls a lot but . . ."

"Let me guess," Harry said. "He has a heart of gold. He's a real pussycat."

"No," Sylvie replied. "He's a mean son of a bitch. Mean, but fair."

"Oh," Harry said meekly, watching a gaggle of guests making their way to the dais. Hawkins was followed to his seat by Anson Young. A drab-looking gentleman, later identified as Communications Officer Mullins, followed. A bald, bespeckled stoop-shouldered gentleman with the look of a professional wet blanket nearly tripped over his chair. ("Communications and Control Chief Harley Thorton," Sylvie explained. "Cataracts.")

Motley outfit, thought Harry.

Last to mount the platform was a short, stocky man, standing about 5′ 8″ and with a quizzical expression on his face that alternated between boredom and fright.

"That, I take it," said Harry, "is Governor Russell Vallory."

"On the button. Russell Vallory: ex-astronaut, space shuttle pilot, and one of the earliest driving forces in the colonization movement."

Vallory wore the look of a once active man now haunted by office work and clerical responsibilities. His expression was intensely banal, that of a badly aging hero. Stalwart and dull. His body was still athletic in spirit but rounded in flesh. His complexion was ruddy, his brown eyes deeply set under bushy, reddish eyebrows. Vallory moved to the edge of the platform and took stock of the audience. Without blinking, his entire demeanor underwent a startling transformation. Harry would not have been surprised if the guy had pulled a knife and, bellowing a Tarzan yell, leaped into the crowd, slashing. Vallory nodded at the guest tables and, turning on his heel, returned to the table on the stage.

"He doesn't seem too happy to see us up here," Harry remarked.

"Why should he be?"

"Why shouldn't he?"

"Look," Sylvie explained, a bit too patiently for Harry's ego to take. (He wasn't an idiot, just a stranger.) "The

89

colony is his whole life. He believes this type of habitat is the only hope for the future of the human race. Right now, he's surrounded by a horde of jackals who see nothing beyond an upcoming presidential election."

"It can't be that serious," Harry chided, attempting to regain a bit of verbal footing.

"Oh, but it is. The president's party is in control of both houses of Congress. With the president's urging, they could shut this place down within a month."

"And that decision is based upon what these delegates report back to Earth?"

"Entirely."

Harry was sobered by the thought of this group of sociological misfits passing judgment on, what amounted to, the entire American space program. No one on Earth was aware that this visit was *that* serious a matter. It was a mere formality, a ritual. *Island* was celebrating its tenth birthday. The president's men were here to judge the colony's merits, to take part in the celebration, to make recommendations for the future. If there was fault to be found on the habitat, they would publicly condemn it and, slapping the colony on the wrist, rectify it for all to see. But to shut the place down completely? Harry folded his arms and glanced at the diminutive governor. "I wouldn't want to be in his shoes," Harry sighed. "Crockett had more of a chance at the Alamo."

"Crockett didn't have Harry Porter," Sylvie smiled.

"Come again?"

"That's part of the reason why you're up here," she said. "We thought that the habitat would impress you so much that you media mavens would send glowing reports Earthside to help turn public opinion around."

Harry flashed a sickly smile. Great. And here he sat, the hope of the future, attempting to track down a missing murder victim. Great publicity in that. Sylvie seemed to sense his mood. "You wouldn't write about the phonebook, would you?"

Harry shrugged. "What can I say about it? My phonebook was snatched and replaced by a newer, leakier edition? That would look good in print, wouldn't it? You could visit me at the home on weekends."

Sylvie patted Harry's hand. "You're so honorable."

Harry grimaced. The lights dimmed and Anson Young stepped up to the podium. As he did so, Tony Safian and his guide slithered into their seats at Harry's table. Harry's eyes focused on the girl's right breast. Damn. Number 9!

"Sorry I'm late," Safian leered, winking knowingly to his female accomplice. "We were . . . unavoidably detained."

"Quite all right," Sylvie smiled back.

"Stop somewhere to get your hair polished?" Harry muttered.

Young began to speak, taking great pains to point out all the rosy benefits of space habitation. Having read all the pamphlets on *Island* life at least six times, Harry did not feel compelled to listen. His eyes wandered around the room, noting the reaction of his fellow guests.

Frantz of NASA nodded in heartfelt agreement.

Congressman Ferron twisted his fleshy mouth into a frown. Archibald Curtis scraped his teeth with a swizzle stick and, then, meeting Harry's gaze, let the stick drop with a self-conscious cough.

Howard Retson smiled confidently, whispering something to his fish-eyed lawyer . . . who promptly laughed into his drink on cue.

Tony Safian applied a thick coat of lip balm.

Governor Russell Vallory stared straight ahead, an immobile figure, his line of vision focused on the furthermost corner of the room. His jaws slackened and tightened regularly.

Young continued his speech, oblivious to the individual reactions occurring around him.

Harry nuzzled a drink. A dozen or so individuals of a variety of temperaments, possessing a variety of goals, all were confined to one vessel, isolated in space. A handful of people whose actions could, literally, alter the future of the human race.

Harry shuttered, realizing that, politically, all would be taking part in a life and death struggle during the next week.

"Life and death," he repeated softly.

"What's that?' Sylvie asked.

"Oh, nothing. Just a figure of speech."

He hoped.

8

Never could find his keys. Rooms all looked alike, too. Made matters worse. Too much to drink tonight. Where was his room? Hands grope through pockets. Keys. Damn his stomach. Doctors had told him to lay off the booze. Hurt like hell? What's this?"

A note?

A note addressed to . . . Porter? What was Harry Porter's mail doing tacked to his door? He didn't like the looks of that Porter fellow. A wise guy. A know-it-all. Inflated reputation. He could be a distinct pain in the ass up here. Could ruin everything. Look at the keys. Look at the door. Match up the numbers. Don't match. Wrong room. They all looked alike, anyhow.

Wonder what sort of mail Porter had delivered at this hour? Anyhow, no harm in looking.

Hand-written. Good to see traditional values upheld. Let's see. Great god almighty! A real nut case! Slow down, now. Take it in. Uh-huh. Yes. Yes. Quite exploitable, this. Use is.

Thank you, ammit.

Lighter. Where's the lighter? Got it. Clickity. Click. There we go. A little fire in the hallway never hurt anybody. Dump the letter in the ashtray near the elevator. Look at it burn.

Now, to find the right room.

Very productive evening after all.

Never could find his keys.

Rooms all looked alike.

9

When Harry woke at seven in the morning, he got out of bed and made a perfunctory check of his bedroom windows. He was so accustomed to the noise and congestion of the city that the quietness of space struck him as violent and alien. Muzak tinkling faintly in his ears, pajama bottoms falling toward his knees, he lurched to the windows facing east.

He saw the strong sun lighting the trees on the hills below, pouring its light onto the flat water of the lake above his head. Walking to the windows facing west, he witnessed an identical sun shining brightly on the clusters of buildings on his left. The reflective mirrors of the colony certainly made sunrise a challenge to the senses. The terra firma hanging aloft didn't make things any easier for a visiting Earthling, either.

Harry opened the door a crack and wheeled in his breakfast tray. It had been delivered, as requested, at seven-ten on the dot. Harry pulled the tray to the writing table and spread the silverware out next to his battered typewriter. His sluggish body screeched for coffee. Last night's fete had gone on a little longer than expected with quite a few attendees getting more than a tad drunk and more than a tad nasty. It was the Earth contingent that displayed the most open hostility. The Islanders, space stoics that they were, just put up with the abuse. The arguments mainly concerned themselves about life during the coming centuries and the socio/political/economic ramifications of space habitation. Such a lofty brand of exasperation both amused and puzzled Harry, who had a hard time getting excited about today's lunch let alone lunchtime habits of the distant future.

Harry admired the Islanders' patience, especially Vallory's. Harry would have punched out some of those loudmouths last night if he was in charge, or at least swung at them with a chair. Harry lifted the traytop from his breakfast platter, stifling a gasp as he did so. He caught a full glimpse of his breakfast. The coffee was there. So were his two eggs and

93

toast. Also onboard was the traditional mummified cheese Danish. But his fruit juice was . . . well, different.

It was blue.

He held the glass of juice to the light. It looked like watered down Indian ink. "What the hell do they make blue juice from?"

He held the glass beneath his nose and sniffed cautiously.

Didn't smell all that bad.

Your basic citric odor, tangerinesque, actually.

Still, it looked like ink.

Maybe water paint.

Since his mouth was currently inhabited by a taste sensation usually associated with a week-old sweat sock, he decided to risk the juice. He took a swig. Surprisingly enough, it didn't taste bad. In fact, it tasted delicious. He gulped the remainder of the glass down. A vaguely tropical tang made its way through his digestive system.

Settling down for his eggs, he removed a copy of *Future Times*, the small newpaper printed on the colony; an eight-page affair, little more than a bulletin, really, which mixed local news with Earth wire service entries. Nothing abnormal seemed to be happening anywhere, it seemed. Scattered warfare in the east and parts of Africa on page one. Black market baby ring discovered in the children's programming department of a major network. Local protesters in Cairo stormed the prestigious Trotwood Institute and leveled it claiming it "brought them disfavor from the heavens." A small puff piece on the president speaking before a convention of antifamily planning fanatics on page three.

Harry chuckled to himself. Two full pages were filled with a very glamorized account of the Earth delegates' arrival on the habitat. "Bounding from the spacetug, the delegates were met by their colony guides, a cadre of professionals trained and picked for their mission by Lt. Governor Anson W. Young . . ." Harry laughed out loud. *Bounding* from the tug? How about *cascading*?

After a quick shave and a shower, Harry returned to the business at hand. Somehow, while in the midst of getting a prescribed guided tour and visiting a host of sites he probably would care absolutely nothing about, he had to solve the disappearance of a young *Island* policeman from the face of the habitat.

Donning a pair of slacks and a particularly space-patterned

tunic he had picked up Earthside, he grabbed the phone and pushed for information.

An anemic-looking young man's face filled the viewscreen. "Raymond Cooper here. May I help you?"

"Yes," Harry answered. "I'd like a residence listing for a Mr. Jeffrey Harden."

"Have you tried consulting your directory?"

"Yes, he doesn't seem to be in there."

"Just trying to save you a phone credit."

Harry knew he had gotten a real live one, a regular maiden aunt. "Maybe he's a new listing," he suggested.

"Spell it, please."

Harry couldn't resist. "I-T."

"We're in a playful mood for so early in the morning, aren't we?" Raymond Cooper remarked not-too-nicely.

"Sorry," Harry said, "H-A-R-D-E-N."

Cooper scanned his computerized listings. "There's no such residence listed."

"How about Seabruck, Ernest?"

"Residence?"

"Uh-huh."

"Nothing on him, either."

"Are you sure?"

What little civility Raymond Cooper retained for his early AM phone inquiries deserted him altogether. His pasty face turned positively flesh toned with anger. "Sir. I am a professional. I trained in viewphone computerized information gathering. If I say there are no listings under those names, there are no listings. The computer file simply does not have a record of them."

"Could they have moved?"

Cooper could not help but sneer. "Where to?"

"Good point," Harry conceded. "Well, if they were shipped back to Earth, for, let's say, medical reasons, would there be some record of their old listings in your files?"

"Of course."

"And there isn't?"

Raymond Cooper was now at the end of his rope. His voice began to break. "No!"

"OK. Thanks," Harry said. "Sorry to bother you."

"No bother," the man hissed from between clenched teeth. "HAVE A NICE DAY!"

"Yeah, you too." Harry walked across the room and

returned the phone to its resting place on the writing table. He had done it again. Stepped right into something. Whatever it was he was up against on *Island* was of a slightly larger proportion than he had originally anticipated. Someone tampering with his phone directory was one man. Someone having the facilities to reprint pages of a phonebook was a few men. Someone having access to a master computer in order to alter records was a group of men. Harry nibbled on a piece of toast. He wasn't all that hungry. He didn't like the odds up here on *Island*. They seemed to multiply against you everytime you turned your back.

The hotel room's peepscreen buzzer emitted a gaseous errrrp. "Who is it?" Harry called, knowing full well it would be the very hungover Sylvie Dunbar.

"Open the door before I throw up," came a wan voice from the hall. "I hope you have coffee in there."

Harry moved to the peepscreen. He'd teach her to flirt with Tony Safian. "Now, let me see who it can be at my door," he sang, fiddling with the dials on the small door screen. "I can't seem to get a good picture."

"Open the goddamn door," Sylvie whined. "I was only teasing last night."

"Whatever are you talking about," Harry wondered innocently. He swung the door open, his sense of sarcasm withering when he glimpsed her face. It was chalk white. "Are you OK?"

"Uh-huh," she said, shuffling toward the coffee like a zombie. "Just a slight case of premature death."

"There's toast under the debris there if you're interested," Harry informed her. As she poured a cup of coffee, he sat down and began making notes in a small spiral notepad. "Guess what I found out this morning?"

Sylvie sipped her coffee. "What?"

"My missing policeman never existed."

"Says who?"

"Telephone information. Their computer shows no record of him."

"Maybe your talkative friend imagined him."

"Maybe. But, according to your computer, I imagined my talkative friend as well."

"There's no record of him, either?"

"Not a trace."

Sylvie buttered a piece of toast. "Mysterious."

"Very. That's where you come in."

96

She put her toast down. "I was dreading this."

"Well, you are my guide, correct?"

She nodded apprehensively. "So?"

"So. Do you know what I'd really like to see?"

Sylvie poured a second cup of coffee . . . black. "I'm afraid to ask. What would you like to see?"

"*Island*'s big computer."

"*Island* has lots of big computers."

"No. I mean the colony's one master computer. Don't you have one? A nuts and bolts bureaucrat? The keeper of the records? Who's been born who's died, who lives where and does what?"

Sylvie returned to her toast. "Maybe we do and maybe we don't. If we did have one of those items up here, it would probably be off limits to you."

Harry flashed a look of utter bewilderment. "To me? Inquisitive, hard-working me? Me? Who could, as of now, raise enough of a ruckuss concerning this place's irregularities to embarrass the whole titanic test tube and cost you your job?"

Sylvie tossed the toast into the wastepaper basket. "We'd have to make an appointment to get in."

"Today?"

"Maybe tomorrow."

"Better than a poke in the eye, I guess."

"Actually, it's more than you deserve," she said. "You're a real security risk up here, you know. You haven't been here a day and you're running around conducting some half-assed investigation of a nonexistent murder."

"Just one of those annoyances that, if I don't check out, will spoil my appetite for the entire trip."

"Why don't you just get dressed and we'll be on our way."

Harry ran a hand along the folds of his dizzily colored tunic, slightly affronted. "I am dressed."

Sylvie emitted a horse-laugh. "You can't go anywhere dressed like *that!*"

"Why not?"

"Why don't you just wear a sign on your back that flashes GREENHORN AT LARGE every few seconds."

Harry scrutinized his outfit in a mirror. "Too Earthy?"

"Slightly." Sylvie fished through Harry's bureau and pulled out a pair of dull blue slacks and an equally drab short-sleeved tunic shirt. "Here. Put these on. I ordered them just

97

for you." She tossed them into Harry's outstretched arms.

"I thought they were pajamas," he said. "How lackluster."

"It's ColCloth," she said. "Everyone wears it up here. New material is hard to come by on the hab. We recycle all the old Earth clothes, mixing the results with mineral fibers mined from the Moon. It's not very stylish, I grant you, but it's lightweight, comfortable, sturdy, and allows for free movement."

Harry walked into the next room and donned his suit. "It looks like a karate outfit to me."

"We always wear this design," she stated, "except when we attend formal occasions, like last night's banquet."

"I thought that shindig was too normal to be true." He stepped out of the bedroom, feeling ridiculous. He was dressed in an outfit that was, indeed, reminiscent of suits worn by martial arts students of Earth. "I hope today's agenda includes some board-splitting."

Sylvie opened the door and stepped into the hall. "Come on, Harry. We have a lot of territory to cover."

"Don't I know it," he replied. "Just a second." He dashed about the room, placing objects in seemingly random positions. He carefully placed the phonebook on the edge of the bureau, dangling at the letter N of ISLAND ONE DIREC- TORY. He leaned a pen precariously against its binding. A necktie was draped over the side of the closet doorknob with four fingers worth of the thin side hanging on the right. He left the lights to the room on. Harry took one last look at the room before leaving. If the person or persons unknown who changed his phoning habits the previous day paid another visit to his room while he was away, he'd know about it.

10

Sylvie knew that Harry would instinctively loathe the idea of traipsing around the habitat grounds. He was an impatient man. No, actually, it was more than mere impatience. Harry seemed to be genuinely frustrated that he was only one ordinary mortal, capable of being at only one place at one time. He resented being tied down to a single location, occupation, situation, or person. At times, she felt that his entire spirit railed against its corporeal host. There was something within him, some essence, that was never meant to be tethered to any stationary object.

Sylvie remembered Harry's impatience quite clearly. And so, it was with more than some small measure of malicious glee that she insisted they make their first morning's rounds on foot. She genuinely admired his independent streak but she also bitterly resented the casual manner with which Harry meted out pain to those close to him by accommodating that very same independence. In his own, low-keyed way, he was a selfish bastard. "If you're going to get used to our artificial gravity," Sylvie said, "you really should rely on your legs and not one of our cars."

Harry grunted but agreed. To put him off even more, she denied his request to see the agricultural cylinder on day one. "One tube at a time, old chum," she grinned impishly. "Today, we'll confine ourselves to the inhabited half of Island."

She saw the look of total exasperation on his face and took great pleasure out of being the direct cause. How dare he be jealous because of a few remarks she had passed to that TV newsman? Who did Harry think he was, anyway?

Sylvie thoroughly enjoyed baiting Harry. She probably would have lapsed into it today even without the inspiration of his current jealousy. Eight years ago, Harrybaiting had been her favorite sport. She liked to believe that Sylviebaiting had been Harry's prime pastime as well. They had been two of a kind back then. Aggressive. Kinetic. Career oriented. Everything seemed so perfect, so idyllic. Then, whatever dark force they had conjured between them, whatever that intangible factor they had mutually created, entered and destroyed their lives. Their life together, at least. In those days, they had been honest with each other. Today, she felt that Harry was holding back, not taking her into his complete confidence. His hesitation did not bother her as much as it would under normal conditions. She knew that she wasn't being totally honest with Harry. She could never be. As long as he was onboard this vessel, Sylvie Dunbar could never be herself.

Taking Harry by the arm, she led him through the small shopping area of the inhabited half of the habitat. She pointed out the sights while Harry supplied the pointed remarks. Against her better judgment, she encouraged his banter. It allowed her to slip back into the past. She quite enjoyed his lack of respect for practically anything considered respectable. Despite his arrogance and sometimes lethal amounts of cynicism, he was an ingratiating sort. He radiated energy. The type of human being that came along very rarely in one's lifetime. She had watched him slip away the first time around, and now ...

And now she was his tour guide.

She shook off her emotions in a sudden shiver, dutifully pointing out that, although the habitat seemed ultra-futuristic at first glance, one of its prime motivating factors was the old, tried-and-true pioneer spirit. The residents of *Island* didn't have it as easy as most people assumed.

The small shopping mall was located in a recess next to the commuter park, set one story deep. Sylvie took pains to stress the similarities between *Island*'s commerce and that of the Earth villages of old. Most of the basics, in the literal sense of the word, were manufactured aboard the craft out of necessity. Importing goods from Earth was time consuming and expensive. Thus, Islanders had to be very imaginative in planning their diets, wardrobes, and recreational activities.

The main diet was a vegetarian one, with fresh food grown in the sister cylinder. A small poultry farm gave *Island* a steady supply of eggs and fowl. Originally, *Island*'s designers had envisioned herds of cattle grazing about for both meat and dairy purposes, but actual living space had proven that idea prohibitive. (Not only that, but most Islanders didn't relish the thought of slaughterhouses in their neighborhoods.) Most of the meat currently available was shipped from Earth and, therefore, priced beyond outrage. Only the very wealthy could afford a mere beefburger.

Import prices led to the popular acceptance of ColCloth, too. Although colony clothing was as multi-faceted, if not more so, as Earth clothing, it did not impress Harry all that much. Although he did admit that its drabness was well suited for space life.

"This whole mall reminds me of an Army PX," he observed.

"We have designer oxygen masks in the next section," she replied.

While strolling through the shopping center, she attempted to explain the social structure of the hab to her captive audience. He might as well learn the basics now. No telling who he could inadvertently insult if she waited until later. Basically, *Island* was populated by skilled manual laborers and scientists. The laborers toiled at constructing satellites, farming, and keeping the habitat running smoothly in a physical sense. The scientists planned the construction and conducted experimental research dealing with radiation, agriculture, sociology, genetics, the effects of space living on the human aging process, advances in contacting alien lifeforms, and future attempts to come up with new habitat programs designed for the benefit of the human species.

"When it thunders, do these guys take a bow?" Harry wondered.

Sylvie hated him when he was smug . . . which was 90% of his waking hours.

"Isn't there any kind of class rivalry up here?" he asked. "You know, workers out-of-this-world unite?"

"No," she stated flatly. "No one has any time for that up here. We're all working toward one goal."

"What's that?"

"Survival."

Harry frowned. She sensed that he suspected something.

"It doesn't seem normal," he finally said.

"Harry," she countered. "Try not playing devil's advocate for once, will you? Just look at all these people in front of you. Do they look unhappy? Do they look malcontent?"

Harry stared at the ColCloth-suited populace wandering about the hab while she continued to chide him. She demanded to know how he could not be impressed. All morning they had seen nothing but cheerful citizens: smiling, waving, chatting happily about their jobs, their lives, their goals. Finally, Harry turned to her. "That's the problem," he explained. "Everyone is too damned happy. Why do I have the impression that I've just walked into a dress rehearsal for *The Wizard of Oz?*"

"Don't be ridiculous."

"Smells like a set-up."

Sylvie ignored his remark and continued her description of colony life. While the scientists and the workers toiled, their spouses, of both genders, worked at keeping the habitat running in a variety of ways. Day-care centers for the small population of toddlers, shops, grammar schools, and libraries all needed personnel. On this vessel, everyone contributed their fair share.

"What do you do in your free time?" he asked.

"Plan for the future."

"Sounds like loads of fun."

"It can be."

The two left the shopping area and entered a small commuter park. They sat down on a bench. Dozens of people strolled by. Sylvie watched the muscles in Harry's jaw work methodically. He was chewing on a thought.

"What happens when you're tired of planning for the future?" he asked.

"What do you mean?"

"I mean, if you don't like it here, can you go home?"

"Not quite," she replied. "We all sign up for duty in two-year hitches. At the end of your term you have the option to either return to Earth or, should you pass the medical, stay on for another two years. There are some people who have been up here since day one. The Lifers."

Harry began a quick retort but allowed it to wither away before actually hurling it Sylvie's way. She stared at the man sitting beside her. He was unfathomable. He had not aged that much in their eight years apart. But there was something ancient about him now. His eyes. That was it. His eyes were old. Almost dead. Even now, with the reporter in him stirring at the scent of a potential story, those once flashing beacons of exuberance were barely flickering. Sylvie concealed her pity. Compassion would only infuriate him.

An ominous shape rumbled by. Sylvie looked up to see Anson Young striding through the park. "G'morning," he grumbled.

"Seems like a contradiction of terms, the way you say it," Harry called after the retreating figure.

Young stumbled to a stop. Sylvie could sense his unease. He had just ignored one of the Earth delegation. She slouched on the bench. "Uh?" the lieutenant governor mumbled. "Oh. Sorry. Preoccupied, I guess. You know how it is with these political events. I'm chairing the first meeting between the president's men and the governor this morning and I have the feeling that I've neglected something important."

Mistake, thought Sylvie.

"You have," Harry smiled. "You forgot to invite me."

Young, realizing he had already put his foot in it, attempted to back-pedal furiously. "Well, to be frank . . ."

"Don't be frank," Harry cautioned. "Because if you're

going to say what I think you are, I should warn you that I don't want to hear it."

"I . . ."

"Because then I'd have to start thinking that you were barring the press from these casual meetings on this wonderful colony for some unexplained reason. And that, in turn, would set me wondering exactly what that reason could be . . ."

"But . . ."

"And, before you'd know it, I'd be pondering the prospect of freedom of the press in space and government censorship and manipulation of the media . . ."

"Now wait just one minute . . ."

"And rumored secret experiments up here and the One Worldist movement down on Earth and the real reason that the president's men are aboard . . ."

Young inflated his chest. "All right, you've made your point. The meeting begins precisely at eleven o'clock. It's in the conference room in City Hall. Your guide will show you the way, I'm sure." He glared meaningfully at Sylvie. She wilted. "I'll see that your colleague is invited as well," Young added before storming off.

Harry arose slowly from the bench. "Guess I'd better go back to the room for my tape recorder. Coming?"

Sylvie noticed a familiar glint in his eye. "Do I really have a choice? I don't think that I should walk around by myself after that little performance if I want to keep my job. Young probably doesn't think I can control you . . ."

"You can't."

"It doesn't have to be public knowledge."

Arm in arm they walked back to his hotel. Once inside his room, Harry motioned for her to wait by the door. First, he checked the light switch. "Ummm," he hummed. Walking across the room, he stopped and measured a tie hanging from a doorknob. "Seven fingers," he frowned.

He picked up a small pen from the rug on the floor in front of the bureau. "Sloppy." He then examined the phonebook hanging over the edge of the bureau. "S!" he exclaimed triumphantly. "Your second-story men don't waste any time up here. This is twice in two days; a record of some sort, I would imagine."

"Huh?"

"My room has been ransacked again," he announced. "Very neatly ransacked, but gone through nonetheless."

She blinked in astonishment. "I don't see anything different about your room."

Harry led her into the room, kissing her on the forehead. "That's just the point," he said, stuffing his tape recorder into his side pocket. "This was the work of a real professional."

The nice thing about being with Harry, she reflected while he maneuvered her out of the seemingly tidy room, was that one frequently explored that twilight zone located between genius and madman.

"Now what," he asked her, getting into the elevator, "could I have brought up here or stumbled over during the past twelve hours that would cause someone to break into my room for?"

They rode the elevator to street level in silence.

11

The conference room reeked with tension. Harry sat at the far end of the rectangular table, waiting for something to explode. He experienced the same sort of apprehension he had felt while stranded in a mine field. The Earth delegates squirmed in their chairs, expectant birds of prey, awaiting the arrival of Governor Russell Vallory. Only NASA's Ryan Frantz sat calmly in his chair, a beatific spectre, outnumbered and overpowered by the opposition.

Seated adjacent to an apprehensive Anson Young, Harry took note of the look of utter boredom on the face of Tony Safian. It was clear that the TV reporter would rather be somewhere else. Anywhere else. Eventually, Harry guessed, Safian would beg out of the meeting, stating that there would be nothing going on worth filming inside the claustrophobic chamber and his camera crew would be doing everyone a lot more good outside, recording the preparations for the Tenth Anniversary fete. It took Safian approximately four minutes to reach those conclusions. Young muttered something about the meeting not being vital to Safian's coverage, adding a nice verbal riff which included an "extending the invitation out of courtesy." He then gave Harry a very hateful look.

Safian slithered out of his chair and through the conference room door tailed by his two cameramen.

Harry reached over the table and tapped Young on the wrist. "Do you mind if we set up a short interview session this afternoon?"

"I suppose so," Young glowered. "With whom?"

"You. I want to pick your brains a little bit about the social order up here."

Young was flattered despite his anger. "All right. After this meeting breaks, give me a couple of hours to regather my wits. Meet me at my apartment at three."

"Fine."

Harry sat back in his seat and surveyed the room. He did not envy Vallory. This seemed to be the space-aged version of Little Big Horn. Sylvie walked into the room, taking her place next to Harry. She handed him an envelope. "This was at the door for you."

Harry opened the envelope, a standard letter-sized container. Inside was a piece of white stationery with the figure of an animal on it. It was unlike any animal Harry had seen before, a collection of different species' appendages.

"What the hell is this?" he asked.

"Let me see," Sylvie said, grabbing the drawing.

"It looks like an ad for genetically impaired animal crackers."

"There's no message with it?"

Harry ripped open the envelope. "Nope. That's it."

"Maybe an out of work cartoonist?"

Harry shrugged and tucked the paper into a pocket. His attention was caught by Governor Vallory who entered the room and stood briefly at the head of the table. Every muscle in his patently all-American body seemed to flex as he rocked back and forth on the balls of his feet. Harry reflected that in heroism there is boredom.

"Good morning, gentlemen," the Governor greeted. "I trust you all slept well last night after our little get-together."

The figures around the table muttered incomprehensible responses. "Good," Vallory injected. "Now, let's get down to business."

Harry smiled slightly. This man had guts.

Vallory sat and removed a sheaf of papers from a file folder. He glanced at them and then pushed them aside.

"Gentlemen," he said, this brow furrowing slightly. "Let me be honest with you. I have been on this habitat for ten years, away from my home planet a decade. Do not presume, however, that because I have been physically apart from Earth for so long that I have forgotten how Earth thought processes work. I have kept in touch with the political developments and cultural upheavals. I have monitored the comings and goings of fads, faces, and fanatics. It is more than obvious to me from the information I've culled over the past few months and from drunken remarks made last night from a few of you that most of you gentlemen are here, not to attend an anniversary celebration, but to attend a funeral ... the funeral of *Island One*.

"Most of you are here, not to honor its accomplishments and make plans for its future, but to cripple it, close it down if possible. Your motives are political, career-oriented and totally absurd."

An angry reaction arose from the attendees.

Vallory took no notice. "Fine. I accept that. It is my job, at present, to find a way to make this colony acceptable to you in a political and power-oriented way. Again, fine. I accept that responsibility. If you will be so kind as to open your folders, we'll begin searching for an ideal way to solve all of our problems."

In the back of the room, Harry stifled a chuckle. In a few short moments, Vallory had succeeded in disarming every delegate in the room. He had backed them into a corner using their own weaponry.

Briefly, Vallory outlined the habitat's scientific accomplishments for the umpteenth time, adding, "But you know all that. You are clearly unimpressed by it all. So, let's turn to dollars and cents, shall we? Let's turn to profit motive.

"During the next fifty years, the world will see an increase in population that will push its resources to the limit. Increased population means strain. Strain means economic chaos. Space colonies represent one possible way out. If humanity is allowed to be fruitful and multiply they will overrun our planet. Increase habitat construction in space and you will give them someplace to go. We can take as many people into space as want to make the journey. Our geographical boundaries up here are endless.

"Plus, think of the industry you would encourage. New types of travel agencies, commercial space travel airlines, real estate bureaus. Granted, these are long-term goals, but they are all realistic goals. And they have to be given a place to start, a time to begin. That time is now.

106

"On a more obvious level, *Island* has, over the past decade, given quite a bit of America a source of cheap electrical power via our solar satellites. In a time when nuclear power is frowned upon, we have provided a safe alternative. Allow us to continue to manufacture our satellites and we will be able to supply *all* of our fifty states with power. Once America has enough for its own usage, the government could contract our satellites to other nations. This would provide a profit, similar to the type made in the regions serviced by the Tennessee Valley Authority. We would take your orders for satellites from France, Russia, China, construct them up here, and position them in locations suitable for your customers.

"Beyond that, there's the profit to be found in space industry in general. There are items that can be manufactured in space much more cheaply than on Earth. Take biological chemicals. In a zero g lab, our productivity in this area would increase manifold, with nutrients and chemicals mixing much more easily without being impaired by gravity.

"On our construction shacks, we could mass produce a new, lightweight form of steel; normal, Earth steel but with many small air bubbles distributed evenly throughout. It would be as solid as its present-day Earth counterpart but weigh only one-tenth as much.

"Think of it, gentlemen. We offer you an unlimited source of income. You need not spend billions of dollars in financing to get the ball rolling. We are already here. We already exist. We are practically self-sufficient. This is beyond politics. It is beyond special interest groups.

"What you see around you is the first step in the next evolutionary leap of humanity. You, as representatives of your government, own something totally unique in the history of the world. Use it wisely, gentlemen, and you can lead the Earth into a futuristic renaissance. Misuse it, my friends, and you will plunge the hopes of all the human race into a dark age unparalleled in its devastation."

Harry felt a lump well up in his throat as the governor finished his speech. He wondered if Vallory ever sold vacuum cleaners.

The room was mute. Paralyzed. Each member of the Earth delegation stared fixedly at his knuckles.

Archibald Curtis cleared his throat and broke the silence. He rubbed his nose nervously and mumbled something about relaying Vallory's message to the president personally. In light of these new developments, he felt that the chief of staff would like to have direct input in the matters at hand. Harry smirked. Even the man's speech pattern lacked spine.

Curtis hemmed and hawed delicately, before concluding. "You must bear in mind, governor, that your elitist stance aboard *Island* has caused quite a bit of resentment back home with a large segment of our hard-working society, who feel that they will never have a chance to luxuriate in outer space. Those people are voters, Governor Vallory, and those voters have rights."

Vallory nodded. "We are all well aware of both their rights and the extent of their political muscle. However, remember, we sold them the space colonization concept once. Perhaps, selling it a second time will prove just as easy."

Curtis's eyes blinked furiously. "Perhaps," he muttered. "Perhaps."

Vallory slapped his hands together, causing nearly everyone in the room to jump. "If there are no more comments, we'll resume this meeting again tomorrow with statements by Mr. Curtis and Col. Frantz."

The delegates verbally agreed and began to move away from the table. Only Congressman Ferron remained, his body, obviously uncomfortable in ColCloth, trembling with indignation. "Go ahead," he sneered. "All of you. Let the dollar signs sway you from the most obvious danger of this colony."

The delegates stopped in their tracks, intrigued by Ferron's unexpected outburst. Ferron licked his oversized teeth, relishing the attention. "You talk about economics," he stated. "You talk about sociology. You talk about lofty ideals. Why not talk about crime? Why not talk about space warfare? This place is an open invitation to every maniac in existence who wants to make a political point. Did you ever stop to think about what would happen if a terrorist organization decided to take this place over?"

Vallory, standing near the exit, remained unruffled. "We have a security staff. They could handle it."

"Suppose these criminals came en masse," Ferron badgered. "And what about one stray nut case, eh? Can you imagine if some malcontent crazy got loose up here with a laser rifle? This place is a psychopath's dream come true. You people would be sitting ducks up here. It would be a waste of life and a waste of the taxyapers' money, too."

"You're overreacting, Wayne," Howard Retson said, in a

soothing tone. "Why don't you organize those ideas and present them formally at tomorrow's meeting."

The once-handsome congressman twisted his features into a caricature of moral triumph. "I'll do just that. I owe it to the American people."

The delegates left the room. Harry and Sylvie exited with Anson Young. "Quite a performance," Harry observed. "He certainly hasn't lost any of his flamboyance over the years."

Young was stunned. "Did you hear him? A psychopath's dream-come-true."

"Not something you'd want in one of your travel brochures," Harry admitted.

12

Porter had learned quite early on that, when it came to life, there was no logic to be found when you really needed it. Nations slaughtered millions in the name of peace. People murdered each other over spoiled dinners and soiled clothes. Perfect couples split. Affluent children turned to crime. Impoverished children won Nobel prizes. Heroes crumbled under pressure while cowards triumphed. To Porter, the observer, day-to-day living was one ill-timed surprise after another.

Following the first day's meeting, he entered his room, expecting to rest before his meeting with Anson Young.

Instead, his day was shattered by an unexpected phone call.

A surprise.

Harry held the phone in his hand for what seemed to be an eternity, listening to the rasping, sexless voice on the other end. When the tirade was over, he replaced the phone on its receiver and stared out the hotel room window. Had he been a wiseman, he probably would have taken a swan dive. He abhorred surprises.

Sylvie walked into the room and saw the lines stretched across Harry's forehead. "You look terrible," she said. "What's the matter?"

Harry continued to stare at the populated test tube outside. "Oh, nothing. I just talked to quite an interesting fellow on the phone."

"Who was it?"

"I don't know. The screen was blank. He asked me if I had warned *them*. When I told him I didn't know what he was talking about, he said he was very disappointed in me. The blood of the baker's dozen would be on my hands. Justice would be done, and the heavens would fall. He hung up. I think he called himself Emmett."

"Emmett?"

"Yeah. I had an uncle named Emmett. Worked for a record company. A real asshole. A rose is a rose . . ."

Sylvie laughed nervously. "A crank call. So what? Maybe it was your crony, Tony Safian, playing a practical joke."

Harry suddenly remembered the drawing in his pocket. He pulled out the caricature left for him at the meeting. "A crank call 250,000 miles from home. Uh-huh."

He sat down at the writing table and pulled the cover off his ancient manual typewriter.

"What's that?" Sylvie asked, pointing to the machine.

"My typewriter."

"Jeez, Harry. That belongs in a museum. Why don't you get one of those computer console models?"

"Because I hate them. Now, be quiet." He started to peck at the keys, trying to fit together whatever pieces he had of whatever puzzle he was assembling. Thus far he had encountered one alleged witness to one alleged murder. The alleged victim had allegedly disappeared. Both the witness and the murder victim did not exist according to Island public record. The witness had, in fact, disappeared from the public record practically before Harry's eyes. His room had been broken into twice. Someone had slipped him a note of a malformed animal during a high-level meeting and a nut case had just called him and blamed him for the fate of the baker's dozen.

Harry read his list aloud to Sylvie. "Not too coherent," he stressed. "Have I left anything out?"

"Just last night's dinner," she shrugged.

"Hell," Harry said, pecking at the machine again. "This diary is shaping up to be Nancy Drew material."

"Nancy who?"

"Professional secret." Harry scrutinized his list. "Do you have thirteen of anything on the colony?"

110

Sylvie thought a moment. "Not that I can think of, why?"

"Well, our Emmett friend talks about a baker's dozen. That refers to the number thirteen. The blood of the baker's dozen will be on my hands. OK. Do you have an organization that has thirteen members."

"No."

Harry began pecking randomly at the typewriter. "OK. I arrive. Meet you. Sleep. Have my phonebooks switched. Go to the banquet. Safian is there. So is Ferron, Curtis, Frantz..."

Harry arched his back, typing more deliberately. "And Retson and Stramm and Vallory and Hawkins and Young and Mullins and... who was that other geezer?"

"Harley Thorton."

"Hell. I'm one short."

"Translate, please."

"All right. Emmett just threatened the lives of thirteen people. Now, try to figure out what thirteen people he'd be threatening. Some organization of important people. Or, how about the thirteen most important people on the habitat at present. Translation: the guests at last night's dinner. The only problem is that there were only twelve VIP guests on the dais and at the first three tables. Ergo, my theory goes down the tubes."

Sylvie placed a hand to her throat. "No... your theory is still afloat."

"How do you figure?"

"I have a title, Harry. I'm director of Press and Public Information."

"Congrats."

"So, I wasn't there merely as your guide last night. I was there as an invited guest, too."

Harry pecked out Sylvie's name on the paper. "Lucky girl, you've just made the official *Island* Who's Who list... many of whom may shortly be Who Wases."

"This all *could* be a prank," she wished aloud.

Harry yanked the sheet of paper out of the typewriter. "I know. It could be one of Safian's tricks. Just in case, though, I'll tell Young about it. Maybe we can at least get the police sniffing around, just to play safe."

Safe. Harry wondered whether there was anyway the members of the baker's dozen would be safe. Thirteen potential murder victims stranded in space on an isolated spacecraft. A psychopath's dream-come-true.

Sylvie, despite her worry, fell asleep on the couch. Harry sat and stared at the phone. What did this Emmett fellow have against the Earth delegation? A chill shot through his body; that all encompassing shiver usually associated with midnight romps through a graveyard, deserted city alley ways, and superior horror movies.

As a rule, Harry never doubted his premonitions. Right now, surrounded by a seemingly infinite amount of confusion, he sensed trouble. More than trouble, he sensed death. In his mind, Emmett was no crank caller. Staring at the phone, Harry decided that the police should know about the caller as soon as possible.

He picked up the directory and found Anson Young's number. He quickly punched it out on the phone. Young must be made aware of the possible danger posed by this loon. Yet, Harry had to take it slow on the phone. He couldn't panic. He had to make Young believe his story. The phone buzzed a few times before the lieutenant governor picked up the receiver at his end. Harry attempted to smile casually at the image of the half-dressed politician on the small screen.

"You're just a little early, aren't you, Porter," the burly man asked somewhat irritably. "I said to give me some time."

Harry walked to his bed, phone in hand. Take it easy. "I have a good reason to call," he informed Young. "Besides, I don't think I'm tearing you away from an army of fans. You don't seem to be too popular right now."

The bearded giant frowned. "What are you implying?"

"Well," Harry said. "Your habitat heaven came under some heavy fire in today's meeting."

Young's face relaxed. "Oh, that. Don't worry about that. A mere grandstand play. Easy to circumvent."

Harry had picked the right man to call about the death threat. Even now, he found himself charmed by Young's brashness. "You seem pretty confident," he said.

"Without confidence in this business, Porter, you're a dead man. When you've been dealing with people as long as I have, you've got to know exactly where your strong points and your weak points are. I can pull this mess out of the fire if I get the chance."

"Can I quote you?"

"I wish you wouldn't," Young admitted. "I'll level with you, Porter. I'm no politician. I have no need for politics. I'm a seller of ideas, of concepts. I was vice president in charge of

112

Public Info in one of the largest communications companies on Earth before coming up here. This place challenged my talents, if you know what I mean. Here I was out to sell something totally *un*real to the American people. And I did it.

"I did it because I know the right words, the proper phrases, the pregnant pauses. But most importantly, I know how and where to use them for maximum effect. I can wheedle any response from the most stubborn of targets. I don't say that to brag. I say that because I want you to know my function up here. You're not like the other delegates, Porter. I can feel that. If I have to trust someone, I'll trust you. Just keep in mind what my job is."

"I'll remember it the next time I don't want a straight answer," Harry said. He wanted to keep Young in a receptive mood long enough to spring the appearance of Emmett on him. If Young trusted Harry and took the threat seriously, Harry might get the police involved. And if the police were involved with Harry in the matter maybe Harry could find out about Ernie Seabruck and the missing cop.

Anson Young laughed good-naturedly. "You do that, Porter. You do that. Just remember that, no matter what happens up here, it's my job to sell you *Island*. If I wasn't selling this, I'd be on Earth selling something else."

"How altruistic."

"*Real*istic," Young replied. "Now, what was so urgent that you couldn't wait an extra half hour to come over here to discuss?"

"Well," Harry said, "I got a phone call this afternoon . . ."

The buzzer to Young's apartment door rang. Harry watched the lieutenant governor turn from the phone and face the door. On the Lilliputian video unit attached to the telephone, it was difficult to judge whether the politician was angry or simply startled at the intrusion. Young looked into the videophone screen. "Will you excuse me for a moment, Porter?"

"Sure," Harry said. "Expecting company?"

"I suppose I'm always supposed to be on call," Young muttered. He placed his phone on a table, giving Harry an excellent view of a blank, sky-blue apartment wall. Harry crossed his legs, Indian style, on his bed and stared complacently at the sky-blue swath on the screen. He heard Young fumble with the latch on the door.

"Hello," the lieutenant governor said off screen.

113

The hair on the nape of Harry's neck began to quiver. A gasp caught in his throat. There was a strange, alien hue making its way into the sky-blue scene before him. The wall's color began to wash out on the left-hand side of the screen, overwhelmed by a wave of harsh, white light. Suddenly, the entire screen was filled with the light. Harry's body tensed. It wasn't the type of light normally found in an apartment dwelling on *Island,* on Earth, or anywhere else. The light nearly wiped out all traces of the wall.

Harry recognized the light. He saw it nightly in his dreams. It was a laser reflection of some sort. "Anson?" Harry yelled at the phone.

"Are you crazy?" Young bellowed from somewhere else in the illuminated apartment.

"Young?" Harry yelled, cursing his own helplessness.

Silence emerged from the other end of the video unit.

The light flickered on the wall. It remained there too long to be the discharge of a short-burst pistol. Harry gawked, nearly hypnotized, at the void. What the hell was he watching anyway. He pounded the phone with the flat of his hand. "Goddamn it, Young? Are you there? Are you all right?"

As if in response to his question, the light on the wall began to flicker and disappear.

The phone screen was once again bathed in a soft, sky-blue.

Abruptly, the screen went dark.

Someone at the other end of the line had terminated transmission.

Harry sat, blinking, at the black videophone screen.

He took the receiver in both hands and throttled it. "Goddamn you," he hissed at the machine. "Goddamn you to hell."

"What's wrong?" Sylvie asked, waking from her nap. "What's wrong with the phone?"

"It sees too much," Harry blurted, tossing the unit onto the bed. He scrambled to his feet and ran to the door. Reaching into his pocket, he pulled out a small piece of paper with Anson Young's address on it. "Call the police," he said, "and tell them to get over to Anson Young's apartment right away."

"Why?"

"Tell them something horrible has happened. I don't know exactly what." He read the address aloud. "How long will it take me to get over there?"

"Ten minutes if you walk. Five if you take a cart."

"Great! Nothing like wasting time. I'll call you later."

Harry left Sylvie in the middle of an interrogative sentence. He ran out into the hallway, punched the elevator, and waited for the lift. It seemed to crawl up the chamber. The elevator took him to the lobby level. He ran out of the hotel, stopped at the hotel for a quick look from left to right, remembered where he was, and quickly ran across the walkway heedless of random pedestrians. He pounded on the car-call device. He pushed the button once. Nothing. He rammed it a second time. Not an empty cart in sight. Harry waited helplessly at the electric car railing. For all he knew, Young could be bleeding to death. Every second could be essential. And here he was trapped in leisure city. No one hurried here. Damn them.

Harry began to walk to Young's apartment. He had taken but ten steps when an electric cart sputtered by in search of a passenger. Outraged, Harry quickened his pace to a trot and, then, finally, a sprint.

Harry ran nearly the length of the cylinder. Young's apartment complex was located at the end of one of the three strips of land. Resting at the base of a small hill, the apartment building was easy to spot from the pedestrian path. Harry, rounding a corner near the top of the hillside, plodded to a halt. Out of breath.

Below, in front of the small dwelling, a white vehicle sat puttering contentedly. The vehicle resembled an Earthly car more than the standard *Island* go-cart. It boasted four rubber tires and worked independent of the habitat's railway system. Harry guessed that it was an ambulance. From inside the rectangular building, two ashen-faced attendants emerged, clumsily carrying an immense body bag. They placed it gingerly in the back of the station wagon. After conferring with two uniformed guards situated at the building's entrance, the medics climbed into the car and sped off silently. Two more policemen appeared from within the building and the foursome stood outside talking somberly.

Harry crouched on the hillside, feeling that a major production entrance would not be the most productive of ideas at the moment. He attempted to find a less conspicuous way of entering the building. Trotting down the far side of the hill, he circled its base and located the rear of the apartment dwelling. If *Island*'s homes were anything like Earth's, there would be a smaller entranceway somewhere in the back.

115

Without too much trouble, he spotted it; a small, single door near a commuter park path. He casually jogged along the path, up to, and through the doorway.

Once inside, he checked the piece of paper in his pocket. Young's apartment was on the third level. He stood under the fluorescent light of the back hallway. He didn't want the police to know he was here just yet. That eliminated taking the elevator to the third floor. There'd be uniformed men all over the front lobby. Harry stood in the back hall. He was in an isolated rectangular vestibule. A flat gray door stood at one end of the waiting area. He pushed it open cautiously. Laundry room. That wasn't what he was looking for. A few steps further, a second door awaited him. He pushed it open. A flight of fire stairs.

Harry ran up the stairway, tiring quickly enough to force him to walk up the last flight and a half. He'd have to start doing those exercises tomorrow. On the third-floor stairwell, he paused to catch his breath and take a second look at the piece of paper. "Apartment 3J."

In the stillness of the stairwell, he heard muffled voices emerge from the other side of the fire door. "See that no one enters the room," a monotoned male voice ordered. A meek chorus of "yessir" sang out in reply. Footsteps seemed to surround him. He flattened himself against the wall and opened the door a crack. Some twenty feet to the left of the door, on the opposite side of the third-floor hallway, a young, pimply-faced policeman stood stiffly outside a door.

Harry didn't bother to strain his eyes to read the apartment's number. He knew it was 3J. A mass of muscles in a sergeant's uniform barrelled by the youth. "Got your story straight," the blue-clad ox snarled.

The guard nodded nervously.

"All right, then," the sergeant said flatly, continuing on his way.

Harry eased the door shut. No use trying to gain access to 3J by asking nicely. Somehow he had to get inside that apartment. He had to find out what had happened. He slumped against the stairwell wall. Half an idea struck him.

Hell. It was lame enough to work on Earth, it might work on *Island* as well. He brushed off his clothes, took out his wallet and pulled out a calling card from a stack of nearly forty different ones. "TIMOTHY PATRICK O'CONNOR: HOLOGRAPHIC FEATURE SERVICE." Harry kissed the card. He was glad he had had these babies run off. Never knew when one would come in handy.

He jogged up another flight of stairs, opened the door, and emerged on the fourth floor. Not a uniformed man in sight. His plan was simple. He'd ring the bell to 4J, flash his credentials and interview whomever it was inside with the promise of a brilliant holographic slice-of-life feature to follow. Then, somehow, he'd get from 4J to 3J.

He walked up to the door and pressed the buzzer.

No one answered.

He pressed it a second time.

Silence.

Harry exhaled slowly, greatly relieved. He tucked the card back into his wallet. As long as he had to act shifty over all this, he preferred to do it in private. He hated to fake interviews. It seemed so dishonest.

Glancing down the hall and finding it completely lacking in traffic, he removed a compact, tuning-fork device from the folds of his tunic. Flicking a switch on the minute machine's base, he activated the vibrating ends of the pick. Harry inserted the pick into the apartment's lock and angled its vibrating action with the skill of a surgeon. Within seconds the latch clicked and the door to apartment 4J was open.

One of the nicest things about being a crime reporter was the memorabilia you accumulated along the way.

Harry opened the door and entered the room. Nice apartment. Smaller than he would have imagined but tidy; filled with modular see-through furniture. All done in white. Must be a woman's dwelling, he figured. Maybe a male dancer's. Harry yanked a handkerchief from his back pocket and closed the door behind him, giving the doorknob a quick rub. There was no sense in leaving his signature all over the place. Ignoring the apartment, he marched out onto the patio.

If this building was designed anything like his own hotel, the roof of Anson's room would be the floor of this patio. Most of the rectangular dwellings were angled slightly, stairstep style, to allow for these overhangs. Harry reasoned that if he jumped from this patio, he would land in Anson's yard below. He looked over the shrub-laden fence and saw a patio beneath it. He hoped that these apartments were numbered logically or else, when he jumped, he might land in some unsuspecting Islander's home unannounced.

Balancing himself precariously on the metal railing, he

117

wiped the fence clean of his fingerprints and leaped forward. He dropped some fifteen feet, hitting the soft dirt with a thud and rolling into the lawn furniture. Without too much of an effort, he tumbled over onto his feet and straightened himself with the ease of a circus acrobat. Young had been right. There were quite a few things you could get away with in *Island*'s lighter gravity that you couldn't even attempt on Earth. Back home, right now, after a similar maneuver, Harry would have resembled a Notre Dame Cathedral employee, his right shoulder jammed somewhere in his midsection, providing for a lot of pain but great bell-ringing potential. Dusting himself off, he peered inside the apartment.

It was indeed Anson Young's. He recognized the sky-blue wall nearest the glass patio doors. Sliding open the door, he stepped into the living room. Everything was in order, if you could call Young's stacking abilities orderly.

Young, a confirmed bachelor, would not have won any housekeeping awards on any planet. *Island* pamphlets were scattered in small clumps about a large writing table in the center of the room. Notebooks, pads, and small pocket recorders littered the sofa. Young was a total professional. That was easy to see. If he had a social life, his apartment certainly did not betray it. Judging from the stacks of papers situated on nearly every piece of furniture in sight, the man lived for his work. Harry tossed a notebook from the sofa onto the desk. He probably died for his work, too.

Harry walked carefully across the room.

The apartment was fairly dark. Under the front door, in the strip of lighted hallway which shone between the doorframe and the apartment's lush pile carpeting, the shadow of two feet solidly stood. The cop was still guarding the room. Straining his eyes somewhat against the total effect of the shadow-filled apartment and the deep blue rug, Harry made out an equally shadowy stain near the doorway.

The stain seemed black in the darkness. Herry guessed it to be crimson. It formed a substantial puddle some three feet from the doorway. Harry couldn't chance turning on a light. In the darkness, he approached the stain. It was some three feet in diameter. He bent over the shiny pool. He dipped his finger into it. The liquid was sticky, cold. He raised his finger to his eyes. He didn't really have to go through the procedure. He knew it was blood from the moment he spotted it. Straightening himself up, he noted that the wall closest to the door was also marred. A scorch mark at least an inch and a

118

half wide and two feet long sliced through its placid blue surface.

Harry glanced at the puddle and, then, at the wall.

Harry's mind raced schizophrenically into the scene before him. On the one hand, he was a reporter. His only concerns should be assessing the facts before him. On the other hand, he had been around so many police cases similar to this that the cop-mannerisms that had rubbed off onto his personality urged him to try to piece together the random elements left in the room. The only benefit of being schizophrenic was that you were never alone.

The cop in Harry walked back toward the patio, to the table where Anson Young's phone was perched. The wires had been sliced. Across from the table, the familiar blue wall.

Harry envisioned the scene.

Anson Young is on the phone, chatting with Harry. Someone buzzes the apartment. Anson puts the phone down, giving Harry a panoramic view of the facing wall. Anson walks over to the door and activates the peepscreen. Someone is calling unexpectedly. It's not a stranger, though. Anson opens the door with a warm 'Hello.' Perhaps it's a friend. Perhaps it's a business acquaintance. Young is constantly effervescent, so it's impossible to judge from the tone of his voice. Then, abruptly, his mannerism changes. 'Are you crazy?' He sees *it*.

But what the hell is *it*?

Harry walked back to the blood stain and the scorched wall. *It* was something capable of illuminating a room and slicing into a wall. Anson must have backed up, retreated hastily from the doorway. Standing some three feet from the threshold he stares at his attacker. *It* fires. Blood. Scorch marks. The end of Anson Young.

Harry walked to the center of the living room. In a way, he has witnessed a murder. A murder wherein the murderer is unknown, the murder weapon is unknown, and the murder victim is not to be found. Harry suspected that Emmett was working overtime this afternoon.

He would have stayed to ruminate further on the situation had it not been for the arrival of two more shadows outside the door. Another pair of flat feet materialized under the doorframe. Probably the sergeant returning. Harry trotted back onto the patio. He stopped short at the fence.

Damn it. He'd make one lousy master criminal. Sure, he

119

had figured out how to get into Young's apartment, but he had never really considered the problem of getting out. How the hell could he get himself back up into 4J?

The doorknob to Anson Young's apartment began to jiggle. Harry shrugged and climbed onto the patio railing. If not 4J, why not 2J?

Harry jumped off the fence and landed on the patio of the apartment below. A blanket was sprawled on the sod, near the entrance to 2J's living room. From beneath the blanket, in an almost magical fashion, two naked young women suddenly emerged, both screaming hysterically. One, an Olympian blonde with breasts that deserved two distinct entries in the *Guinness Book of World Records,* ran into the apartment. Her blanket mate, a thin, birdlike redhead, sensibly remained on the patio. Standing six o'clock straight, she screeched hysterically. "It's not what you think," Harry said by way of introduction. He produced a small card. "Tim O'Connor. I'm here doing a story for the holo network."

The redhead was decidedly unimpressed by the idea. She continued to scream.

The blonde amazon reappeared on the patio, wielding a large and potentially lethal broom. Emitting a primordial battle cry, she charged at Harry.

"Much as I'd love to stay and chat with you girls," Harry gasped, retreating, "I promised the folks in 1J I'd drop in."

Harry dove over the patio railing and landed on the terrace below. Without stopping to notice if he was upsetting the balance of nature in this apartment, he dove off 1J's patio and crashed into the park next to the apartment building. He landed in a clump of bushes with a brutal "thud."

"Jesusgoddamnchristalmighty," he wheezed, biting his lower lip in pain. Light gravity or no, that last leap hurt like hell. He stood up as delicately as possible. Dusting himself off and wiping the sweat from his face, he glanced at his watch. Three o'clock. Time for his appointment with Anson Young. Taking three deep breaths, he affected an air of utter calm and strolled innocently to the front entranceway of the apartment complex. He smiled at the doorman on his way in. He nodded to the police in the hallway. He was still nodding and smiling like a mental deficient as he entered the elevator. When the door closed, he collapsed in pain against the rear wall of the lift. Something that was once an integral part of his back now felt like it was residing in his left foot. He inhaled slowly. Nothing seemed broken ... merely painfully twisted. The elevator door opened on Young's floor and Harry emerged. He strolled to the policeman's post before Anson's door.

"May I help you?" the acne-scarred guard asked.

"I'm here to see Anson Young."

"Mr. Young isn't here," the cop recited.

"But I talked to him not more than a half hour ago," Harry said. "He knew I was on my way."

The young policeman was slowly coming undone. He was clearly not used to arguing a cause. "Well, he, well . . ."

A heavy hand latched onto Harry's shoulder. Harry turned to face the bullish sergeant. "I'm afraid Mr. Young has had an accident," the voice of authority stated.

Harry was almost as amazed as he appeared. "Accident?"

"Heart attack," the sergeant nodded grimly, pointing a beefy finger at his own chest. "Passed away en route to the hospital. He died quickly."

Harry stared at the policeman. "I bet he did." These folks seemed to think of everything. Someone was covering a hell of a lot of tracks. Harry made a honking sound with his nose, expressed his grief and sense of loss, and headed back to the elevator. He'd have to tell Sylvie about this. He had seen the blood. He had seen the scorched wall. Jesus, he'd practically watched the crime over the phone. Harry reentered the lobby. If Young had died of a heart attack, it was brought about by having his entire chest ripped open.

Harry walked toward the exit.

"That's him," a familiar set of lungs bellowed.

Harry spun around to confront two fully dressed, but nakedly angry tenants. The women of 2J were trotting toward him, accompanied by two grim security guards. "That's the man!" the amazon thundered. The thin redhead nodded vigorously. Harry attempted to consider all his options. He could either bolt for the door or stick around and explain the entire incident away with his all-purpose smile. While he was still contemplating his choices, the older of the two guards drew a pistol. "Hey, there's no need for that," Harry was about to say. Instead he raised his hand and took three steps into a full-force blast from a stun-gun.

In between bolts of lightning and peals of thunder, he dimly heard the crackling noise of laughter.

13

When Harry reopened his eyes, the braying blonde was gone. Still, Harry could discern a blurred, hulking presence nearby. At first, he thought it was an enormous bear. The creature bending over him was bulky and blue. Its nose was pushed in and its eyes were nearly enveloped by a series of fleshy bags of skin. They were beady and alert beneath the camouflage. Below its snout, a bull-dog jowl was hidden by a burst of hair. The mouth worked an unlit cigar up and down. Harry's vision cleared and he recognized the figure of Police Chief Josh Hawkins.

Hawkins squinted into Harry's face long enough to determine that the reporter was not seriously injured. Coming to this conclusion, he then turned his back on Harry with disdain. Harry got the impression that the cop was disappointed. "He'll be all right," the chief grumbled.

Harry propped himself up on his elbows. The surface beneath him was firm, yet yielding. He suddenly realized that he was lying, fully clothed, in a hospital bed. Sylvie stood at his side. At least *she* seemed relieved.

"How the hell did I get here?" Harry asked.

"Ambulance," Hawkins said. "Damned unnecessary for a mild stun but your ladyfriend here insisted. Damned unnecessary. I got tire tracks all over that park. I'll catch holy hell for that."

"While we're on the subject of the unnecessary," Harry bantered, "let's talk about the guard who blasted me for no good reason."

"He had good reason," Hawkins said, his jaw jutting out in self-righteous anger.

"Like what?"

"For one thing, he had just spotted a dangerous prowler on the run."

"Who had the chance to run?"

"Chief Hawkins," Sylvie interrupted, "I don't exactly know what you're trying to say about Mr. Porter."

122

Hawkins placed his hands behind his back and rocked back and forth on his heels, relishing every moment. "Miss Dunbar, your charge was spotted bounding around several apartment dwellings, terrorizing the inhabitants of the building."

Sylvie was skeptical. "According to whom?"

Hawkins produced a small pocket computer from his tunic. Squinting his face into a dour, canine expression he read off the small screen. "According to Ms. Jackie Greene and Ms. Terri Reed."

Harry began to climb out of bed. Feeling woozy, he settled for merely sitting up on the side of the bed. "Two dykes," he explained to Sylvie.

"You jumped into their backyard, didn't you?" Hawkins demanded.

"Yeah."

"And then you dropped down into the next yard, right?"

"Yeah."

"So that's two counts of trespassing and possibly breaking and entering."

"You can't be serious," Sylvie gasped. "Mr. Porter is a guest on *Island One*."

"The law's the law," Hawkins stated. "I'm sure Mr. O'Connor here will agree with me on that point."

Sylvie looked at Harry quizzically. Harry shrugged. "Just a joke."

Hawkins regarded Harry with overt disdain. "I'm not going to encourage anyone to press charges, Mr. Porter. But I could."

"I bet you could," Harry said. "I bet you could make them stick, too. If you guys can make Anson Young's death out to be a coronary, I'm sure you can pull off anything."

Hawkins's face reddened, giving him the appearance of a uniformed Vienna sausage. "What are you implying?"

Harry faced Sylvie, ignoring the chief's consternation. "I dropped in on those two screaming Mimis because I was in a hurry to get out of Anson Young's apartment."

"Breaking and entering!" Hawkins thundered.

"And the reason I had to get out of there in a hurry was that the police were returning to the scene of his murder."

"What?" Sylvie gasped.

"Give me a break," Hawkins sneered.

Harry continued. "When I called him on the phone before, I knew something was wrong. Someone showed up at his apartment while I was still on the line. I actually witnessed his

123

murder over the viewscreen. I didn't really see anything, but I heard everything. Then, someone ended transmission. When you were calling the cops, I hightailed it over to Young's place. I got there as the ambulance with his body was leaving. When I arrived at Young's door, two of *Island*'s finest were standing guard outside. I had to get inside to find out exactly what happened. I cut through the apartment upstairs and . . ."

"BREAKING AND ENTERING! FOUR COUNTS!"

"So who's keeping track? I got inside through the terrace. There was blood on the floor and scorch marks on the wall. No Anson Young. Later, the cops outside tell me that he's gone to his eternal reward via a bad heart."

Hawkins nearly inhaled his cigar. "Are you telling me that there's a cover-up going on in my own department?"

"No," Harry said, "I'm telling *her*."

"You have no proof!"

"Take me back to Young's apartment. I'll give you proof."

"You're on, Mr. Porter," Hawkins said, masticating the cigar into a stub.

Hawkins, Harry, and Sylvie took the lift to the hospital's ground floor. "You were drinking quite a bit last night, weren't you, Porter?" It wasn't so much a question uttered by the chief as a statement of incriminating fact.

"I could have consumed my weight in alcohol and still be sober by now," Harry grunted.

The threesome hailed an empty cart. "Drink anything this morning?"

"Don't worry about me dehydrating," Harry said. "I have enough fluid to last me the rest of the day."

After a short trip along the cart track, they pulled up at Young's apartment complex. Harry led the way inside, taking the elevator to the third floor and pushing his way past the two guards at the doorway of 3J.

"This had better be convincing," Hawkins warned.

Harry swung the door open in triumph. He stood in the threshold gaping at the room inside. Everything was in order. There was no pool of blood on the carpet. No scorch marks on the wall.

Hawkins glowered at the shaken reporter. "I hope you have a explanation for this that's as imaginative as your accusations."

Harry stood transfixed in the doorway, gawking at the spotless pale-blue rug and the untarnished wall. "But it was all here," he protested feebly, "just the way I told you."

He marched slowly to the center of the room.

"Then, where's all your evidence now?" Hawkins asked.

"I don't know."

"You don't know," Hawkins snorted.

"It was all here," Harry repeated.

"Goddamn Earthside lushes," Hawkins muttered.

"He's not drunk," Sylvie said, rallying to Harry's defense. "He's been . . . sick."

Harry's eyes nearly popped out of his head. "Sylvie!"

"He was in a hospital for a while," she clarified further, putting a totally debilitating intonation on the word "hospital."

Hawkins deciphered her meaning and backed off a step from Porter. Harry began to pace. "It was all here, Sylvie, so just can it, will you?"

"I'm only trying to help."

"Well, don't help!" Harry snapped. He scanned the room. Everything was perfect. Being a long-time Manhattan resident, Harry was well versed in the art of introspection to the point of paranoia. Like most of the other residents of New York City, the psychoanalysis capital of the world, he was quite capable of conjuring up mental images designed to rekindle every fear experienced since conception. If he ever wanted to drive himself into a state of total apprehension, he could ruminate on being mugged by illiterate giants, being trapped in a burning building with barred windows, watching his loved ones tortured at the hands of crazed drug fiends, or dying alone, at an advanced age, in a seedy hotel, eventually being mutilated by his formerly loyal but increasingly voracious pet dachshund. Normal thoughts for the typical self-tortured New Yorker. This time, however, Harry was not out to drive himself up a wall. It was possible that he had imagined this room's former condition, but highly unlikely. Hawkins glanced at his watch and winked at Sylvie. "Well, no harm done, I suppose. Just keep an eye on Peter Pan here. We like to deal with facts in our end of things, not fantasy."

"Thank you, chief," Sylvie replied meekly. "We'll remember that."

Hawkins stood by the door to the room. "Coming?"

Harry sat down on the sofa. "I still feel a little woozy from the stun gun, chief. Mind if I sit here for a moment?"

Hawkins frowned but acquiesced. "Just don't touch any-

125

thing. There'll be two officers outside the door if you need anything."

Hawkins left the room, shutting the door behind him. Harry glowered at Sylvie. "Thanks a lot, Florence Nightingale. Why didn't you just tell him to coat my hotel wall with rubber."

"I was only trying . . ."

"Oh, excuse him, officer," Harry mimicked. "He's usually in shock therapy at this time of day but my watch stopped and we didn't have time to get him into his straitjacket. He promises not to stab anyone again."

"I was only trying to help," Sylvie stammered, her lower lip beginning to quiver.

Harry watched her cautiously. He was beginning to get some vague idea of what was occurring on this habitat, but he wasn't sure he should take Sylvie into his confidence. After all, she did work up here. He watched her lips tremble. "Aww, I know you were. I'm just a bit pissed off at being such a chump. Come here. Look at this."

"What?" Sylvie said, following Harry to the door.

"Hawkins almost had me turning fruit loops there. He nearly convinced me that I had imagined the whole scene. But I figured that I had to trust my instincts."

He bent down and touched the carpet. "What color is this rug?"

"Blue."

"What kind of blue?"

"I don't know; sky-blue, powder-blue, light blue."

"Right," he answered. "This isn't the same carpet as the one I saw before. The other rug was a deep blue pile. This is several shades lighter. I remember the other was really dark because I had to strain my eyes to see the blood stain on it."

"Are you sure?"

"How long was I out in the hospital?"

"You were there for ten or fifteen minutes."

"No. *You* were there for ten or fifteen minutes. Young called you to tell you about my 'accident,' I presume?"

"Yes."

"And you insisted I be brought to the hospital?"

"You know that."

"Yeah, I know that. All right. Count on me being in the hospital at least five minutes before your arrival. Plus my time in the lobby and en route . . . I suppose you could safely assume I was out for a half hour. During that time, somebody switched rugs in this room. I'd guess that a moving crew of three men could have done it in about ten minutes. There isn't much furniture to play around with in here. A sofa. A writing table. Not much. It could be done."

He walked to the writing desk and stared at the neat stacks of *Island* pamphlets. "They were in a hurry, too. They didn't notice what they were doing. When they moved the furniture, they put things back neater than Young had originally had them."

He tapped a stack of tidy papers. "This place looked as if a small hurricane had hit it this afternoon. It's neatly arranged now, though."

"But what about the wall," Sylvie asked. "You said it was burned."

Harry walked over to the wall. That did have him stumped. A carpet you could yank out. A wall you couldn't replace. You couldn't just paint over a scorch mark without leaving a scar visible, either. Even with some of the instapaints available. They weren't thick enough and plaster wasn't fast enough to conceal a surface mark of that drastic a nature.

Harry touched the wall with his hand. He moved his hand to the edge of the wall, running his finger along it. No, you couldn't paint a wall, but you could paper it. Harry probed until he came to a bump. He ripped a small sliver of plastipaper off. "Here we are," he said. "Wall paper. The new plasticized stuff. Solid in color. One large sheet expertly applied."

Harry took Sylvie by the arm. "Come, dear heart. I think it's time we paid a visit to your computer center."

"But why?"

"Because things seem to be getting a bit surreal up here. Someone is going to an awful lot of trouble to cover up a murder."

"But who?"

"Maybe the computer can help us discover just that."

The two left the room, passing the pair of guards in the hall. "I thought you hated machines."

"Nonsense," Harry said, pressing the button for the elevator. "I have a toaster at home that I'm quite fond of."

14

In order to visit the computer center, unauthorized personnel had to request an appointment at least twenty-four hours in advance. No one could explain exactly why that time period was considered the law in terms of waiting. It was just the way things were done on *Island;* a chunk of protocol as illogical as the cornerstones of social etiquette which required all men to open doors for women, all women athletes to be judged weaker than their male counterparts, and all dentists to have totally repulsive breath. The twenty-four-hour wait annoyed Harry to the point of physical mayhem. Through Sylvie's charm and Harry's frenzy, the time period was eventually whittled down to a mere eighteen hours. Such was progress in the second millennium.

Harry envisioned the computer center as being dark and foreboding.

As dark as an alley filled with dangerous lowlifes.

As dark as a cave populated by blood-sucking bats.

As dark as the old piece of chewing gum firmly affixed to the heel of his right shoe.

Harry stopped near a curbside and scraped his shoe clean. "I thought you people were supposed to be neat and clean up here."

Sylvie shoved him back onto the walkway. "Just keep moving. Sid was nice enough to fit us into his morning schedule. I'm not going to keep him waiting."

Harry returned to the walkway and paced Sylvie's stride. If he was on Earth right now, he'd be sitting in Lt. Garner's office, exchanging information and views about the missing cop, the missing murder scene, and the mysterious phone caller. On *Island,* he couldn't do that. He couldn't exchange anything with the local police except for angry looks. Hell, for all he knew, half the cops up here could be on someone's payroll. It was an unlikely possibility but one worth considering. At present, he felt that he could drag in a dozen cadavers

128

and Hawkins would still insist that they were all figments of his imagination.

Harry hated the thought of consulting a computer about the entire mess. He hated to work hand-in-wall socket with technology. It seemed damned unnatural. But now, in a last ditch effort to dig up some answers, he was about to take the technological plunge. On his way to a computer center ... dark and foreboding.

Sylvie paused before a gleaming white building; rectangular in shape, its top half constructed entirely of glass. "Come on," she said, walking toward the entranceway.

"This is *it?"* Harry said, almost disappointed. Uncomfortably cheery place, this.

They walked into the brightly lit two-story building and down a sunny, yellow corridor. At the end of the hallway they entered a small, comfortable office. Sid Kraft was a slight man, in his fifties, with a round, smiling face and a shock of bright red hair. As Sylvie and Harry entered his room, he stood in front of his console and welcomed them.

"Here to see the master computer, eh, Mr. Porter?" he asked.

"That's right," Harry said, still slightly disoriented. Maybe they kept the mammoth machine in a large pit in the basement or something equally as melodramatic.

"Well, what do you think?" Kraft smiled.

Confused, Harry glanced around the room. The office was no more than fifteen feet by twenty feet. There was one brightly lit console next to a wall. A five by five viewscreen of some sort was built into the wall. The rest of the room looked like an ordinary place of business. A large bay window. Assorted plants. A few chairs for guests. A desk. "Uh, what do I think of what?"

"The computer," Sid said.

"Where is it?" Harry asked.

"You're standing in it," Sid laughed. "Actually, this whole building is the total unit. You're standing in its heart, though. This console here is the key. This is the only room where information may be obtained from the computer."

"You mean," Harry said, "that everything that goes into the computer is fed in through this little thing?"

"It could be," Sid stated, "but the actual programming is done in a number of different terminal areas such as this. There are separate small input areas for different types of

129

information: personal, medical, political, classified, that sort of stuff. But," Sid smiled, beaming at the console like a proud father, "this is the seat of information. This is where the information is actually retrieved from. She can be quite talkative during a good conversation."

"She?" Harry blurted.

"Just a small joke of mine," Sid coughed, slightly embarrassed. "I call her Babe III. She's a Barcroft Artificial Brain Ectype. I worked on two similar systems before coming up here. Thus, she's my third. The biggest I've ever seen, really. Compact by computer standards of course, but capable of storing a nearly infinite amount of knowledge."

Harry sat down in the chair before the console and eyed the buttons before him suspiciously. Positively macabre. A machine possessing all knowledge. "A brain, eh?"

"Oh yes, indeed," Sid enthused. "Babe does possess a limited amount of independent artificial intelligence. But, because of the ideological war between the artificial intelligence boosters and the small minds I refer to as the parrot crops, she has been stifled in her decision-making ability. Still, she's quite a controversial unit."

"How much has she been stifled?" Harry asked.

"I don't understand."

"I mean," Harry continued, "if Babe decided, one fine day, that she didn't feel like giving you the information you desired, could she refuse on her own?"

Sid chuckled and winked at Sylvie, enjoying Harry's naïveté. "Oh. I see. You mean could the computer one day decide to eliminate my functions and strike out on her own?"

"And link up with the other minor computer systems on the hab," Sylvie encouraged.

"And then," Sid theorized, "overpower the humans onboard and take over the habitat!"

"And then the entire communications center!"

Sid licked his lips. "Eventually hooking up with the major systems on Earth with the intention of dominating the entire human race!"

Harry sighed and rested his chin on his hands. "Why is it that I get the feeling you two are not taking me seriously?"

The red-haired programmer slapped Harry on the back. "Just a bit of fun at your expense, Mr. Porter. You see, even today, most people are inherently suspicious of major computer networks. They still view them as monsters. In these days of micro-processing, it's not the size of the computer that throws them (indeed, most systems are totally compact), but rather, the extent of their intelligence, the scope of their knowledge. As humanity becomes more and more lax and apathetic in terms of education and general thinking abilities, the computers continue to expand their horizons, to accumulate more knowledge. This building houses all the knowledge accumulated since the dawn of recorded history. Imagine that. Every fact you could ever want is somewhere in this building, etched on an, er, electronic brain cell, if you will, no bigger than one-quarter of your thumbnail."

"Awesome," Harry agreed. An interesting concept. In a world of mass illiteracy, a house with a plug knew all the answers. There was a very profound philosophical letter to the editor in there somewhere.

"Yet, " Sid said, "Babe is as agreeable as a tabby cat. I ask questions. She answers them. I give her facts. She remembers them."

"And if you take away the facts?" Harry asked.

"Then, she forgets them."

"Forever."

"Forever."

Harry ran his fingers across the sleek console. "And if anyone wanted to remove facts from Babe, the request would have to go through you?"

"Oh no," Sid laughed. "You overestimate my importance. My superiors have to OK the request, there's a logical chain of command to go through. Then, either myself or one of my two colleagues must process the request here."

"Is your immediate supervisor a fellow named Mullins?"

"Why, yes. Do you know him?"

"Just by reputation," he shrugged. "Do you keep records of all the additions and subtractions handed to the computer's memory bank?"

"It's required by law."

"Is there any situation where a log entry wouldn't be kept?"

Sid ran five stubby fingers through his red mane. He wore the expression of a man attempting to conjure up a vision of armageddon. "A situation that would be above the law? Well, technically, yes. But I can't really imagine it happening up here. Such an action would have to take place during a national emergency. Something along those lines."

"Couldn't happen up here?"

"Unlikely. Still, there are pieces of information that Babe

131

holds that she doesn't give out to just anybody. Classified stuff. Top secret. In one sense, Babe is first cousin to her agency peers on Earth. Every fact about the colony is residing in her brain, but not every fact will be revealed to anyone who asks."

"Rank has its privileges in space, too, eh?"

"That's right."

Harry noticed that, during the entire conversation, Kraft had continuously stroked the shiny console before him; much in the same manner as a person would normally caress his pet dog or lover or, if you hailed from the lower west side of Manhattan, both simultaneously. "Could anyone tamper with Babe without your knowledge?"

Sid was visibly stunned by the thought. "Tamper?"

"Yeah. Break in here and tamper with her memory banks."

"My God!" Kraft exclaimed. "It's unthinkable. Such a wanton act carried out by a nonprofessional could destroy Babe's circuitry."

"But could it happen?"

"I suppose. But I'd know about it. I'd see it in the way she functioned the next day. She'd be damaged, maimed, perhaps beyond repair. Murdered." Kraft worked himself into a verbal frenzy, his words tumbling forth with increasing speed. "And you could be sure that if I ever found out who the culprit was, I'd make sure that they paid in full! Laws today don't acknowledge the severity of tampering with computers. But a computer has all the components of a human being. It has intelligence. It has beauty. It possesses life! It's more than human!"

The programmer's face had taken on an uncharacteristically grim look. Harry noticed the first glistenings of sweat forming on the man's forehead. Even in the sterile environment of *Island One* there was room for passion, albeit slightly misguided passion. In a way, Porter envied the man his one-sided love affair with his machine. By human standards, it was a perfect relationship. No misunderstandings. No falsehoods. No one left the room feeling cheated.

In an effort to soothe the man, Harry patted the console gently. "I quite agree. Would you mind if I asked Babe a question or two?"

Sid was pleased by Harry's interest. "Not at all." He adjusted a lever beneath a small speaker. "And, for you, Mr. Porter, Babe will go all the way. You won't even have to use the keyboard grid. You two can converse vocally."

132

"You're kidding."

"No. Try it."

Kraft pointed toward the small speaker. Harry moved his chair in closer to the intercom. "Babe, can you hear me?"

Within seconds, the machine boomed in a monotoned, but distinctly female voice. "Affirmative."

Harry recalled his annoying home computer unit and, before he knew it, was overcome by a bizarre strain of homesickness. "Babe, how does the law enforcement on *Island* compare to that of Earth?"

"Taking an overview," Babe replied, "it is an identical system, with minor modifications, founded upon the same judicial principles."

"How do the statistics regarding crimes committed tally?"

"*Island* has a much lower percentage of lawlessness than Earth."

"What's the worst crime ever committed on *Island*?"

"Assault with a deadly weapon. February 23 of this year. The perpetrator, one James Wallace Doohan, attempted to persuade one Milton Reethcliff to pay him an overdue amount of money owed. Aiding him in his argument was the use of a large lead pipe. Suspect apprehended by police. Doohan was tried, found guilty, and sentenced to five years in an Earth prison."

"Pretty stiff sentence."

"*Island* justice is unyielding."

"Why's that?"

"The eyes of the world are upon *Island*."

"Sounds like a national anthem," Harry acknowledged with a grin.

"Sir?" Babe inquired.

"Humor," Harry informed the machine.

"It eluded my circuits."

Harry rubbed his eyelids with his thumb and forefinger. Headache coming. "Now, what do you think would happen if a serious crime was committed on *Island*?"

"I am not programmed to respond to inquiries requiring conjecture."

Harry patted the speaker. "Spoken like a true gentle ... brain."

Sid gazed at the console fondly. "Isn't she marvelous?"

"A regular Einstein," Harry agreed. "A few more questions?"

Sid nodded positively. "Once you start, it's hard to stop."

"Like eating peanuts," Harry said. "Babe. Has any information been removed from your memory banks lately?"

An alarmed look flashed across Kraft's face momentarily. Babe, however, set him at ease. "I am not programmed to respond to questions concerning measures taken for security reasons."

Harry's expression did not change. Inwardly, however, he realized that he had just scored a few points. Babe was programmed to yield to unorthodox, albeit officially sanctioned, additions and deletions of facts and figures. She was smarter than Sid would ever imagine. "Well, tell me this, Babe. If some information *was* removed from your databank and I wanted to get hold of that information, how could I go about it?"

"I am not programmed to respond to questions concerning measures taken for security reasons."

Harry stood up. "Well, she's certainly no gossip."

Sid grinned and chatted for several moments, extolling the virtues of Babe the omniscient. Harry experienced the same nauseating feeling he got after running into an old school chum loaded down with snapshots of his runny-nosed children performing such Herculean stunts as eating, sleeping, crying, and falling over. Eventually, Harry and Sylvie shook hands with Sid and left the computer center. The pair began their walk back to Harry's hotel. Harry paused at the curbside. The gum was still on his shoe.

15

Harry sat in his hotel room, guzzling blue fruit juice. The more he drank, the more he craved. He made a mental note to find out exactly what the hell it was. Despite his contented stomach, he was depressed and uneasy. That in itself was not unusual. Harry was constantly depressed and uneasy. This arose, in part, from the nagging realization that, in his own eyes, he was a failure. He had wanted to make something out of his life, be a world-shaker. He had wanted success beyond articulation. Here he was, on a floating space tub, running around totally confused.

His divorce had also affected him more than he really cared to admit. He was tired of the solitude, of the long walks taken at midnight to help him relax, of the marathon TV-watching sessions which lasted until three in the morning.

He projected the image of a seasoned, world-wise reporter which, in essence, he was. But there was a larger part of him, totally unpublicized, which was slowly driving him out of his mind. It was the part of him that yearned for emotional tranquility, that demanded fulfillment, that mourned the loss of experiences and feelings unrealized. At times, the futility of his longing overwhelmed him in Olympian waves, causing his eyes to tear and his knees to shake; giving him the appearance of a landlubber afloat at sea for the first time. During these periods, the seasoned world-wise reporter took over; beating back the insidious uprising with a decidedly masculine club. The process was simple. Plagued by self-doubt and loss, he would bite down hard on his lower lip and mutter "damn, damn, damn" until he was in control once again. As a result of his last ten month's anguish, his bottom lip was perpetually chapped.

He was running on empty and he knew it. To make matters even more depressing, he had yet to actually file a news story about his space voyage. Thus far, he had wasted nearly all his time investigating a far-fetched murder scheme which alternately struck him as grotesquely real or totally absurd. Nothing added up. Harry suspected that the space colony was slowly coming apart at the seams. Yet, all those around him proceeded about their business as if nothing was happening whatsoever.

Threatening notes. Strange phone calls. Purloined phone directories. Just thinking about his first three days onboard gave him indigestion. He glanced at his wristwatch. It was eight P.M. Sylvie was going to pick him up at half past the hour. They were scheduled to attend Anson Young's funeral. According to the local newspaper, it was a closed coffin affair. Young's heart attack had irrevocably contorted his features. His coffin would be jettisoned into space; an honor reserved for an elite few.

"Bullshit," Harry muttered, pacing the length of the room. Either he was crazy or everyone else up here was. In five days, the tenth anniversary celebration of the colony would occur. And, if he had interpreted this Emmett fellow's phone

135

message accurately, within five days, thirteen people, himself included, would be quite deceased. This fact did not sit well with his intestinal track. He wished that someone other than himself, and Sylvie, was privy to this information.

Brushing aside his hourly attack of self-pity, he attempted to untangle what he knew as fact and what he felt was mere supposition. He couldn't. Anson Young was murdered. Maybe. If Young was murdered, the police didn't want to know about it. Hence, the police must have been involved in a cover-up. Hence, the governor must be involved in a cover-up. That, in turn, would explain how the computer managed to erase the lives of two of *Island*'s citizens from all records. But what if Young wasn't murdered? And, even if he was, what could Harry do with his suspicions? Logic told him that, should he voice his theories, he wouldn't be too popular a boy up on the hab with the local authorities.

Harry uncovered his typewriter and attempted to bang out a short feature on the life and death of Anson Young. He stopped after a few moments. Three sentences. Lately, whenever he sat down to the typewriter he felt the seductive calls of the couch caressing his mind. "Nap. Nap." It would advise. No matter how much stamina he thought he possessed, the couch always emerged the victor.

Harry sat on the couch. Now what? Murder, madmen, and corrupt officials. He didn't consider himself a hero. He could walk away from the entire affair. But there was his own ass to consider. He had grown quite fond of it over the years and would truly hate to part company with it prematurely. Harry left the couch and entered the bathroom. He stepped into the shower and turned on the water full blast. Damn. He couldn't make sense out of any of it. There had to be some way to trace this mess to its point of origin. But where did it start? Where would it end?

Harry allowed the speeding droplets of hot water to plow into his flesh unmercifully. It relaxed his muscles on most occasions. Now, however, it had just the opposite effect. His body was growing tenser. He felt his muscles tighten. It was as if his entire body was being stretched length-wise on a psychic rack. His head began to throb. He felt an alien presence slice through his thoughts. No. Not again.

A peeper was nearby. Closing fast.

Harry shut off the shower, wrapped a towel around his waist and scrambled out of the room. Damn it. There weren't any peepers registered on the habitat. He had checked that

136

fact out earlier this afternoon. His stomach contracted violently, nearly doubling him over. Why did he have to be so empathetic to those creeps. There was a mind probe emanating from someplace close. It was a fierce but clumsy attempt. Tumbling onto the sofa, he grasped his head. He had to fight back. Maybe some of those prescription migraine tablets he picked up earthside would help. He reached for the small bottle on the coffee table before him.

A buzzing noise filled the room.

The walls took on an eerie, yellow-white glow.

Harry popped two pills into his mouth, glancing at a full-length mirror on the opposite wall as he did so.

"Cheezus!" he choked, spitting the pills across the room into the mirror like machine-gun pellets. Harry rolled over the sofa as a luminous blade sliced through the air, neatly cleaving a pillow in two. Poised over the chair was a white robed figure; a warrior straight out of medieval mythology. It was Death itself . . . or a close relation.

The figure's robe was studded with patterned layers of jewelry, giving the shift a regal look. He wore a golden face-mask beneath his cowl. The figure was wielding some type of pulsating sword, possibly of laser tech origins. The light it emitted was painfully bright. Harry had never seen anything like it before. He was curious about its design but was in no hurry to ask for a sample demonstration of its power. A pain shot through his head like an arrow. Here was his peeper; his killer; Emmett.

Sprawled on the floor, Harry scrambled back to his feet in an attempt to avoid certain death. He clutched the towel to his waist, desperately playing for time. "You here to turn down the bed?" he prattled. He had to try to make it to the door. The eyes beneath the mask flickered and made contact with Harry's mind. The warrior leaped in front of the door, effectively blocking Harry's proposed exit. The light beam sliced past Harry's ear,

Harry realized the full extent of his danger. He mustn't think. The maniac with the sword could hear every thought. Harry dodged the next blow with awkward precision. "That's OK," he blurted. "It's no trouble. I'll fix the sheets myself."

Harry's vision blurred momentarily under the weight of the mental probe. God. The man in the room with him was the most powerful telepath he had ever encountered. The psychic potency was staggering. Yet, somehow, at its root was an inbred clumsiness. The force was anything but professional in character. An untrained presence. An uncontrollable fury. Harry guessed that his swordsman wasn't a trained parapsych but, rather, a natural. He stumbled over the weight of that discovery. A NATURAL?

"Correct," the hooded figure hissed.

Harry mentally kicked himself. He mustn't think. He mustn't think. Sing a song. Recite a rhyme. Peter Piper picked a peck of pickled . . . Jesus God. The time. The time. It was almost 8:30. Sylvie would be arriving at 8:30. Death waved his sword in the air dramatically. "Excellent," said the rasping voice from beneath the shroud. "You shall watch me dispose of her before I turn my sword on you. Two in one night."

The buzzer to Harry's room sounded. Sylvie's face appeared on the peepscreen. "Harry?"

Harry gaped at the screen. Damn her. Not only was she punctual, tonight she was actually early. The robed figure moved toward the door handle. Harry was about to watch a murder. Sylvie's murder. Something inside him snapped. There was no time to think. No time. His body convulsed, summoning up a sudden surge of energy. He emitted a piercing yell and dropped his towel. He had no idea what he was doing even as he was doing it.

Harry ran toward the swordsman. The robed assassin, not understanding Harry's plan of attack any more than Harry, instinctively tensed his body, allowing his fingers to slip from the doorknob. Obviously stunned by the mobility of the naked reporter, the killer grabbed his weapon with both hands and aimed a thrust in Harry's direction. Harry tumbled backward, the sword zipping by his chest harmlessly. The killer continued his advance, the pulsating weapon heating the air before it.

Harry backed toward the patio. He was operating on remote control now. Impulse power. With the swordsman not five feet in front of him, half an idea entered his head. He spun around, grabbed his ancient typewriter, pivoted and tossed the machine at the advancing demon. The effort, however, cost Harry his balance. Cursing his stupidity, he tumbled out onto the patio, stark naked. He landed on his stomach, sliding a few feet. Clutching his abdomen, he reasoned that, no matter what happened now, his procreative days were over.

Harry flopped over on his back and watched helplessly as the figure lurched headfirst toward him, sword upraised. Also in Harry's line of vision was the still airborne typewriter. A resounding "clunk" brought the tableau to a fitting conclusion as the killer's head unexpectedly met the machine's shiny surface. The assassin let out a low moan. The sword seemed to sputter in his hand. The light faded. The weapon now resembled nothing more than a piece of glass tubing in a handle. Blood dribbled from beneath the cowl. Reeling unsteadily, the killer hobbled onto the patio, nearly tripping over Harry's body. The assassin swayed dizzily above Harry. "Until our next encounter, Mister Porter," he rasped, jumping over the patio railing and tumbling into the awaiting night below. Harry's body stiffened, mentally absorbing the intruder's pain and fear. After a few seconds, the psychic anguish dissipated. Only Harry's physical pain remained. He clutched his stomach and struggled to a standing position.

The door buzzer was still humming impatiently.

He limped across the room, reached the doorway and grasped the doorknob firmly. With great effort, he swung open the door. Sylvie stood in the hallway, dumbfounded by the sight of Harry, naked, numb and bruised before her. She caught him as he started to slide down the side of the threshold. "Harry, what happened?"

He attempted to steady himself, weaving bravely on his knees. "You just missed a t'riffic experiment," he muttered, "in which I conclusively proved that the pen is still mightier than the sword."

Against his better judgment, he passed out.

16

He hated being in a weakened condition. Being sick or injured annoyed him almost as much as it did those caring for him. He made a rotten patient, complaining constantly. His attitude was justifiable, however. He knew that the individuals charged with taking care of the infirm secretly abhorred their task and, as a matter of course, their task-makers. He always remembered how Anne used to treat him on those rare occasions when he came down with a cold or the flu. There was one part concern mixed with nine parts resentment hovering around his sickbed.

He pushed the cold compress from his forehead. Opening his eyes, he found himself stretched out on the sofa, wearing a pair of trousers. He patted the trousers reassuringly. "All dressed up and no place to go."

"Just relax until the doctor gets here," Sylvie said, appearing from the mist swirling next to the bed.

Harry sat up suddenly, sending the facecloth flying onto the rug. "Shit! You called a doctor?" He blinked his eyes furiously. The fog in the room disappeared.

Sylvie retrieved the facecloth and threw it at Harry's head. "Of course I did, you ungrateful lout. When I came in here you were as white as one of those sheets."

Harry stood unsteadily. "Lout? Is that any way to talk to someone who just saved your life?"

Sylvie crinkled her nose, obviously unimpressed. "How did you save my life?"

"That Emmett nut was in here waving some sort of laser sword in my face. He was just about to decapitate this intrepid reporter when you came charging in like the U.S. Cavalry. That was him opening the door for you just now. He figured he could get a double-header going."

Sylvie touched her throat lightly with her left hand. "I-I didn't see anyone."

"Of course you didn't," Harry said, grabbing a tunic and slipping it on. "It was all a figment of my imagination again." He motioned toward three drops of blood out on his patio. "Only this time, my figment must have gotten injured during my brainstorm."

Harry tried not to get upset. Sylvie had not only summoned a doctor, but the police as well. He looked at his watch. It wasn't nine yet. Young's funeral service wasn't scheduled to start until 9:15. Offering no explanation, Harry told Sylvie to contact Police Chief Hawkins and tell him to get over to the hotel in a hurry. Emergency. "And when you have him on the phone," Harry advised, "make sure to check out the buttons on his uniform. Shape and color."

Sylvie frowned and dialed the phone while Harry systematically rummaged through every one of his bureau drawers. Finally, he came up with a small billfold. He opened it. Inside was a sheet of buttons. He took the billfold and laid it open on the surface of his bed. Sylvie hung up the phone and entered the bedroom.

"How soon will he be coming over?" Harry asked.

"Right away."

"I thought he might. What color were his buttons?"

"Gold. Or yellow, anyhow."

Harry took Sylvie's hand and drew her to the bed. "Which one of these buttons comes closest to the ones on his uniform?"

Sylvie shook her head in disbelief. "Why are you carrying around a wallet filled with buttons?"

"Zippers are too bulky."

She pointed to a small, bright yellow button in the middle of the collection. "That one, I guess."

"Good." Harry picked up the billfold and carefully removed the button. "This one should do it, then."

He closed the case and placed it in the drawer of the night table next to the bed. Sylvie watched him place the button on his pillow. "Are you going to tell me what you're really doing with the buttons?"

"They're not really buttons. They're micro-transmitters of mine. Bugs. A little souvenir from an old story I did about Washington D.C."

"Why do you carry them around?"

"Emergencies. Like now. Someone is being slightly dishonest with me, dear heart, and I intend to find out why. Suffice to say that, when Hawkins leaves this room, he'll be wearing an extra button on his jacket. And we will be with him, in spirit and in microphone, wherever he goes."

The door buzzed. Harry humped under the sheets of the bed while Sylvie admitted Dr. Estelle Jerrow. An aging, stoop-shouldered woman who wore a patented scowl and a hair-do outmoded for years (metallic blue bun), Jerrow walked with a stiff, arthritic gait. She reminded Harry of a great bird of prey.

She was a figure yanked out of her own time, a time long gone, and thrust into the future. She seemed to radiate a somewhat genial contempt for all living creatures around her . . . most notably Harry. She stooped over the bed and twisted her scowl into a pucker. The pucker then metamorphosed itself into a tight-lipped smile. "What seems to be the matter?" she asked, not really wanting to know. Her breath smelled like week-old milk.

"Someone just tried to murder me," Harry replied cheerfully.

The paralyzed smile of Jerrow's face didn't waver. She

nodded and stuck two fingers into Harry's right eye, yanking it open wide. "Pupils seem to be all right."

"Except for a finger or two," Harry pointed out.

Jerrow moved to the other eye and, after yanking that open and shut, felt Harry's pulse. "A little rapid but nothing extraordinary."

"No, you missed the extraordinary part," Harry informed her. "An audience participation performance of *The Mark of Zorro*. I was the mark."

Jerrow turned to Sylvie. "Is your friend a comedian?"

"No," Sylvie said.

"I didn't think so," said the doctor, shining a small flashlight into Harry's eyes. The woman was so Old World, it was frightening. Harry detected a slight, middle-European accent lurking beneath the surface of her sharp, clipped speech pattern. He also detected a large dose of sadism as she reached under the covers and poked and prodded him with a passion usually reserved for ripe tomatoes.

Between winces, Harry caught sight of Police Chief Hawkins shambling into the room, obviously displeased at having been dragged away from the funeral. "What's the trouble?" he asked.

"Harry was attacked by a burglar," Sylvie explained.

"A murderer," Harry corrected.

"Were you killed?" Hawkins queried.

"No," Dr. Jerrow replied.

"Then it was a burglar," the chief stated.

"Or a nightmare," Jerrow said reassuringly, cutting off Harry's irate response.

"A what?" Harry finally sputtered, reaching under the pillow for the button.

"A nightmare," Jerrow repeated, patting Harry on the head, much in the same way a kindly school teacher does to a mental deficient. "My dear young man, you have just had a terrible nightmare. Incoming Earth residents often experience very unsettling feelings shortly after their arrival. They are tense. On edge. Sometimes they hallucinate. It's a symptom of arrival."

"Right," Harry said, pointing to the two halves of the sofa pillow strewn upon the living-room floor outside. "Only this hallucination almost turned my arrival into a farewell."

As if on cue, Jerrow produced Harry's vial of pills. "I

picked these up in the other room. Did you take many of these before seeing your ... burglar?"

Harry struggled to sit up, his anger getting the best of him. These people had all the answers, even before the questions had been asked. "No, it wasn't like that at all. I didn't even get a chance to put any of those into my mouth before Ivanhoe showed up behind me, batting clean-up with his sword."

A tremor rumbled across Hawkins's deeply lined face. "A sword?"

"Yeah, a sword. Some laser weapon or particle beam weapon. I don't know. The guy was a total loon. He was dressed up like death itself. Robe and all."

Jerrow frowned and placed a bony hand to her forehead. Shaking her head sadly, she stood up with the dignity of a mortician and handed Sylvie two small white pills. "Why don't you try getting a little rest, Mr. Porter." She executed an elaborate stage wink for Sylvie's benefit.

"Yeah," Harry grunted. "After a deflected decapitation, there's nothing like a nap to put you straight."

"We'll see that your pillow is replaced," Hawkins mumbled, lost in thought. Without warning, Harry reached out and grabbed him by the sleeve of his tunic. He pulled the police chief down to the bed. "It wasn't a nightmare, Hawkins. You and your people know that for a fact!"

Hawkins struggled to pull himself away from the bed. Harry pushed the transmitter onto the man's tunic, at the end of a long row of golden buttons.

Hawkins broke free of Harry's grasp. Jerrow puckered her lips into a sour expression. "See that he takes those two pills," she told Sylvie, "and gets a good night's rest."

Dr. Jerrow and Hawkins left the room together, the police chief glaring angrily at Harry. As Sylvie closed the door behind them, Harry vaulted out of the bed. "Perfect!" he exclaimed.

"Perfect?" Sylvie repeated, amazed. "They both think you're crazy. They both think that I'm crazy for letting you get this crazy and you call that perfect. It's my job that's on the line, you know."

"I know. Now, why don't you just flush those two little pills down the toilet while I set up here." Harry removed a small valise from his suitcase and pulled out a minute radio speaker.

143

"Isn't it illegal to carry stuff like that around?" Sylvie asked, peeking out from the bathroom.

"Totally," Harry admitted. "So I would appreciate your keeping all this out of the *Island* gossip columns."

"I thought you were part of an honorable profession."

"Honor is relative," he said, placing the speaker on the coffee table in the living room. He pulled up a chair, opened a magazine, and sat directly in front of the transistorized console. Sylvie entered the room and sat down on the couch. "Now what are you doing?"

"Waiting."

"For what?"

"Revelations, my dear. Tonight, we're attending a listening party. Everyone will be getting together for Young's funeral right about now. I'm simply going to eavesdrop on the proceedings. Physically, of course, I cannot be in attendance due to my current tranquilized state. Ergo, I will not be missed. You, on the other hand, still have the option to attend or stick around here and play nurse."

"Nurse?"

"Don't worry, it's not the same as playing doctor."

Sylvie stretched out on the couch, folding her hands on her lap. "Wishful thinking on your part."

Harry ignored the subtle curves of Sylvie's body and concentrated his gaze on the speaker. He was sure to be a hot topic of conversation at some point during the evening. He'd be conspicuous by his absence. Someone was bound to ask what had happened to him. It would be interesting to hear the answers given. Someone might even slip and tell the truth. "I guess we might as well order some coffee," he said, adjusting the volume on the speaker's controls. "This may be a long night."

The pair spent what seemed to be hours sipping black coffee, huddled around the innocuous amplifier. After a point, the coffee lost all of its taste and potency. It succeeded only in filling the stomach and burning the tongue. Sylvie was dozing when the conversation started. A sharp poke in her side jolted her into wakefulness. "W-what?" she exclaimed.

"Here it comes," Harry said, pointing reverently to the speaker.

"What did I miss?"

"Nothing. A lot of praise for Young. Wasn't it a shame. That sort of crap. But we're down to the nitty-gritty now.

144

Hawkins and Vallory. I think they may be in Vallory's office."

"This is just so illegal," she protested.

"So's sodomy in New Jersey," Harry replied.

"Even between consenting adults?"

"Especially between consenting adults."

Hawkins's voice droned through the speaker. It was clear, strong, and angry. "We've got to get help up here, Russ. If we don't, we're going to have a real bloodbath here."

"We can't get help," came the calm reply. "You know that. It would mean the end of *Island*."

"*Island*'s not going to mean a hell of a lot with nobody left alive to enjoy it," Hawkins countered.

"You're exaggerating," the governor offered.

"We can't be sure that I am, though, can we?"

Vallory's voice was level, firm. "We cannot acknowledge this little problem of ours publicly. We are the hope of the future ... of everyone's future. We are looked up to as an example of high moral fiber. And now ... this."

A hand struck something solid. Harry envisioned Hawkins slamming his fist down on Vallory's desk. "All right, so we might tarnish our image. But we'll save a few lives. Look, Russ, I wouldn't take this nut as a personal offense. This sort of freak can turn up anywhere?"

"But the habitat is not just anywhere. People expect more from us ... much more."

"Russ, I know you have everyone's best intentions at heart, but we can't cover up murder. These aren't random acts of violence. These are executions of some sort. Look at this note we found near Anson's body. What's all this *children of light* stuff? I don't know what it means, but whoever wrote it is damned serious about avenging them."

"You know nothing," Vallory stated. "Nothing."

"All right. I'm no genius. But what do you think is going to happen when someone finds out about all this. Someone like one of those reporters."

"We'll take precautions."

"Precautions? One of them is already onto it. He thinks he's seen this guy. I can't, in good conscience, keep him away from this when, for all I know, he could help us track this guy down."

"I assume you're talking about Mr. Porter?"

"Yes."

"Well, he hasn't been very healthy of late, has he? His word is not exactly taken seriously these days, is it?"

Harry felt his face redden.

Another resounding thud. "Can you hear yourself? Why are you protecting this creep?"

A loud crash. Harry conjured up a mental picture of the governor standing so quickly that the chair at his desk toppled backward.

"I'm protecting us! US! What do you think would happen if we publicly admitted this situation? We'd be ruined. Earth would close us down in a second! Especially now, during an election year when we need votes! We still have to prove our worth to the good people below. The power satellites weren't enough. We're still too different, too far removed from the norm, for a lot of people to accept us. We have to provide them with constant miracles.

"All right. Fine. We'll play on their level. We'll give them all the miracles they want. But to do that, I need time. I need this entire week. And while I take that time, while we entertain our guests, the habitat has to generate as much positive publicity as is possible. Anson was right about that. We have to snow them. And that is the only reason those reporters are up here. We have to sell the hab to the people down there all over again. We have to make them believe that we are their only salvation. And I will not lower ourselves to Earth standards by wallowing in lurid cops and robbers terminology!"

"Cops and robbers? These are real people dying up here. By covering it up you're creating an even bigger scandal. You're dipping into the very same type of Earthshit that we fought against years ago. And if anyone does find out about this, it will be one hundred times worse for us to have the news leaked than it would be to go public. Is it so horrible to admit that we have one, single maladjusted individual aboard, one in a population of 10,000?"

"No one on the hab should be maladjusted," Vallory said sternly. "We take precautions."

"No one anywhere is *supposed* to be maladjusted. It happens. Even on *Island*. Hell, we're just beginning to learn about the psychology of space, about isolation, about radiation."

"I appreciate your interest, Hawk, but I must insist that you keep a lid on this."

146

Hawkins's thundering voice shook with rage. "My man-power is already pushed past the point of endurance. This place is teeming with visitors just begging to become political martyrs. Earth politicians. Reporters. Businessmen. One quick shot would guarantee headlines around the globe. I can't protect all these people and track down a killer at the same time. I don't have the men."

"Double your guards on all visitors for the time being," Vallory instructed. "Twenty-four-hour plainclothes duty."

"If we do that, we'll be giving that asshole carte blanche to kill!"

"No one has to know how you deploy your men."

"Give me a break, Russ."

"Hawk," Vallory persisted. "The future of Earth's space program rests upon the daily lifestyle of our Islanders. I'm not saying that this situation is either fair or unfair. But it stands. Someday, through our example and performance, a fleet of space habitats may be created by dozens of govern-ments. A United Nations of space may make its way through our galaxy. *Island* is not just responsible to one government. It is responsible to all of humanity."

Hawk's voice was getting lower, muttering obscenities between sentences. "Great. You hang in there and keep humanity in working order. I'll try to see if I can stop a lot of insignificant little people from being butchered like goddamn cattle."

Vallory's voice faded. Apparently, Hawkins was leaving abruptly. "It will only be until the president gives us the go ahead, Hawk. As soon as I get the green light, we'll go after your killer. I promise. Just give me time."

A burst of static howled from the speaker. A thud ended transmission. Harry reached forward and turned off the speaker. "Must have lost our button," he whispered, his mouth dry from tension. He took a quick gulp of coffee and sat in front of the speaker. "Holy shit," he muttered over and over again. "Holy shit."

Sylvie simply stared at the ceiling.

"Do you know what this means?" Harry asked aloud. "Do you know what this means? I'll tell you what it means. It means that there is a murderer running around up here and no one is going to try to catch him. The guy's already threat-ened me. He's challenged me. It's a contest. This Emmett guy thinks it's me against him. I'm supposed to come to

147

terms with this guy and no cop on this whole goddamn barge is going to lift a damned finger to track this sonofabitch down."

Sylvie continued to gaze at the ceiling.

"Do you know what that means?" Harry muttered. "It means I'm all by my goddamned self up here, that's what it means. It means that if I don't do something, no one will. Oh Jesusgodandchristalmighty."

Harry stood up and plodded into the bedroom. He fell into the bed. Lying on his back, he closed his eyes. Sylvie followed him into the room. "Now what?" she asked.

"Now, will you stay with me tonight?"

She flashed a puzzled look in his direction. "Only if you promise not to jump on me."

Harry slipped out of his pants and slid under the bed-clothes. "You're such a romanticist," he said, turning on his side and facing the wall. Behind him, he heard Sylvie remove her tunic and slacks. He felt her nestle into bed next to him, her firm breasts pressing against his back as she wrapped an arm around his chest.

"Do you feel vindicated?" she asked softly.

"Not particularly." The feeling of her erect nipples caressing his body stirred up memories in the inner recesses of his mind. But they were dim and fairly timeworn. Tonight, the emotion which reigned supreme was anger. Anger and fear.

"What are you going to do?"

"Nothing. Goddamn it. I've got my story."

Sylvie nearly pushed him out of bed. "Your story? You mean you're going to print all of this?"

"It's good copy," Harry stated. "I've lived up to my promise to Ernie Seabruck. I've done my part. I've proven that he's not crazy. I've proven that there's a killer running around lose up here and the local government is trying to hide that fact from the populace. Has all the ingredients of a bestseller. People love to read about corruption."

"But it's not real corruption," she countered. "It's not a *malicious* cover-up."

Harry didn't stir. There was a certain amount of twisted truth in what she said. The governor's actions were selfish, in a sense; but in a larger sense, they were almost altruistic. Were the lives of a dozen individuals of greater concern than the future of humankind. Some choice. Harry sighed, longing for the days of good and evil, black and white and neatly delineated sides. He placed his face in his pillow. "A cover-up is a cover-up."

Sylvie pounded him on the back. "Where's that knight in shining armor I once knew?"

"Rusted to death about five years back."

She leaned over his shoulder. "Say it."

"Say what?"

"Say that all you care about these days is yourself."

"All I care about is myself."

Sylvie wriggled away from him. "What a horrible thing to say."

Harry rolled over to face her. "What do you want me to do?"

"Anything but what you're thinking of doing," she said. "If you print that story just think about what it will do to our space program. Granted, it's the story of a lifetime for Harry Porter, but your cheap shot at fame would positively destroy over three decades of planning and work. The people up here would be thrown into a panic. The U.S. government would shut the hab down. Eventually, the killer would be caught . . . maybe. In the meantime, there'd be martial law, mass evacuations . . . "

Harry mentally envisioned the widespread confusion aboard the well-tailored craft. He hated her when she was right.

"Suppose you just went about your business as if nothing was happening," she suggested. "You'd spare the colony embarrassment and allow the whole affair to run its course."

"Yeah," Harry replied, "and lose my head in the process. Yours too, I might add."

Sylvie shrugged innocently. "Well, is there *anything* else you can do?"

Harry pulled Sylvie to him by the shoulders. Nose to nose, he glared at her. "You know damn well there is."

"Like what?"

"Like I could play hero. I could snoop around on my own and try to pull all the puzzle parts together. Who's our Emmett doodler? What's his beef? Who are the children of light?"

"You could do that, I guess."

"Yeah, but I'm not." He shoved her away. "I don't particularly care about any of this."

Sylvie cuddled up to him. "Thinking like that makes a lousy reporter."

149

"No. It makes for a good reporter but a lousy humanitarian."

"Well, before you make a final decision, Harry, think about it. Why are you up here? What do you really want out of your visit? What are your priorities?"

Priorities?

He had none. In a very real sense, he didn't care too much about any of all this. He had seen his share of murder and mayhem. He had stuck his neck out for the best of them. And what did it get him? A dead-end career and an empty house. This habitat business didn't offend him. He was simply pissed off that he was stuck in the middle of it. All he wanted to do was get off the tub alive. Still, that Emmett clown practically challenged him. That was hard to ignore.

He supposed that, while he was still onboard, he'd do whatever he had to do to stay healthy. And, if that included some freelance snooping, he supposed that he'd do it. He wouldn't be doing it for *Island*'s sake, though. He had a tough time sympathizing with its plight. It's one thing when an innocent man, a lone individual like Ernie Seabruck, gets caught up in a larger-than-life deceit. One innocent victim is a reality. Humanity is sheer fiction.

"Hell," he whispered into the night. He wouldn't file his big story. He wouldn't send the goddamn habitat into panic. He'd just do his job and pass the time. On that thought, he turned to Sylvie and fell asleep. That evening, his nightmare featured a double feature of devilry: two men, one stout and sweaty, the other robed and gaunt, waved laser weapons before him.

Such were the ways of progress.

PART FOUR

"All cities are beautiful,
but the beauty is grim . . ."
—Christopher Morley

1

Harry sat on the patio sipping a glass of blue fruit juice when the habitat's control center turned on the morning sun. In the glow of the filtered sunlight, the female figure in the next room stirred under the bedclothes. "You're up early," Sylvie said, stretching. She slowly arose from the bed, allowing the bedclothes to slide to a heap at her feet.

Harry stared at her naked body, memorizing every detail and cross-checking them with decade old facts. He crossed his legs quickly, attempting to hide his growing interest. "If you're going to flaunt yourself," he smiled by way of greeting, "you're going to have to rescind your 'no jumping' law."

Sylvie placed her hands on her breasts and walked haughtily toward the bathroom. She pointed a finger at Harry's crossed legs. "Don't exaggerate. You're not excited. I know for a fact that all men go through that when they first wake up in the morning."

"I've been awake for an hour."

Sylvie ran for the bathroom.

Harry followed her to the door and leaned against the frame. "I've been meaning to ask you," he began, juice glass still in hand. "What the hell is this crap I'm drinking?"

151

"Don't you like it?"

"I love it . . . but what the hell is it?"

"We call it Harmony Juice."

"Distilled from old gurus?"

"It's just a name," Sylvie said, emerging from the room with Harry's robe on. "I don't know what it is in technical terms. It's a mixture of a lot of different fruit juices plus some juice that's made up here on *Island* exclusively. I guess 40% of it is indigenous only to the hab. That's the blue stuff; a citrus hybrid they've been working on."

"Is it plentiful?"

"It's everywhere up here. It's like space cola."

Harry gulped down the rest of his juice. "Hurry up and eat your breakfast. I want to catch Sid and Babe before he elopes with her . . . it."

Sylvie stared at the alarm clock next to the bed in disbelief. "My God, Harry! It's not even seven o'clock!"

"I wanted to see the sun get switched on."

Muttering under her breath, Sylvie ate a quick breakfast and donned her clothes. Within minutes they were on their way to the computer center.

"What's the rush?" she asked him.

"I figure I'm living on borrowed time. Might as well use it constructively before old Emmett comes a' calling again."

"You're cheerful."

"It's the bottled morning air."

2

Harry and Sylvie found the wild-haired Sid alone in his cubicle. He was obviously pleased to have company. "Here for another bout with Babe?" he chuckled.

"I couldn't get her off my mind," Harry said, pumping the affable gentleman's hand unenthusiastically.

"Yes, indeed," Sid said. "She can do that to a person." He made room for Harry at the console.

"It's her cologne," Harry said, taking a seat. He leaned

forward toward the speaker grille. "Now, Babe. I want to ask you a few questions about the habitat's populace."

"Affirmative."

"Let's talk about mental stability, shall we?"

The machine purred. "It's your dime."

Harry looked up from the console and turned to Sid in shock. Sid shrugged. "Sometimes I get bored with her programming . . ."

Harry patted the console. "Can you briefly outline the steps *Island* takes to insure the mental health of its citizenry?"

"Affirmative. From its inception, the government of *Island One* has determined to maintain a healthy atmosphere for the human spirit to thrive and prosper within . . ."

"What do you mean, from its inception?"

"Even during the initial planning stages of *Island One* years ago on Earth, a series of psychological studies were conducted to calculate what lifestyle would offer minimal mental risk to space colonists. It was common knowledge that a space habitat, in its purest sense, would have qu'te an adverse effect on certain human personalities. A list of operations designed to counter these effects were drawn up and implemented during the construction of the craft. For example: all of the workers who built the habitat were sent Earthside once the craft was completed. None were allowed to live on *Island*."

"Why not?"

"The theory was that if one was aware of every possible structural flaw or hazard of the space habitat, one would subconsciously dwell upon them until a condition of monomaniacal proportions arose. To exist aboard the habitat in a state of mental well-being, one must be able to relax and have faith in the colony as a space vessel of the highest caliber."

"Interesting."

"Once an initial grouping of citizens was subsequently chosen for duty, the United States government then picked a strong leader/father figure to rule as governor."

"The governor was picked? Not elected?"

"Affirmative. Studies conducted by psychological researchers on Earth prior to actual construction of the habitat concluded that the best form of government for an isolated space dwelling would be that of a benign dictatorship; a government led by a strong, charismatic leader. This leader would give the space-dwelling populace a reassuring paternal role model to emulate and believe in, thus alleviating some of the inbred tension caused by a life led in an isolated and alien environment."

"But the governor still reports directly to Earth. He's not really an independent leader."

"Affirmative."

"That's nice to know. And the people all bought it. Amazing. Now, what about this muzak? I mean, the government uses that to keep the populace in line, too, right?"

"Crudely put, but affirmative in substance. Psychologists found that by playing innocuous, incessant melodies constantly, they could lull the human subconscious into a relaxed, tension-free state."

"How Machiavellian."

"Freudian."

"Keep going."

"This music can, of course, be altered to subtly manipulate the general mood of the people."

"A potential weapon."

"Negative. The music is designed to alleviate stress, not to cause it."

"And all this adds up to a fail-safe formula for mental health?"

"In regards to the continuing maintenance of a mentally stable community, the governor and his staff of physicians have made sure that every possible precaution is taken in screening potential citizens in order to avoid any and all possible mental problems. Psychological profiles are done on all incoming members of the habitat populace. In addition, two-year assignments of duty are given, with options renewable only at the individual's request. At that point, yet another psychological profile is taken. The request for extended duty is judged on the basis of said report."

"Do you have these profiles in your memory banks?"

"Affirmative."

"Let me guess. They're classified."

"Affirmative."

"Have people failed these tests often?"

"As of 7:56 AM today, some 1.79% of the populace has failed to pass these psychological surveys."

Harry looked at his watch. "I have 7:54."

"You're slow," the computer replied.

"It's one of his strong points," Sylvie informed Babe.

"All right," Harry persisted. "One last question. Now, despite these tests and their wonderful results, how many people have actually cracked up on *Island* over its ten-year history. Give me numbers not percentage points, please."

The computer paused to calibrate. "120 citizens."

"Not many," Harry muttered.

"Affirmative. The average, rounded off to the nearest tenth numerically, is 1 citizen out of every 3,345 grouping."

"Thanks, Babe," Harry said, rising from the chair. "And thank you, Sid," he added, once again pumping the man's hand up and down. "This has been a most informative session."

"Leaving so soon?" Sid smiled. "You didn't even get into Oedipal complexes or penis envy."

Sylvie pushed Harry toward the door. "Why is it I get no respect?" he moaned loudly.

"I am not programmed to respond to inquiries requiring conjecture," Babe replied, her console still on audio.

"Smart circuits," Harry grunted, leaving the room and heading toward the exit.

"Find out what you were after?" Sylvie asked.

"I'm not sure what I was after," he answered. "All I can say, at this point, is that we can safely assume that our nut case is, statistically, a very rare breed up here."

"Insanity is never considered common," she said.

"Maybe," Harry admitted. "But on *Island*, a controlled environment which caters to mental hygiene ... I wonder what would cause someone to become unhinged?"

"The usual stuff, I suppose. Depression. Anxiety. Isolation. Anger."

"How about stress?"

"Stress, too."

The two people walked along the pedestrian pathway. They approached the electric cart track. "All right. Before our cartoonist killer gets another chance to wield his fiery swift sword, let's see if we can figure out what his gripe is. He just doesn't cream a select cadre of habitat dwellers for no reason whatsoever. Depression and anxiety I think would have been caught on those shrink profiles. The same goes for isolation. Those traits seem to be ingrained in your personality permanently. But, I've seen a lot of 'normal' people just go to pieces because of their jobs, or the responsibilities of home-life. Stress. Some people just can't take it. And if our friend is

155

a product of too much stress, it wouldn't hurt us to check out some of the jobs that offer the most pressure up here. Maybe we can trace him through his environment."

"So you've decided to hunt for him on your own?" Sylvie smiled.

"For the time being," Harry muttered.

"Why?"

Harry shrugged. "For the sport."

She hugged him suddenly, causing him to blush. "It has nothing to do with you. He's out to kill me. I tend to take those kinds of threats personally."

"Why don't you just become a cop?" she said.

Harry was forced to laugh. "The pay is lousy. Now, you're going to have to help me out with this sleuthing. No one will notice my snooping around if you give me an official OK. Take me to as many job locales as possible. I'll file a bunch of puff pieces on *Island* life profiling the workers, the scientists, and anyone else we have to sniff at. While I'm doing my 'stories,' I'll be looking for our pal as well."

"But how will you spot the killer? Are you expecting him to wear a big scarlet 'K'?"

"No." Harry smiled. "But he might as well be. Our friend is a telepath of some sort. A Cro-Magnon caste peeper. Unless he can control his mental output, and I'm not sure that he can, I'll find him. I'm more sensitive to his aura than most. I'll recognize it right away."

"You think of everything, don't you?"

"If we're both alive in four days, I'll let you know."

Sylvie shuddered slightly. An electric cart puttered by. "Let's walk to the spaceport."

"What for?"

"For your first contact with stress-laden Islanders. We'll visit some of our factory workers."

"Why the spaceport?"

"Because all our factory work is done on the shacks." She pointed a finger toward the colony's large mirrors. "Out yonder in space."

Harry automatically rubbed his stomach. "Gee. I was just getting used to things here."

"Relax, Buck Rogers, it's a short trip."

The twosome moved to cross the pedestrian walkway. Harry stood on the curb watching cautiously for nonexistent traffic.

"Jeez, but you're a creature of habit," Sylvie said, pulling him along.

3

The space shack spun lazily in the distance, an armor-plated basketball suspended against a black backdrop. Porter sat in the spacetug and brooded. He couldn't shake the feeling that he was to be the killer's next victim. He wondered when he would once again face the deranged shadow shape. Perhaps on the tug. Perhaps on the space shack.

He couldn't even attempt to understand just what it was that drove one human being to kill another. In that sense, he was very naïve about matters concerning violent crime. Oh, he had confronted an assortment of murderers in his time. Talked with them. Profiled them. Relived their hideous deeds in print. But he could never isolate, never comprehend that all-consuming passion that would drive a man to murder.

That passion both revolted and attracted him. To be able to experience such a sudden wave of intense feeling just once... He pushed the thought from his head immediately. Sick. He was resigned to the fact that he would never know such passion, any kind of passion. In a sense, his profession precluded that. He was a paid observer of events. He noticed things, memorized details. It was his job to impartially dissect a situation and parrot the findings. He was a man in control; a being who could neither love nor hate. He wondered which originated first; his lack of feeling or his professional stoicism. Someday he'd have to figure that one out. Not today, though. Today was a time for irony. A man whom passion eluded was now in pursuit of a passionate man; a dangerously passionate man.

He felt the ship dock. The trip had been a mercifully short one; this type of small tug resembled a space bus with no more than forty seats in the entire cylindrical rig. Sylvie took him by the arm and led him to the deplaning area.

The construction shack itself was not the Utopian type of

157

structure one dreamed about when envisioning space exploration. Like its earthly counterpart, the factory, the shack was a sweatshop; as unglamorous as an armpit and equally as ripe. A circular craft slightly more than 100 yards in circumference, the globe was actually a two-layered structure: a sphere within a sphere. Its outer hull contained a layer of small offices and corridors. Its hollow, inner core was the construction area proper. In this interior sphere the assembly of power satellite parts took place on a daily basis.

Harry and Sylvie were greeted at the docking station by plant foreman Ian Cartwright, a no-nonsense British expatriate who had achieved fame on Earth earlier as the foreman of the crew that had paved over Florida's Everglades as part of the U.S.'s "expand and multiply" program. ("Tough job, that," Cartwright was wont to repeat every so often, "dozens of bulldozers lost. Tragic, really.")

Cartwright was at least six feet six inches tall and at least half that size around his middle. Standing upright, he resembled a jumpsuit-wearing grizzly. His face had that comfortable, pushed-in look that is found so often at construction sites. He would have been downright all-American rugged-hero looking had it not been for the fact that he possessed but half a nose. Harry could not help but gape at the sight.

"Saves on hankies, this," Cartwright smiled, shaking Harry's hand and noting where his gaze was riveted. "Happened when I worked on a sanitation truck, if the truth be known. A freak occurrence. There are ways to pick up those trash cans, you see. Always take the cover off before you pick one up. My boss always told me that. 'Always take the cover off for a quick peek inside,' he said. Well, I didn't listen. Then, one day, I pick up this can and what comes out from under the lid but a rat the size of a bulldog. I don't know which one of us was more surprised. He took off half my nose as a souvenir of the encounter."

Harry couldn't decide whether the foreman was kidding or not. "Still," Cartwright reflected. "I got off luckier than most. Take old Crazy Alex. He was just plain old Alex until a truck tire blew and sent a hubcap slamming into the side of his noggin. Tragic, that. Good driver at one time. One of the best."

Harry nodded in mute agreement. Sylvie said nothing. "I expect you'd like a tour of this place, then," Cartwright said. He led Harry and Sylvie down a short hallway leading from the docking area to the outer hull. As it turned out, the tour

158

of the outer area was lackluster and brief. The shack's top section was a maze of steel-blue corridors which seemed to twist and turn endlessly, dotted with small doorways that led to offices and locker rooms. Before the trio had gone too far, Harry noted that a figure was following them at a discreet distance. Far enough behind to be faceless, yet close enough to pose a threat.

Cartwright was seemingly oblivious of the stranger to the rear. He pointed to the shiny azure walls. "All this was manufactured in space," he informed Harry. "It's called bubble steel. It's as strong as any steel you'll find on Earth but lighter. Air bubbles interspersed throughout. You manufacture the stuff in zero g plants. Piece o' cake."

Harry felt uneasy walking through the blue corridors which gave no signs of having any ultimate conclusion. One hallway after another. One turn after another. Mentally, he attempted to hone in on the figure behind him. He wondered if it was the peeper killer. Cartwright made a sudden gesture, pointing to yet another blue wall. He swung his massive arm wide, catching Harry in the side of the jaw. Harry's head whiplashed into the wall with a resounding thud. He almost blacked out from the sudden burst of pain.

"Damn," Cartwright said, pulling back his arm instantly. "Sorry about that one. I get carried away sometimes. Let's have a look at that head. Quite a nasty bump you got just then."

Harry's head pounded like an epileptic drummer. He allowed Cartwright to probe the back of his head while Sylvie stood by. "You'll be all right," Cartwright pronounced with a grin. "Just have a goose egg up there for a bit. Does it hurt much?"

Harry touched the back of his head gingerly. The tip of his index finger touching his scalp caused a bolt of pain to erupt above his eyes. "Naahh," he sighed. "Not too much."

He wondered if Cartwright had orchestrated that swoop purposely. His head now throbbing, his senses shriveled in pain, Harry would not be able to pinpoint a peeper if his life depended upon it. Which it did. He glanced suspiciously at the ever-smiling Englishman. He was tall and strong. Could this be the killer? Was it one of Cartwright's men?

Harry humbly followed the big man's lead, wishing the foreman would just stop grinning. He was beginning to look like the Cardiff Crocodile. After a few more moments of walking, the trio emerged from the infinite passageway and

159

walked out into a large catwalk-laden platform; a sort of ledge. Harry could not supress a gasp of surprise at the sight before him. Cartwright merely chuckled. "I know. Something to see, isn't it?"

The ledge formed a complete circle, outlining the innards of the second sphere. Below was the circular, hollow "guts" of the shack: a massive factory. Harry watched at least two dozen construction workers take part in an eerie industrial ballet. Floating around in zero and light g in the center of the shack, they assembled a large, seemingly cumbersome piece of satellite equipment.

"The inner core," Cartwright explained. "The working area. Everything is built right here."

Harry watched the men hover about the satellite component below, riveting pieces together effortlessly. "Incredible."

"That's not the half of it," Cartwright added.

Harry made a move to walk down the flight of stairs leading to the center of the core. "I wouldn't do that," the foreman cautioned. "You'd go flying. You might not have noticed it all that much but you've been losing weight the entire time we've been walking. It's a gradual lessening of gravity caused by our traveling toward shack midpoint. You don't feel it too much because of the way our corridors spiral. Trot down that stairwell, though, and it will hit you quite nicely. I don't think the boys would appreciate a visitation from above, either, if the truth be known."

Harry gulped, hesitantly lifting a foot. He did feel a bit more buoyant, come to think of it. "Your men are serious about their work, eh?" he stated.

"It's more than mere work, Mr. Porter. It's a way of life, that. We're unique up here. Specially trained. A lot of us are on our fourth and fifth tours of duty."

"You wouldn't want to go back to Earth I take it."

"Not while there's still a breath of life in me."

"How about your men?"

"That goes double for the men. We're special up here, you see. We're one of a kind, doing a job that's one of a kind. It gives us a sense of purpose. Put us back on Earth and we'll be quite ordinary again, wouldn't we? Just another group of hardhats. But here, man, here we're making a contribution to the world that you can see, we're making things that count. And God help anyone who tries to take that away from us."

He shot a meaningful glance at Harry, the grin never fading

160

from his face. "You can quote me on that, Mr. Porter. I'd be very pleased if you do so in the near future."

Harry swallowed, his mouth suddenly dry. "Here," Cartwright said, stepping into an office nearby. The room's most distinctive feature was a large picture window overlooking the construction area. "Let's watch the fun safely."

The office was a control base of some kind. On the wall opposite the window were rows of dials and instruments that were quite alien to Harry . . . as were any mechanical objects more complex than a rubber band. Cartwright closed the door behind them. Harry noticed that it wasn't an ordinary hatch. The door was at least eighteen inches thick and closed with a latch locked from within.

"Once that piece of machinery is completed down there," Cartwright said, "my men will leave the factory area and head for their pressurized cabins. Rooms similar to this one. You might have noticed the doors in the hallways. Right about then, we'll hook that piece of satellite down there to a drag line attached to a tug hovering outside. Then, we start the show!"

"Show?"

"Spectacular event, really. We slow the rotation of the shack through small jets. Then, the shack, this whole craft, actually separates in two. There are three hydraulic beams that expand and push the two halves of the shack apart. From a distance, this place would look like a halved orange during the process, the two sides stuck together by three toothpicks. While we're all huddled in our cabins, hanging on to these stirrup things for support, the tug tows out the piece of equipment. Later, it brings it to the satellite that's under construction in space. Our two orange halves will slowly be drawn back together, the shack will begin its rotation again, be repressurized and, like good workers all, we will scurry out of our cubbyholes and get back to work."

"You don't sound too excited about your show," Harry smirked.

"Once you know the general plot, the action gets a bit tedious," Cartwright explained. "Here, look. All the fireworks start right in this room. This panel of switches here. They all get pushed in succession. Rotation. Depressurization. Beam expansion. You want to close the shack, you just pound the series above them. Beam retraction. Repressurization. Rotation. I'm sure it's a very intricate console but for blokes like me to use them, they've oversimplified everything. On my

161

days off, I think they bring a trained ape up here to take my place; Bonzo Einstein or something to that effect."

Harry found himself smiling despite his aching head. "Don't kid me, that's quite a dangerous maneuver."

"Oh quite, yes. Dangerous, but routine."

"Hasn't anyone ever been injured here?"

"Nothing serious. A broken toe or a sprained wrist. I got a nosebleed once. Most of the injuries happen when we stop and commence rotation. Zero g is a tricky addition to anyone's life."

"But what if one of those slabs of machinery fell on top of one of your men? Those things must weigh tons."

"On Earth, certainly. Up here, they're light as a feather. You could dance with a hippo down there and she'd be as graceful as a ballerina."

Harry watched the workers below. He concentrated his thoughts, hoping to send out a sudden mental vibration in their direction. He deliberately envisioned scenarios of death, destruction, and despair. He rubbed his forehead vigorously. Hell, even if the peeper was down there and responded to his mental feeler, he wouldn't know it. His head was on fire. The lump on the back of his scalp emitted a steady, piercing pain. He tried one last time to conjure up a mental portrait of an unsettling nature for the benefit of any neighborhood telepath. "What would happen if one of your men was caught down there after the shack opened?"

"Not a chance of that, if the truth be known."

"Why not?"

"Well, first we sound an alarm. That's a five-minute affair. And then, we depressurize. That takes another few minutes. A man would have to be deaf to ignore all of that."

"Suppose he did."

"Well, technically, he could survive for a few precious seconds by exhaling, getting all of the excess air out of his body and diving like hell for the nearest cabin."

"And if he didn't make it?"

"Bad news, that."

"Would he be hurt?"

Cartwright nodded vigorously. "Oh, yes indeed. But he'd never know how badly."

"And why not?"

"He'd die first. The difference in pressure involved between his own body and space . . ."

162

"Oh yeah," Harry said, feeling more than slightly ignorant. "A vacuum."

"Right," Cartwright replied. "Basic science. Gawd, remember those classes? And the teacher always looked like an anemic owl? Anyhow, get stuck out there and you'd have quite a nasty death on your hands. Your skin would bubble first, quite painful I'd guess. Then, your insides would burst, bit by bit."

"Nasty death," Harry repeated, "wonderful murder."

Cartwright smiled at Harry. "Perfect murder."

Harry stepped away from the window momentarily, his stomach rejecting the scene described by the foreman. "Is there a drinking fountain around here?"

Cartwright pointed to a second door on the inner side of the control room. "There's a water dispenser in the hall. Just 'round the corner."

"Thanks." Harry wandered off, leaving Sylvie and Cartwright chatting by the glass pane. His head ached so much he couldn't tell whether he was feeling the effects of a concussion or a malicious mental marauder. He rounded the hallway corner. There wasn't a water dispenser to be seen. Perhaps Cartwright had gotten his directions confused. Harry strolled down the hall, past a few doorways and rounded a second corner. Still no sign of the fount. Maybe he'd simply taken a wrong turn somewhere. The next corner took him to a "Y" split in the corridor, a steel-blue fork in the road. Harry stood before the division and listened closely to the sounds around him.

Footsteps echoed dimly in the distance.

There was someone else in the corridor. Although his initial reaction was one of panic, he made a brilliant try at rationalizing the sound. Of course there would be footsteps resounding nearby. He was on a space shack, populated by dozens of men. The footsteps came to a halt. Harry began to walk once again, softly and slowly. The footsteps mimicked his gait. Someone was following him. Was it one of Hawkins's plainclothes cops or was it the killer?

Harry didn't particularly desire to find an answer to the question while roaming about on his own. He had to make it back to the glass-paned room. No one would dare accost him in the presence of the plant foreman. He began retracing his steps. He came to a familiar looking door. Was it the control room already? He grasped the handle and pushed inward.

The door wouldn't budge. He trotted quickly down a side corridor to where the massive catwalk was no doubt waiting. There was nothing there but a wall . . . a wall and a small monitoring screen. The screen showed the hollowed core of the shack. The workers had departed. A tow line had been attached to the satellite piece. Harry felt his chest grow tight. The construction shack was about to open!

A buzzer sounded ominously above Harry's head. He assumed it was the signal for the workers to double-time it to their pressurized cabins and safety. He ran for the nearest door. His fingers slipped round the doorlatch. He yanked on it furiously. It was locked. Furthermore, there wasn't a sign of any of the returning workers. The buzzer droned on. Harry leaned against a wall, wheezing. Had he been set up? Was this how he was destined to go? A small splatter in space?

Somewhere beyond the buzzing sound, a rhythmic pounding arose. The footsteps persisted. Harry was still being pursued. Harry gleefully tossed logic out the window and gave in to sheer panic. He darted blindly down the first hallway he could find. There were no doorways in sight. The steady, plodding pattern rumbled behind him. Harry continued to run madly. He was a dead man. He realized that as a fact. But how did he want to die? Laser blasted from behind? Attacked by air bubbles from within? He rounded another aimless corridor corner. Had he his druthers, he'd prefer to die of old age, thank you. The footsteps behind him picked up speed. Harry skidded to a stop, deciding that it was time to meet his assailant head-on.

He ran to a small archway at the far end of this section of hallway. Crouching in the recess, he surveyed the corridor. He had no idea where he was or even if he had passed this way before. The corridor, like so many of the others he had darted through, branched out into a "Y" at the opposite end. The footsteps echoed relentlessly through one of the two hallway stems before him.

He held his breath, seeing the shadow. It began as a small dot emerging from the left branch of the corridor. Soon, it grew into a titanic twisted, shapeless form. As the steady pounding of leather on steel grew louder, the indistinct shadow gradually took form. It was the figure of a man, gun poised in hand. The shadow gradually receded to life size. Suddenly, the shadow-caster himself emerged from the hallway. Harry's pursuer, a solidly built man in a gray uniform charged down the hall, oblivious to Harry's presence. Harry counted under his breath to six before leaping.

As he dove through the air, he wondered why he had counted to *six*. Fairly odd number to base any plan of attack on.

The guard whirled around instinctively, eyes wide with surprise. Harry crashed into the runner's side. Both men ricocheted into a wall and slid onto the floor, the wind knocked out of them. A shrill bell began clanging loudly. Harry could not tell if this was the final alarm or whether he had merely punctured an eardrum. He attempted to wrap his hands around the assailant's throat, somewhat clumsily. The assailant slammed a fist into Harry's nose, causing his already aching head to explode with pain. Harry attempted to come up with a logical, well thought-out plan of attack. After a fist slammed into his nose a second time, he abandoned logic altogether. Like most civilized men caught in a totally unexpected, high-tension situation, he relied on sheer animal instinct to see him through. Unfortunately, like most highly civilized men, his animal instinct was about as lethal as that of a toy poodle's. In a word, Harry was outmatched.

Still, he fought valiantly onward, grunting, wheezing, clawing for his life, and feeling both frightened and foolish all the while. The two men rolled through the hall. The guard raised his gun to strike Harry. Harry sent his closed hand slamming into the butt of the pistol. His assailant's finger brushed the trigger mechanism, sending the gun jerking into action. A blinding burst of laser light zipped across the corridor. Blinded by the light, Harry relaxed his body. The guard, noting Harry's reaction, slammed a fist into the reporter's stomach. Harry scurried away in a fetal, nearly crablike crawl. Scrambling to his feet, the guard loped after Harry and, collaring him easily, lifted him off the floor and pushed him toward a door. Punching the door open, the guard shoved Harry inside. The door closed behind them with a resounding thump. From the hall outside the room, a whirlwind sound could be heard. Depressurization.

Harry slowly picked himself off the floor. He found himself staring at Sylvie Dunbar and Ian Cartwright. "Now where the devil were you two?" Cartwright asked. "We were getting a bit worried. A bad time to go exploring on your own, I'm afraid."

Harry clutched his stomach.

The guard wiped a trickle of blood from his nose. "Don't tell me, tell your explorer pal here."

Harry was too exhausted to be very embarrassed. Paranoia was a trait he'd have to curb in the future. He smiled lamely at Sylvie and Cartwright. The foreman returned the grin easily enough, but Sylvie regarded him with an icy stare. Through the near wall-sized window, Harry watched the shack's factory section slowly open up like a globe being pried apart from its equator. Harry was given a breathtaking look at sheer space. Outside the window spanned endlessness, infinity.

In the distance, a spacetug appeared. It slowly glided by the shack, pulling the piece of satellite out of the factory area and into the endless sky.

Harry's stomach rumbled. Jeezus. Another minute or so in that hallway and he would have been . . .

The guard, obviously struck by the same thought, simply leveled a contemptuous look Harry's way. "Asshole," he whispered passionately.

Harry pressed his nose up to the glass, the star-studded void outside completely mesmerizing him. "None of this would have happened if you kept your water coolers out in the open," he muttered.

4

The two figures climbed up the embankment to the man-made hilltop from where *Island*'s pedal-plane enthusiasts soared. Pedal planes were one of the most popular leisure diversions on the habitat, and also one of the most dangerous. Small, lightweight vehicles, a cross between a bicycle and an Earthly hang-glider, the planes were designed for graceful flights in low gravity. Launched from a strategically constructed hilltop runway, the brightly colored craft regularly took Islanders on topsy-turvy tours high above the habitat's rooftops . . . or below its rooftops, depending on your point of view.

"I like the way you just sort of *blended* into the crowd on the space shack," Sylvie remarked, a smirk causing small creases around her lips. "Very inconspicuous."

Harry simmered in silence.

Sylvie's smirk broadened. "Didn't they refer to you in the newspapers as 'The Chameleon' at one point?"

Harry wanted to arrange her pixie-ish features into a state worthy of a large facial cast. He thought better of it, however, and gritted his teeth instead. He would much rather have been tying one on, by himself, right about now in one of the habitat's bars. The memory of his father, however, usually kept him fairly unsoused if not totally sober. Nice fellow, pop. Started out as a school teacher and ended up as a sponge. Future shock they called it. Bloated belly, red-freckled face, paper bags with leaky bottoms, the works.

Dozens of such cheerful thoughts filled Harry's bruised head as he stood on the hillside. He'd made a complete fool of himself on the shack, but of course he'd never admit that. Besides, there were somewhat mitigating circumstances involved . . . like that bone-crushing blow to the skull. "All right," he answered after a while. "I made an awkward entrance, but that Cartwright fellow wasn't exactly making things easy for me."

Sylvie's smirk melted into a puzzled pout. "What do you mean by that?"

"I'm talking about that little love tap. With my head aching like that I couldn't have located a peeper up there if I tripped over him."

"You don't think that he did that intentionally, do you?"

"I'm not ruling out that possibility."

"You're being silly."

"Perhaps."

Harry and Sylvie walked across the runway to a pair of pedal planes. "Are you sure you want to try this?" she asked.

Harry sat on the bicycle seat and nodded. "Don't worry about me, just shove off."

Sylvie boarded her plane and, pedaling slowly to the edge of the small runway, accelerated, sped to the hilltop's end, and sailed off into the air. Harry was impressed. He wasn't all that crazy about following her out there but he felt he had to. In the wake of the space shack incident, he was sure that he was being followed by at least one of Hawkins's men. And if they were close to him, they could be carrying short-range pinpoint microphones. He really didn't want to have all of his conversations monitored when it came to the subject of Emmett.

Harry pedaled furiously. His plane bounced toward the cliff. As the plane soared into the air, leaving the hillside with a single, ungainly bound, his legs instinctively froze. His plane dropped into a sudden tailspin. Regaining his composure, he pedaled as he had never pedaled before. Within seconds, his plane was gaining altitude.

Sylvie was soon gliding beside him. "Easy there," she cautioned. "You don't want history books to call you the habitat's first kamikaze pilot, do you?"

Harry didn't answer. Actually, he couldn't answer. So laborious was the constant action of his legs that he found himself totally winded, incapable of speech for the time being. He cursed himself silently for suggesting such a foolhardy maneuver in the first place. After all, his idea of a physically exerting sport was checkers. Noticing Sylvie's concerned look, he renewed his pedaling with increased vigor cum madness.

"Be careful," he barely heard Sylvie warn. He did not know it at the time but, as he exercised both his legs and his pride, he was deliberately maneuvering his craft headfirst into the habitat's zero gravity strip; an encounter Sylvie visualized with visible dread. Zero g was an experienced pilot's delight; an exhilaratingly euphoric experience. However, if the zero g area, located in the exact middle of *Island*'s sky, wasn't entered properly, an inexperienced flyer could find himself stuck precariously in mid-air. It was all a matter of angle and momentum.

Of course, Harry was unaware of both momentum and angle when he hit the strip. He hit it hard, like a fly rebounding into a spider's web. He was soaring upward when, without warning, he felt his body lift upward, nearly leaving the bicycle seat. Attempting to push himself back down, he somehow succeeded in yanking his craft upward instead. His body still seemed to be rising. So was his plane. He pushed down on the pedals frantically, attempting to accelerate. Encountering no resistance, his feet plunged downward, missed the pedals and hung, uselessly, alongside his vessel. He began to tumble slowly. He couldn't gather enough speed to move either up or down, left or right.

He was stuck.

"Goddamn it," he hissed. "Goddamn this crazy place to hell."

"Just hang on," Sylvie called.

"The thought had occurred to me," Harry muttered, vainly attempting to discern which direction was indeed up and which direction down.

From below, Sylvie built up a solid burst of speed and soared, angelically, through the zero g strip. Extending an arm, she lightly shoved Harry's plane to one side during her pass. Once propelled in a single direction, his craft continued to move, further and further away from zero g and into a heavier gravitational area. He felt his body regain some sense of weight. Composure at hand, he replaced his feet on the plane's pedals and continued flying.

"I was only resting up there," he shouted to Sylvie as she approached him.

"Right," Sylvie replied, slightly disgusted. "You were thinking about the reasons you took me up here to chat."

"Exactly," he said, allowing her to pull up alongside of him. "I've been thinking about our space nut. As of now, he could be anybody, right? I mean everyone employed on that space shack, for instance, could have a pretty damn good reason to wipe out the people responsible for the end of their careers."

"Not too likely, but go on."

"Now, as far as we know, Vallory doesn't want to admit to the killer's existence for purely publicity-related reasons. But, suppose he has other, more subtle causes for his hesitation?"

"Continue."

"I've got another theory about our space nut. This Emmett could be someone who's slightly out of whack because of stress, because of job pressure. But, suppose he isn't a pure mental. Suppose he's a *physically* aberrated guy. I didn't see what he looked like. Suppose he's a victim of a horrible accident."

"No way. There has never been a major accident aboard *Island.*"

"How about the shacks."

"Nope."

Harry continued to pedal. "All right. Let's leave the physical scars behind for a moment. How about a victim of cosmic radiation? Hawkins mentioned it briefly when we eavesdropped."

"I can't imagine that," Sylvie answered. "It's a possibility, I suppose, but a very remote one. The colony is equipped with a pretty effective cosmic radiation shield. It's a layer of Moon minerals spread out over every inch of *Island*'s outer hull. During times of solar flares, which are pretty infrequent, when the radiation increases, there are also special suits to wear and pre-designated shelters available to shield citizens from any harmful rays if things really go haywire."

"Sounds dangerous to me."

"Not really. We take those precautions because no one knows the full effects of cosmic rays. It could very well cause genetic or mental instability. So why take chances?"

Harry watched the electric carts sputter along the tracks below. If cosmic radiation could cause changes in physiological growth, perhaps it could also alter mental growth. Mental stability. Mental prowess. Perhaps it could drive a man to murder. "No one has ever become ill from these rays?"

"No one."

"No accidents and no radiation victims."

"Zero."

Harry lapsed into silence. He was back to square one. He had a killer tailing him with no origin and no clearly defined motive. Just a shopping list of victims-to-be.

"How do we land these things?" he asked.

"I was wondering when you'd think about that," Sylvie laughed.

The two airborne figures glided downward through the *Island* sky. One landed on the hilltop runway as gracefully as a feather, the other as delicately as a rock.

5

Harry now knew the meaning of the word "pain." His pedal-plane romp had awakened entire sections of his body heretofore never heard from. Not only were those sections awake, they were fairly disgruntled about being disturbed. Stopping off at his hotel room to change, Harry had time for a stiff drink before attending that afternoon's meeting of the

Earth delegation. The drink helped him retain his sense of detachment. No matter how the battles between the delegates and Vallory shaped up, they were strictly small potatoes when compared to Harry's problems with the killer.

He hopped a cart to the government building. As during the first meeting, the room was once again charged with emotional electricity and not too much logic.

Sitting at the oblong table next to Sylvie, Harry was struck by the thought that he simply didn't care about the Islanders and their plight. He couldn't really identify with their lighter-than-air lifestyles. In terms of priorities, he was much more concerned with the well-being of one totally deranged assassin. None of the multi-million-dollar space colony's aspirations particularly impressed him.

He was beginning to regard both the habitat and many of its inhabitants with disdain. Vallory, of course, was on the top of Harry's shit list. Vallory, the pious leader, currently up to his neck in deception; deception of the variety that could cause the death of a dozen innocent people. Harry slumped in his chair and allowed the warmth of the drink to pulsate through his aching body. He wouldn't piss on any of these people if they were on fire.

The arguing around the table had already grown in volume to near fist-fight status. Harry paid it no mind, concentrating instead on the killer. Motive. If Harry could pinpoint the motive, he probably could come up with a fairly good character sketch of the assassin. Was Emmett's motive revenge? Was he protecting his job? Avenging a miscarriage of justice? Or could this group of people represent something that Emmett despised, like capitalism? That might be an angle to check out. Perhaps the killer was a jaded political idealist.

He glanced around the room. And maybe an interview or two with some of these pirates would reveal what sordid plans they had on the back burner that might offend a political purist. He watched the men bicker. The various attendees had perfected the verbal strut to an art form, inflating their chests and their egos with each pronouncement. Harry stifled a smirk. Some of the most powerful and pompous men on Earth, all marked for death and not even knowing it.

He caught Sylvie gazing at him. He knew she was wondering what was on his mind. Let her wonder. The pressure of this situation was finally beginning to affect him. He felt trapped. Her being at his side every hour didn't help any, either. He felt constrained. Hampered. Maybe today, he'd see if he could give her the polite slip. He returned her gaze. She was undoubtedly one of the most beautiful women he had ever met. He'd miss her company. Cancel thought. He had some intense investigative work to accomplish and he'd rather do it solo.

The men at the table glowered at each other, giving the brightly lit room a dark and ominous feel. Science Advisor Curtis was blubbering that, despite its altruistic gameplan, *Island* was a distinct liability to the president on Earth. Some recent polls showed that the chief of staff was losing political ground because of the habitat's existence. Harry noted the fellow's well-developed whine. Curtis's rotund face and extended nose seemed to clash with each other throughout his tirade. Harry watched with morbid fascination as the seemingly boneless jowls flapped up and down with increasing intensity. He silently wondered if Curtis's lower lip would ever flop closed hard enough for it to overshoot the upper lip and hook itself on the end of the science advisor's dangling proboscis. It was obvious to everyone gathered that, in spite of Vallory's persuasive arguments of the previous day, the perpetually worried politician was in favor of an abrupt discontinuation of *Island* activities.

Curtis began to calm down. At that point, Wayne Ferron, coming to life suddenly like the semicomatose doormouse at the Mad Hatter's tea party, licked his oversized teeth expectantly and proposed an infinite number of "what if" disaster scenarios. They were clearly designed to frighten the wits both out of the assembly and the citizenry of Earth, portraying *Island* as the bane of humanity.

"What if this thing suddenly stopped turning?" he demanded, jabbing a finger in Vallory's direction like a prosecuting attorney on the attack. "What if the gravity was simply shut off? Everyone would be killed. We'd all be flying around like leaves in a whirlwind!"

Harry took a pencil and jotted down a single word on his notepad: "Idiot."

Vallory, summoning up a great deal of patience, calmly explained that the habitat was not powered by a motor or any type of instrument that could "break down" and bring the colony screeching to a halt. In space, a body in motion would simply remain in motion until acted upon by an outside force. Initially, both cylinders of the habitat were sent into rotation at a desired rate by two small sets of booster rockets. That rate of spin was now virtually perpetual. On infrequent occasions, a small rocket at either end of the craft was put into use to prevent an infinitesimal wobble.

Ferron's fears refused to be explained away by Vallory's knowledge. "And what if an enemy government attempted to take over *Island?*"

The room buzzed for a moment as delegates allowed that thought to sink in. "You have no adequate defenses to speak of," Ferron declared. "A fleet of ships could come around the Moon and have you cornered by the time you knew what was going on!"

Ferron had obviously been doing his homework. Vallory sighed audibly and began, once again, to placate the headline-happy politician. "But *Island* is not located in terms of strategic military placement, we're not all that important."

Ferron was unmoved. "You know that and I know that, but suppose THEY don't?"

Harry shook his head and returned to his doodling. He hated these sort of bull sessions. In the middle of a fairly nice sketch of a very famous mouse being attacked by a flyswatter, a thought crossed his mind. Suppose Emmett wasn't one man, suppose he was a part of a terrorist organization? An organization representing a foreign government bent on taking over the habitat. Before he realized it, Harry's doodled mouse was uttering a single, one-word thought balloon.

"Sabotage."

Vallory was still verbally dancing with Ferron when Harry looked up. ". . . and any major launch emanating from Earth would automatically be detected by the U.S.'s spacecraft defense unit. There would be enough time for the armed forces to attack the invaders from home!"

The meeting lapsed back into monosyllabic muttering. Harry toyed with the sabotage idea. He'd have to look into that angle. The meeting dribbled to a stop. Harry was determined to spend the rest of the afternoon sleuthing on his own. All things considered, Sylvie took the news fairly well. "I'd really like to roam around up here by myself for a while," Harry told her.

"Sure," she said. "Drop dead."

Harry launched into an intricate and highly melodramatic song and dance concerning his feelings of isolation, his yearning for freedom, and the psychological effects of these strange, new surroundings upon his psyche. Sylvie mulled over this information and informed him of the existence of a

173

biologically improbable act, encouraging him to partake of it at his earliest convenience. After some haggling, the two went their separate ways. Sylvie traipsed over to the computer center in search of information concerning any possible cosmic radiation poisoning cases and/or accidents. She was also to compile a list of any *Island* personnel with the first or last name of "Emmett."

Harry wandered off in search of experts on both radiation poisoning and the psychological make-up of your typical Islander. According to Sylvie, most of the top men of *Island*'s scientific community had offices in a single unit on the habitat; a three-storied think tank. These men of thought were encouraged to bounce ideas off each other regularly for the betterment of both Island and Earthly living conditions.

Harry walked slowly on his way to the science center. He wanted time to think clearly. Dressed in a conventional *Island* jumpsuit, he attracted no attention from passersby. Even so, their attitude bothered him. Everything up here bothered him. The place was too pat. Too orderly on the surface. Since his arrival, Harry had noticed that the populace went to and from their jobs like cattle; lobotomized cattle at that. Smiling faces. Sparkling uniforms. They were flawless. *Island* seemed flawless. No frowns. No tears. No fears. That kind of perfect blandness struck Harry as being impossible to pull off where living, breathing human beings were involved. He briefly entertained the notion that everyone onboard was some sort of super-android. He caught himself in the midst of that thought and, declaring himself more asinine than usual, he conjured up a vision of Sylvie standing naked in the morning light and dismissed the robotics completely. There were just some things that you couldn't duplicate in plastic . . . yet.

He glanced at his watch. It was nearly 3:30. Thus far during this marathon day, he had made an ass of himself aboard a space shack, taken part in a slightly psychotic meeting of minds, and gotten himself stuck in the middle of the colony's sky. Harry abruptly decided that he needed a drink more than he needed the think tank. The brains of this outfit could wait a few moments.

Harry passed the doorway of Robeur's Retreat, the biggest (and sole) night spot on the habitat. What the hell, he thought. After all, this was the first time to himself he had had since arriving. Harry stepped inside the bar, noting that its design was clearly similar to most of its Earthly counterparts and that it was just as seedy. Somehow, the seediness comforted him. He was expecting glass and chrome. He peered at the darkened establishment. Nearly empty, the main room was a series of abandoned tables and chairs highlighted by the presence of a seemingly endless bar, roughly based upon the control sector of Jules Verne's legendary airship, *The Albatross:* a lighter-than-air warship piloted by the exceedingly power-mad Robeur.

Harry sat at the bar and ordered a sunrise. Made with the habitat's blue fruit juice, however, the finished drink would have been more aptly tagged a moonrise. It looked like an ink well. In the middle of the bar sat Howard Retson and Wayne Ferron, apparently in the middle of a not-so-pleasant conversation. Drink in hand, Harry decided to play reporter. After all, anything he picked up along the way could always be used as background information for the fluff pieces he had to hack out for rent money.

"Gentlemen," he said while approaching the pair, "I don't think we've been formally introduced. I'm Harry Porter, *Herald-Times-News.*"

Retson flashed a barracuda grin. "Howard Retson of Kingdoms, Inc. Very nice meeting you, Mr. Parsons. I've read your crime pieces on Earth. Very ... entertaining."

Ferron continued to glare at Retson. He reluctantly shot a hand in Harry's direction. "Wayneferron ... I'veseenyouaround."

"I'm up here for the Tenth Anniversary story," Harry smiled artificially. "Reporting on the overall lifestyle of *Island.*" Harry continued grinning. Ferron managed a thin smile.

The three men grinned at each other like idiots, each trying to outdo the other in hypocritical graciousness. Although this exercise made his mouth muscles hurt like hell, Harry was glad for the chance to meet Retson face to face. The man could out smile a crocodile. That smile coupled with the fellow's ever-moving eyes gave Harry a bit of insight into the man's character. Retson was smooth but devious. Probably was as shrewd a businessman as one could find. "And what do you think of *Island* life so far?" Retson said, teeth gleaming.

"Nice," Harry said almost honestly. "Nice but very dull."

"Oh yes," Ferron smirked, assuming his legs-apart political crusader stance. "The whole habitat is *nice.* And it's very pretty. And it's a total waste of the American taxpayer's money. People are starving back down on Earth and our government is pouring millions into this orbiting Disney-world!"

Retson leveled an accusing finger in Ferron's direction. "I can see by your hysteria that you're upset by this space colony, Wayne. But, honestly, your viewpoint is very myopic . . . characteristic but still disappointing. Just think of the profit that a Disneyworld like this could produce in a single day."

"Horsefeathers," Ferron replied tersely.

Retson, ignoring the senator, turned to Harry. "Properly managed," he confided, "this place could be a goldmine."

"Then you're is favor of continuing with *Island?*" Harry asked.

Retson pursed his lips and pondered that query, giving his delicate features that Madison Avenue inscrutable look. "Totally off the record, of course?"

"Of course."

"Well, let's just say that with a little bit of creative input from Kingdoms, I could think of quite a few reasons why *Island* should stay put."

Ferron, reeling at such a public betrayal by a fellow Earthling, jerked his once-handsome face back and forth, glaring at both men. "Horsefeathers!" he restated emphatically. "Horsefeathers!!!!"

Ferron slid off the bar stool and trotted toward the exit. "Wayne," Retson called, "please don't leave angry."

Retson paid the tab for all three men and excused himself, following the offended politician. "We can't have the Earth delegation fragmenting this early." He winked at Harry.

"I'd like to talk about your plans for *Island* sometime," Harry called after him.

"Oh, we'll talk . . ." Retson replied over his shoulder. "I'll give you a story that will win you a Pulitzer for journalism."

He stopped at the doorway and turned toward Harry. "They do still give prizes for something along those lines, don't they?"

Harry shrugged.

"No matter," Retson commented, leaving. "We'll fix it."

Watching Retson trot out of the room, Harry noted that the man constantly worked at retaining his aura of dignity. Even slurping down a drink at a cheesy bar, he projected aloofness. The guy would probably come off regal in a pay

176

toilet. Retson was never "off," either. The wheels of craftiness were always spinning. Ferron, in his own monomaniacal way, was equally energetic albeit in a much more common fashion.

Harry glanced at his drink. It tasted great. But, now, with the ice melting, the liquid was a shade of blue you usually found in your hotel toilet bowl after the damned plastic flower thing had remained in the tank a tad too long. He pushed the drink away, left the bar room and sauntered out onto the walkway. He nearly tripped on the curbside, still twisting to the left and right for fear of oncoming autos. He really wished he could drop that Earth habit. Another quick stop like that and he'd give himself whiplash.

He was already in a less than exceptional mood so the habitat's muzak annoyed him more than usual. He said a silent prayer to the patron saint of ear plugs and proceeded to the think tank.

The tank was, in reality, called *The Island One Science Center*, a brilliantly mundane title for an equally stunning architectural edifice. The building was square. Period. From a distance, it looked like an empty cardboard box. Harry was getting tired of all these rectangular and circular exercises in nouveau nothing. Everything was so damned efficient and streamlined. He longed for a funky tenement building. Los Angeles tackiness. Anything.

He entered the center and marched through the lobby . . . much to the annoyance of the guard on duty; a reed of a man with a belabored afro hairdo. Harry read the guard's name tag. Mickey Moskowitz. Had a nice ring. "What do you want?" Mickey Moskowitz demanded with the sort of self-inflated whine used by young snots who have never seen a real fist fight in their life.

"My name is Harry Porter. I'm a newsman with the *Herald-News-Times*."

"State your business."

Harry thought he had just done that. What ho! he theorized, yon Mickey Moskowitz never had to pass an IQ test to wear that nifty little gun around his middle. "I'm working on a story," Harry said, slowly enough for a mental deficient to understand.

The guard did not seem overwhelmed. "You just can't walk into this building and talk to anybody."

I just did, you little prick. Harry smiled beatifically.

"You're right. I was, in fact, relying on someone in a position of authority, such as yourself, to put me in direct contact with the proper interviewees."

Mickey thought hard on that last one, eventually concluding that a compliment had indeed been given to him somewhere along the line. His skinny face almost became human. "Well," he snorted condescendingly, "I guess I could see what I could do."

"I'd be forever grateful." Pencilhead.

"I'm not making any promises, now." Harry watched the guard lope to a desk in the center of the small lobby. Behind him, a roster listing the names and room numbers of all the tank's residents was affixed to the wall. The guard picked up a small microphone and threw a switch. The names of all the scientists were immediately illuminated on the roster.

"I have a reporter down here from Earth," tactful Moskowitz intoned with obvious disdain. "Anyone wanna talk to him?"

A great buzzing noise erupted from the roster plaque. Harry half expected the wall to go into orbit. He was more than a little disappointed when, one by one, the lights on the wall flicked off abruptly. "Negative . . . negative . . . negative . . ." Mickey Moskowitz reported dutifully with each fading name. After a moment, all of the names had lost their luster but one . . . one Dr. Paul Harper. His name stubbornly retained its glow.

It was Harry's turn to gloat. "A positive?"

"Yeah," the guard grunted. "Looks that way, don't it? Dr. Harper will see you, I guess. He's on the third floor. Room 306." The guard sounded terminally disappointed at Harper's response. "The elevator is on the right," he said glumly.

"Thanks," Harry said, walking toward the lift. "If you ever get reassigned earthside, look me up. I think I can get you a job with the UN Diplomatic Corps."

Harry rode the elevator to the third floor and, alighting, attempted to find Dr. Harper's office. It wasn't all that difficult. It was the only room in sight with an open door. Orthodox symbolism, Harry surmised. He stuck his head inside the doorway. "Dr. Harper?"

"Ahuuuh," the doctor replied. Harper was short, about five feet four inches tall, and the possessor of a pear-shaped body. His face was jovial, ruddy, and topped by a crown of wispy sandy hair. In his late sixties, the man conveyed a sense of genial eccentricity. He wore glasses, square framed wire-rims, which he seemed to take great delight in balancing on the very edge of his nose. His clothes seemed to be in a permanent state of disarray, despite their loose-fitting, futuristic cut. Surrounded by the sterility offered by *Island* architecture, the red-faced gnome seemed not only out of place, but out of time as well. Harper looked up at Harry over his spectacles. "Ahuuuh," he repeated. "Mister Porter, isn't it?"

Harper toddled across the room and shook Harry's hand in one, precise, downward stroke. He then turned his back on his visitor and returned to a chair perched next to a large, spotless desk. Harry followed the little man across the room uneasily. "Dr. Harper?" he asked again.

Harper crinkled his face into a small grin. "Ahhh. I thought we had gotten that out of the way."

"I-I wasn't sure," Harry said lamely. He wasn't sure whether Harper was going to be a good source of information or simply another waste of investigative time. He began to verbally fence with the old man. "So this is the think tank, eh?"

"Only if you acknowledge it as such," Harper scowled. "I much prefer calling it the Science Center."

"Why's that?"

"Oh, a personal quirk, I suppose. People in, uhhh, your field, your profession (?), enjoy words like 'think tank.' Labels like that are very handy and convey a fairly concise meaning. But myself ... I hear the words think tank and I envision a rather large aquarium loaded with all this brain matter. Enough to ruin my lunch, thoughts like that."

Harper spoke slowly and seemed to take great delight in playing with the English language both in terms of usage and delivery. His speech was exaggerated, melodramatic but crisp. His movements complemented his verbal pattern perfectly with phrases and sentences punctuated with arched eyebrows, winks, frowns, head-nods, and expansive hand movements. Within minutes, Harry found himself mesmerized by the small man's inflated delivery. Harry's questions were blunt and to-the-point. Harper's answers were vague, good-natured and exceedingly slow in coming.

The twosome was still debating the pluses and minuses of life in space when the sound of approaching footsteps could be heard in the hall. "Aha, yes," Harper sighed. "This should be one of my concerned colleagues, young Dr. Simmons perhaps, warning me, in a very dramatic manner no doubt, about the dangers of talking to you."

As if on cue, a stern young man with a pock-marked face stuck his head in the door and stared first at Harper, and then at Harry. He finally turned his gaze back toward the old man. "Have a care, Dr. Harper, have a care."

"I would much rather have an apple," Harper said cheerfully. "Do you think you could swing that for me?"

The young face scowled and disappeared from the doorway. Harper settled back into his chair. "I do enjoy playing the eccentric every so often," he explained matter-of-factly. "It, ahhh, enhances my reputation within the building. Puts some zest into life as well. Lord knows that you need all the excitement you can muster living up here."

"Boring, huh?" Harry asked.

"Deadly so," Harper winked. "Not that I am complaining, you understand. Oh-ho no. I suppose ennui is the price you pay for being one of The Saviors of Humanity, eh? That is what you call us in your stories on Earth, isn't it?"

"Something like that."

The old man's stomach shook with silent laughter. "Well, goodness. Had I known you were coming I would have snatched my halo out of the dry cleaners. You really should put a stop to my feeble attempts at humor, Mr. Porter. Left to my own devices, and with very little encouragement, I will pun away an entire afternoon. I assume that you've come to talk to me about something in particular?"

"Well, yes and no," Harry replied sheepishly. He quickly explained how Harper was the only resident of the building who would see him and that he didn't really have any specific questions to ask of the man. "No matter," Harper shrugged. "We can use the old hit and miss technique, I suppose."

"You'll still talk?"

The old man folded his hands on his lap. "Oh yes, my ego is not what it used to be. I love to talk. I'm old. I'll probably die fairly soon and get shipped off this tube in a space baggie or something equally as glamorous. Talking passes what time I have left creatively and, between you and me, most of my peer group aboard do not make for scintillating conversations."

"Hard to believe."

"Isn't it, though."

"You were a psychologist on Earth?"

"Sometimes they even call me that up here."

"Sorry," Harry said, checking himself. "I guess what I'd

180

really like to know is this: what could drive a man out of his mind up here?"

Harper furrowed his brow. "Oh, any number of things. *Island* is not all that different from Earth in that respect. Humans are humans. Pigs is pigs. Etcetera. However, the colony has taken steps to keep its citizens mentally relaxed."

"The muzak and that kind of stuff?"

"Yes indeed. Rather Pavlovian, don't you think?" Harper leaned forward. "I will level with you, Mr. Porter. There is one element of danger aboard this craft that could, almost literally, cause it to burst apart at its seams. The biggest threat to this craft and, I suppose, any large vessel is one of sameness. The sense of routine up here is almost overwhelming. In the very beginning, you see, most of the people onboard were hand-picked for duty. Consequently, most of *Island*'s citizens were very well educated, even socially and financially well off. Upper class and upper middle class types. They came to the habitat positively brimming with, ahhh, misguided idealism. They were ready to take on any and all possible dangers for the good of humanity. They were prepared to ward off space demons, wrestle comets, anything, everything."

The old man cocked an eyebrow. "Once here, however, oh my goodness, they found that they didn't have to make any grand scale sacrifices. No one had to kill their first born or donate their brain to the master computer. *Island* was a veritable suburb of space. Unglamorous end to great ideals, eh? Realistically, there was no more a need for individual heroics up here than you'd find living down in the Hamptons on Earth.

"And so, the armchair explorers suffered in silence. No great sacrifices came their way. However, the little, everyday denials began to get on many of the first crew's nerves. Many of them fell into a deep state of depression. Deprivation. They had lost all their familiar touchstones, you see. The material things. Earth cloth, for instance, was simply too expensive to import on a regular basis, so they had to do with this wretched material we now wear. Liquor couldn't be imported regularly for the same basic reason. They missed their first-run holography shows. They missed the noise. The smog. The violence. The pollution."

"They missed Earth."

"Exactly. Now, as obvious as that may seem to you and me

right now, back then, it took everyone by surprise. Most of the first crew had come up here under the delusion that they were, indeed, elite. They would never succumb to such a common trauma as homesickness. But, that's life, eh? Full of little unexpected plot twists. Needless to say, everyone was in a state of shock. They could see what was happening to them, but they didn't have the emotional fortitude to do anything about it. They grew tired of seeing the same faces in the streets everyday. Tempers got shorter and shorter. Fist fights erupted in the streets. This place looked like Dodge City."

"We never heard about that on Earth."

"Not exactly the type of image one would want to capitalize on, is it?" Harper said, eyes twinkling. "Well, Vallory turned to the think tank to come up with solutions and we did. Short term, we had the entire populace tranxed. We then set about finding ways to keep the populace permanently calm, to give them physical constants to identify with. We managed to come up with a whole list of space anchors for their drifting emotions. The buildings were repainted in bright, cheerful colors. More trees were planted. More pedestrian parks were built. A radio station was inaugurated, a TV station christened, a local theater group organized . . ."

"And the muzak started . . ."

"And the muzak started."

Harry shook his head. "That piped-in sing-song-shit doesn't calm me. It annoys the hell out of me."

Harper smiled, pulling out two earplugs. "Aha, yes. I never venture outside the building without them."

The two men shared a laugh. Harry watched the old man curiously. Harper seemed to be an almost magical figure, devoid of any political or personal prejudices. He actually seemed to enjoy himself at all times. "Dr. Harper, do you think that all those things worked? Do you think that the populace is happy now?"

Harper crossed his arms, tilting his elfin face to one side. "Well, what a perfectly silly question to spring on me, Mr. Porter. Happiness. Happiness. Ahuh. Think about it. Most people refer to happiness as a quality of the past tense, don't they. They say 'my goodness, I was happy then' or 'I certainly was very happy before I made that last mistake.' The more imaginative ones occasionally even get off a 'If you do this for me, I will be very happy' or 'If I win this, I know I will be happy.' But it's a very rare person indeed who runs around saying things like 'Gaawwd, am I happy NOW!' The point is:

it's hard to define happy, isn't it? I would venture to say that most people aboard *Island* today are content. Maybe they were happy yesterday. Perhaps they will be happy tomorrow. But today? I'm afraid I couldn't tell you."

"Is madness possible aboard the habitat?"

"Madness is always possible."

"How about murder?"

The old man nearly toppled from his chair. "Murder? Now, what on Earth, if you'll pardon the expression, are you getting at?"

Harry backed off. If the old man knew anything of import, it wouldn't pay to tip him off to everything this early in the game. "Nothing, really. I was just wondering whether such an act of extreme violence would psychologically fit in with the hab's lifestyle."

A glint of understanding flashed through Harper's eyes. "Aha. Of course, you are not taking me into your confidence. You are bullshitting me. Well, fine. I will bullshit you back, OK? Here's my line: 'Murder? Out of the question.' Now, you must present me with a grisly 'what if' situation and I will nod gravely and say, 'You win. Yes, Mr. Porter, I suppose that murder is possible. You are dealing with people in a confined environment. Despite all our efforts, it is theoretically possible that someone could snap.' "

Harry smiled. "Snap from pressure?"

"Snap from anything."

"How about from cosmic radiation."

"Bingo," Harper said, exhaling. "The crux of your visit, I would assume. Well, I have my doubts that cosmic radiation would make you snap. It might melt you more than crack you in half. A bit of humor there, if you hadn't noticed."

Harry suppressed a groan. Harper took it in stride. "Now, assuming that you are not sitting here with me just to exercise your right to random pessimism, let us conclude that you are interested in the effects of cosmic radiation on the human mind. Well, congratulations, sir, you have stumbled across an area that I, too, am direly interested in. However, thus far, our experiments in that area have merely scratched the surface. Dangerous stuff, this radiation. Fearful. But here on the habitat, I should point out, the levels of cosmic radiation are substandard. And, if you have already been checking, as I am sure that you have, you already know about the drills, the shelters, the protective shields. Etcetera."

Harry couldn't help but laugh. "Can you read my mind?"

"Your face," Harper said, rubbing his hands together. "You think in headlines."

"OK. So I'm not as subtle as I'd like to think. But what if something went wrong with your shields, shelters, and drills?"

The old man slid a hand across his chin. "Well then, I suppose we'd all be lying on our backs with very small x's across our eyes. Very dead. Now, if something along those lines happened in our past history aboard the habitat, I certainly would not be able to answer your questions now, would I?"

"You run circles around me in logic."

"That's why I am kept in this little room. My job, you see."

Harry sighed and made a motion to leave. "Oh no, you can't leave yet," Harper said in genuine dismay. "I've just begun to tolerate your brashness. I haven't been grilled like this in years. Invigorating to say the least. I know what. Let's talk about Earth for a moment, shall we? Is the sky still as blue as I remember it?"

"Charcoal gray," Harry replied.

"Of course," Harper nodded sadly. "Well, I ahh, see that you really wish to leave. A shame, really. I could tell you all you need to know about *Island*. I'd love to, in fact. I don't get around as much as I used to, but I have a remarkable memory."

Harry stared at the psychologist. The man obviously had enough energy to outdo most of his younger peers onboard. He probably went overlooked, for the most part, because of his age, too. Harry was about to launch into a series of off-hand questions when yet another noise emerged from the hallway. With surprising speed, Harper darted across the office and shut the door. "How can anyone concentrate in the midst of such chaos?" he muttered.

Harry stood and faced the door. A man was screaming wildly outside. There was the sound of footsteps pounding up and down the hallway. Soon, other voices and other footsteps resounded in a cacophonous collage of sound. Harry approached the door with curiosity. He placed a hand on the doorknob. "Oh dear," Harper sighed. "I really wouldn't open that door if I were you."

Harry smirked and opened the door. A wild-eyed man in his seventies stood there, shaking in a white smock. His body convulsing, a pair of oversized false teeth protruding from beneath his upper lip, the bald-headed apparition leveled his gaze at Harry. Harry felt as if he had been hit in the forehead with a brick. Clutching his forehead in pain, he reeled backward across the room...the recipient of a telepathic haymaker.

Harper, however, was quite unaffected by it all. Standing up to his full five feet four inches height, he marched to the intruder with a sense of total calm. "Relax, Martin."

The apparition tilted its head, recognizing the voice and recalling it as friendly. The man in the doorway calmed down slightly, his body movements slowing appreciably. The pain in Harry's head subsided almost as suddenly as it had begun. He struggled to steady his liquified legs. If these types of encounters continued up here, he'd have to start buying aspirin by the truckload.

The wild-eyed visitor stepped into the room and walked in a brisk, circular path. His movements were quick, birdlike, nervous. "God! God!" he whined.

If the fellow's behavior startled Harper, the psychologist showed no evidence of it. He took the visitor by the hand and faced Harry. "Harry, this is Martin. Martin, this is Harry. Say hello to Martin, Harry."

"Hello, Martin," Harry whispered.

The bald-headed bundle of nerves stopped pacing. He turned toward Harper and, towering over the small man, stammered. "I—I must find God. Need him. Have y-you seen him today?"

Harper shook his head negatively. "Have you tried the chapel?"

"Too obvious," Martin said smugly. He spun around and gawked at Harry. "God subtle. But I'll find, find him and tell him about the light. He'll help. Help his children. He'll put out the light!"

Martin's body dropped into a crouch, its lanky, angular shape assuming an almost-grasshopper look. "The light," he muttered. "Light gave life to some. Death to others. Monsters...life."

Poised like a reptilian runner about to embark on a pond-to-pond dash, his head swung back and forth in quick, spastic movements. "Listen," he hissed.

Arching his back suddenly, Martin shot up into human posture. "They're here!" he cried, fleeing the room.

Harry and Harper stared at the open door. "Where did he come from?" Harry wondered aloud.

"He used to work here," Harper said softly.

185

"He was part of the think tank?"

"His name is Martin Graff."

"Graff," Harry muttered. "Graff. Sounds familiar."

"One of the Earth's greatest psychotherapists. Part of the militant Self-Help group."

"The *I'm OK, Fuck You* Martin Graff?"

"Yes."

Harry's mind reeled. It indeed was possible to go bonkers on the hab. He had just seen his first bona fide basket case. "What happened to him?"

Harper toddled to his chair and sat down. "I don't really know," he explained. "One day, he saw the face of St. Theresa in a dish of jello at lunch. He never was the same after that. Ahhh, brilliant mind, too."

"He just flipped out?"

"No," Harper said. "It was a gradual process. It took several weeks. We finally noticed that his mental faculties were, er, eluding him when he continued to introduce his 'toe theory' at our conference sessions."

"Toe theory?"

"Martin came up with a plan to genetically alter the structure of the human foot for all city dwellers. He wanted to completely eliminate the big toe. Called it 'excess baggage' as I recall."

"I don't understand."

"Well, think a moment. What's the very first part of your body that gets stepped on in a crowded city street?"

"Right," Harry nodded in appreciation of the daft logic present in the theory. "How long ago did all this happen?"

Harper thought for a moment. "Four, maybe five years." He motioned for Harry to sit in the chair next to his own. "Are you all right? You still look a little pale."

Harry sat in the straightback chair. "Just a headache. It's nearly gone."

Harper giggled softly. "You don't really have to continue your charade for my benefit, Mr. Porter. I assure you I won't betray your confidence. You're a sensitive, aren't you? His telepathic power hit you directly between your orbs."

Harry reddened slightly. "Yeah, well, it isn't something I like to brag about. I had some treatment involving parapsychs and . . ."

"No need to explain."

"But he didn't affect you," Harry suddenly recalled.

"I've had time to practice evasiveness," Harper said.

Harry was astounded at the implication. "You mean you've actually come up with a way to ward off peepers? You've developed a mental power that strong?"

Harper shrugged modestly. "It was just a little brainteaser I cooked up to pass the time."

Harry slumped down in the chair. Natural telepaths. Counter-peeper powers. It was simply too much for him to assimilate all at once. Why the hell hadn't he refused this assignment?

Harper arose and patted Harry on the shoulder. "We'll talk about everything another time." He padded across the room to the door. "Right now, however, we had better leave the area. Dr. Jerrow and her aides will be arriving momentarily. No sooner does Martin escape than Jerrow catches up with him."

Harry followed Harper to the door. "Martin is kept somewhere?"

"The hospital."

"How often does he escape?"

"Every day around lunchtime," the old man said. "I think the meal triggers memories of the original jello incident. I don't know."

In the distance, Harry heard Martin shrieking. Harper fumbled in his pocket, producing a second set of earplugs. "Here," he advised. "Not only will these save you from the muzak but from the sounds of the hunt and the capture outside. Martin gets a bit loud sometimes."

Harper jabbed a set of earplugs firmly in his ears. Harry did likewise. The two men walked down the hall together, oblivious to the avalanche of voices and door slammings arising from another part of the floor.

"I hope we'll be able to talk again," Harry bantered.

The old man looked up at Harry's determined face. "What?"

6

Harry could have sworn it was a gust of wind that gave an extra bounce to his step as he left the think tank. But wind was, of course, impossible within the closed confines of the habitat, so he chalked it up to mental ebullience. He was onto something at last.

He now knew for a fact that there was at least one mental case under wraps at the hospital. And, if there was one, it was decidedly possible that there were others. Harry hummed a sprightly tune as he walked, the earplugs completely blocking out the everlasting melodies dished up by the omnipresent muzak. He looked at his wristwatch. With a little bit of luck, he'd be able to catch up with Sylvie at Babe's. Maybe the computer would have a record of Martin Graff's activities prior to his sudden crack-up.

Maybe Graff's illness would, in some way, hook up with Emmett. Graff had mentioned light and he had mentioned children. Emmett seemed to be obsessed with the phrase "the children of light." But Graff's mention of "monsters" really threw Harry for a loop. Creepy stuff. Harry increased his pace, arriving at the computer center in record time. He entered the building and was on his way to Babe's domain when he was stopped by a guard; a brick wall in a blue jumpsuit.

"I'm afraid you can't enter this area, sir," the man grunted politely. "Restricted."

Harry was dumbstruck. "I don't understand. By whose orders?"

"The governor's, sir," the guard answered stiffly.

Harry didn't flinch. "I was on my way to see Mr. Kraft. Mr. Sidney Kraft. He might not be on duty right now, but I'm sure that one of his associates will vouch for me. The name is Porter. Harry Porter."

The guard moved to a phone affixed to the wall. Picking up the receiver, he talked sternly into the viewscreen. Within a moment, he returned to Harry. "Sorry, sir. Mr. Kraft is no longer employed at this facility."

Harry smiled politely, masking his surprise. "You guys sure don't believe much in job security up here."

"No, sir," the guard deadpanned.

The guard had the personality of a sandlot backstop. "When was he reassigned?" Harry inquired.

"Couldn't say, sir."

"Where was he reassigned?"

"Couldn't say, sir."

"Do you know who *could* say?"

The guard clenched his jaw. "Couldn't . . ."

"Never mind," Harry said, turning on his heels and marching out of the center. Despite the guard's ominous presence, he left the building almost elated. If the governor was interfering in his routine prodding, then he was surely close to discovering something big. The only problem was, Harry had no idea what he was onto. That didn't matter for the time being. Sylvie would be proud of his deductive reasoning this time out. He'd make it up to her for that gaffe aboard the space shack. Not that it mattered, of course. Better watch it there, old boy. Once emotions get in the way of logic . . . pfffht.

Harry paused along the walkway. If the computer terminal was closed to him, perhaps he could use the local library's microfilm index. The habitat did have a newspaper (of sorts) and, if anything of importance did happen to Martin Graff, the event would be on record along with the date of its occurrence.

He hailed an electric cart and, duplicating Sylvie's actions of the day of his arrival, he punched out his destination on the computerized dash. Since he had no idea of where the library was or even what it looked like, Harry decided to sit back and enjoy the scenery. The small cart traversed the entire length of the strip of land housing the computer center. At the end of the landmass, at one end of the cylinder, the cart made a sharp left and headed for the next strip of land. The cart executed a steep climb along the rounded edge of the cylinder. Harry felt like a fly crawling along the bottom of an overturned drinking glass.

Holding firmly onto the dash, Harry watched his cart slide from one strip of ground onto another in a snail's paced roller-coaster turn. Much to his surprise, he didn't grow dizzy

189

from the maneuver. There was no "up." There was no "down." There was no wind movement. Everything just "was."

Marveling over the maneuver, Harry turned to trace the path his cart had just taken and caught sight of a second cart, not twenty yards behind him, executing an identical move. Harry instinctively tensed, suspecting the presence of a tail. He quickly relaxed, however, noting that, at one point or another, every electric cart had another directly behind it during a ride. It was a natural occurrence.

Still, Harry couldn't shake the feeling that the cart behind him was deliberately pacing him. His cart pulled up in front of a one-story rectangular building, painted a cheerful yellow. *Public Library* flashed on the cart dashboard. Harry quickly punched the dash once more, requesting the machine to take him to the far end of this landmass. The cart responded sluggishly. Harry feigned total calm, turning his body around in the seat to a three-quarter profile position. With his face now nearly facing the rear of the vehicle, he was able to watch the cart behind him slow down to a halt outside the library.

The driver did not exit the vehicle. Before too long, the cart behind him picked up speed and, once again, began following Harry. From the manner in which the pursuing vehicle slowed down, stopped, and then resumed the chase, Harry surmised that the driver was aware of Harry's destination. The driver behind him had access, in some way, to the master computer. Whoever was tailing him had programmed the second cart's dashboard identically as Harry's. Ergo, he or she had to be aware of Harry's every move as Harry made them.

Harry relaxed slightly, realizing that his tail must be one of Hawkins's men and not the killer. He watched the far side of the cylinder draw near. Harry pounded the dash, sending his cart into a sputtering stop outside a nondescript apartment dwelling. Wanting to attract as much attention as possible, he dramatically darted out of his cart and into the front entrance. He then slowly made his way to the rear exit of the building where he slipped out unnoticed.

That would keep his guardian angel busy for a while. Trotting a few blocks behind several large apartment complexes, Harry finally made his way back to a public walkway only a few hundred feet away from the library entrance. He entered the sunny building. Its interior was appropriately mundane. The librarian, a woman who resembled a horse, was very anxious to help Harry in his search through the microfilm files. He smiled and flashed his dimples. She laughed and produced ugly snorking noises with her nose.

She brayed at him for several minutes, detailing the care and maintenance involved with keeping up a solid micro-library. Harry dutifully screwed on an admiring grin and "yes, ma'amed" her and "really, ma'amed" her into a state of ecstasy. The horseface woman herded Harry to an empty cubicle and nodded with regal approval as he carefully placed the first spool of film into the projector. Much to his surprise, he actually began viewing the contents of the roll without tearing the damned little thing to bits. How he longed for paper pages that one could flip over with a push of a finger.

All the while he researched, the librarian hovered nearby. She reminded him of the girls he had gone to college with back in the Dark Ages. He had attended an educational institution, a teacher's college, where the ratio of females to males was seven to one. Harry had considered that to be a decided benefit until he caught a glimpse of five out of the seven. Library science majors. Elementary education majors. They hunted down men with everything but snares and flint-tipped arrows. They learned early how to cover their sofas with clear plastic seat covers, how to smile shyly when a fellow offered to pick up the check, and how to rid them-selves of any and all original thoughts. God. He wondered how he had stayed married so long. More interestingly, he wondered how lesbians survived?

After an hour of viewing reel after reel, he came to several conclusions:

1) He was crazy for ever coming up to this space tube.

2) He was even crazier for sitting here in the library in search of clues concerning a murderer when he could have been hiding under his hotel bed.

3) When he got back to Earth, a good pair of reading glasses might be in order.

Harry yanked yet another spool out of the projector and replaced it with its twin. Hell. *Island*'s newspaper clippings made the Daughters of the American Revolution's newsletter read like hot copy. Nothing in the news files reflected *Island* life realistically. It was candy-assed. Worse yet, it was badly written. (Remember, folks, a verb is an *action* word.) Even the wire service stuff picked up from Earth was watered down to printed pablum.

Even more frustrating was the discovery that, apparently, Martin Graff was the first cousin of the Invisible Man. Two mentions in five years and then . . . nothing. Five years ago he was involved in the planning of a fifth anniversary plant-in public service project; part of a beautification movement designed to increase the variety of foliage on the habitat. More than likely, the whole thing was a publicity ploy. See how the mighty minds of *Island* get back to the soil for the benefit of all. That sort of concept piece. Anson Young would've loved it.

And then . . . zilch.

No mention of Graff after that. Harry drummed his fingers on the desk. "Shhhittt," he hissed between his teeth. The librarian across the room looked up from her desk. Startled, she made short, snorting sounds. Harry smiled endearingly and went back to his film. The woman flashed a lopsided grin in return. He felt like the only beer in a desert oasis.

Harry gazed at the headlines. Graff had disappeared from view during that fifth anniversary time period. Harry continued his search. Oddly enough, the plant-in ceremony had vanished from the newspaper's pages as well. Harry threaded the film quickly. No further mention of the festival as page after page fluttered by on the viewscreen. A non-event in anybody's social calendar. Something must have happened to force the happening's cancellation. Perhaps it was the same "something" that cancelled out Graff's mental capacities. Harry twirled through the remainder of the reel. Blank-o. He gathered the reels together and returned them to the horsey woman. "Many thanks," he grinned boyishly. You buck-toothed busybody.

Harry felt so elated with his progress that he walked home, even hazarding the stairwell leading from land strip to land strip; a definite human fly endeavor. He knew he was getting close to something. What he needed now was a good drink and even better company. He'd sort out some of the pieces of the puzzle later.

Harry returned to his hotel. When he entered his room, Sylvie was already there. Standing in the entranceway to the patio, she was a vision befitting heaven let alone space. Her long black hair was illuminated from behind by the setting mirrored sun. She wore a long, shimmering gown that sent him into a state of sensual shock. Where the neckline of her dress should have been, a mere fold of cloth dangled. Shaped in a deep "v" and plunging to her waistline, it revealed the presence of two well-rounded breasts. Her nipples were taut beneath the light fabric. She walked toward him, her bare legs easing in and out of her slit skirt.

"How did things go today?" she asked.

The back of Harry's neck twitched. This was too good to be true. This type of thing might happen to other men, more glamorous men, but definitely not to him. Damn it, he was really beginning to care about her. "Fine," he stammered. "I did some interviewing, some checking. Didn't come up with too much, though."

He nearly ran to the bar, making himself a large drink. He wondered why she had never married. He wondered why he had. "How did things go at the computer center?" he asked.

"I didn't have much luck," she said. "Babe and Sid either didn't have any information on cosmic radiation or else it was classified. I came up with zero on Emmetts, too. Fairly unusual name. By the way, I've made plans for us tonight . . ."

Harry's stomach went numb. He stared at his drink sadly. Sid? "Sid couldn't pry it out of Babe?" he asked weakly.

"No," she answered. "He was as helpful as could be but not helpful enough, I guess."

Liar! Harry's insides screamed. He took his drink and moved to an armchair near the patio. He slid into the chair and stared at the beautiful woman before him. A woman he had trusted. Goddamn it. Sid wasn't even at the computer center today. He'd been ousted. Of course, Sylvie didn't realize Harry had been there. She didn't suspect he knew the truth. His bottom lip trembled ever-so-slightly as rage and disappointment collided.

Why couldn't she have been honest with him? Why couldn't she have played it straight? If she was lying to him now, that probably meant she had been lying to him all along. His chest turned to stone. Who was this woman, really? Who was she working for?

Sylvie stared at Harry, fully aware of his sudden shift in mood. "You look awful."

"I feel fine," he muttered.

She walked across the room and pushed herself into the plush chair with Harry, wrapping one of her fingers around a lock of his hair. She leaned forward, her breasts barely

193

contained by the folds of her gown. Her perfume overwhelmed his nostrils. Her body radiated warmth. He was a young boy again. A young boy totally enamored with his first love. He felt awkward. He felt intimidated. Angry. Hurt. Damn her.

"Do you know what you need?" she asked him.

Something that's impossible to find, he thought. "No," he said.

"You need to unwind," she smiled, standing. "I've booked a room for us tonight at Robeur's Retreat. It's the greatest night spot on the colony. Bar. Casino. And light gravity bedrooms for the . . . adventurous."

Harry stared at her. Right, and who programmed you today, miss? "Fine," he nodded. "Why don't you just give me a little time to get ready. I think I'd like to take a nap. I'm pretty exhausted."

She slid a hand under his chin. "Harry, aren't you feeling well? I'm serious, now. You look as if your best friend just died."

Harry chuckled grimly. "Naaah. That happened a long time ago. I just need some rest, that's all."

"Well, you *did* have a long day," she admitted. Harry sat on the couch. Sylvie walked toward the door. "All righty. I'll call you in a little bit." One hand resting on the doorknob, she paused in thought. "Oh, you know what? The strangest thing happened today when I was leaving the computer center."

"What was that?" he asked, stretching out on the couch.

"As I was leaving Sid's cubicle, I saw a group of guards heading for his door. I was going to hang around for a while, just to see what was going on, but one guard practically ordered me out."

Harry blinked and stared at the ceiling. "That *is* odd."

"I thought so," she agreed. "Well, maybe it's nothing."

"Maybe."

"Feel better." She left the room. His longing for her returned. He was relieved that she had mentioned the guards. It gave a ring of authenticity to the rest of her story. She really could have talked with Sid, left his cube empty handed, and then bumped into the goon squad on the way out. Sid could have been carted out after Sylvie's departure. Harry, arriving later, could have missed them both. Yeah, that made sense. Damn it, Sylvie had always insisted that Harry created problems out of thin air just to have something to agonize over during an angst lull. Maybe she was right. Maybe he was allowing his imagination to get the best of him. Then again, maybe Sylvie was lying.

Harry closed his eyes and drifted into a light, restless sleep. He had to watch himself. He was getting too emotionally involved with Ms. Dunbar. That wasn't particularly healthy. And, on the off chance that she wasn't leveling with him, it could be somewhat more than unhealthy.

It could be fatal.

7

He was sitting on the edge of the sofa, rubbing the sleep out of his eyes when the phone rang. *"Nothing* makes *no* sense whatsoever," he theorized, shambling toward the phone. He reflected on his stay aboard the habitat thus far. "There has to be some logic here, some pattern that I'm missing."

He picked up the phone and watched Sylvie's face materialize on the screen. "Almost ready?" she asked.

"Yeah," he yawned. "I'll meet you at the club in an hour."

Harry hung up the phone. As he did so, he calmly noticed two men slip into his room via the patio. The two men were both muscular and of medium build. Neither of them appeared to be friendly and they had the kind of jaws you could break walnuts with.

Harry was too exhausted to panic. "Are you with the bus tour?"

The taller of the two pushed Harry into the armchair nearest the patio. "Just shut up and stay put."

The second man, a scar-faced chap, pointed an accusing finger at Harry. "Get up out of that chair."

Harry crossed his legs and sighed. "I wish you guys would get together on this."

"Shut up," the first man barked.

"What did you say to me?" leered the second.

"Look, do you want some time to rehearse this?" Harry offered.

The man with the scar pulled Harry out of the chair.

"Listen, Porter. We came here to give you some good advice. We want you to forget everything you've heard up here and who you've heard it from. We want you to just hand in your nice little stories and butt out of everyone's business."

Before he could muster a glib reply, Harry was spun around by the first man. The second intruder hammered several blows into the small of Harry's back. Harry clenched his teeth and groaned. He would have collapsed from the pain shooting up his spine had it not been for the fact that the first man was holding him straight. "No marks," the first man cautioned the second. "No marks."

The larger of the two spun Harry around again and the scarface threw several additional punches into Harry's stomach ."All right," the first man said, "that's enough."

He released his grip and Harrry crumpled to the floor. "Any chance you guys are in the wrong room?" he wheezed.

"Look, Porter," the first man said. "We don't know exactly what it is you're after up here or what you're telling people, but you just cost a good friend of ours his job."

Harry attempted to straighten up. The spirit was willing but the flesh said no. He remained in fetal position on the floor. "Who?"

"Sid Kraft."

Harry pulled himself up into the armchair. "He was fired?"

"Worse," the first man said grimly. "Sent Earthside."

"What for?" Harry coughed.

The two men looked at each other, puzzled. "You don't know why?" the scarface asked.

"No."

"We thought you had arranged it," the first man said.

Harry rubbed his stomach. "I didn't even know the guy."

"That's a lie. You were seen entering his office several times in the last two days."

"I was visiting his computer. It's background for a story I'm working on."

"Rumor has it you were out to set him up."

"Rumor has it wrong. What the hell would I want to do something like that for? I just met the poor slob yesterday. He was okay."

"Well," the first man hesitated. "Sid has always been a bit of a closet reactionary, you know? Sometimes he's a little too outspoken for his own good. Usually, he manages to keep a lid on it. We figured that he'd slipped up this time, said something to you that you considered insulting or unpatriotic. We figured you turned him in to the locals. Sid was technologically oriented. He didn't know from shit about political dos and don'ts."

Harry hobbled over to the bar. "You guys are a pair of real morons, you know that?"

The intruders stiffened.

"At ease," Harry hacked. "You come in here like two rabid dobermans with half a thought between the both of you, try to kill me, and then wind up insulting me. I should turn you over to the goddamn cops. Instead, I think I'll help you out."

The scarface took a step forward. "How are you going to help us?" he asked suspiciously.

"What's your name?" Harry inquired.

"Tom Kenny," the taller of the two replied. "This here is Joey MacManus."

"My friends call me Mac," the scar offered sullenly.

"Well, I won't," Harry answered. "Now, you two Einsteins will probably be interested to know that Sid was fired because he was helping me out. He was letting me use his computer to check out a couple of theories I had."

"Theories about what?" Kenny demanded.

Harry was deliberately mysterious. "About this scam you people have going up here."

Kenny and Mac exchanged shifty looks. "Then you know about it?"

"Of course, I know," Harry smiled. "What do you take me for . . . a total idiot?"

"When did you figure it out?" Kenny asked.

"As soon as I got up here," Harry smirked. "It was pretty obvious, really."

The two men walked over to the bar. "And you haven't printed anything?" Mac asked.

"Not a word," Harry said. "Small potatoes. Do you think I'm a dummy?"

"I guess not," Mac replied. "Glad you didn't write it up. You could have knocked the entire habitat for a loop. Not that this place is all that hot, you understand, but it's a damn nice place to work."

Harry poured two shots of tequila for his guests. "Here," he offered. "Drink up. Earthside stuff. No blue juice in it."

He perched himself on a stool on one side of the bar while

the two men climbed on stools facing him from the other. He began to periodically refill their glasses as the conversation continued.

"Don't you guys get bored working up here?"

"Oh, sure," Kenny stated. "But you get used to it. The pay's good. The location is pretty off-the-wall and the tour of duty looks great on a resumé. You get used to the routine."

"Yeah," Mac laughed. "But when they announced you guys were coming up here, the routine hit the fan. Everything went haywire. We started those drills. Phew!"

"The drills," Harry repeated knowingly. "They started that recently, eh?"

"Of course they did," Mac said smugly. "What did you think, we do this kind of stuff all the time? It's no bed of roses, believe you me. The whole mess would never have started if it wasn't for you Earth guys."

"It was really strange," Kenny reflected. "Working up here has always been like, well, working on a military installation, I guess. A lot of discipline, a little bit of fun. Humdrum, you know? But suddenly, there we all were, being instructed about how to act cheerful whenever you guys were walking around. We were taught how to smile, what to say, where to go, how to behave. We all had to read those goddamned pamphlets that told you all what *Island* was really like. We had to memorize them. It was pretty eerie."

"Scary," Mac added. "It was like being in a big high school production, you know? And you couldn't screw up because your parents were in the audience ... even though the script really sucked."

Harry slid off the stool and made himself a moonrise. The whole thing was a sham. "Unbelievable."

"I'll say," Mac agreed. "But it had to be done, I guess. It was important for us to make a good impression."

"But it was hell," Kenny injected. "The pressure you feel during a time like that is overwhelming. Hell, we're *still* feeling it. Everyone is tight. Tense. Mentally on edge, you know? Drinking has become quite the rage during the last few weeks."

"Where were you indoctrinated?" Harry asked.

Kenny made a sour face. "I don't know whether we should tell you that or not."

"Oh, come on now," Harry replied, refilling their glasses. "I knew about the drills and I didn't say anything. It would just be a matter of time before I found out the rest. I mean, I had guys like Sid helping me with my research, right? I can find other people to supply information. You two can save me the time."

Kenny and Mac exchanged shrugs. "Well, I suppose you're right," Kenny finally acknowledged. "We worked it in shifts every night from seven until ten. The public parks were used. So were the theater and banquet halls."

"Ten thousand people were taught how to behave and nobody objected?" Harrry wondered aloud.

"Oh no," Kenny stated. "A lot of people objected. But it didn't take long to change their minds. OK. We all knew it was dishonest. But the choice was this: either everyone took part in all of this or the habitat would be closed down and we'd all be out of our jobs."

"People would kill to keep this place open," Mac said off-handedly.

"A 10,000-peopled fraud," Harry whistled.

"A 10,000-peopled 'charade' sounds a lot nicer," Kenny said.

"Either way," Mac added, "we really appreciate your keeping your mouth shut about it. Anyone else would have hit the Earth wire services with this by now. He'd be famous and we'd be ruined. But you didn't do that. You're a real trustworthy guy."

Harry nodded absent-mindedly. "A regular saint."

"Say, what is it you were working on with Sid, anyway?" Mac asked.

"Yeah," Kenny slurred, "what could be bigger than this scam?"

Harry attempted a bluff but actually stumbled into a half-truth. "I think someone onboard the colony is trying to shut it down."

The two intruders sat in shocked silence.

Harry glanced at his watch. "Hey, I have to get going. I have a date. Why don't you guys leave through the door. You might hurt yourselves jumping off the patio."

Kenny reached out and shook Harry's hand as if he was expecting butter to appear. "We're truly sorry we beat you up," he blurted. "It was a clear mistake in judgment on our part."

"We'll never do it again," Mac vowed, swaying slightly as he stood up. "Thank you also for the drinks that we have partaken in . . . of. They were nice."

"Think nothing of it," Harry said, meaning it. "Tell you

199

what, though. If I need any background information for my stories, can I count on you two guys?"

"Sure thing," they both agreed.

He led the two of them to the door. Once they had staggered out of the room, he shut the door and sat on the patio with his drink. Night had angled in. He added a pinch of blue juice to his liquor.

He had never felt so alone.

At this point, he no longer knew who was lying to him and who wasn't. Or: who was lying and why. Or: who was lying a lot and who was lying just a little. Jeezus. He wished Leonard Golden was up here with him. At least he'd have someone to confide in that he could trust. Hell, he'd even settle for his nagging home computer unit.

8

Robeur's Retreat, in all its nighttime glory, was a four-storied edifice cheesey enough to fit into any Earth singles neighborhood nicely: a top-notch combination of noise and physical excess. Kenny and Mac hadn't exaggerated to Harry about the recent increase in *Island* bar traffic. The spaceship bar, nearly deserted earlier that afternoon, now teemed with tired-eyed Islanders of both sexes. Walking into the congested bar/lounge, Harry imagined that he had just jumped into a time warp, leaving a chrome and steel present and winding up in an Alaskan dive during the great Klondike gold rush.

Conversation around Harry ceased as he strode into the room. He was wearing a short-sleeved sports shirt, Earth shoes, Earth trousers, and a denim Earth sports jacket. It was his own small way of saying "in your ear" to the largest fraud in the history of the United States. Let them put on airs with their space garb. He was comfortable in his Earthly attire. The bar patrons were somewhat unsettled by his entrance. Rather than being ridiculed, however, Harry found himself the object of envy. He was wearing real cloth, real material; not that mundane hab crap.

He walked up to the bar and ordered a shot of tequila.

Sylvie was nowhere in sight. Just as well, he reasoned. He was working on a good argument with her. He had quite a few things to say that she probably wouldn't be overly enthused about hearing. He downed the shot quickly. At least Sylvie could have leveled with him about the behavior drills.

Without thinking, he ordered a sunrise. A few moments later, he once again found himself the recipient of an inkwell on the rocks. As good as these things tasted, the first appearance of the glass always took Harry aback. The bartender, a round man with alabaster skin, noticed Harry's reaction.

"We use our own juice up here," he pointed out. "Orange juice is too expensive."

"Yeah, I know," Harry said above the din.

"It's just as good," the bartender assured him.

"I'm sure it is."

"Better even."

"I feel like I should be putting it on a canvas, not drinking it."

"It's very good," the bartender assured him.

"I'm sure it is. It's very pretty too."

"So," the bartender wondered. "Why don't you drink it?"

The bartender watched the glass. Harry watched the glass. The bartender stared at Harry. Harry stared at the bartender. The bartender returned his gaze to the glass, waiting for Harry to pick it up. Harry didn't.

"What's the matter?" the barman said. "Not good enough for you?"

"I'm a sipper."

"So sip, already."

Harry finally picked up the drink. He closed his eyes and took a sip. It was, of course, excellent. "It's good," he pronounced.

"What did I tell you," the round face behind the bar grinned. "That one is on the house."

Harry leaned on the bar, still under the scrutiny of the barman, and attempted to relax. No use. He was just too caught up in the day's events. He was working on his third moonrise when he heard his name being slurred across the room. "Misster Parlor," a baritone voice boomed. "What a plessent surpisse."

Harry looked up to see Howard Retson stumble suavely across the dance floor toward the bar. The tall gentleman looked commanding even when inebriated and dressed in the

201

bulky strain of space colony clothes. Watching the tycoon move his blue-jumpsuited frame easily through the gyrating bodies, Harry was overcome by a feeling of distaste. He really didn't want to talk to Retson right now. The guy was as shallow as a midget's fingerbowl. Retson was shadowed by a nervous Ira Stramm who weasled around the dancing couples with the easy determination of a garden snake on the prowl.

Retson strode up to Harry and grasped onto one of his denim lapels. "Goodness," he exclaimed. "You sss-certainly stand out in a crowd."

"I felt like being comfortable for once," Harry answered, removing the clammy hand from his jacket.

"You don't like thessse little sumpjuits?" Retson exclaimed.

"Let's just say I got tired of playing by someone else's rules and leave it at that," Harry smiled. He stared directly into Retson's bloodshot orbs. Back off moneybags or you'll see how comfortable the dance floor can be when it's encased around your head.

Retson was too drunk to notice Harry's menacing look. Stramm, however, caught on and attempted to maneuver his employer out of Harry's possible striking range. "Come on, Mr. Retson," Ira said in his usual whine. "You wanted to mingle with the Islanders, remember?"

Harry heard the panic in the man's voice. Stramm's normally oversized eyes were even larger and more frantic than usual.

Retson shoved his sniveling assistant aside with a single, fluid arm movement. "To hell with them! I'm tired of them! I need a break. I need a chat with an *Earth* man!"

Retson flashed his crocodile smile. Harry did likewise. Stramm attempted one, conjuring up a look straight out of *The Joys of Internal Injuries*. Harry gazed at Stramm, noting that the man's inordinately large eyes and high forehead gave his face a top heavy look. He reminded Harry of a psychotic egg.

Retson latched onto Harry's arm. "Have another drink."

"I haven't finished this one."

"Well, finish it and then have another!"

Harry shrugged. What the hell. Company was company. At least he wouldn't have to listen to the music. Harry and Retson began to fence verbally about the pros and cons of *Island* life. Harry found it the pits. Retson saw it as a potential goldmine. Harry attempted to pry a few details out of the mercantilist concerning the possible motherlode to be found on the habitat. Whenever Harry probed too deeply, however, Ira would come to life.

"Uh, Mister Retson," Ira would periodically inject, "maybe you should step outside for a little while. You look rather flushed."

"Shut up, Ira," Retson would reply curtly.

And Ira would shut up.

Finally, after what seemed hours of babbling, Retson began zeroing on the plans he had for *Island*. "Think of its potential in terms of commerciality," he began. "Endlessss possibilities . . . endlessss."

Harry was intrigued with the revelation but far from satisfied. He needed details. "But will the United States government actively support a purely financial scenario?"

Retson executed a parody of a wink. "That'sss what I'm here to find out. If they do decide to expand their way of thinking, I'm sssure there would be ways available to sssway public opinion on Earth in *Island*'s ffavor. And that'sss what they're worried about, isn't it? It's all a matter of image. Believe me, Mr. Portal, I'm an expert at molding imageses," his voice trailed off in a drunken mumble.

"Mr. Retson . . ." Ira cautioned.

"Later, Ira," Retson continued. "I can see by the way that your nose is turned up that you doubt my ssscheme would work. Well, let me tell you, Parsons, this *Island* place is an entrepreneur's dream come true. In many ways, it is exactly what they say it is in their brosh—broshh . . . pamphlets. It is a *paradise!*"

"Mr. Retson," Ira persisted.

"What *is* it, Ira," Retson demanded.

Ira cleared his throat and offered a humble observation. "You're sliding down the side of the bar, sir."

And he was, too.

The distinguished businessman looked up into Stramm's knee. "By God, you're right."

Harry extended a hand and helped the fellow to his feet. "Sorry about this, Prodder," he apologized, regaining his composure. "Too many of these blue juicers. They sssort of sssneak up on you. Taste so damn good you can't feel the alchs . . . alchso . . . the booze. Maybe a ssstroll outside in the canned air would be in order, eh, Ira?"

"Good idea, sir," Stramm quickly agreed, the weight of the world now definitely off his stooped shoulders.

Harry patted the weaving Earth delegate on the back and

watched Retson and Stramm find their way to the exit door. There were two members of the Earth party that were pro-*Island* at any rate . . . for whatever mysterious reasons they had.

Harry ordered another drink and studied the faces of the Islanders crowded into Robeur's Retreat. It struck him that there was a certain universality to be found in the visages of those trapped by routine. (These days that was practically everyone.) Tired faces were tired faces whether they were the product of a Pennsylvania steel mill, a smog-encrusted Los Angeles office building or a space colony factory shack. And routine was routine whether it entailed typing invoices, straightening bent fenders, or devising perfect panaceas for humankind eight hours a day. The exhaustion caused by such routines was an exhaustion arising from within. The sparkle in the eyes dimmed first. Then, the smile showed signs of sagging. The voice became tired, lackluster.

Harry guzzled his drink. Somewhere, along the line, in the search for a bigger and better society, some element of humanity, of human-ness, had been lost in the process . . . or, at least, effectively hidden from view. The creative spirit seemed to have been muted somehow; to have been lost in the general stew of lifestyle trends and quirks. The thrust of the total society completely dwarfed the feelings and goals of the individual. Harry stared glumly at the dancefloor. There had to be a way for the rights of a single human being to fit into it all.

A very drunk girl with very red hair squeezed herself into the barstool next to Harry and attempted to giggle at him. The noise which emerged sounded like a death rattle. Harry managed to mimic the sound and, making brief eye contact with the woman, returned his attention to his drink. He caught her image in the wall-sized mirror behind the bar. An interesting looking woman. She was very young and very attractive, despite the efforts of her bulky jumpsuit. A round, shapely female, with large blue eyes, she noticed Harry's gaze in the mirror and met it evenly. Perhaps it was just his Earth clothes, he theorized. She was simply too attractive for him to even consider. Yet . . .

Before long, Harry and the woman were locked in mortal eye-to-eye combat. Who would back down first? Who would shift their eyes? Certainly not Harry. There was honor at stake here. He recalled tales of the early American pioneers who would stare down bears and cougars. No mere female was going to stare him down ... even if she was at least four inches taller than he.

The woman took a large celery stalk from a nearby platter and dipped the tip in a container of salad dressing. Still observing Harry, she placed the stalk to her lips and slowly licked the dressing off the top. Harry began to sweat ... for two reasons, actually. He was exceedingly horny and exceedingly hungry. Unfortunately, the tray containing the celery was beyond his reach. Just as well. His joining her in a celery break would have Freudian connotations Harry would rather not give rise to. The woman continued to slowly devour the stalk, never breaking eye contact, bite after lick after bite.

Harry's face seemed flushed enough to burst from inner pressure. As much as he loved the fine art of communication via body language, this woman was exceeding the boundaries of good taste with her vocabulary. She was chewing her way through paragraphs of purple prose and there was just so much a man could take.

While he inwardly debated how to tactfully stage a retreat without appearing to be a coward, a homosexual, or worse, he caught a mirrored glimpse of Sylvie Dunbar entering the club. She spotted him immediately thanks to his Earthly apparel. Sizing up the situation between Harry and the buxom vegetarian, Sylvie wordlessly walked by Harry's stool and yanked him away from the bar. She moved him bodily to a table at the far end of the room. "I hope you haven't been too bored waiting for me," she said.

"Uh, no," Harry replied. "You know us reporters, always soaking in the scenery."

"That scenery appeared fairly moist."

"Whatever are you talking about?" Harry asked, being shoved into a chair. Once seated, his sense of anger and betrayal began to surface once again. "What kept you?" he began.

"I decided to change my outfit. How observant of you."

Harry saw that she was now encased in a silver jumpsuit that was nearly see-through. Sylvie watched his eyes take in the contours of her body. "I also picked up our key for later," she said, dropping the small metal object onto the table.

Fighting his growing need for her, Harry pushed the key back toward her purse. "Save it," he said flatly. "There won't be a *later*."

"I-I don't understand."

"There will be no *later* because there will be no more Harry and Sylvie after tonight."

She looked as if she had been hit by a clenched fist. Her lips trembled once and her eyes glistened. Harry couldn't tell whether she was genuinely upset or merely worrying about her professional guide status. He fought to remain aloof. "No more us," he repeated. "Let's talk about us, shall we? Let's talk about trust. Let's talk about deceit. Let's talk about how you've been playing me for a real chump, all right?"

Harry watched her crumble beneath his words. "Let's talk about how this whole *Island* trip was a set-up, a hype junket, with all the happy Islanders rehearsing their lifestyles for the benefit of us hapless assholes from Earthside."

She attempted to take it all in stride. "Oh, I was really going to tell you about that, Harry. Eventually. I was just waiting until the right opportunity presented itself."

Harry ordered a drink from a passing waitress. He had forgotten how convincing Sylvie could be under pressure. "Right," he sneered. "Right. Sure you were. Just a small oversight on your part, forgetting to tell me that the whole purpose of my being up here was a sham. You probably haven't been straight with me since I landed on this tub."

"Are you calling me a liar?"

"Let me put it to you this way. Some people get through the day by telling little white lies. In less than a week, you've gone through the entire color spectrum at least twice."

Sylvie wiped a solitary tear from her right eye. "You have your nerve."

"And I have my brain as well, so let's stop playing verbal badminton and cut the shit."

Sylvie glared at him in silence, the tears welling in her eyes. Harry instinctively began to feel defensive. Hell, he hadn't started this. She had. But, damn it, why did she have to be so beautiful. Why did he have to care. She sat across from him, fighting to keep her head erect, small tremors shifting her face from side to side every few seconds. Harry swallowed hard. "Who are you working for? Whose side are you on?"

"You've always been a suspicious bastard," she finally hissed. "Paranoid. Jumping to conclusions. You've never trusted anyone in your life. I should have expected you not to trust me, to run away again." She stood up abruptly, trembling with rage and indignation. "Go fuck yourself, Harry!"

She threw the keys across the table at him, hitting him hard in the chest. The keys slid onto his lap. "Or better yet, why don't you go fuck that cow at the bar, the one who looks like the proverbial good time had by all?"

"Maybe I will," Harry shouted, taking the key in his left hand. "Maybe I will."

Sylvie ran off.

Harry stalked over to the bar, seating himself once more next to the celery stalker's stool. "May I sit down?" he asked politely.

"Oh sure," she replied catatonically, "there's ample room for your space."

Harry stared at the bosomy woman. This close, he noticed that, apparently, she had put on her make-up with a trowel. He couldn't think of one damned clever thing to say. "Come here often?" he finally blurted. Jeez. He didn't believe he had actually said that. Next he'd be asking her what her sign was. This was awful.

"I go with the flow," the girl replied. "I can see that you don't, though."

She gestured toward his Earth suit. "Oh yeah," he explained. "I'm just visiting."

"I can accept your visitation."

"Oh. Right. Uh, what do you do up here?"

The woman sipped a large drink languidly. "I'm a psychotherapist."

Oh K-rist! Harry nearly slid under the stool. He had this attraction for potential disaster that he really wished he could shake.

"A psychotherapist," he coughed. "Interesting field. Fascinating field. Uh, how's business?"

"Picking up," she replied, a noncommital Mona Lisa look on her face.

Harry attempted a witticism but, coming up with nothing of a spontaneous nature, offered a nasal "ahahahahah" instead.

"My being a shrink has you uptight," she said, placing a hand on his. "I can accept that."

"No, not uptight," Harry insisted. "Just slightly uncomfortable."

"I'm sorry," she said. "I just can't get behind words like 'uncomfortable.' They have no meaning."

" 'Uncomfortable' has no meaning?"

"I mean, I *hear* you but look, perceive what it is you're

doing. You're creating unnecessary space for dealing with a problem that is equally as unnecessary."

"Space," Harry repeated. "You mean like physical space. Outer space?"

"Space," the woman said slowly, "is where your head is at if it's in a good place. Space creates a context for impacting the environment."

"Uh, right. But suppose your head is in a bad place?"

"Then you've run out of space and into a wall."

Harry raised a free hand to his eyes and gave them a vigorous rub. A headache of the first magnitude on the way. "Uh, do you talk to a lot of people up here? Patients, I mean."

"Quite a few, why?"

"Just planning for the future," he said. "I think I'll try to come back as a fig bar or something."

"A beautiful fantasy trip," she complimented. "Simplistic, natural, but still beautiful."

"Thanks."

"How did you feel telling me that?"

"Telling you what?"

"About coming back as a fig bar. How did you feel?"

"I didn't feel anything, really."

"Maybe not consciously, but subconsciously you did."

"I did?"

"Certainly. You must have."

Harry thought a moment. "No . . . I can honestly say I didn't feel anything. I just said that. Really."

"Aha. You don't think that you felt anything but, subconsciously, you *know* you did."

"How can you be sure?"

The woman at the bar giggled graciously. "My dear, Freud was talking about the subconscious in the nineteenth century!"

"But Freud was a goddamn cokehead!" Harry exclaimed.

The woman smiled, leaving a solid line of lip gloss on her teeth. "You're still uptight."

"No I'm not."

"It's my being a shrink that does it to you. Before you knew about my occupation, you were quite ready to give me a quick boffing."

"Bof . . ." Harry was stunned. "Now, wait just one minute . . ."

The woman raised a finger to his lips. "That's all right. I

208

realize that my breasts are an incredible turn-on to most men. It's a combination of the American male's fascination for oversized mammaries and a mother fixation that most males harbor in general. In the United States, I find this combination extremely common. I think it arises, in part, from the American man's refusal to deal with male-initiated oral sex as a viable part of intercourse. They hone in on the breast as an alternative measure. In Italy, this just isn't the case, however. They love bottoms."

"What the hell are you talking about?" Harry finally asked.

"You have a room here?" the woman asked.

"Well, yes," Harry admitted.

"Well, then let's go," she smiled. "I've been hot for you since I caught sight of your lapels."

"I-I don't even know your name."

"Just call me Dawn."

"Just call me Harry Porter."

"All right, Harryporter, let's go."

Harry slid off the stool. This was ridiculous. Still, he had been dumped by Sylvie and he did have that room upstairs. He began to relax. His ease was shortlived, however. He bumped into Sylvie Dunbar on the way out and was given a token of her esteem. She had apparently spied him leaving with the woman from the bar and had decided to take action. Walking slowly up to him, she took a drink from a nearby table and dumped it onto his left shoulder. The drink cascaded down the front of his Earth jacket.

Sylvie smiled and walked away.

"Friend of yours?" Dawn asked.

"Acquaintance," Harry said, dabbing his coat of many colors.

"Lapel envy," the woman concluded.

Harry and Dawn ("Like in the new DAWNing of an experience.") walked through the hallways of the Retreat's hotel sector. Glancing at his key, Harry theorized that their room was on the second tier.

"Good," Dawn said, "then we aren't near the zero g level; simply light g."

"You don't care for zero g?"

"Negative connotations," she answered thoughtfully.

Harry nodded, wisely choosing not to press the point. After five minutes of exhausting walking, they still hadn't located their room, although they had unintentionally eavesdropped

209

on the sounds emerging from a few dozen doors; an auditory panorama that reminded Harry of a book by DeSade he had read once. (It still boggled his imagination.) Lost and directionless, Harry was getting very annoyed. Dawn was growing very comatose.

"Lose your bearings?" called a voice from behind. A young bellboy bounded down the hallway, obviously adept at light gravity movement. "I sure have," Harry said. "Could you help us out?"

"No problem," the boy winked, giving Dawn a quick once over. "I've been working here two years. I know my way around."

His eyes moved to Harry's suit. "Great threads. Earthside?"

"Yeah. Came up here a few days ago."

"With the Earth delegation," the boy said, snapping his fingers. "Should've guessed." He pointed to the stained shoulder. "Been using the jacket for a towel."

Harry was beginning to grow weary of the kid's jocular attitude. "Had a little accident downstairs."

"I can get it cleaned for you. Good as new."

"Really? Now?"

"Sure. Downstairs at the laundry center. I'll take it down and bring it back in ten minutes . . . half hour tops. Delivered to your door."

Harry was beginning to grow fond of the kid's altruistic attitude. He quickly took off the jacket and handed it to him with a fiver. "Here you go."

The boy grabbed the jacket tenderly. "Gee. I haven't seen one of these in months," he whispered. "Mind if I try it on? We're about the same size."

"Go ahead," Harry laughed. "Run up and down the halls in it for all I care. Just don't . . ."

"Use it as a towel?" the boy grinned.

"You got it. Now, where's our room?"

The boy took Harry's key and hopped off. "Just follow me!"

Harry and Dawn did just that, with some minor difficulty caused by the woman's failure to move her legs in a logical manner. ("Right. Left. Right. Left," Harry encouraged.) Two hallways later, they were both standing in front of their room. The bellboy had opened the door and was holding the key. "Here you are sir," he said, palming a small pamphlet into Harry's outstretched hand. Harry glanced at the book:

The Kama Sutra of Space. He slipped the kid another five and watched the boy leap on down the hall, still wearing Harry's jacket. Maybe there was hope for this younger generation yet.

Harry and Dawn entered the room, a standard hotel set-up of the decidedly carnal motif. Circular bed. Overhead mirror. Grotesquely ornate starfield drapes. Large sunken tub in the middle of the living room. Holography unit if you were interested in homemade pornography. Harry sat down on the rim of the bed and undressed eagerly. He watched Dawn slip out of her tunic with an exaggerated sense of modesty. Her figure was solid and rounded. She had the largest breasts he had ever seen in a situation he didn't have to break a fifty for.

Dawn padded into an adjacent bathroom and Harry stretched out on the bed. Surreptitiously flipping through the pamphlet the bellboy had left, he began to clinically map out his strategy for the lovemaking to come. He'd begin with conventional arousal techniques: kissing, nibbling, fondling, squeezing, etc. Then, once they were both suitably aroused, he'd place her astride him, her breasts dangling over his face as he entered her. He'd use short, deep thrusts. She would climax. He would not. With them both covered in sweat, he would ease her onto the bed next to him. He would roll over on top of her and, folding her legs up around his neck in a scissor hold, he would climax in a series of slow, deliberate movements. And that was just for openers. He carefully closed the book and slipped it under his pillow, grinning. What an animal he was.

The stillness of the room was broken by a series of tiny, almost animal squeals coming from within the bathroom. After a few seconds, they subsided. After a time, Harry wasn't sure that he had even heard them in the first place. Shortly, they began again.

"What's that?" he called.

"I'm expelling negative components from my body," Dawn whispered softly.

"What?"

"I'm expelling negative components."

Harry was still puzzled. "How's that?"

"I'm puking my guts out," she whined. "I'm really not supposed to drink. You know? Doctors orders. But every so often, I like to have the toxins of alcohol flow through my system and ... brrreeeka ... eeeka ... eeeka"

211

Harry pulled the covers over his fast-fading manhood. Yet another night of uninterrupted slumber.

He stared blankly at his face in the mirror above for several minutes before becoming aware of the ominous silence arising from the bathroom. "Are you all right?" he called. No response. Putting on his pants, he tiptoed to the bathroom door and peeked inside. The woman was asleep in fetal position on the room's lush carpeting. She had the face of an angel. Most women did when they slept. No matter how much of a pain in the ass they were when awake, asleep they were a reflection of heaven itself. Hell, Lizzy Borden probably even looked saintly when dozing. Gazing down at the sleeping psychiatrist, Harry stifled an empty sigh. He pulled a large bath towel from the linen closet and draped it over her supine form.

He gazed fondly at the graceful folds of her body. His senses were yanked from the room when a horrifying scream split the silence of the hotel with the speed of a hot knife.

A yell.

A crash.

Glass exploding.

Unmindful of the light gravity, Harry made a leap for the door, intending to fling it open and dash outside into the hall. The light gravity of his hotel suite caused him to misjudge, however, and his hand merely grazed the doorknob before his body crashed headlong into the door. Precious seconds lost. Quickly recalculating his sense of distorted balance, he slid the door open and limped into the corridor. Other doors along the hallway were beginning to ease open, with drowsy heads appearing peek-a-boo style from within.

The screaming had long since stopped.

Harry ran down the hall and rounded a corner. He stumbled to a sudden stop. His stomach twisting in revulsion at the sight before him. At the beginning of the next corridor was a window.

That window was now shattered.

Hanging from the jagged panes of glass left in the window frame was the body of the young bellboy, still clad in Harry's jacket.

His neck had been impaled by the long slivers of glass. His body was leaning forward against the window, his feet still touching the hotel's floor, as if he was staring at the ground outside.

The body was headless.

212

A crowd began to follow Harry down the hallway. "Stay back," he cautioned. "Call the police. Please don't come any closer. This isn't very pretty."

His stomach still convulsing, his mouth devoid of all moisture, Harry walked up to the shattered window and stared at the walkway below. He shouldn't have. The boy's head stared back at him, its eyes wide open in terror. The boy's mouth was twisted into an oval shape. Harry heard his screams once more. His stomach shuddered. A second bell-boy, white faced and wobbly, appeared on the scene, carrying a sheet from a nearby room. He was about to drape it over the body when Harry waved him back. "Don't touch anything until the police arrive."

"What a horrible accident," Harry heard one guest declare from somewhere behind him. The man's manner of speech was too pat, too confident for Harry's taste. He looked up into the faces before him. One man, solidly built, his tunic neatly pressed, stood out from the crowd. "Horrible accident," the fellow repeated.

Harry smelled a cop. So that's how the poor little bastard's death would be written off.

"Stupid place to put a window," a second voice in the crowd agreed, picking up the torch. "Horrible accident."

The word "accident" caused Harry's teeth to gnash.

The first man in the crowd continued to speak. "I saw this kid running around here before like a wild Indian," he stated emphatically. "Hell, any one of us running down this hall could have lost our balance and gone through the glass like that. That kind of momentum in this kind of gravity? Whew!"

"Yeah," a third voice said timidly. "Surprised this kind of thing hasn't happened before."

"All of us would have trouble negotiating that turn," the first man declared.

"Right," Harry muttered. Only with you or me, Mack, our clumsiness would arise because we just weren't used to this light g set-up. This poor kid worked up here two goddamn years. If anyone was able to bounce around these halls without fear of injury, it was this bellboy. Harry stared at the hacked off section of neck impaled on the glass. Something was strange. The neck wasn't ragged. It was smooth. Clean cut.

Burn marks lined the boy's neck. A sickening suspicion became an even more nauseating fact in Harry's mind. The kid had been beheaded . . . from behind. Chased and attacked from behind. Pushed forward into position. He stared at the body. Clad in Harry's coat, the boy did resemble Harry from a distance. What was that he had said. We're both the same build? Harry had given the boy his jacket. He had told him to wear it. Harry turned his back on the scene and, pushing his way through the gaggle of guests, plodded back to his room. The bellboy hadn't been the intended victim this evening.

Harry had.

Harry had just sent a youth barely out of his teens to a most horrible death.

Dawn was standing dreamily in the doorway when Harry returned to the suite. Saying nothing, he gently nudged her out of his path as he walked past the sunken tub and into the bathroom.

For the next fifteen minutes he crouched over the toilet, expelling negative components from his body.

PART FIVE

"A hero cannot be a hero
unless in a heroic world."
—Hawthorne

1

There were times when Harry doubted his own sanity. Since his arrival on *Island* four days ago, however, he had been doubting everyone else's. There was simply no reason, no matter how noble, to allow a murderer to have the freedom to stalk and kill his victims with the ferocity exhibited in Robeur's Retreat. Harry had been the killer's target twice. He had been spared twice, pushing, what Harry believed was a very succinct schedule of death back two days. In the three days left before *Island*'s massive anniversary celebration, the murderer had to dispatch twelve people. Harry cringed at the thought of the bloodbath to come.

Following the bellboy's death and his own stomach's demise, he returned to his hotel room. Unable to sleep, he began to type although it was approximately three o'clock in the morning. He was angry. He was tense. He was frightened beyond description. Lining up the stacks of publicity handouts Anson Young had provided the Earth delegation with, Harry quickly cranked out six colorful, happy-go-lucky, and totally fictitious slice-of-life pieces dealing with the habitat. Let them eat pap.

By the time eight o'clock and breakfast rolled around,

much of Harry's fury had subsided. His eyes were puffy. His cheeks were drawn. His back ached from sitting in front of the typewriter and his breath smelled like the body of a badger. Harry glanced at the mirror hung across the room. What a noble visage. Impotent, totally outmatched by the habitat's power structure on the matter of murder, but noble nonetheless. The kind of face that, in those old nuclear warfare movies, belonged to the guy who got everyone to safety before manning the controls himself seconds before personal armageddon and the closing credits appeared. Noble but stupid.

Harry showered and shaved and consumed what seemed to be his weight in coffee. Slipping on a jumpsuit, he bundled up the innocuous copy under his arm and strolled over to the communications center. He picked up the copy of the *Island* newspaper from outside his hotel room door and took it with him on his walk. Scanning the front page, he found a small story dealing with the unfortunate death of a very clumsy bellboy. Such a tragic accident. Harry was too exhausted to be angry. Truth was simply an unknown commodity up here.

Harry spotted the communications center across the walkway. He paused on the curbside to look left and right for imaginary traffic before crossing. A woman pedestrian bumped into him from behind.

"Sorry," he muttered.

"My fault, really," she said.

"No," he explained. "It wasn't." He wished she would stop smiling at him. "I'm from Earth, you see. I keep on thinking the walkways are like streets. You know? I keep on waiting for cars to sneak up on me."

"I should have recognized you, Mr. Porter," the woman said, smiling still. "And taken that into consideration."

Harry managed a shadow of a grin and continued on his way. He was growing tired of the enforced politeness. If he stabbed one of these people, would they apologize for bleeding on his knife? Harry entered the center and asked for instructions to the Earth transmissions desk. A guard pointed the way.

He was greeted by an intensely perky transclerk. She wore a bright orange uniform, a hat cocked to one side that reminded Harry of a twentieth-century ice-cream salesman and had a smile bright enough to make a blindman blink. "I'd like to send these Earthside," Harry said, handing the girl the stack of papers.

"Certainly," she chirped.

"To a Mr. Leonard Golden. Cable #NTH 3X5, Sector 45. My name is Porter, Harry Porter. I'm staying at the hotel down the road apiece."

"I know." The girl's smile, already reaching dinosaur proportions, widened even more when Harry mentioned his name. "Why, Mr. Porter, we've just received a transmission for you from Mr. Golden. Small universe, isn't it?"

"Frightfully," Harry answered. She handed him an envelope. Before he could open it, the girl blurted happily. "He says that your cousin is just fine."

Harry nodded and placed the envelope, still unopened, into one of the jumpsuit's pockets. So much for privacy. At least Seabruck was safe. He watched the girl take his stories to the scanning machine. It took her some time to get them through, however. Longer than usual. He couldn't swear to it but it appeared that the girl was speed reading them, word for word, before sending them Earthside. If that was indeed the case, then Hawkins and Vallory had alerted the powers-that-be to monitor Harry's every action. It also meant that the pieces were bland enough to pass official inspection. Hell, they were practically rewrites of Young's pamphlets with a few quotes jammed in to effect a sense of local color.

Harry decided to check out his censorship theory. Taking a piece of stationary from the girl's desk, he hastily printed: "Leonard. There's something fishy going on up here. Could be the story of the century. Please contact. Advise."

"Oh, miss," he called. "I'd like to send this out too. A little postscript for the last story."

The girl, ever vivacious, grabbed the slip of paper between her thumb and forefinger, as if it was alive, and brought it to the machine. She stood over the scanner/transmitter. The machine didn't buzz. Didn't quiver. Didn't light up.

Harry leaned against the desk. "Something wrong?"

"I'm afraid we can't transmit this," the girl said, her smile sagging slightly in order to convey a deep sense of dismay. "Our equipment just went out. Solar flares, I suppose. It happens every so often."

"What about my stories?"

"They got in just under the wire!"

"How lucky."

"Excuse me?"

"I said, how fortunate for me. Say, I don't suppose you'd know just how long you'll be out of whack in here, do you?"

"No, sir. These little flares can last moments, hours, or sometimes, days."

"Oh my goodness," Harry said. He wrote down his address and phone number on a slip of stationery. "Let met know when we're no longer incommunicado."

"Excuse me?"

"Let me know when the flares subside."

The girl nodded obediently. "Oh, certainly, Mr. Porter."

Harry left the building and sat outside on a bench. Now he was really stuck. Sylvie had lied to him. He couldn't really trust her. His communications were being censored. There was a nut loose on the habitat and the government was involved in the biggest cover-up since the delivery of the Trojan Horse. Harry was depressed. He was not given the chance to sink to new mental lows, however, in that his train of thought was abruptly derailed by the sudden appearance of two uniformed policemen. Harry stared at their lupine faces. They didn't resemble the school crossing guard type.

"Porter. Harry Porter," the more verbose of the pair grunted.

"Present. Harry Porter present," Harry said.

"The chief wants to see you."

"Sitting Bull or Geronimo?"

The cop was not amused. "On your feet."

"Onyourfeet? Is he back in town?" Harry asked, standing. Hell, he might as well play it their way. There wasn't all that much of a choice, anyway. Apparently, his audience with Hawkins was top priority. He was driven to the police station in one of those independently automated mini-vans. The van resembled the ambulance he had seen outside of Young's apartment building. The ride was smooth but not exactly speedy and he felt vaguely uneasy about not traveling along the habitat's trackway.

The car pulled up in front of the station and Harry was somberly guided to Hawkins's door. The officer at Harry's left swung the door open. The inside of Hawkins's office was fairly Earthlike in decor. One large desk stood at the back of the room. Two chairs for guests and/or prisoners were placed directly in front of the desk. American flag on one side of the

218

room. *Island* insignia, an outline of the cylinders on a black starfield, draped on the other. Various presidential portraits and official documents hung from the walls.

When Harry entered the room, he noticed that one of the two desks reserved for guests was already occupied. Sylvie Dunbar turned around and faced Harry as he walked in. Harry nodded in her direction. "Here for the reading of my will?"

Sylvie made an instinctive movement to rise. Harry waved her back down. "Oh Harry, are you all right?"

Harry ignored her and sat in the empty chair facing Josh Hawkins. "Who knows? Let's take a vote on that. What do you say, chief, am I all right?"

"You've got a smart mouth," Hawkins muttered.

"Part of a set."

Hawkins folded his hands on his desk and glared at Harry. His drooping hair and sagging mustache accented his bulldog jaw. Every line in his face, and there were dozens, furrowed downward. The man looked even more exhausted than Harry. "Truce, Porter. OK? I didn't call you here because of your comedic talents."

"Nuts," Harry said evenly. "I had worked up a whole new routine, too."

"About last night . . ." Hawkins began.

"That's what my routine was about," Harry said. "Really funny stuff. It's about this accident that's no accident. About this bellboy who accidentally blasts his head off from behind while diving through a window he hasn't noticed for two years. Now, stop me if you've heard this one before."

Hawkins's eyes turned heavenward. "I don't have enough problems, right?"

"Oh, you've got problems, all right," Harry said. "But you don't seem to have the guts to do anything about them."

Sylvie stomped a foot onto the floor. "Harry, will you please shut up for a moment! That's why Chief Hawkins sent for you."

Harry crossed his arms. "All right."

Hawkins heaved a prolonged sigh. "I know that you've stumbled on to what's going on up here. Ms. Dunbar has told me of the bugging device you planted on me the other night."

"A regular Mata Hari," Harry chided.

Hawkins was not to be deterred. "She did it for your own

219

good. She's worried about you. I'm worried about you. You simply can't charge around on the habitat like some one man commando unit and expect to come out of it in one piece."

"Well," Harry countered. "If I don't, who will? Vallory seems to have all the rest of you neatly sewn up by the balls."

Hawkins reddened slightly. "You know the circumstances surrounding our present stalemate. There is just so much I can officially do right now for various political reasons. I am not allowed to even acknowledge the fact that there is a problem aboard. I'm stuck, Porter. I admit it."

Harry and Hawkins faced each other over the chief's desk. The policeman raised a finger at Harry. "But you, on the other hand, are not."

Harry didn't like the direction this confrontation was taking. "I know I shouldn't ask this, but what are you getting at?"

Hawkins leaned back in his chair. "I'm simply opening up a concept you came up with yourself. I can't operate openly on this investigation, but you can. You have the freedom, denied me, to move around this habitat practically unchecked and with Ms. Dunbar here as your guide, there's no door closed to you."

"I no longer wish Ms. Dunbar to be my guide."

"Harry!" exclaimed Sylvie.

"You lied to me," Harry blurted, his hurt rising to the surface.

"Everyone's lied to you," Hawkins interrupted. "Don't take it out on her. It'll cost her her job."

Harry slumped down into his chair. "Who can argue logic?"

"Well," Hawkins asked, "what do you say?"

"About what?"

"About working with us . . . undercover, of course. Vallory must never know."

Harry whistled through his teeth in a pitch that annoyed Sylvie. "Hold on. Stop the music. You're actually asking me to act as a plainclothes detective on your behalf?"

"Unofficially."

"Unofficially," Harry swallowed, envisioning the danger involved. "Uh, no offense, chief, but I've never been much for charitable causes. What's in this for me?"

"Your life."

"Good point," Harry admitted. "I don't know, though. It sounds pretty risky."

"No more so than your present actions," Hawkins assured him. "We're prepared to take every precaution possible to lessen your own personal jeopardy." He fumbled a hand into his top desk drawer, producing a gun and a small wristband. He pushed the laser pistol toward Harry. "Ever use one of these?"

"I try not to but, yeah, I can handle one."

"Good. It's yours."

"You shouldn't have."

"You can pick up a shoulder holster on the way out."

Harry picked up the pistol and held it in his hand. The plastic butt of the gun had an alien feel to it. It didn't belong in Harry's possession. He held the butt next to his face and turned to Sylvie. "Nice. It almost matches my eyes, don't you think?"

"Drop dead."

"I love it when you're loathesome." Harry returned his attention to the chief's desk. "What's that?" he said, gesturing to the wristband.

Hawkins held out a square, ice-blue wristwatch/video unit. "It's a two-way communicator."

Harry picked it up, laughing. "Oh my God! So it is! I haven't seen one of these turkeys around in years. Jesus. Remember when they were going to be the next big thing? When was that, the 1990s?"

"Well, yeah, around that time," Hawkins admitted.

"Little bastards," Harry chuckled, gazing at the machine. A standard wristwatch, the wrist device also had a ten push-button dialing system, a speaker microphone, and a three-antenna system for receiving and sending signals. "Boy, these were a real boon to mankind, eh? They put up that switchboard in the sky satellite and every yahoo in the world went out and bought one. A personalized phone system. These things jammed the airwaves better than the CB radios in the '80s. How long did it take them to pull these off the market . . . six years?"

"About that," Hawkins said, steaming.

"What the hell are you doing with one of these fossils up here?"

"Just stow it, Porter," Hawkins said. "This is a new model. Ours don't need the overhead satellite system to work. They use the communications center as a base. All our cops use them. It's a two-way device. You can talk to me and I can talk to you. The videoscreen can relay facts and figures to you visually. You just strap it on and activate that little switch next to the . . ."

"Yeah, I know how to work one," Harry said, putting the watch on with unusual care. "Next to the watch nub. My dad had one of these. One of the few pleasures he had in his last years. Makes me feel like a kid again."

"Try to curtail your enthusiasm," Sylvie said, attempting to dampen Harry's spirits. "We're not on our way to a homecoming, we're trying to track down a killer."

"And prevent a possible massacre," Hawkins added.

"No kidding," Harry said, lapsing back into his stoic self. He folded his arms once more. "Now what?"

"Now you just continue doing what you were doing," Hawkins stated.

"Which was?"

"Snooping around and making a pain in the ass of yourself," Hawkins said.

Harry picked up the laser pistol. "Only this time with official approval, eh?"

"That's right. You just report everything to me with that little communicator of yours."

"Right." Harry looked at the watch. "But, now that I'm a junior G-Man, I'm afraid that I'm going to have to have a few answers from you about a few things that have been bothering me since I arrived here."

Hawkins tightened his jaw. "Let's hear the questions."

"I heard that you people drilled the citizens up here before the Earth delegates' arrival, taught them how to act 'serene.' "

"That's true," Hawkins muttered.

"Have you people been trying to censor my copy?"

"Affirmative."

"Was Sid Kraft dismissed for associating with me?"

"Yeah," Hawkins grunted, "we never figured that you'd be hooking up with us."

"That makes two of us. Have your men been tailing me for the past two days?"

"Affirmative."

"And it was one of your guys who followed me on the shack?"

"Yeah."

222

"And the library?"

"Yes," Hawkins said, growing weary of the cross-examination.

"All right," Harry said, satisfied, "I want them off."

"Huh?" Hawkins's face took on the shape of a question mark.

"I want your dogs called off my tail. If I'm going to do any good around here, I have to do things my own way."

Hawkins drummed the fingers of his left hand on his desk top. "Nice try, Porter, but it doesn't wash. No one, I repeat, no one outside the people in this room will ever know that you're working for me . . ."

"With you," Harry corrected.

"With me. If I call off your tail, that will arouse suspicion. I'm sorry, but to the plainclothes squad, you're still just another sitting duck needing protection."

Harry mulled that one over. Hawkins was right. Any deviation from the norm would only attract attention to Harry's movements. "There's probably a lot of truth in that last statement anyhow," he said, getting out of the chair. He walked to the door, Sylvie trailing silently behind. "Let's see," Harry muttered, "gun, communicator, official status . . . anything missing? Oh yeah," he faced the already flustered police chief. "Can I have the keys to the car tonight? Heavy date."

"Get the fuck out of my office," Hawkins said politely.

Harry and Sylvie left the police station and walked solemnly back to his hotel. Sylvie stared straight ahead during their trek. Neither spoke for what seemed an eternity.

"Mad at me?" Harry finally offered.

Sylvie walked in silence.

"Was it something I said?" Harry asked.

"Drop dead."

"Well, we're making great progress communicating, anyhow." He grew serious. "Look, if it's about that remark I made about you not being my guide, you have to understand that . . . I trusted you. I don't trust a lot of people. I leveled with you from the outset and you, well, you just stuck to the government spiel. I took you into my confidence and you lied to me."

"I had to."

"Bullshit."

"Harry, it was my job to present the colony in a certain light. It is still my job to do that."

223

"And if the circumstance arose again? If I stumbled onto a skeleton in the hab's closet, would you still lie to save your job?"

"I suppose I would."

Harry shrugged. "Well, at least we know where we stand."

"It's not as awful as you make it sound." Sylvie frowned.

"Right. You lie when I trust you."

Sylvie quickened her pace. "And I loved you a long time ago and you never did a damn thing to make everything right."

Harry jammed his hands into the jumpsuit pockets. "Yeah, well, that was *then*. I was a little young and a little stupid."

"Now you're a little older and a lot stupider. You could've gotten yourself killed last night. I was worried about you." Sylvie attempted to mutter the last phrase, but her sincerity caused her voice to break.

"Thanks," Harry said sheepishly.

"Chalk it up to the current nostalgia craze."

The pair walked to the hotel without talking further. They marched through the lobby and onto the lifts without looking at each other. Entering Harry's room, Sylvie went to the bar and made a drink. Harry sat at his writing desk. "Let's see if I can ring up old smiley on this thing," he said, pointing to his wrist communicator.

Sylvie came the closest to a smile than she had had in the last twenty-four hours. "You've been dying to try that out since Hawk gave it to you, haven't you?"

Harry flashed a lopsided grin. "Yeah, I suppose so. Makes everything seem so . . . *official*." He played with the buttons on the communicator, punching out the number to the police station. "Here goes. Hawkins? Porter here. Come in, Hawkins." He felt foolish parroting the semimilitaristic drone used in awful TV crime shows for over a half-century. He felt even more foolish at his efforts at communication being greeted by nothing more than a steady, pulsating yellow light on his viewscreen.

"I think my communicator is having an attack of some sort," Harry muttered.

Sylvie stood at his side. "What's it doing?"

"I haven't the vaguest idea. Maybe it has a crush on my wrist or something."

Suddenly Hawkins's voice emerged from the minuscule wrist-speaker. "What the hell are you doing?" he barked in a tinny voice.

224

"Watching my communicator wink at me."

"Damn."

"It likes me."

"Look," Hawkins offered. "Your device is on yellow alert. It's designed to register the presence of any unauthorized transmitting device within a twenty-foot area."

"Translation: an electronic bugging device."

"You got it."

"Great," Harry mumbled. "About this concept of privacy you folks have going up here."

"Walk around the room," Hawkins advised, "and watch that wristscreen. The yellow light's pulsations will increase in frequency the closer it gets to the bug. When you're on top of the bug, it will simply shine solid yellow. When it's solid, check to see what the nearest object in the room is."

"Then what?"

"Then tear that object apart and remove the bug."

Harry held his right arm before him and marched around the room. The wristscreen pulsated docilely. Near the couch, the communicator's flashes increased in speed. Harry ran his arm along the length of the sofa. The flashes remained constant. He approached a small end table. The light beats fused into a solid beam. He aimed his arm at a lamp on the table. Solid. Harry grabbed the lamp with two hands and smashed it onto the ground. The lamp broke into six large pieces. Harry held each piece up to his communicator for visual confirmation of the presence of a transmitter. Four pieces into the process and the light shone solid on his screen. Harry unscrewed the lamp's shattered lightbulb and found a small electronic bug attached to its base. "Gotcha," he beamed.

He tossed the bug onto the floor and stepped on it several times with obvious glee before walking over to the bar. "Got it," he told Hawkins, joining Sylvie for a quick drink. "It was in the lamp."

"Any idea how long it could have been there?" Hawkins asked.

"Hell, with the traffic I've had in this room so far, the tooth fairy could have walked in here unnoticed with the damned thing."

"That's not good," the chief said.

"Explain."

"Well, you know a lot about the murderer and the political climate up here. I know a lot about it, too. And now, whoever

225

owns that little bug knows as much as we know, too. It looks like we have ourselves a whole new ballgame, Porter. Either the killer had taken a very big interest in your comings and goings or a third party has taken a very big interest in our killer."

"I hate crowds," Harry exhaled. "OK. That settles it. Get Ms. Dunbar out of here."

"What?" Sylvie exclaimed in surprise.

Harry addressed both the communicator and Sylvie. "Look, at this point we have no idea who this killer may be or even if it's an individual. We may be dealing with a solitary fanatic or a group of loons. Let's just say that Emmett has some sort of pecking order in terms of who gets it when. He's missed me two nights in a row. He doesn't have much time left to catch up, corpse-wise. If I'm his next target, I don't want Ms. Dunbar near me. Especially in light of finding out we've been monitored for god knows how long. I think she should be put under police protection."

"She is now," Hawkins countered.

"I want her out of here," Harry repeated.

Harry gazed at the communicator, ignoring Sylvie's angry face. "Keep her in a safe spot unless I say otherwise. Increase the guards around the other delegates, too. And get your men off my ass."

"You're crazy," Hawkins fumed.

"Maybe, but unless you do exactly as I say, every delegate up here is going to know about my dealings with you, your government, and your resident psycho."

A steady crackling sound emerged from the wrist device. "All right," Hawkins said, "have it your way. Just don't go getting yourself killed."

"It's the furthest thing from my mind," Harry said. "Send one of your plainclothesmen up to my room and we'll get Ms. Dunbar home."

"Will do."

Harry broke off communication and, catching a bright reflection out of the side of his eye, ducked. The ashtray sailed harmlessly over his head and smashed into a wall. Sylvie stood facing him, her arms stiff at her sides, her hands clutched in white knuckled rage. "How could you?" she steamed.

"You have a good head on your shoulders," Harry smiled. "I'd like to make sure it stays there."

She flashed a contemptuous look in his direction. The

226

doorbell sounded. Harry swung open the door and greeted a barrel-chested detective. The cop nodded in wordless greeting and took Sylvie by the arm. She left the room still staring at Porter.

"Tell you what," Harry said by way of a peace offering. "While I'm out pounding the pavement, check out the names of any Island citizens with parapsychological training, OK? A quick run over to the computer center."

"Drop dead."

Harry chuckled and closed the door behind them. He stood in the middle of the room, trying to figure out what he was going to do next. He knew it was important to find out as much about Emmett's possible background as he could before a trap could be baited. He also had to find out exactly who had bugged his room.

Harry stepped into the bathroom and turned on the cold tap. He unstrapped his wrist communicator and placed it on the side of the sink. Splashing cold water onto his face, he took no note of the communicator's viewscreen. It shone with a solid yellow hue.

2

"Well, my goodness, all of this certainly sounds mysterious . . . and very exciting," Dr. Harper said, his eyes widening in a show of excitement. Harry had decided that he needed some expert help in tracking down Emmett and turned to Harper for help. He outlined the events of the past week . . . deleting quite a bit of political information in the process. Harper placed a finger to the nosepiece of his glasses and pushed the wire-rimmed spectacles from the tip of his proboscis back to eye level. As soon as he removed his finger, the glasses slid back down to the edge of his nose. "Exciting," he repeated, "and positively volatile."

"You don't seem too surprised about it, though," Harry stated cautiously.

"My dear young man," Harper informed him, "as you get older you will find that there are very, very few events which can elicit genuine surprise . . . with the possible exception of one's mail being delivered on time."

"But murder?"

"Murder happens daily."

"But here on *Island?*"

"Aha, yes," Harper said. "I suppose I should be shocked at that fact, eh? Well, were I in your shoes, I suppose I would be. Utopian *Island One*. But I've lived on the habitat for close to a decade, Mr. Porter. It's anything but all-perfect, as you now know. It's filled to the brim with living, breathing people. And people have very many flaws. Who's to say that one of our all-perfect residents, angered by some alleged injustice, couldn't turn to murder? Really, haven't you ever wished harm on someone who has done you a disservice. I know I have. There's hardly a day that goes by when I don't simmer at one of my colleagues and wish him dead."

"But you don't actually go around knocking them off," Harry countered.

"I don't have the height for it," the old man shrugged. He cocked his head thoughtfully. "But why have you taken me into your confidence? Surely I am just as suspect as anyone in taking part in this cover-up."

"To a degree you are," Harry admitted. "But my guess is that the powers-that-be wouldn't exactly want you boys in the think tank to find out about this killer. After all, you are the morale boosters, are you not? It wouldn't pay to sour your sunny outlook."

"Yes, you're quite right there," Harper sighed.

"So," Harry continued. "I thought you might be interested enough in the situation to help me do some detective work."

Harper waddled across his living quarters, a small studio apartment littered with books and pamphlets. Opening the door to his refrigeration unit, he took out a chilled bottle of blue juice. He offered a glass to Harry. Harry refused politely. "I'd be delighted to help you," Harper said. "I enjoy a challenge. Yes, I do. But you must tell me exactly what it is I am to do."

"I don't know yet," Harry said lamely.

The elderly fellow poured a small glass of juice for himself. "Then, uh, what exactly is it you are looking for?"

"I don't know," Harry stated.

"Well, good grief, man," Harper cringed. "If I'm to play Watson to your Holmes, you should have at least some idea of our course of action!"

Harry pushed his chair against a wall. "I know that, I'm thinking. This is what I know. Emmet is either part of an organized strike force or a lone looney. No matter what he turns out to be, he is not what you'd call a stable character. He is also a telepath. He has it in for me, personally, and he has forty-eight hours to systematically kill twelve people."

"Ah yes, I see, I see," Harper chuckled, sitting down across from Harry. "You are bullshitting me again. Well, that's fine. It doesn't pay to trust too many people completely. And, it's a pleasant diversion for me to try to spot the small glimmers of honesty in your statements. Let *me* tell *you* exactly why you're here. You have taken me into your confidence because you know your Emmett fellow is a telepath. Now, in my office, you met a natural telepath, one Martin Graff, a former colleague. You also took note of the fact that I have the ability not only to ward off his mental darts but to actually calm his feverish brain down. You would like a meeting with Graff, I presume, for whatever reasons. You would also like me to be present as a sort of mediator."

"Watson," Harry smiled, "you amaze me."

"Remedial, my dear Holmes," Harper cackled. "You wear your thoughts in neon letters across your face." Harper grew serious. "Do you suspect that Martin may be the killer?"

"No," Harry admitted. "I got the feeling that he was, and is, a very gentle man. But I do think that he may be able to point us in a direction leading to the murderer. It's logical. Graff didn't go mad and develop his telepathic abilities just by chance. Something happened to him. Some catastrophic event must have actually altered his physical and mental state of being."

"But surely we would have been informed of such an event here on the habitat."

"Not necessarily. It would have been bad press. Especially if it was something strong enough to change a man's physiological make-up."

Harper ran a gnarled hand over his chin. "Yes. Yes. I see what you're getting at. Why didn't I think of it before. You think that something actually invaded Martin's body and mind simultaneously. But that something would have to be very strong. Something as powerful as ..." He gaped at Harry.

Harry nodded. "Cosmic radiation."

"But it would have to be a massive dose."

"True."

"And that would mean that this event would have had to have been a tremendous accident."

"Right."

Harper raised a protesting hand. "No. I really cannot accept that. There is no possible way for an accident like that to occur up here without the general populace knowing about it. Even if the government attempted to whitewash the affair, there would have to have been witnesses."

"Right."

"And you think that your killer . . ."

"May have been one of them. He may have seen the entire accident occur."

"Impossible," Harper insisted. "Dozens, perhaps hundreds of citizens would have seen such an event occur. The news would have spread like wildfire."

Harry leaped to his feet. "But there must have been a way to cover it up, nonetheless. There had to have been an accident. The cosmic radiation on this habitat isn't strong enough to drive one lone individual batty without affecting the rest of you. Something had to have happened to Graff and it had to have happened five years ago . . . on a single day."

"Conjecture."

"There's only one way to prove it otherwise."

Harper stared at the glass of blue juice in his hand. "The meeting would be dangerous, you know. Especially for you . . . a sensitive."

"I realize that."

"Martin is mad."

"Perhaps."

Harper was startled. "Perhaps? You saw him yourself."

"I saw a man mentally displaced," Harry said. "That doesn't make him a lunatic. He has cunning. He has an intelligence. And, beneath the surface, he has the ability to make rational judgments."

Harper chuckled softly. "You should have entered the field of psychology."

"I did," Harry said. "I became a reporter."

"All right," the little man sighed, putting the empty glass on a nearby table. "You wait here. I shall endeavor to smuggle our dear friend Martin out of the hospital. It shouldn't take too long, security being as lax as it is."

The gnomelike fellow got to his feet, walked to the door, and exited his apartment. Harry, still tired from the events of the last day, stretched out on the sofa and napped. He

230

couldn't have been sleeping more than a moment, or so it seemed, when he felt a soft tapping on his shoulder. "Mr. Porter," a voice hissed. "Mr. Porter."

Harry opened his eyes. Harper was leaning over him. "No time to sleep," he whispered. "I ran into a little bit of trouble 'rescuing' Martin."

"What kind of trouble?" Harry asked, propping himself up on his elbows.

"A few guards came trotting down the hall quite unexpectedly as we were making our way out. Martin panicked. He let out a mental blast that knocked them off their feet, quite literally. I've never seen anything like it. He's still quite agitated, so please be very careful. I fear that he is quite capable of crippling one's mind if he sets his will to it."

Harry glanced over Harper's shoulder at the wild-eyed man in the white smock. "Great," he mumbled. "Just swell."

Harry sat on the sofa. Harper went to the door and returned to Harry with the elderly, bald-headed apparition Harry had encountered previously in the think tank. The reedlike figure in white allowed himself to be led by his diminutive peer to a plush chair. Harry sat immobile, staring at the figure of Martin Graff. Graff wore an expression of perpetual shock. Slack jawed, he stared vacantly into space. Somehow, Harry sensed that despite his outer appearance, the man's intellect was intact; trapped in a body that defied logical movement and saddled with a verbal network that wallowed in gobbledygook. Harper took Martin by the hand and held out his right arm. "Martin, this is Harry Porter. You met him in my office. He is a good friend of mine. Do you understand?"

Graff shook his head in a painfully slow, albeit affirmative manner.

"Good," Harper responded. "He is going to ask you a few questions. Please be so kind as to answer them as best you can."

Harry tentatively took Martin's outstretched hand and gave it a firm shake. It was like grabbing a dead fish. He allowed Graff's arm to slip back down to the man's lap.

"Gently, Mr. Porter," Harper advised.

Harry faced the deranged man of science. "Martin? You are kept in a hospital?"

An affirmative nod.

"Why are you kept there?" Harry probed.

Graff's mouth began to flap open and shut, the movements

231

of a slobbering dog or a grazing cow. A hissing sound emerged from his throat. Gradually, short, guttral syllables took shape; catching up with the exaggerated lip movements. "Because . . . because fibly hit mecoldly light . . . light . . . made me not remember what I should to be like used. I sure was, yes."

Harry took the man gently by the hand. "Martin. Dr. Graff. Slow down. Listen to me. I know what you are going through. I know that you can understand everything I say. I know that you are not mad . . . up here," Harry pointed to his own forehead.

"Not mad," Graff repeated, a glimmer of understanding flashing in his eyes.

"My god," Harper muttered, leaning forward in his chair. "He understands."

"Not mad," Graff stated, his eyes slowly focusing on the room around him.

"All this time I thought," Harper stuttered. "My dear Martin . . . you . . . you must forgive me."

Harry turned to the flustered Harper. "That first day I met Dr. Graff, I, of course, made the assumption that he was completely insane. But then I remembered how he phrased his words. There was some sort of inverted logic there. Ill-trained logic. Whatever caused Dr. Graff to enter the hospital has caused a condition not unlike those experienced by individuals who have suffered a stroke. My father was one."

Harry let that train of thought go. "I've had a little experience with it. My guess is that no one up here has bothered to deal with Dr. Graff's condition on a therapeutic level."

Harry faced Martin Graff. "I know that you are whole in there," he said, once again pointing to his head. "I know you can tell me what you feel. But you must tell me slowly. I want to hear every word."

Graff nodded quickly. "Every word, I say will hear but I cannot you . . ."

"Slowly," Harry repeated. "Give the words time to catch up with your lips."

Graff contorted his face into a mask of painful determination. "I can hear my words, up here," he said, alluding to his head. "But can't you . . . cannot you. Speak no more like usedto I killminsilf if . . . could."

"No," Harry said reassuringly. "Now that we know how

you are, Dr. Harper will help. He'll tell the people at the hospital what's wrong."

"That's right, Martin," Harper injected. "I never realized ... I'm sorry."

"Sorry," Graff smiled thinly. "It is ..." His voice trailed off. "Sorry."

"Tell us about the accident," Harry asked. "The accident that made you like this."

Graff focused his eyes on Harry. His mouth moved slowly, forming each syllable carefully. As he spoke, his words alternately accelerated and decelerated, giving his speech pattern a roller-coaster effect. "Accident ... were t'me ... couldn't helppit ... triedbut couldn't getout ... Hit usover ... wantedtoscream ... light ... cannotsee forthelight ... in brain ... feelit ... tasteit ... thinkit ... godhelpus ... god help the children of light."

"Slowly," Harry reminded. "You were hit with something. Where?"

"*Island*. We were in the other tub ... tube. Grouping of us. In glasshouse ... greenhouse. Look out. I looked up. Tubberway. Crashing from above. The shielding parted. Starting at the sky. Satellite breakthrough. Trapped below. Ohgod. Floodlight. Feelit."

Harry interrupted in a clear, calm tone. "Something hit the greenhouse."

"Yes," Graff answered, his breathing slowing down. "Part of a satellite ... towed through space, yanked by a tug out of space shack. The mooring came loose. Satellite part slicked smoothlyslowly through the sky until it hit the shielding above heads ... our heads. The shielding cracked open eggy. We tried to tubbaway, run but couldn't. Greenhouse hit by debris and downwego. All of us trapped there ... exposedtosky. Seemed hourslike to me. I thenafter began to lose gripping on my being. Tried to not to do it. Tried to think but thoughts runaway before mouth catches them. Get smallchunks. Began to seethings. Seethings I knew couldn't be. My insides stayed strong but my outsides just wouldn't stay like used t'be. Slipped down and put away."

Harry stared into the haggard face. A powerful mind trapped in a spasmodic body. The ultimate hell. He attempted to smile at Martin Graff. His jaws never felt heavier. "The others from the greenhouse. Are they all like you?"

"Others?"

"You said there were a group of you in the greenhouse."

Graff licked his lips. "Some die screaming on me. They see no longer. The scream up here," he remarked, rubbing his forehead haltingly with his right fist. "No longer say, just scream. They died. I wishto as well. Sometimes can't want to live."

Graff's body seemed to deflate, sinking lower in the chair. He heaved a long, lonely sigh. "But, with me, live others. Survivors. Some are like me, strong inside, not outside. Others soft in both sides. If I could just find God . . . tell him to turnoff light. Cosmic light."

Harry patted the man on the knee. "Soon, Dr. Graff. The light will soon fade forever."

"Good," Graff grinned weakly. "Should fade. Have to. Living like this . . . horror. The children of light. We are the mutants." He laughed softly to himself. It was a dry, hollow intonation. "Never thought of that. Worried also about outside. And now, we, the brainymen, aremutants."

Harry looked at Graff's sagging features. "It will be all right, doctor."

"No," Graff said sadly. "We mutants are. But, monsters are, too."

"Monsters," Harry asked startled. "Yes, you mentioned monsters."

"Right," Graff said. "Maiden monsters during the slippery crashing. Grew taller than the highest fountain. Still live here. Still here. Bigger than I or you head to foot. Blessings in disguise. Some good comes out of all rotteny."

Harry glanced at Harper. The little man looked bewildered. Neither understood what Graff was alluding to. "There are *monsters* here on *Island*? Physical mutations?" Harry asked.

Graff emitted a sudden, shrill laugh. "Yessiree. Crazy, huh?" He drew his both hands up to his mouth, obviously startled at his own quick and abrasive response. He withdrew his hands slowly as if waiting for a second noise to flow from his lips. When he was convinced that his answer was, indeed, finished, he placed his hands on his lap.

"Where do these monsters live?"

"Home."

"Home?"

"Wherelse?"

Harry shrugged his shoulders. "Where else? Right." He leaned forward and looked Graff directly in the eyes. "Dr.

Graff," he said, "you must help me. You have power in your mind that Dr. Harper and I cannot come close to matching. There is someone aboard the habitat who is trying to harm people. Trying to kill them. He does this in your name. He murders in the name of the children of light."

"Noshit?" Graff chuckled.

"Who is this man, Dr. Graff? Who can he be?"

Graff shook his head from side to side in a terse manner. "Can be ... jackripper ... satan ... whoknows ... allbad. Jussaminute musthink. Sometimes jumbled it all."

Graff's speech began increasing its speed of delivery. "Manyknow. Manyknow us. Who can be. Know not. Try to readminds. Can't. Hell. Can't hardly think on my own. Please don't ask me readminds. Can't findfor you. Willy wish I could. Can't read but can feel. Felt you try to drawme out. Drawmy words, thoughtsout. You try to makeme whole for little bitta time. Thankingyou. Wish I could helpback. First talking to someone since smoothyslidingcrashing. Feelgood."

Harry sighed and pushed back his chair. Graff was silently crying. Harry felt a warm presence on his left cheek. He touched it with his fingertip and found it to be a tear. "Thank you, Dr. Graff," he said. "You have helped me a great deal. Dr. Harper will take you back to the hospital now. I will visit you soon."

Harper struggled out of his chair. He raised Graff to his feet. "Come, Martin, we'll go home now."

Graff remained stationary. "Wrong. Toodle harm is wrong. Will try to help. Dobest. Dobest."

Harry gave an encouraging nod to Graff. He fidgeted in the sofa as the two men left the room. He wanted to lash out at those responsible for that brilliant mind being trapped in that enfeebled body. He wanted to weep for all those trapped in their own private hells. Instead, he walked across the room and made himself a cup of coffee.

He took the coffee black. He needed something to shock his body back into action. Lack of sleep and emotional exhaustion had taken its toll. His body ached with every move. He longed for sleep. He was finishing his coffee when Dr. Harper reentered the apartment. The lift had gone out of the spry little man's step. He looked more his age now. He looked ancient.

"Any problem getting Graff back inside?" Harry asked.

"No, none whatsoever," Harper replied with a casual wave

235

of a hand. His mind was obviously somewhere else. The two men sat in silence for a few moments. Harper was the first to speak. "It's an outrage, Mr. Porter, a total outrage."

As he spoke, the elfin figure clenched his hands into fists over and over again. "If you could have seen him five years ago. He was brilliant. Absolutely brilliant. It's a crime, you know. Just look at what has become of him up here. We, all the citizens of *Island*, are guilty in this crime. We may not have caused his condition, but we have ignored it. We have forgotten his spirit, his essence. That spirit is alive, too. Alive in that ghostlike body. How is it I never saw it? How is it I watched him pass through my life almost daily and never saw what he was, never noticed how he cried out for mental and physical contact? All alone, trapped within himself, calling out for help. And I never saw it. Yet you, you sensed it right away."

Harry brushed aside Harper's self-criticism. "It's no sin to be human, doctor. You missed what was right in front of you, what was commonplace. I saw something strange and picked up on it. That doesn't make me a genius nor you a villain. It just makes us people. Shortsighted . . . as usual."

"I suppose in your own glib way, you're right."

"Enough self-pity. Now that we know Graff's condition, there are a couple of things we have to take care of. First and foremost, you're going to have to stick your nose into things and make sure he gets proper treatment. That's not going to win you any popularity awards with the think tank troupe."

"Don't worry about that," Harper said, clenching his jaw. "I'll make sure that Martin gets the best care possible. Let someone attempt to hinder my attempts and I'll make myself a nuisance physically."

"OK. Now, the next thing we have to work on is how to get me into that hospital."

"Why?"

"Figure it. Martin is a natural peeper. His power was caused, more than likely, from that accident. Our killer is also a peeper. Perhaps he is a victim of the same accident. I have to get inside that hospital and find out where Martin is kept. More than likely, the survivors of that greenhouse accident are kept in the same area. If the killer is there, he'll slip telepathically when he sees me and I'll sense it."

Harper made a sour face. "But Mr. Porter . . ."

"Harry."

Harper crossed his arms belligerently. "Harry, while your

detective instincts are without peer, I feel that your sense of self-preservation is slightly lacking. Should you indeed stumble across the killer within the confines of the hospital and that man's telepathic skills are as raw and as powerful as Martin's, he might do more than merely slip telepathically. He might attempt to kill you."

Harry swallowed hard. "Mentally?"

"Precisely. By concentrating all his efforts on your mental facilities, which are admittedly sensitive to peeper powers, he might, quite literally, cause a rupturing in your cranal area. Telepathic power is quite a young science as of yet. We are not quite sure of all of its physical manifestations. It could, indeed, be used lethally if honed properly . . . or, rather, improperly."

"You mean, the killer could cause me to have a stroke."

"Or something similar in nature. It's entirely possible."

Harry folded his hands on his knees. "Well, what the hell. If I don't take the chance, I very well might wind up dead in a day and a half anyway."

"Spoken like a true fool," Harper said with admiration.

"Fine. Then, it's to the hospital."

"They're not just going to let you stroll in there as if you were part of the bus tour," Harper pointed out.

"Oh, I know that," Harry grinned. "That's where you come in."

Harper squinted his eyes warily. "What role can I possibly play in this scheme of yours?"

Harry left his chair and roamed across the apartment. He spied a heavy frying pan in the corner of the kitchenette. Some sort of space alloy. Lighter than iron. Still, with enough momentum behind it, it could generate a pretty good-sized wallop. He picked up the pan from its resting place, walked across the apartment and handed it to Harper. "I'm not going to the hospital as part of a tour group," he said. "I'm going there as a patient. Here. Give me a good shot on the back of the head."

The little man was horrified. "My dear Harry, don't be absurd. It's out of the question! Do you really expect me to resort to barbarism simply to allow you to conduct some half-cocked experiment in masochistic deductive reasoning?"

Harry held out the pan. "I do have my heart set on it."

"Well, I won't do it!"

Harry shoved the pan into the old man's hands. "Let's cut the crap. In a couple of days, there'll be thirteen corpses

237

littering this habitat. One good crack on the skull could help stop that. Now, when you call the hospital, tell them that I've had an accident; tripped over a chair or something."

"Why don't you just trip over a chair yourself?"

"Because I want a bump on the head, not a broken goddamn leg . . . now will you just slug me?"

Harper held onto the frying pan as if it was a diseased reptile. Harry knelt down before the elderly man like a knight awaiting to be rewarded by his kind. Harper raised himself to his full height. He lifted the frying pan high above his head and brought it down with a sudden "clang." Harry clenched his teeth, closed his eyes, absorbed the echoing blow, and remained in kneeling position. Pain shot through the back of his neck and down his spine.

Harper pulled the pan back and held it to his chest, blinking. Harry looked up, annoyed. "What the hell do you call that?"

"Well, I'm really not in the habit of doing this sort of thing."

"Come on, now," Harry groused. "That swat wouldn't have put out a light."

"If you're asking me to repeat my performance I'm afraid that I simply won't."

"Come on, you pot-bellied old coot, put some muscle into it."

Slightly annoyed by Harry's outburst, Harper raised the heavy pan a second time. This time, he sent it slicing down onto the back of Harry's head with a solid "thud."

Harry fell to the floor with a contented groan. Blood began to dribble from beneath his hairline. "I knew you could do it," he wheezed. "Now call the hospital."

Harper ran to the phone. "Oh dear. Violence has come into my life." Dialing the hospital extension, he alerted the emergency squad. "Come quickly. One of the Earth delegates has had an accident. It looks serious."

"It *feels* serious," Harry said, holding his bleeding head. "Were you ever a professional baseball player?"

3

Within minutes Harry was ushered via a four-wheeled ambulance to the hospital. His priority rank as a visiting delegate from Earth assured him the finest of care. Hence, for a second time, he was brought face to face with the dour Dr. Estelle Jerrow. The stoop-shouldered administrator still wore that nonchalant grin so often associated with vultures.

"We meet again, Mr. Porter," the blue-haired woman smirked. "You just can't seem to keep yourself out of trouble, can you?"

The doctor's fingers probed the back of Harry's head harshly. "I guess I'm just a hyperactive hypochondriac. Ouch! That's not a melon you're squeezing there."

Harry's body twitched on the emergency cot. The doctor, clad in a traditional white jumpsuit, looked down upon him with obvious distaste. "If it was, I would change my diet. As usual, Mr. Porter, you are in nowhere near as bad shape as you would probably desire. The wound is quite superficial. It will close itself without the aid of any stitches. Your X rays show no concussion, nor fracture of any kind. In short, you have sustained a rather nasty bump on the head. The type of wound that any child would have been given a lollipop and dismissed for."

"Gee. It sounds so reassuring coming from you," Harry said, sitting up. "What flavor lollipops you got here?"

"Please don't be a goldbrick, Mr. Porter."

"But my head hurts!"

"Suffering is good for the soul."

"Is that the kind of stuff that's in your Hippocratic oath?"

Jerrow reacted sourly. "My dear Mr. Porter, in some circles I assume your humor is regarded as quite the rage. Up here, however, it is simply a tedious time waster. I am a very busy individual and you have just robbed me of approximately four and a half minutes of my time."

"But who's counting?"

Jerrow left Harry on the cot. A male orderly applied an

adhesive bandage to the back of his head. Harry got to his feet. "I can find my way out, thanks," he said, shaking the young man's hand.

Outside the emergency room, Harry veered left, turning his back on the exit. He began to walk deeper into the building. The hospital hallways, like those of Earth, were appropriately sterile, metallic blue in color. Sauntering through the corridors, he aroused no more than casual interest from the hospital staff. Seeing the bandage on the back of his head, they assumed he was either on his way from or to a doctor's office. After a few moments of walking, he found himself in a nearly deserted section of the building. The small hallway before him led to a single doorway. He felt a slight twinge in his head. It could have been from the wound, but he didn't think so.

He cautiously walked toward the door, a swinging portal with a single, round window in its center. He gazed through the windowpane. Inside, in the low light provided by a single ceiling fixture, a dozen beds were lined in a small room, six on each side. The beds were occupied by dozing patients. He pushed open the door gently. He stepped inside the room. It smelled of death and decay, possessing that perceptible, yet ambiguous morbidity associated with the workroom of a mortuary.

The figures in the beds didn't stir. At the far end of the room, Harry spotted Martin Graff. The fellow was apparently heavily sedated, his heavy lids struggling in vain against drug-induced sleep. Harry walked softly to Graff's bed and placed a hand on the man's arm. "Dr. Graff? It's me. Harry Porter."

Graff sat straight up in a spasmodic lurch. It was as if a button at the base of his spine had suddenly been activated. "God! God!" he bellowed. "The light! The light! Slippery crashing into my eyes. Out it! Turn out it!"

Graff's emotional discharge was mental as well as verbal. His pain slammed into Harry with the force of a tidal wave. Harry staggered backward, clutching his head with two hands. "Dr. Graff! It's me, Harry! Stop it, please!"

Graff, his eyes wide with horror, continued to screech at the top of his lungs. Harry continued to reel. His eyes watered. His temple throbbed. His entire body felt as if it was wracked with a sudden fever. Eyes squinted under the force of Graff's torrent of emotion, he dimly caught sight of a frightening phenomenon. One by one, the other patients in the ward set bolt upright as well. They began to scream; each subsequent mental surge of anguish hammered into Harry's forehead like a molten fist. Harry watched the howling men helplessly. Their faces were haggard, drawn, nearly void of all life. Yet each possessed the shadows of their former lives; faint traces of high intelligence, learning, refinement. Their civilized visages now propelled by the memory of stark terror and the reality of continuous suffering, they drooled, screeched, and babbled into the stoic walls around them. Harry desperately attempted to appeal to the traces of the men they once were through Martin Graff.

"Martin, it's Harry. We talked before! We reasoned before! Martin, I know you're in there, listening. Come out of it, Martin!"

Graff's screaming continued, his intelligent side subverted by the sedative. His emotional, illogical self was clearly in control and it was now, quite literally, squashing the life out of Harry Porter. Harry tumbled back into a wall. He attempted to remain upright. His vision began to blur. Bursts of color appeared in his mind's eye. The room began to slowly dissolve in a shroud of deep purple. He slid down the wall to the floor. "The light! The light!" the men chattered. "Out! Out it!"

Harry sagged under the mantra of pain.

He was just about to explode from the pressure when, as quickly as it had started, the shouting in the room ceased. Bowed in fetal position on the floor, Harry slowly opened his eyes. He took his hands from his ears and stared at the doorway. There, staring wild eyed in the entrance, was Dr. Estelle Jerrow. The doctor glared at Harry. Porter, experiencing a wave of genuine shame, averted his eyes. Jerrow's face was ashen, taut, and hard. Harry had never seen this side of the doctor. Posture straight, shoulders flung back in rage, the stoop-shouldered bird of prey was now a grandiose eagle of a woman. Tall. Angry. In command. Jerrow stared at each one of her patients. They slid back down into their beds, turning their faces away from her demonic gaze. Jerrow was unyielding. She walked defiantly among them, peering at each patient individually. She walked to Harry in silence. Extending a bony hand, she yanked the shaken reporter to his feet. "Of all the impudent . . ." she hissed between barely moving lips.

"I can explain," Harry offered, his head still swimming.

With one of Jerrow's hands supporting him from behind the shoulder, Harry stumbled out of the room. The woman tossed him into a chair outside. "I should have known that, somehow, you'd be responsible for this disturbance."

"I'm sorry," Harry muttered, rubbing his head.

"As well you should be. These men require constant sedation. Have you any idea what you could have done?"

Harry shook his head clear of the mental reverberations unleashed moments before. "Why do you keep them sedated? They're capable of so much. At least Martin Graff is. I talked with him this afternoon."

Jerrow's expression softened slightly. She sat down in a waiting room chair across from Harry. "Without sedation that ward is a telepathic time bomb just waiting to go off."

"But Graff . . ."

"One of the saner ones. Did he tell you . . ."

"About the accident? Yeah."

Jerrow remained passive. "In that room, you have eleven of the finest minds ever to grace this habitat . . . all prematurely destroyed."

"But," Harry countered. "They're not destroyed. At least Graff isn't. With proper care . . ."

"Proper care?" the doctor snorted. "And who's to give them such care? You saw what kind of power they possess! How many people do you think could withstand that type of telepathic power? I don't have anyone up here who can deal with it. I need parapsychiatrists up here to treat these men properly. They need therapy."

"Then why not put in a requisition?"

Jerrow smirked at Harry's innocence. "Do you think I haven't tried? Do you think I don't ache to see those men bedridden like that? They were all my friends, my colleagues. I've tried to help them. But I'm not allowed to enlist the proper medical personnel up here because it would arouse suspicion on Earth! 'What do they need PSI therapists for?' I'm not allowed to send them down to Earth for treatment, either. Our governor would then have to acknowledge the fact that here has been an accident. So, all I can do is keep them sedated."

"It's inhuman," Harry mumbled.

"Indeed," Jerrow spat. "But we must keep the facade up, mustn't we? The good citizens of *Island* know nothing of this, of course. As a matter of fact, very few of the doctors and orderlies employed here are even aware of the contents of this ward. It is not only inhuman, Mr. Porter, it is a crime. A crime against these men and a crime against the dignity and

242

sense of justice of all men. These poor unfortunates, these offsprings of light are representatives of all those who have suffered on this habitat."

"All those?"

Jerrow rubbed her eyes. "I'm sorry if I sound harsh, if my manner is brusque. But you see, I've watched these men disintegrate. I've watched two of them die screaming. Thirteen men were trapped under that rubble that day. One moment they were standing there, preparing to praise the glory of the habitat. The next moment they were trapped beneath an avalanche of debris, their bodies twisted into totally unreal shapes, their brains bombarded by a flood of cosmic radiation. I couldn't help them. I tried, but I couldn't remove them in time."

"You?"

"Yes," Jerrow nodded sadly. "I was there to pull them out of the wreckage."

"And you've cared for them ever since?"

"Yes. And I suppose I feel rather guilty for not residing in one of those beds myself. By all rights, I should be on the other side of this door. But I was running behind in my appointments that day and I arrived just a few minutes too late. My tardiness saved my life, in one sense, and ruined it, in another. Such is the way of God."

"God?"

Jerrow looked up with a faint smile. "Yes, God, Mr. Porter. You do believe in God, don't you? Some god? Any god?"

"I-I suppose so," Harry replied, "subconsciously."

Jerrow relaxed a little. "Fine. Fine. Yes, a man in your position would have to have a very strong faith to survive. Faith. An admirable trait. Faith used to be one of the foundations of a man's existence. In those days, a man's life had meaning. It had purpose. It had romance. Today, traditional values wither within the confines of a permissive society."

"I never would have taken you for an old-fashioned philosopher."

"Being human can never be old-fashioned, Porter. It can, however, lose its footing to dozens of fads. Look around you. People today have lost their faith both in themselves and in their creator. They worship newness, they worship progress, no matter in what direction it may lead them. They have no concept of love. They have no concept of justice. They never consider the fact that all of their actions are being observed by an omnipotent force and will be rewarded or punished accordingly on the day of reckoning."

"But it's always been like that," Harry offered. "I mean, religion and technology, progress, have never exactly gone hand in hand."

"More's the pity. Today, more than ever, they *need* to coexist. We need a renaissance of faith, Mr. Porter, not to replace technology, not to subvert it, but to enhance it. God is timeless. We must unite the old with the new. Bring the old gods back to life, give humanity a sense of faith and fair play and you just watch what progress will arise from the union . . . meaningful progress, not merely aimless movement."

"You've thought about this a long while, haven't you?"

"Oh yes. In my own small way, I've tried to promote this concept in all of my endeavors." She ran a gnarled hand through her ice-blue hair. "I've had to promote faith, you see. I've had to rely on my belief in something *better* in order to deal with the tragedy which surrounds me on a day-to-day basis. Such tragedy. Such waste."

Harry stared at the closed door. "Could any of these patients escape their confinement?"

"It's not likely, but it's possible. Martin, for instance, takes a stroll nearly every day. It's almost part of his exercise program at this point. He thinks of a new way to slip by us daily. He always was quite the sly one," Jerrow added with a slight grin. "What a mind."

"And the others . . . could they escape and return unnoticed?"

"It's doubtful . . . why?"

"Curiosity . . . I guess."

Harry stood to leave. Jerrow grabbed him by the elbow, pulling him down to her still sitting frame. "Are you going to write about all this?"

Harry couldn't decipher the look in her ancient eyes. "I don't know, honestly. Do you think that I should?"

"It would be the best thing you could do in order to save these men! It would end their five years of solitude. Reveal their circumstance and you would set them free!"

Surprised by Jerrow's liberal response, Harry fumbled for a reply. "B-but, well, I wonder. If you draw attention to them and bring them back to Earth, they might be treated like space-bred freaks. You could have every scientific community in the States crawling all over them."

Jerrow's face fell. "Yes, you might be right. I hadn't thought about that. Compassion, justice, those were the old ways, weren't they? Well, still, the people should know the truth, I suppose."

The doctor's hand slid off Harry's arm. Harry walked toward the hospital exit. "As soon as I figure out what the truth is, doctor, I'll let you know."

Jerrow leaned forward in her chair and watched Harry walk down the hallway. "Keep the faith, Mr. Porter."

4

"Oh, come on now, Hawkins. What do you take me for, a sap?" Harry turned his eyes heavenward. "You never heard about any of this?"

"Never," Hawkins said, running a stubby hand through his long, stringy hair. "I can't believe it."

"Believe it," Harry sat on the park bench between Hawkins and Sylvie. "Thirteen men permanently disabled because of an unpublicized accident. Thirteen people about to be executed publicly in retaliation. How's that for significance?"

Dozens of preprogrammed Islanders walked by the commuter park, all smiling at Harry as they passed. "I wish they'd knock that off," Harry grumbled, smiling back. "This set-up is beginning to strain my facial muscles."

"Do you have any idea who this Emmett character could be?" Hawkins said.

"Sure," Harry nodded. "Anybody. Anybody who knew about the accident or anybody involved in it. I need more time to get a positive ID."

"Time's the one thing you don't have." Hawkins cracked his knuckles carefully. "It's like tap dancing on dynamite."

"Another day and a half and it will all be over," Sylvie said optimistically.

"One way or the other," Harry grunted. It was at times like

245

these that he wondered if *Island* was worth all the trouble he was going through. He could just blow the whistle on the governor, get the place shut down, and save a whole lot of lives quite easily. But he had only to look at Sylvie's concerned face and Hawkins's sagging pockmarks to know that he couldn't betray their cause. Well, what the hell, maybe he could sell the movie rights to the whole mess for a cool million later on. He'd do the best he could.

"Do you really think that Emmett could be one of those men in the hospital?" Sylvie asked.

"It's possible. If he is, he's a lot more cunning than I had thought. This killer is a self-taught peeper. He releases his mental energy in short, sporadic bursts. I didn't think he could control his power. If he is one of those men then, apparently, he's mastered his art quite well. None of those patients revealed themselves to me telepathically."

"Then we're really no closer to stopping this lunatic than we were three days ago." Hawkins stared at his reddened knuckles.

Harry tapped his foot impatiently on the grass. "No. I think we're right on top of him. We're just too stupid to notice."

He glanced at Sylvie. "How did your hunting go?"

She pulled a small list out of her handbag. "Here you are, general. Every *Island* citizen known to have had some contact with parapsychological classes."

Harry took the slip of paper in his hand. There were over a hundred names there. He scanned the list for any familiar monikers. Unfortunately, there were too many of them. Russell Vallory, presently governor of *Island One*. Dr. Harper. Harley Thornton. Jerrow. Hawkins. "Jeez," he hissed. "It looks like everyone in a position of authority up here has had a brush with the paranormal."

"Popular stuff," Hawkins shrugged. "Policemen take at least one course in it these days. In some of the larger cities on Earth, where the parapsych education centers are located, crimes involving peepers-gone-astray have been on the increase. Cops have to know how to deal with it."

"Great," Harry said from between clenched teeth. Using this list as a possible key to Emmett's identity, he had just narrowed the field down to include most of the society page of the local newspaper and the entire police force. Great detective work. Harry folded the paper in an exaggerated motion of decorum and jammed it into his hip pocket.

"How'd you like to be a working tour guide again?" he asked Sylvie.

"I was just beginning to enjoy my job as bookworm."

"How much time do we have before the next meeting of the Earth delegation?"

"An hour. Everyone was taking a tour of the space shacks this morning."

"Great. That should give us enough time."

"For what?"

"To take a couple of pedal planes into the agriculture cylinder."

"Why the sudden interest in farming?"

Harry walked away from the bench. "I've always been a country boy at heart. Also, there's the little matter of a ruptured piece of shielding in there."

Sylvie gave a "I can't figure him out, can you?" look to Hawkins. Hawkins merely grunted and shook his head from side to side in mock sadness. Sylvie shrugged and trotted off after Harry. "So what?"

"So I want to see exactly where this accident occurred." Harry glanced at her inquisitive face. As much as he wanted to trust her completely, he knew he couldn't. It was too late. He'd have to play the game out himself. "Don't ask me why," he added. "I'm not sure myself. But maybe just being there will jell something in my head. Shake some piece of logic loose that I'm aware of but haven't deciphered yet."

"There are too many things in your head that have already been shaken loose."

Harry walked on in silence, pondering the reasoning behind keeping the shielding fiasco secret. As cockeyed as *Island*'s governmental policies had struck him as being thus far, there was something sensible about them. The areas of *Island* life it had hidden, had been hidden from Earth's populace for purely political reasons. Why would anyone want to hide an accident from *Island*'s populace? They were supposedly a very dedicated bunch. The accident had nothing to do with Earth and its influence on the hab's future. The accident only had to do with the colony's immediate lifestyle, its safety. Harry wanted to see the accident site. Whatever Emmett's gripe was, it probably had a lot more substance to it than anyone expected.

Sylvie took Harry via electric cart to one of the ends of the cylinder. They boarded a small, enclosed ski-lift device which took them from one tubular ecosystem to the next. Disembarking at the agricylinder's docking station, they quickly boarded two pedal planes and soared off.

Harry adjusted to the light gravity quickly this time. He managed to maneuver his pedal plane through the sky without losing either his breath or his shoes. Gliding through the air, he was amazed at the differences between the two halves of the colony. The agricylinder was, like its sister tube, divided into three sections of artificial turf. These new land masses below, however, were untarnished by the presence of buildings and any overt signs of civilization. The agricylinder's land strips were green, lush, almost tropical in appearance. A single roadway ran along each land mass and only a few workers could be discerned below. The tube was a veritable garden of Eden.

Pedaling easily, Harry noted that the greenery below was dotted by occasional greenhouses, gigantic in design. Overwhelmed by a latent sense of professionalism, Sylvie began to explain the inner workings of the agricylinder in her staunchest, tour guide voice. "All our vegetables and grain are grown in the farmlands below," she stated. "There are a few livestock regions tucked away down there as well. Originally, the plans for the colony called for cows and pigs to be shipped up as a source of meat. We settled for chickens, however. They're smaller and easier to manage. You might be able to make out herds of goats as well. We keep them for our dairy products."

Harry peered down at the hillsides below. Indeed, he could see a few goats grazing under the watchful gaze of an orange tunic-clad shepherd. The irony of this pastoral portrait in the midst of wall-to-wall hardware did not escape him. "What are the greenhouses for?" he asked, pointing a finger to one of the large, domed structures below.

"That's where our fruit is nurtured," she replied. "Much of our fruit is tropical in nature, sunbelt items. By controlling the temperature and the sunlight inside those buildings, we can duplicate the climate of nearly every geographical region on the face of the Earth."

"And you can therefore duplicate their natural resources as well, eh?"

"Right. Some of the greenhouses are used by our agriculturists for experimental purposes as well."

"What kind of experiments do they work on?"

"I don't know, really," Sylvie said, tilting her glider toward another strip of land. "I guess they work on crossbreeding and things like that."

Harry angled his plane, following her lead. "All right, now. We're both going to have to pay attention. We don't have all that much time to pinpoint the exact spot."

"What are we looking for, anyway?"

"Any irregularity in the cylinder's outer surface. It should be a pretty big patching job from what Graff told me."

"His story might not even be true," Sylvie said. "He's crazy."

"So's an entire hospital ward. Just look for the scar."

The two planes swooped low over the land mass. Harry knew he was looking for the space equivalent of a needle in a haystack. Gliding above the greenery, he and Sylvie were also gliding above the three strips of paneled shielding. From the air, there was no way to observe the shield as closely as he would have liked. Trying to zero in on the individual panels required the utmost concentration. Harry was constantly plagued by a feeling of total disorientation. From the air, *everything* was below you. Pedaling across the sky, there was no top nor bottom to the cylinder. It was like observing the inner surface of a round doughnut from the middle of the hole. Which direction was up and which direction was down?

There was really no way for Harry to land on the shielding's surface, either. From the air, it was totally impossible. From the land, it was also quite a feat. None of the shuttle carts or walkways extended across the paneled shielding strips. There was no real reason for them to. Only maintenance crews, wearing special suits and outfitted with adhesive shoes designed for traveling across the slick surface, were allowed on the shielding. All Harry could hope to do from the air was spot the ancient wound and try to calculate where the most resulting damage was done on "ground" level.

After buzzing two out of the three land masses and adjoining paneled strips, Harry and Sylvie moved on to their last target area. "There," Harry suddenly pointed. "Look down there."

Sylvie spotted the break immediately. Four entire panels of the shielding had been replaced, an area some forty feet in diameter. The tint of the new panels was a slightly different hue than the rest of the surrounding squares.

Harry tried to imagine how the violent, unexpected event must have looked from all the three strips of land. On the two strips of land flanking the shielding, the crash must have resembled a stainless steel volcano erupting. A massive piece of machinery exploding upward from a swath of see-through sea. The satellite wing, pushing higher and higher from the "ground," sending chunks of glass and glimmering matter shooting upward. Harry banked his pedal plane and turned his imagination to the remaining land mass, the strip of greenery directly opposite the ruptured section of shielding. Or, from its inhabitants' viewpoint, directly below the crash site.

The satellite fragment must have whipped through the paneling with incredible force. Harry tried to envision the scene from the point of view of the trapped scientists. A deafening crash must have filled the air; both the hunk of steel and the panel particles tumbling down toward the center of the cylinder's sky—the zero strip. Perhaps the zero g sector slowed down the smaller fragments momentarily. Indeed, perhaps, the small chunks of debris came to a complete halt. For the men trapped below, this avalanche must have appeared surreal. The debris, passing through the zero g strip, might have appeared to dance a grim ballet of impending doom.

Maybe a wave of the small chunks hovered in the sky momentarily before regaining momentum and slamming into the greenhouse below. And the satellite section, the monster in search of a resting spot, might never have appeared to slow down. It probably just fell like a stone, plowing into the thirteen scientists caught in its path.

Harry swooped lower and lower, attempting to follow the path of the debris. As the gravitational pull increased the nearer he got to the ground, the harder he had to pedal. His efforts were worth it. At what he imagined to be the impact point, he discovered a greenhouse. It was the biggest greenhouse of the agricylinder. He calculated it to be some three city blocks in circumference. Much of its domed shape was covered by vines and deceptively "natural" greenery. Harry buzzed the building and noted that it was under the protection of several uniformed guards of an exceedingly armed nature. He pedaled furiously in an effort to regain altitude. He nosed his way up toward the center of the sky. Sylvie pedaled alongside. "Find what you were looking for?"

"I think so," he said. He knew he had to talk to Harper again . . . and Graff . . . and Jerrow. But first, he had to waste time and play reporter.

5

Howard Retson sat at the conference table, proudly caressing a small sliver of paper, when Harry and Sylvie strolled into the room. The fish-eyed Stramm sat at his mentor's right hand, attempting to summon up an equal amount of rapture on his face. His efforts produced a look closer to kidney disease than ecstasy. "Good news?" Harry asked, sauntering by.

Retson immediately assumed a poker player's stance. "Hmmm, well, yes, in fact," he admitted. He pointed to the paper and asked in a conspiratorial tone. "Do you know anything about art, Pauper?"

"I had a painted turtle when I was a kid."

"Well," Retson said, gazing lovingly at the paper. "Kingdoms, Inc. has just purchased the entire treasure of King Tutankhamen from the Egyptian government."

Harry took a seat across from the industrialist. "What made them sell?"

"The government is going bankrupt," Retson replied. "Religious warfare, financial chaos, the usual sort of Middle East nonsense." His eyes took an added sparkle. "But do you have any idea of what this means? Why, Kingdoms can roadshow the entire treasure all over the world! Every major city! Rome! Paris! Madrid! Peking! Moscow! Cincinnati!"

"Cincinnati?"

Stramm peered over Retson's shoulder. "Mr. Retson was born in Cincinnati."

Harry leaned back in his chair. "How fortunate for St. Louis."

The room began to fill. Harry prepared for yet another long-winded bull session between the Earth delegation and the Islanders. So far, the habitat was holding up under the pressure imposed by Earth politics, but Harry saw that defiance as being short lived. With all the members present, Governor Vallory called the meeting to order. Harry immediately began to draw doodles of rocketships and big breasted

251

female nudes on his note pad. Sylvie, noticing his sudden artistic flair, took her pencil and, leaving the rocketships intact, concentrated her efforts on the nudes; drawing large and cumbersome brassieres on the women. Harry sketched more women. Sylvie drew more brassieres. Ten minutes into the meeting, they were engaged in a marathon tic-tac-toe session. Harry wondered if they had gotten married whether they would have spent countless evenings at home doing this sort of thing. It would have saved on theater tickets, anyhow.

Harry was barely taking notice of the meeting. Vallory was being attacked from all sides. Curtis, the president's main flunkie, stuck to his hard-line political liability shtick. Congressman Ferron insisted that the colony represented an aberration in the human condition. NASA's Ryan Frantz attempted to get a few positive points across but didn't have the necessary mania needed for such an effort. Harry glanced up from his notebook from time to time to catch the reactions of the various delegates. Finding them to be quite predictable, he concentrated on the note pad, not wanting to give Sylvie the chance to cheat. The entire quagmire was videotaped by Harry's favorite moron, Tony Safian, whose chin was still very dimpled.

After some sixty minutes of tedium, the proceedings lapsed into verbal coma. The delegates sputtered and fumed but made less and less sense. It took Howard Retson to bring a sense of animation to the stagnant encounter. "Gentlemen," he stated, exhibiting a wonderful example of perfect posture from his chair. "I believe I have come up with an ideal solution for *Island's* present woes."

Harry lost the sixtieth game in a row. He put his pencil down and concentrated on the meeting. "Sore loser," Sylvie admonished.

"I am not."

"You are too."

Retson gazed solemnly at the mildly interested faces around the table with a beatific look on his face known only to popes and Jewish mothers. Harry yanked the pencil out of Sylvie's hand. "Am not."

Retson cleared his throat. "It's quite simple, really. All you have to do is turn a liability into a viable commercial reality."

"Quite simple, really," Stramm echoed.

Retson chose, as usual, to ignore his gangly assistant. "The

252

people of Earth resent *Island* because they just don't know enough about it, correct? They have been fed your Utopian line of PR for a solid decade now and they feel that the colony is just too far removed from their day-to-day existence. Your lifestyles seem to be worlds apart. Why, they don't even remember that you people are flesh and blood, ordinary humans, just like they are. You might as well be Martians as far as they are concerned."

A thin smile played across the dapper businessman's reptilian lips. "In order to win back their attention and encourage their devotion, you must enter their lives on a less grandiose scale. And, for your own benefit, in order to continue working and expanding in space, the habitat must begin to make money . . . quite a bit of money. I believe that I, on behalf of Kingdoms, Inc., can show you a way to do both."

The room remained silent. Retson got to his feet, drew himself to his full six foot two height and, silver hair gleaming in the reflected sunlight streaming in through the room's window, began to circle the table, thus attracting the attention of all involved. "I believe, gentlemen, that the answer lies in *franchises*."

"Franchises?" Vallory repeated, pronouncing the word like the name of a social disease.

"Franchises," Retson repeated cheerfully. "Commercialization. I propose that Kingdoms, Inc. pay *Island* for the right to offer a series of franchises to the colonists themselves. Think of it, gentlemen, modernization, urbanization will come to the habitat!"

Stramm, still seated at the table, appeared to be getting misty eyed at the very thought. "Urbanization," he sighed. Harry chalked it up to a religious experience.

Retson placed his hands on a portion of the table and leaned into the inner circle of delegates. "King Kone ice cream parlors dotting the countryside. King Kastle Burger Kastles. King Kakes in every supermarket and Kingdom Kola at every soda fountain. And if there aren't any soda fountains, then by God, we'll *build* soda fountains!"

Vallory's copper skin reddened slightly. "While your intentions are laudable, Mr. Retson, I don't see how this proposed influx of junk food . . ."

"Fast food," corrected Retson, slightly annoyed.

"Fast food," Vallory amended. "I don't see how this will help *Island* at all. And, in terms of profit for Kingdoms, our

253

population is too small for you to realize much money up here."

"I didn't think you *would* catch on," Retson said smugly. "But a business mentality would see the point immediately. In return for our franchises being allowed to bring goods up to the colony, we would ask for an agreement from the habitat, a tacit endorsement agreement. In short, we would want *Island,* as a single unit, to endorse any and all Kingdoms, Inc. products present on the colony. The community, in effect, would give us a stamp of approval.

"We would then bring up our TV crews and film a series of commercials touting our products using the habitat itself as a backdrop. Think of it, governor. Your colony would get more favorable publicity in ten days than you have garnered in ten years! Hundreds of beautiful, artistically breathtaking commercials filmed aboard this luxurious craft being shown daily in billions of homes across the nation, nay, across the world! *Island* would no longer be seen as a cold, unknown, alien terrain. Its presence would be linked irrevocably to some of Earth's most beloved and best known fast food products. People would welcome *Island*'s presence in their homes, much in the same way as they do King Kola now. You would become a household commodity."

Retson returned to his seat, obviously pleased with his grand eloquence. The room sizzled with excitement. Various delegates whispered to each other in cautious bursts of approval. Harry tapped his pencil on the desk. It would seem that *Island* had just been saved. Debased, but saved nonetheless. He could sense trouble brewing, however. A hardboiled idealist like Vallory would never swallow such a cheapshot. Harry turned to the head of the table. Much to his surprise, Vallory was grinning like the proverbial Cheshire cat.

The former astronaut clasped his hands behind his head and tipped back his chair in a folksy manner. "All in all," he sighed, "I'd say your plan was excellent, Mr. Retson. It's very well thought out and, indeed, a sound one from both a financial and a public relations point of view. I believe that everyone in this room would agree to that."

Both the Earth delegates and the Islanders grunted in affirmation. "However," he continued, "what I frown upon in the connection between *Island* and the Kingdoms line of *junk* food. No offense intended, but Kingdoms products are infa-

254

mous for their great abundance of calories and their total
lack of nutritional value."

Retson glared angrily at the governor. Stramm fluttered his
eyelids so much that Harry was worried the aide would start
to hover above his chair. "But," Vallory stated, "your suggestion does bring to mind a plan I was going to introduce at
tomorrow's meeting, at the eleventh hour as it were. I agree
with all of Mr. Retson's basic points, gentlemen. *Island* does
need to make a favorable impression on Earth. But I don't
believe it has to be via a partnership with Kingdoms, Inc."

Vallory pressed an intercom button on a panel next to his
chair. "Melissa, take the refreshments out of the fridge, will
you please. Yes, you can bring them in."

In a moment or two, a young woman and a young man
entered the room, wheeling a tray before them. The tray
contained a pitcher of the blue fruit drink that intrigued
Harry so, as well as a platter filled with blue pieces of cake.
The refreshments were distributed to those assembled. Vallory encouraged the puzzled gathering to nibble and sip
freely. "Now," he explained, "you've all seen our Harmony
juice before and I'm sure you'll agree with me when I say it's
quite delicious. And that cake you're eating is equally tasty.
My suggestion is this: if we are going to try for a big
impression Earthside with a mass appeal marketing campaign, why not design a campaign related to products indigenous to *Island?* What you have before you are examples of
home grown *Island* foodstuffs; both created by a new strain
of fruit grown exclusively aboard the habitat. It's tasty, with
enough natural sweetness to give it both a soft drink and a
dessert appeal. An added plus is that it contains a horde of
essential vitamins and minerals."

A look of horror spread across the poker face of Howard
Retson. "You mean to tell me that this stuff is actually *good*
for you?"

"Afraid so," Vallory replied with a chuckle. "Now, what I
propose is this: why not allow *Island* to make a profit
Earthside entirely on its *own,* devoid of any ties to Earthbound industry and products. Think of it, Mr. Curtis. Think
of the benefits *Island* exports could bring to the sagging
economy!"

The blind, banana-nosed Curtis studied Vallory's words
carefully, turning them over in his mind. Harry nearly returned to tic-tac-toe-ing. Finally, the Earth politician spoke.

255

"There *are* possibilities to such a plan," he admitted. "If *Island* could export these goods to the United States and turn a profit, then the government wouldn't have to subsidize the habitat financially at all."

"Think of it, Curtis. The habitat could become totally self-sufficient! We'd export our food to the States. The U.S., in turn, could sell the goods to foreign countries at a mark-up."

"We could actually realize a profit in trade." Curtis said.

"Certainly," Vallory agreed, "and our gearing up for mass production would cause an economic snowball effect. Independent advertising, marketing, and distribution companies would get involved, too. We'd give the economy a pretty big shot in the arm, job-wise. Plus, we could sign a profit with a U.S. subsidized space freighter outfit and create a regular *Island*-Earth run, thus increasing the need for available ships."

"Which means an increase in construction," Curtis injected.

"*Island* could even sell franchises on Earth to small businessmen who want to get in on the ground floor, so to speak. Now, while we're making strides in this area, the work on the power satellites would continue. We could construct enough to fulfill America's needs and then sell the excess satellites to other nations. The U.S. would benefit financially since, in reality, our space shacks are government owned and operated factories."

"Talk about monopolies," Retson whispered angrily.

For the first time since his arrival, Harry watched a grin appear on Archibald Curtis's face. "You know, governor, your plan does have possibilities. Merchandizing *Island* products could both improve your image and help the president better his. If you can't bring the people to paradise, bring paradise to the people. I'm very impressed."

"Well, I'm not," Retson blurted, his composure crumbling at an accelerated rate. "It's preposterous. Why, your products would be dead on arrival. As far as marketing is concerned, you people are babes in the woods. You'd be up against some of the Earth's real heavyweights in the fast food line."

"Granted," Vallory replied. "But think of the exotic appeal of the *Island* line. The American public has always been willing to try something new. Now we have the opportunity to give them a taste sensation that is, literally, out of this world!"

The room erupted in laughter. Retson stormed out of the room. Ira slithered out seconds later. The meeting adjourned until the following day. Following the formal closing of the gathering, the attendees lingered in the room, launching a wave of handshaking and back-slapping. Vallory seemed elated. So did Frantz. Even Curtis and Ferron seemed pleased with themselves. Sylvie was overjoyed. Harry was skeptical of the whole affair. He was confident that there'd be a monkey wrench tossed into the machinery of joy somewhere down the line. That wrench just might come in the form of Emmett.

"What's bothering you, now?" Sylvie asked, picking up her notebook and pencil from the table.

"I suppose I just can't absorb the fact that I've just seen the tide of war hang a quick 180 degrees." Harry picked up his pad and headed for the door.

"It happens," Sylvie stated.

"I wonder. I keep on listening for the other shoe to fall."

"You almost sound eager for that to happen."

At the door, Harry was handed a note from one of the guards. "This came for you during the meeting, sir."

"Thanks." Harry slit the envelope open with his left index-finger nail. The handwriting on the letter was familiar. A small chuckle emerged from his throat.

"Is that your other shoe?" Sylvie asked.

"Let's just call it a sock."

"Emmett?"

He showed the note to Sylvie.

Dear Mr. Porter

Despite your persistent refusal to right the wrongs of this habitat, I sense that you are a fair and just individual. I will cease my reign of terror for exactly one day: twenty-four hours. You must act in that time period, however. Communicate with your peers on Earth. Expose *Island* as the hell it is. If you do not perform this function, the condemned will die before the celebration can begin. You will be the first to be executed. Until our next meeting,

Ammit.

Sylvie shuddered, returning the note to Harry. "Not exactly a Hallmark Card."

"No," Harry said, "but it's the thought that counts. We now have an extra day to stop that loon."

"If we don't find him, the night before the celebration is going to be too busy for my taste."

"Look at his signature. Is that an 'A' instead of an 'E'?"

Sylvie stared at the scrawl. "It could be. It could be a sloppy 'E,' too."

Harry puzzled over the letter. From the tone of the note, he caught the inference that he had actually met or spoken with this aberration's alter-ego during the past twenty-four hours or so. If that was true, Harry could now narrow the suspects down from one to two hundred people to one or two dozen.

6

Night fell on schedule.

Porter sat in his room alone and sifted through the computer notes Sylvie Dunbar had gathered during the day. He was beginning to doubt if he would be able to make enough progress on the killings to make any difference in the short amount of time left. He simply had too many people with too many possible motives.

Complicating matters was the fact that Sylvie's list of *Island*'s citizens having a brush with parapsychology read like a Who's Who of the habitat. Hundreds of citizens had some dealings with the subject, but only a few had crossed Harry's path within the last few days. Pencil in hand, he sat at his writing desk and methodically crossed out the names of all strangers. The final list of familiar faces included:

Russell David Vallory, governor of *Island One*. He had dealings with parapsychs during his astronaut training program.

Joshua Henry Hawkins. He trained with department ESPers at the New York City Police Institute.

Dr. Anthony Harper. He observed a series of classes conducted by Earth's leading paranormal expert, Arthur Loweb.

Dr. Estelle Jerrow. Attended two dozen seminars on telepathy at the renowned Trotwood Institute.

Dr. Martin Thomas Graff. Earth psychiatrist and media personality, he was one of the leaders in the paranormal reform movement on Earth before moving to *Island*. He studied under Arthur Loweb for a short time.

Sylvie Marie Dunbar. She served as a publicist for the National Lobby to Increase the Funding of PSI Research.

Harry scanned the list, frowning. Practically everyone he had met on the colony since his arrival was connected, in one way or another, with the subject. Mullins, Thornton, Kraft, even the late Anson Young had some knowledge of PSI. He supposed that made sense. Parashrinks were used in high government circles and most of these people moved in those circles. He tossed the papers onto the desk top. He was back to square one . . . almost.

There were certain names on the list he could dismiss. Young certainly was not the killer, unless he was truly knowledgeable in the field of psychic phenomenon. Sylvie wasn't involved, either. Hell, she had almost walked into her own funeral three nights ago. But Graff, Vallory, Harper, and Jerrow? He didn't really know them well enough to form concrete opinions. He wasn't positive about the medical conditions of the residents of *Island*'s impromptu insane asylum, either. One of them could be faking it. He had a gut instinct that Emmett was connected with the accident, either its cause or result.

Harry fiddled with the list a second time, coming up with a series of alter-egos. If Emmett was a victim of the accident, he could be any one of the patients at the hospital or the doctors or nurses involved, and that included the very moralistic Jerrow. If Emmett was a guilt ridden cause of the accident, he could be Ian Carmichael, the foreman of the space shack, or the tug pilot, or any one of the factory workers involved. Or, suppose the killer was a remorseful government official tired of the cover-up? Vallory and Hawkins fit into that subhead. Harry knew he was staring at the killer's true identity but was too ignorant of the facts to spot it. He picked through the listing again, attempting to unearth any further clues. The New York Police Institute trained its students to match wits and power with strong-willed ESPers. Arthur Loweb was a radical PSI booster, a militant, whose followers were trained in an almost militaristic manner. Trotwood was one of the most controversial scientific research centers ever constructed. Harry closed his eyes for a moment. He knew something else about Trotwood. The name had crossed his path during the past few days. He thought hard. Ah yes, the place was just destroyed. Built in a suburb near Cairo, it was destroyed by angry religious fanatics. After so many years of peaceful coexistence, too.

"Nuts," Harry muttered, frustrated by the blind alleys continuously manufactured by his mind. The videophone in his room jingled. He pushed the chair away from the desk and walked over to the instrument. The swarthy face of Tony Safian appeared on the screen.

"Porter," he stated flatly, "my stories are being censored!"

Harry relaxed. Just what he needed: comic relief. "By TV critics or viewers with taste?"

"Neither," Safian pronounced. "By *Island*."

Harry feigned surprise. "That's a pretty big accusation there, Tony boy."

"It's the truth, Porter. I tried to beam my tapes Earthside and they told me that the communications center was on the fritz."

"The whole center, eh? Well, I suppose those things happen."

"Yeah? Well, I smell a rat."

"Probably something you ate."

Safian glanced meaningfully into the phone. "Let's meet."

"Let's not."

"We can discuss old times."

"I'm not into nostalgia."

"We can discuss mutual friends."

"I'm an orthodox misanthrope."

"We can discuss one mutual friend . . . Ammit."

Harry took a deep breath, effecting a sense of calm. His insides were turning. If Safian got involved in this mess at this crucial point, everything could take a turn for the worse. "Who?"

"Ammit."

"Is this like a knock-knock joke? Am I supposed to ask who ammit? And you say it am I?"

"I'm not kidding around, Porter," Safian smirked. "I received a note from a fellow calling himself Ammit this evening. He spilled the beans. Told me about the rub-outs. The cover-up. The works. He told me you were in on the scam. You were a smart cookie on this one, Porter, but not smart enough for this reporter. You want to talk about it before I blow the whistle?"

"Will you talk sense?"

"Robeur's Retreat in one half of an hour."

Safian hung up, giving Harry the impression he had just engaged in conversation with an Edward G. Robinson film festival. He got dressed in a hurry. He hated it when idiots attempted to act hard boiled. Well, he could always do with a good night's outing in colloquialisms. Fully dressed, he realized that he had enough time to walk to the bar.

When he arrived, he found Safian seated in a painfully obscure table in the corner furthest from the bar. Since it was early evening, the night trade had yet to make an appearance. With the bar nearly deserted, Safian's presence in the shadowy corner was exceedingly conspicuous. Harry gazed into the murk. Safian's famous face looked like the profile of a well-bred sewer rat. His hair was styled. His *Island* jumpsuit looked tailor-made. Harry stood next to the bar, praying to the patron saint of terminal zits to give this guy at least one good one by the end of the evening. Just one small lesson in humility, please god.

Safian noticed Harry and made an exaggerated nod in Porter's direction, signaling that the "coast was clear." Harry ignored him, ordered a drink from the bar and, at his leisure, strolled over to the table in the corner. "Jesus, Tony, you need a miner's helmet to find your drink over here."

Safian kept his jaw firm as he spoke. "You never know who could be watching."

"Oh yeah, I forgot. Who ammit."

"Don't play dumb with me, Porter. You're a tough bird, but I'm stronger."

"You're mixing metaphors."

"Let the chips fall where they may."

Harry blinked. Seemed like a good idea to down his drink. "You're inscrutable, Tony."

"Damn straight. I've been sitting here trying to suss this one out. The way I see it, this Ammit is a terrorist organization out to discredit all of *Island*. That's why it's been systematically murdering everyone and backing the hab locals into a cover-up situation. Then, when it stages its big blowout on happy B-day, it will blow the hab's cool in public. Live, for everyone to see."

Harry put down his glass. "You mind repeating that in English?"

"I'll spell it out for you, Porter. I got a note from this organization. The writer tips me off to the murders. It also fingers you in the cover-up. Savvy?"

"I repeat: *English*."

"You're a cool customer, Porter, but . . ."

"You're tougher?"

"Right."

"How did I guess?" Harry signaled for a second drink. "Now, who's this Emmett guy?"

"It's not a guy and it's not *E*mmit. It's *A*mmit. I figure it to be a Middle Eastern terrorist group."

"How so?"

"Ammit is an Egyptian deity, wise guy. A whiz. A chief. A god. The guy who calls the shots."

"Are you sure?"

"I check my facts, Porter. Ammit was a hot little number who also went by the monicker 'The Eater of the Dead.' His m.o. was mondo disgusto. He ate men's hearts out after they'd been weighed in the hall of judgment and found lacking."

"An Egyptian judge . . ." Harry muttered.

"The guy was no raving beauty, either. In mythology, he's pictured as part crocodile, part hippopotamus . . "

". . and part lion," Harry said, mentally kicking himself for being so damned ignorant about the situation.

"Who tipped you off?" Safian asked suspiciously.

"I'm a friend of King Tut's."

Safian jutted his chin out to an almost gravity-defying angle. "The way I see it, Ammit figures that you've dropped the ball, you've fumbled on the three-yard line, you've fouled out."

"I never was much good at sports. Daddy wanted a girl."

"You were supposed to sing to the people of the Earth about the murders and the whitewash. But you don't come through. You dummy up. So now, Ammit turns to me, the last hope for humanity. The organization says that, now, it's my turn to blow the whistle and make like a canary. I have thirty-six hours to contact Earth with the true story or else all hell breaks loose."

"What kind of hell?"

"How many kinds are there? They told me they'd blow up the entire colony."

Harry received his second drink and took a large gulp. "The whole colony?"

"You got it. They plan to punch everyone's ticket up here pronto."

"Just when is all this punching going to take place?"

262

"Wouldn't you like to know," Safian said smugly.

"Tony, if you're going to play games, I'd prefer scrabble. If you're going to talk, then talk. I wouldn't have asked you if I didn't want to know."

"How do I know I can trust you?"

"You don't. Take a chance. Live dangerously."

"Well, all right," Safian answered. He ordered a scotch from the waitress. It was blue upon its arrival. He stirred the drink with his finger. "The note says that the massacre will take place during the big B-day celebration the morning after next. When everyone gathers in the one cylinder . . . ka-blooie."

"Kablooie?" Harry repeated.

The second scotch began to affect Safian in a semicomical way. His jutting jaw became exceedingly slack. "One habitat . . . el snuffo."

"Tony," Harry offered. "That's a pretty impressive scenario, really and truly exciting, but I just don't buy it."

"Why not?"

"Because it makes no sense. Why would this Ammit character . . ."

"Group."

"Character kill people one by one, stop, and then threaten to blow up the entire habitat?"

Safian considered Harry's objection. "To test me!" he suddenly exclaimed.

"Come again."

"You know, like Sisyphus searching for an honest man."

Harry winced in silence. Safian continued. "Ammit told me that only I can save the colony now. I have to broadcast the truth within the next twenty-four hours. I have to give Ammit my response by 7 P.M. They said to leave a message in the commuter park next to the Retreat. Next to the fountain."

"All this was in that note, huh?" Harry grunted. "Did it come hardbound? Sounds like a veritable encyclopedia of knowledge."

"Hah! Hot under the collar? You blew it, Porter. They came to a pro this time 'round. Sure the note was long. But I read it. The whole thing. I picked it apart. And when I finished, I clutched it in my hand, my heart pounded like a jackhammer. I looked at the note . . ."

"It felt good to your touch . . ."

"It sure did. So I looked at it and figured: 'Tony, it's time to put up or shut up. Sure, it's dangerous. Sure, you can get your own ticket punched in the process, but hell, everyone bites it sometime.' "

"Some more often than others," Harry smiled. "Getting back to the note. I don't suppose you have it with you?"

"Hell no. You got rocks in your *cabasa?* I destroyed it!"

Harry's jaw dropped with a resounding click. "You ate it, right?"

"No. I burned it and then flushed it down the can. You can't take too many chances . . ."

"Yeah You never know when an autograph hound with a plunger is going to show up. Now, listen, in that note, Ammit said he was a terrorist group?"

"Right."

"And that the group had approached me . . ."

"Yeah. Told me everything. The killings. The cop. Anson Young. The bellboy. You're hushing it up. They spilled their guts to me."

"And you, in turn, agreed to cooperate."

"I don't like what you're getting at," Safian fumed. "You make it sound fishy," he said, his eyes dwindling to championship b-b size.

Harry ignored the TV newsman's attempt at macho. Safian look too much like a ferret to make Harry sweat. "Here's what I'm driving at, hammerhead. It's now 8 PM. You were supposed to contact them at 7 P.M. Did you?"

"Who are you calling hammerhead?"

"Well, I can eliminate *me* right away," Harry said, his anger mounting. "Did you contact them or not?"

A puzzled look appeared on Safian's face. His voice assumed a slightly nasal whine. "Sure I did, why?"

"And you told them that you'd cooperate?"

"Well . . ." Safian was lost now. Harry could see the wheels working above his eyes and he was quite aware that they were spinning aimlessly. "No . . . no . . not exactly."

Harry heaved a sigh. "What exactly did you tell them, Tony?"

The newsman's lower lips twitched slightly. "Well, well, I told them that, well, I tried to get the story out to Earth, but they wouldn't let me send it. They closed up the communications center on me. I told them that I'd try again tomorrow with another story. As a gesture of good faith, I even left them the video report I was trying to send back."

Harry folded his hands across his chest and shook his head sadly. "Forget I ever said you were a hammerhead, Tony. You don't rate that high. You're a putz."

The newsman attempted to swagger in his seat, correcting his sagging posture as much as possible. His lip, however, was still at half-mast. "A what?"

"A putz. A jerk. A reallll asshole," Harry explained cheerlessly. "Will you think just one moment about what you have just done? You've been contacted by a killer who threatens to blow this place out of the sky unless you do something. You, then, go back to the killer and tell him that golly gee, you'd really like to play hero, but no one here will let you. Then, you destroy all the evidence that proves this Ammit exists. You rip up the note the killer gave you and you turn over the tape to the killer himself. Jeezus, Safian, a demitasse would fit your head like a sombrero."

Safian's face collapsed. "I never thought of that."

"You're putting me on," Harry said. "Well, never mind that now, just get up and let's get you out of here."

Harry stood. Safian remained slouched, looking very much like a teenage lothario just jilted for the first time. "Where are we going?"

"I'm going home. But, on the way, I'm dropping YOU off at the police station."

"What for?"

Harry yanked Safian out of the chair. "To save your ass. I don't know whether this lightning bolt of info has struck you as yet, sport, but you've just left yourself wide open for a quick trip to the Pearly Gates?"

"Huh?"

"Your ticket is in danger of getting prematurely punched by your pen pals, Bogie."

"How d'ya figure?"

"You blew it, Tony. You screwed up. You can't help Ammit anymore, and if you go around talking it up, you can only hinder his, her, or their plans . . . And if your very existence threatens their kablooie on the day after tomorrow, what do you think they will do to lessen that threat?"

A brief glimpse of panic appeared in Safian's squinted eyes. "Oh, yeah."

"Come on, Sherlock, let's get you to Chief Hawkins." Harry pulled the reluctant TV reporter out of the bar. Standing outside the front door, Safian limped into another wave of bravado. He shook himself free of Harry's grasp. "I'm not going," he declared petulantly.

Harry faced Safian more than a little annoyed. "Look. I'm not doing this for my health, Tony. You make a lousy escort, especially for someone who is allergic to slime, so let's go."

Safian rocked back and forth on his heels. "Why are you so interested in my well-being, all of a sudden, eh, Porter?"

"Old boy scouts never die."

"Bullshit," Safian smiled, his self-imposed tough guy image slowly rising from the ashes. "I got you pegged, you two-bit hack. You scrapped your story, lost it. I still have a shot with mine. You want in."

"Oh, for all the . . ."

Safian pulled in his chest and, patting his hair back into place with a delicate flick of his wrist, swaggered up to Harry. "Well, I'm not cutting you in, see? Why should I go fifty-fifty with a has-been?"

"Will you come off it, man?" Harry shouted. "Keep this ego-stroking up and you're going to find yourself el snuffo a lot sooner than this colony!"

"You're lying."

Harry grew serious. "Look, Tony. There's something seriously wrong about all of this. What I know and what you've just told me just don't jibe. I don't know what it is that knocks this out of kilter but maybe, if you and I and Hawkins can sit down and try to figure all of this out, we can come up with a logical, orderly pattern."

"I do my own figuring, old timer," Safian sneered. Harry watched dumbfounded as the TV idol stalked away from the bar and onto the walkway. He crossed the pedestrian path and walked to the electric car station. He had no need to push the call button for a vehicle since one was already sitting on the track.

A thought flashed through the back of Harry's mind. Why would a cart just be sitting there like that? Harry watched the newsman get into the car. Hell, those carts were never around when *Harry* wanted one, why should Safian be so lucky? A sudden shaft of fear imbedded itself in Harry's train of thought. He began to run toward the car.

"Safian!" he screeched. "Don't touch any . . ."

He had time to see Safian turn toward him and sneer one last time before pushing the computerdash defiantly. The cart and the newsman exploded in a sudden eruption of smoke and flame. The fireball that had once been a cart and rider

266

shot over Harry's head. He dove to the ground, choking on the smoke.

"Kablooie," he whispered.

7

Once, many years ago, he had witnessed a small funeral ceremony in a small Italian town in the Alps. The hamlet, a picturesque collection of rustic homes surrounded by ice-blue mountains and unbelievably green fields, smelled of death despite its visual charm. Every bird that sang seemed to emit a mournful sound. Every gust of wind echoed mournfully through the colorful town square. It was as if you could feel the presence of the deceased's soul as it made its way from one place of rest to the next.

Harry felt that presence now. Dawn bathed the police chief's office in a wave of carefully contrived orange light. Harry sat before Hawkins's desk, drawn and tired. Death was in the air. Harry couldn't sleep. Death was behind him. He couldn't eat. He even tasted the presence of death; the food turning to ash in his mouth. He rubbed the sleep from his eyes and looked around the room.

A very pale Russell Vallory sat, slumped, in the far left corner of the room. Sylvie Dunbar stood protectively beside him. Behind the desk, in the center of the room, Joshua Hawkins cursed a litany of apathetic and totally useless saints. In front of Hawkins's desk, Harry attempted to relax; not that hard a trick to accomplish physically following a night without sleep. Mentally, however, the task proved impossible.

Once again, he found himself the center of attention. Putting it nicely, he would have just as soon avoided the spotlight for the rest of his stay on the habitat. It was beginning to make him more than a little paranoid.

"Exactly what did he say about the note?" Hawkins cross-examined.

Harry drummed his fingers on the arm of his chair. "Look, I've told you all this before . . . at least six times."

"Well, tell me again, maybe there's something you've forgotten . . ."

"Like what? The color of the ink it was written with? I didn't even see the damned letter." He raised his hand in protest, noticing the strip of ruptured metal around his wrist. He took off the remains of the wrist-communicator and tossed it on Hawkins's desk. "I hope you have a warranty on this," he muttered.

Hawkins suddenly pounded the desk with his fist. "I thought you said this guy was going to lay off!"

"Ammit? That's what he told me in his note yesterday."

"Well, he lied to you!"

"He's a murderer, Hawkins. That class isn't exactly known for its sense of honor and fair play." He was growing weary of Hawkins's neo-Nazi cross-examination approach. He glanced at Vallory. Vallory did not meet his gaze. The man looked beaten, lost. He was bent forward in his chair. He cupped his face with his hands. Sylvie instinctively reached out and grasped the governor's shoulder from behind. A simple move, yet one that filled Porter with a sense of bitter betrayal.

Harry didn't like this tableau at all. What was Vallory doing there, anyway? Wasn't Hawkins supposed to be running this investigation without the governor's knowledge? Harry had the feeling that the chances were good to excellent that he had been played for a primo chump.

"All right," he announced abruptly. "I'm through playing *Witness for the Prosecution!*" He pulled out a cigarette from the tunic. "Before I say anything else, why don't you try leveling with me . . . for a change?"

Harry looked at the cigarette in his hand. It was nearly broken in two. Still, he had already pulled the damned thing out of his pocket for the sake of melodramatic effect. He was now obligated to light it and smoke it tough-guy style. He tried straightening the busted butt with his fingers. No luck. Hell, he could always say it was good for smoking around corners.

"Say what you mean, Porter," Hawkins said, glancing at Vallory. Porter knew the policeman realized what Harry was getting at. Hawk was a lousy liar. The man simply had too many crevices in his face to coordinate simultaneously into a mask of innocence. As Hawkins struggled to effect a look of composure half of his face twitched under the weight of near panic.

"What I mean is this," Harry said, attempting to keep his cigarette on his lip and off his lap. "Why doesn't some bright boy or girl in this room tell me exactly what I've been chasing my tail around for during the past few days. I have a feeling I've been conned."

Hawkins reddened and peered into the surface of his desk top. "Bullshit."

"I'm right, chief, and you know it," Harry said. "I've been playing secret agent for your departmental pageant, haven't I?"

Vallory slapped his knees with his hands and straightened himself in his chair. He emitted a prolonged sigh. "To a degree you have been dealt with in a dishonest fashion," he said somberly. "At my behest."

Harry shot a withering look at Hawkins. The chief was still entranced by his desk top.

"I apologize for getting you involved in this very ugly situation," the governor continued, "but, in a sense, your personal involvement preceded your official participation."

"My official participation?" Harry repeated. "In other words, all the time that I've been working with Hawkins, I've been working for you?"

Vallory nodded, his face tight. "It was my idea to get you involved on our side. You had seemed to be making more progress than our men with this Ammit individual so . . . You see, I couldn't publicly or even privately acknowledge your connection with the case because . . . well, because of political ramifications."

Harry had heard this song before. "I've been counting bodies while you've been lubing the wheels of progress, right."

The veins in the governor's forehead began to throb and take on a purple hue. "Please, don't judge me quite so glibly. We both know that this Utopian portrait of *Island* life promoted for the past decade is a hoax and has always been a hoax. But in this case, lies were necessary to help the people being lied to. The *Island* dream had to be created in order for us to get the proper funding from Earth to get the project going: funding that had to be taken from the taxpayers' dollars.

"People have never been very interested in scientific research in America, Mr. Porter, only with results. They love their electric lights, their energy efficient cars, their wall-sized TV screens. But do you think they would have supported the

269

years of long-term research that led up to those inventions had we asked them? I'm afraid not. It wouldn't have seemed immediate enough for them. Yet, this research has always been necessary and, almost inevitably, has not been very glamorous. That's the nature of technology," Vallory stated firmly.

"*Island* was, and is, the biggest research project ever proposed. The first step to what can be a leap into space. In order to sell it to the public, to convince them to back it, we had to create a romantic lifestyle; a lifestyle that would appeal to the latent dreamer in all Earth people; a lifestyle that would rekindle the pioneer spirit of America.

"And it worked. By God, it worked. Do you remember the *Island* fever of a decade and a half ago? Can you recall what it was like ten years ago when the first *Island* citizens set foot in this habitat? The crowds went wild on Earth. We were heroes, Mr. Porter, we had dreams big enough to share with everyone. But, somewhere along the line, the dreams faded. We should have realized that they would. It's only natural. If America has been consistent through the years, she has been consistent in her love for anything new and her disdain for anything commonplace. And, within a decade, we had become commonplace." Vallory heaved a slow sigh.

"Yet, we had to keep our sheen. We had to revamp our image. With you Earth people coming on board we had to actually begin to live up to the myth we had created years before. We had to make you people believe that our dreams were still very, very real and very, very important. You, in turn, would bring this message to the populace Earthside. Islanders were called upon to dispense with their everyday lives, which were quite ordinary, and play act for your benefit. It was necessary. The lies were necessary. There could be no flaw in our perfect presentation. If we had to offer illusion in order to keep hard-core science afloat up here for another decade, we would do so gladly. Everyone aboard knows the potential benefits this habitat can offer humanity. Everyone up here decided to cooperate in our charade."

"Everyone but Ammit," Harry injected.

"Yes," Vallory admitted with a slow nodding motion of his head. "But I couldn't allow that one sick mind to bring everything grinding to a halt."

"One is all it takes," Harry said.

"You must see how it was for us," Vallory insisted. "We were suddenly trapped, Mr. Porter. Trapped in our own

270

myths. We had to trap you into helping us. We had to prey upon your own sense of justice . . ."

Harry slowly stood up. Surrounded by a roomful of beaten individuals, he suddenly appeared very tall. "I don't suppose it ever occurred to you to just come out and ask me for my help."

"We couldn't risk it," Vallory offered lamely. "You're a . . . reporter."

Vallory had muttered the last word as if it were connected with a sewage process. Harry began to pace the length of the room, his footsteps echoing with every sentence. "You couldn't trust me enough to tell me what the score was, but you could trust me enough to do your dirty work . . . under false pretenses. Is that it?"

"I'm sorry, Porter," Hawkins said softly. "I really am."

"So am I, chief, because I think this exercise in play acting has probably cost us a lot of time and, perhaps, a lot of blood." Harry placed his hands on Hawkins's desk and leaned over the paper-laden blotter. "You people have manipulated every honest feeling I've had since arriving up here. You knew how I felt about impersonal political set-ups and you used it against me. You staged this whole loyal police vs. corrupt government match to suck me into this case, didn't you?"

"Yes," Hawkins said, averting Harry's intense scrutiny.

"You suckered me. You flattered my ego. I suppose you realized I planted that bugging device on your coat."

"Afraid so," Hawkins admitted. "It registered on my wrist communicator."

"And you and Vallory staged that entire Punch and Judy radio show for my benefit?"

Vallory smiled weakly. "We had to make the situation as real as possible for you. And, in all actuality, we were actually dramatizing what the facts were."

Harry faced the governor. Vallory slumped lower in his chair. Harry stared at Sylvie. "What about Mata Hari here? Was she in on everything?"

Hawkins glanced nervously at Sylvie and, then, at the governor. "Ms. Dunbar cooperated without fully realizing any of the particulars."

"Just along for the ride, eh? Recreational activities plus cheerleading practice."

"You could say that," Vallory said from between clenched teeth. "Although that's a fairly crude simplification."

"Let's deal in crude simplifications, gov.," Harry fumed. "You people have been fucking with my head for a week. You've pushed me and pulled me every which way from Sunday because you knew I was here to check out one poor kid's story about a murder. My female companion, I assume, kept you abreast of my every thought and action. You used my personal feelings to try to save your own asses. Is that crude enough for you, governor?"

"We were doing it for the good of the community!" Vallory insisted.

Harry was about to tell the governor to stuff his community when he sensed a sudden emotional reversal taking place behind Hawkins's desk. The police chief began pounding the blotter in a slow, rhythmic manner with a closed fist. Harry and Vallory stopped bickering. They watched the police chief's fury rise to a quick peak. Finally, Hawkins sent his fist crashing onto the desk top, sending a wad of paper cascading onto the floor. "Goddamn your philosophy!" he bellowed at Vallory. "Goddamn your sense of honor. And goddamn this whole goddamn shithole!"

Hawkins shot up from behind his desk, his eyes hard, his mouth trembling in outrage. "We have a goddamn killer loose up here. He just blew away someone else last night. The first member of the Earth delegation has been slaughtered . . . and that's after our sly little friend promised to lay off for a day. We now have twenty-four hours to prevent eleven more deaths. I don't want to hear about community. I don't want to hear about publicity. I don't want to hear about politics. From anybody. Is that clear? And you, Mr. Porter, I don't want to hear about your hurt feelings. You're either in this or you're out of this. Which is it?"

Harry didn't speak. He walked to the chair before Hawkins's desk and sat down. "Let's get back to basics. We have one day, folks. Let's not waste any more time."

Hawkins attempted to calm himself. "You're with us?"

"As much as I can be." He still wouldn't piss on any of them if they were on fire.

The chief sat down and sniffled. "We can chalk Safian's death up to a malfunction in the electric cart. We'll make up some nonsense that will wash. It will horrify the rest of the delegation, of course, but it will be a hell of a lot simpler to explain than murder."

The governor broke his silence. Harry didn't bother to glance in his direction. He knew that the man was still sitting

272

sorrowfully in the corner. "We have to do everything in our power to keep this maniac in abeyance for the remainder of the day. I know I can salvage the fate of the colony today. After the headway we made at yesterday's meeting, we don't have much further to go. I can cinch everything within hours. I know it. Economics will prevail."

"Sentimental fool," Harry muttered, directing his eyes at Hawkins. "I have to admit, chief, I understand this case less today than I did yesterday."

"What do you mean?" The police chief played with a pencil on his desk top, spearing random sheets of paper with a vengeance.

"I can't figure Ammit out at all. We know now that his killings are indeed ritualistic. He's a dispenser of justice. But I've tried putting a psychological profile of the guy together, but I just can't hammer it out. In the last twenty-four hours, he just sent all of my theories down the toilet. It's like he's two distinct personalities. First he says he's going to kill me. Then he says he's taking a day off. Then he breaks his word and blows up Tony."

"Schizophrenic?"

"Seems that way." A sudden idea flashed through Harry's mind. "Hey, during your Shakespeare festival over the communicator, did you two plant that bugging device I found in my room for added effect?"

Hawkins shook his head vehemently from side to side. "Now THAT we had nothing to do with. Swear to God."

Harry cut short the expected tirade. "You sure?"

"Positive," Hawkins snorted.

"Shit," Harry said, crossing his legs in a gesture of nervousness. "Then we've got some additional problems."

"Problems?" Vallory echoed.

"Use your head, gov. Someone's been using my apartment as a listening station for real. Something you folks might have forgotten about with all your acting classes and all."

Hawkins mumbled something that had something to do with Harry and a few rolling doughnuts.

"I'll pretend I didn't hear that," Harry said, smirking at Hawkins. "I'll help you guys out but, as of now, I want all plainclothesmen off my tail and everyone in this room out from under my feet. Agreed?"

Hawkins looked at Vallory. Vallory, his eyes a mirror of uneasiness, stared back. "Agreed," Hawkins replied sullenly.

Harry walked toward the door. "Fine. Until later. Ta-ta."

Sylvie stepped between him and the doorway. "Harry..." she began.

"Don't worry about it," he said, almost meaning it. "I never should have expected more."

Harry left the room knowing that the trio inside was still using him in some way; still keeping information out of his reach. But that was the way things were everywhere. It was the individual who was constantly drained for the betterment of the system. Harry smiled to himself. He didn't mind really. There were quite a few puzzle pieces still known only to him. Fuck them all. Right now, his top priority was making sure that his head and the rest of his body left the colony in the same space ship.

He stopped in the library. The horse-faced librarian was still conducting her one-sided love affair with her desk. "Hello, darling," Harry smiled. "Show me everything you have on Egypt in the twenty-first century."

"That research will take you some time, mister..."

"Harry," he said.

"We have spools and spools of current events."

"Oh gee, you see I'm with the Earth delegation and I don't have a lot of time. If I gave the specific information I wanted to a staff researcher could he or she..."

"Out of the question," the woman replied, a traditional showing of librarian aloofness coming to light. "We have no staff researchers."

Harry shifted gears on his smile, showing even more teeth. "Well, golddarn it. I have this important meeting with the governor and the rest of the delegation in an hour or so and I really need that information. It's a matter of life and death."

"Well," the librarian said, her coldness thawing, "*I* might be able to look up a *few* facts for you."

"Could your messenger them over to the meeting?"

"I suppose I could. It's not on my budget."

Harry produced a twenty-dollar bill and thumped it onto her desk. "Tell the messenger to have a moonrise on me." He scrawled a few lines on a piece of paper. "Here's what I need and here's where I'll be."

He made for the door.

"B-but, Harry," the woman called. "I don't even know your last name."

"Porter," he replied.

"Harry Porter?" the librarian called.

A small, elderly man perusing a shelf of reels behind the

librarian's desk poked her sharply in the ribs. "Shhhhhhh!" he said sternly.

8

"He certainly sounds like a fairly sick individual to me," Dr. Harper wheezed, padding alongside Harry on a stairway leading from the think tank to the walkway.

"Most killers are somewhat less than your model citizens," Harry said, stepping closer to the walkway. He lurched to a stop on the curbside, looking left and right.

"Don't bother," Harper said with a wave of the hand. "No cars. Just pedestrians."

"Old Earth habits die hard."

"Yes, it takes a few months, a few months."

"I'll be off of this pleasure palace long before my ninety-day warranty expires."

"Let's hope so," Harper panted. "I read in this morning's newspaper about your friend Safian."

"Acquaintance."

"It's not customary to belittle the dead."

"I never had to belittle Tony. He always did too good a job of it himself."

"You sound as if you didn't like him."

"I loathed him."

"Enough to kill him?" Harry stopped dead in his tracks. He stared at the little man at his side. Harper, red faced from exertion, met Harry's gaze with a sly grin. "Just wanted to show you how you sounded."

"That bad, huh?"

"Worse, mostly."

"Someday I'll come back for a class reunion and you'll see me off duty. I'm a regular delight."

"I can imagine. You know, your acquaintance's death has caused quite a stir within our little scientific community."

"Why, do they like TV?"

"Not especially. But no one believes it was an accident. Electric carts just don't blow up, you see. They're transportation devices, not land mines. If anything happened to their circuits, they'd short out . . . or slow down . . . or speed up. At best, they'd fall over on their sides like poor wounded cows and derail. But, oh dear no, they'd never explode like that."

"Yeah. I figured that story wouldn't sit well with the locals. The Governor's lucky most of the Earth delegates are mechanical morons. You could tell Curtis and Ferron that a can opener blew up and they'd believe it."

"I don't doubt it. Most Earth people seem to take technology very much for granted. A very odd concept. They regard so many marvelous inventions as almost natural resources . . . until there is a power failure or a faulty outlet. Then, these very same inventions take on the aura of the mysteries of the ages."

"I must admit that I'm guilty of that approach."

"So am I," the old man chuckled. "I couldn't tell you how my TV set worked if my life depended on it. Life," he sighed. "Blowing someone up in an electric cart, to take a life like that, was a very demented endeavor."

"And totally unexpected." Harry grunted. "He fooled me with that letter."

"Don't feel bad," the psychologist said. "He would have fooled me as well. The killer's sudden reappearance does puzzle me. From what you say, he vowed to cease his plans for retribution. His resumption of his killing spree strikes me as a most serious breach of character. It's almost as if he had two minds, two personalities."

"Maybe he's two people," Harry said.

"An organization?"

"Maybe. Imagine an organization of some sort wherein the members have a disagreement. One side says stop the killing, the other side says keep it up! After a while you have a very dualistic movement going."

Harry suddenly became aware of Harper's labored breathing. He slowed his pace down, allowing the elderly thinker to catch up with him. "Your killer seems intensely motivated," Harper wheezed. "I believe that, basically, he or she or they is or are just. The killer, and I shall refer to him as a he, is righteous in his own way. He isn't attacking, mind you, simply dealing out justice in the biblical sense. Old Testament. Within his own framework, he's acting with the very best of intentions."

"Dr. Harper, since I've come up here, I've met dozens of lying, cheating phonies who are all operating with the best intentions. That doesn't make them all honorable or right, for that matter."

"True. Now, as to his motive. I believe you're onto something with this greenhouse accident. But, bear in mind, if the killer is insane, he may have no connection with that fiasco. This 'children of light' business may just be a coincidence. Or, perhaps it is a phrase that the killer picked up from another party. If this is indeed the case, then the killer could be avenging anything from a broken romance to a personal insult or a faded career. It could be anything."

"Doc," Harry said. "I respect your opinions and I love you for offering them, but I think you're wrong. The killer's connected with the greenhouse business. He was driven mad by his knowledge. That narrows our suspects down to a handful of people who know of the incident. Unfortunately, they're half of the ruling class of the habitat. Ah, here we are."

The hospital stood before them. Harry and Harper climbed up the front stairs. Without any interference whatsoever, the men made their way toward the ward where the survivors of the accident were kept. Harry stopped at a gift cart along the way and picked up a picture-filled magazine.

"For Martin?" Harper queried.

"Yeah," Harry said. "I sort of like the old guy. I have a theory that I'm going to test out on him right about now. If he comes through, we'll have solved this whole mess. This is just a 'thank you.'"

"Good choice," Harper commented. "Martin will love it. Before his mind went, he was very much involved with the great outdoors. Ecology and the like."

Harry rolled up the magazine and continued on his way. "You see, I have this feeling that if he concentrated really hard, Martin could tip us off about Ammit, telepathically of course. Subconsciously, he may realize who our killer is. All he needs is the proper stimulus to produce the response we need. He needs someone to take him out of his shell a little bit. We made real headway at your apartment. He knows we're his friends. That we care about him."

"Yes, yes," Harper said enthusiastically. "At any rate, you'll be testing the limits of telepathic communication."

"I just hope he isn't totally sedated."

"Perhaps he is even in contact with the killer telepathically at all times. I studied parapsychology very briefly on Earth. At that time, they were envisioning networks of PSI possessors,

277

able to communicate at will over vast distances of time and space, through the use of their minds *only*."

Harry smiled to himself. Harper, through his babbling, totally eliminated himself as even a remote suspect in the hunt for the killer. Ammit, if confronted, would probably attempt to conceal his history of telepathic study. Harper simply recalled it as a matter of fact. A brief note of suspicion sounded in the back of Harry's mind. Harper was clever. Suppose he was having deadly fun at Harry's expense? Harry tossed out that thought immediately. Paranoia would serve no purpose now.

The two men heard the screams from beyond the doorway at the hall's end. "Martin!" Harper whispered. Harper ran for the door, his stubby legs pumping like abbreviated pistons. Harry followed close behind. His mind didn't dare attempt visualizing the horror beyond the door. The two men burst into the ward unannounced. Two young nurses, numbed with shock, made a feeble effort at waving them back. Their faces were white beyond belief. One of them made soft, gagging sounds.

The men in the ward were all sitting in their beds, mouths agape. Toy soldiers in a trance, swaying from side to side in a uniformed, pendulum motion. From their mouths emerged a deep-throated, elongated moan. More of a hissing noise than any note realized. The sound of wind rattling through a dead tree's branches. The sound of a coffin lid closing for the last time.

At the far end of the ward, two doctors stood over Martin Graff's bed. Harry and Harper approached the scene warily. Sensing the inevitable, Harry motioned the psychologist back with one hand while continuing to move forward himself. Martin Graff had been covered by a hastily applied white sheet, crimson stained from beneath. Only an outstretched hand was visible in the sea of wrinkled linen. Harry wormed his way in-between the doctors. He lifted the sheet slowly. Graff was dead. His face had been seared away. Laser pistol. Close range. Harry let the sheet drop clumsily. His stomach lurched. He left the bed, leading Harper away from the site. He maneuvered the man out of the ward and, as tactfully as possible, verbally recreated the experience.

"Murdered," Harper repeated. "Murdered."

"Brutally," Harry added.

"But why? Why Martin?"

278

Harry attempted to rationalize the killing while walking through the hospital corridors. "Maybe our idea about Martin being able to telepathically tag the killer was right. Too right. My guess is that someone else thought of it slightly before we did. They approached Martin and asked him to perform, to test his PSI prowess."

"But who?"

"Beats me. The killer himself, most likely. With Martin the only clue to his identity, he couldn't take any chances. Martin performed. Martin was killed."

"How primitive."

"Not at all. The latest in hardware was used."

"You persist in referring to the killer as a lone individual."

"Yeah. I just can't swallow this organization story. It's too complicated."

Harry stopped at the nurses' station nearest the exit. "Excuse me," he asked a rotund woman behind a small counter, "is Dr. Jerrow in?"

"I'm afraid not," she grinned, revealing a mouthful of nicotine-scarred teeth. "She called in sick this morning."

"Thanks," Harry said, crossing the corridor.

"What do you want Jerrow for?" Harper asked.

"The more questions I come up with, the more answers I find that somehow connect Jerrow with all of this. She's been part of this mutant bunch since their creation. Maybe she's one of them herself, I don't know."

"You think she's your killer?"

"If not, I'm sure she knows who the killer is."

Harry stepped up to a video phone booth and plunked in a half-dollar. After flipping through the directory, he dialed Jerrow's home number. He quickly replaced the receiver. "No answer."

"Maybe she stepped out."

"That's what I'm thinking." The two men left the hospital. "What kind of a person is Jerrow, anyway?" Harry asked the psychologist. "She strikes me as being sort of a cold fish."

"She's not exactly your party type," Harper nodded. "But she's a dedicated human being. She's worked day and night to get that hospital in shape. She believes in saving lives, not taking them."

"You don't believe she's involved."

"Not particularly."

Harry was about to argue that point when a small police van pulled up on the hospital lawn. Joshua Hawkins was at the wheel. "I've been looking all over for you," he rasped.

"Well, you found me," Harry said. "You here for the deceased inside?"

"No, a second unit's on the way. We have to get back to the delegation right away."

"What's going on?"

"Your pal Ammit has just paid a call on the delegation, in a manner of speaking."

"Any harm done?"

"Nothing much. I think he's just killed the entire habitat, that's all." Harry shook hands with Harper and dove into the police cart.

"He's an acquaintance, not a pal," he muttered as the cart scooted across the lawn, siren blaring.

9

Harry and Hawkins were met in the vestibule outside the conference room by a near hysterical Sylvie Dunbar.

"Where have you been?" she asked Harry.

"At the hospital. Ammit has eliminated a key lead . . . literally."

"Who?"

"Dr. Martin Graff. Our greenhouse survivor."

Harry opened the door leading into the meeting area a crack. The inside of the room resembled a bus terminal on the Friday before a three-day weekend. Delegates moved in and out of their seats aimlessly. Armed guards marched about, almost in circles. In was beyond chaos; a panic found only in classical national disasters or Saturday morning cartoon shows.

He closed the door. "What's going on inside?"

"Everything," Sylvie prattled. "The meeting was just getting started when one of the delegates brought up your friend's death last night."

"Acquaintance. Which delegate?"

"Ferron."

"Figures."

"The governor managed to convince them all that the entire incident was a tragic accident; something to do with a malfunction in the cart's motor. Things started going smoothly after that. They began to talk about the financial aspecs of the colony during the decade to come. Everything was looking really good when a messenger brought *these* to the door. Each delegate got one."

She handed him a bright orange envelope. The type of container that usually held a festive party invitation. Harry opened it. A small, neatly typed piece of paper was folded inside. He removed it, unfolded it, and read: "Surrender the habitat by dawn or perish . . . Ammit."

"Charming," Harry remarked.

"All hell broke loose in there," Sylvie said.

Harry shrugged. "There's nothing that can be done now, I guess, except roll with the punches."

Hawkins shot him a withering look. Harry guessed that there was nothing much he could say that would please anybody right then. He opened the door to the meeting room and was about to enter when a messenger handed him a plain white envelope. He stuck it under Ammit's note absentmindedly and stepped into the carnival grounds. Shouting seemed to be the rule of the day around the table. Vallory sat, Buddah-like, at the head of the table. A look of hastily enforced tranquility was affixed to his face. Only the rapid movement of his eyes beneath their sleepy lids betrayed the turbulence existing within.

Nearly every delegate was in an advanced state of hysteria. Only Ryan Frantz, the weary emissary of NASA, retained his composure. He stared dumbly at the note, apparently expecting to erase it from reality through the power of positive thinking. You could always tell a good administrator by the degree of fantasy employed in his performance, Harry surmised. Frantz would go to the top some day. Harry moved to the back of the room and observed the proceedings objectively. He mentally calculated Ammit's score for the week. Four dead and one 10,000-peopled habitat tossed in the toilet. Not bad for a beginner maniac.

Harry reached into his pocket for his notebook. It wasn't there. Somewhere along the line, he had misplaced it. He pulled out a slip of paper to take notes on. The scrap he pulled out was the dog-eared list of all the PSI-oriented

Islanders Sylvie had assembled. He turned it on its blank side and began to outline the meeting in progress.

Sitting two seats from Harry was the most outraged of all the delegates present, Wayne Ferron. "This is an outrage," the once and future political hero pronounced. The fading public figure attempted the ultimate in macho delivery. While his effort was laudable, the finished performance was anything but Hemingway material. He simply did not possess the bass profundo ambience needed for the role. His noticeable overbite also lessened his heroic stature a bit. What should have emerged as a resonant declaration left his sneering lips as a high-pitched whine. "Our rights have been transgressed! An invader has set foot on United States property and has threatened our very lives!"

"No shit," Harry snorted from his seat. This whole scene reminded him of a well-worn B-movie. All they needed was Godzilla at the window.

Surprisingly enough, it was Archibald Curtis, the president's pet amoeba, who put the gathering in its proper perspective. Although obviously scared to death, his normally bland countenance now reduced to the robust color of chalk, he clenched his hands together on the table top and asked, politely but firmly, for a full assessment of the current situation. "Exactly who or what is this Ammit?"

Vallory opened his eyes. The commotion in the room slackened off to a mere buzz. "We're not sure," the governor admitted, hating every word.

"Is this some demented individual?"

"It could be."

"Could it be a terrorist organization?"

"Possibly."

Harry began to doodle on his note paper. Sorry, folks, we'll have to throw over all the cards. Our Ammit could be any and all of the above. That's fifty points for the blue team. Next topic: famous faces for forty, please.

"Who cares what he is?" Ferron spat. "I say we get off this tub. Abandon this project now while there's still time!"

Ryan Frantz spoke in a calm, assured tone. "We can't do that for two reasons. One: there is no viable plan for mass evacuation. Two: if we formally abandon this colony, according to the Space Salvage Act of 1987, any sovereign government who has signed the treaty has the right to reclaim it as their own after a thirty-day waiting period. In other words,

Mr. Ferron, you'd be wasting all the technology onboard, costing the American people billions of dollars in losses."

"It's already lost."

Silence.

Archibald Curtis shook his head sadly. "Under the circumstances, governor, I'm afraid I have no choice but to report this entire incident to the president. And, as his official representative, I must formally demand the immediate capture of this terrorist."

Harry watched the muscles around Vallory's eyes twitch with each subsequent sentence delivered by Curtis. Some men were good at rolling with the punches, others could squirm out of any situation. Vallory seemed good at neither; an oak tree immobile in a windstorm.

"And furthermore," Curtis declared. "I must formally request military assistance in the matter. This is now a matter of national security. The rights of the United States have been violated by a perpetrator or perpetrators of unknown origin."

Harry himself winced at the thought of the habitat being put under martial law. He was amazed that Vallory had not slithered under the table at this point. His futuristic dream was now resting securely around his ankles. Finally the governor spoke: "Mr. Curtis, while I appreciate the validity of your statements, I must point out that, unless otherwise notified by the president himself, I am in charge of administering to the wants and needs of this habitat. At present, I do not see the need for calling in military assistance. What you tell the president is, of course, your business and feel free to portray this situation in any manner you feel appropriate. I should mention, however, that our communications center has been closed down for twenty-four hours because of a rather major malfunction and will probably be shut down for at least twenty-four hours more."

He was stonewalling it! Harry admired his tenacity.

"You mean we're being held here incommunicado?" Ferron shouted.

"No," Vallory explained. "You are free to leave here at any time. What I'm saying is that, for the past day, communications with Earth have been terminated. It is an inconvenience we experience up here with marked regularity."

Island will pay dearly for this," Ferron cautioned.

Vallory did not bother to look at the man. "Perhaps. In the

interim, however, may I suggest that we conduct business as usual?"

"But there's an insane person running loose up here!" Ferron yelled.

"Does New York City shut down every time a murder is committed?" asked Vallory.

Harry couldn't help himself. As much as he disliked the governor, he instinctively rooted for the underdog. "If that were the case," Harry said, "Manhattan would have been paralyzed for the last seventy-five years."

"Precisely, Mr. Porter," Vallory acknowledged.

"Your attitude does not lend itself to a favorable portrayal of this incident in my report," Curtis said "When communications with Earth are resumed, I am very much afraid that I must recommend that this craft and its mission be terminated."

"I understand completely," Vallory nodded.

The silence enveloping the room was interrupted by Howard Retson. The industrialist cleared his throat not-too-delicately. He spread his hands out on the desk top in a near parody of The Last Supper. "If Messrs. Ferron and Curtis will allow," he began. "I believe I can offer a mid-ground solution to this sordid affair that will keep all concerned parties happy. Granted, we are now faced with a thoroughly despicable situation. We are being taunted by an exceedingly deranged character. A character who may have permanently sullied *Island*'s image in the eyes of the United States government." He glanced meaningfully at Ferron. "But, gentleman, one bad apple does not spoil the entire bunch!"

Harry rolled his eyes, waiting for the business tycoon to produce a Bible to go along with the homily. "If the United States abandons *Island* then, as Mr. Frantz pointed out, a great deal of scientific research will be wasted, as well as a tremendous source of potential income."

Curtis appeared to be open minded. "What do you suggest?"

Funny he should ask, Harry sighed. Retson extended both hands in an I-am-the-Good-Shepherd-give-me-your-wallets gesture. "I can fully understand why the president will have to publicly disassociate himself from the project after this debacle but, rather than let *Island* die altogether, why not keep it alive in another format. Why not lease this entire construction to Kingdoms, Inc.?"

"Lease it?" Curtis was obviously taken by surprise.

"Certainly." Retson cracked the smile of an ingratiating barracuda. "This business about your murderer may spoil *Island* for the president who is, let's be candid, quite worried about his chances for reelection."

"Politics has nothing . . ."

"But for Kingdoms, Inc., this affair would amount to a mere inconvenience. Anything can be blotted out with enough time and money. Should the United States agree to a lease, we would assume total responsibility for the well-being of the structure. We would, of course, use the habitat to manufacture and promote Kingdoms goods in a manner I mentioned at yesterday's gathering. The U.S. government could thus sever its overt ties with *Island* but continue its scientific research onboard during our leasing period. Governor Vallory would, of course, continue to run *Island* operations and the habitat's entire population would be invited to stay on and to maintain whatever work schedule they are currently involved in."

Curtis's dour expression remained unchanged. After a few seconds' thought, he nodded gravely. "It sounds feasible to me."

Vallory said nothing. It was clear from the steely expression in his eyes that he was not at all pleased with the turn of events. Retson regarded the governor with characteristic élan. "Any thoughts on the subject, governor."

Vallory folded his hands on the table top and squeezed his fingers until his knuckles turned white. "I am interested in seeing *Island* survive," he said in a leisurely tone, "but I am also interested in seeing its philosophy, its principles, remain intact. And I am very much afraid that those principles do not include cheapening the habitat with the presence of junk hamburgers and high calorie colas."

"But those principles allow you to cover up murder, I take it," Retson smiled, blinking demurely.

Vallory sputtered into silence. Retson directed his gaze on the delegates seated around the table. "Gentlemen, since communication with Earth is at a minimum at present, may I suggest that we sleep on this proposal? I can see by the look on your faces that you still have your doubts. Well, I for one have every confidence that the governor and his intrepid law enforcement team will apprehend this vile individual by tomorrow's meeting. Let's not act hastily. Let's allow the Islanders to go about their day-to-day activities. Let the anniversary celebration take place as planned tomorrow. If we try to encourage complete normalcy, we'll lessen the blow to *Island*'s image Earthside when this news eventually is made known."

"Yes," Curtis nodded solemnly, clearly relieved that the burden of leadership was no longer resting on his stooped shoulders. "That does seem to be the proper course of action. I'll talk to the president as soon as possible. If we can carry off this transference of public control smoothly, perhaps these unfortunate killings won't make all that much of a difference in the eyes of the U.S. population. Why, perhaps by leasing the habitat to Kingdoms, Inc., we'll even bolster the government's image . . . and the space program, of course. Here we are, cooperating with private industry in space. Very modern. Very democratic. Free enterprise and all that."

Vallory sat at the head of the table, seething in silence.

Harry continued to doodle on Sylvie's list, drawing small rockets next to the names of Dunbar, Vallory, Harper, Jerrow. He suddenly stopped mid-doodle, remembering the parcel delivered to him before the meeting. He opened the envelope hastily, discovering three single-spaced sheets of typewritten information.

He scanned the report until he came to the section he was looking for. *"One of the most controversial elements in modern Egyptian history has been the Trotwood establishment near Cairo."*

He read through the report quickly. He had it! He couldn't believe it! All the missing pieces were in these papers. He knew who Ammit was. It all fit now. Harry stuffed the papers into his hip pocket and left the room in a hurry. Let the politicos battle it out concerning the future of dollars and cents, he had to get a killer off the streets. He ran into Hawkins in the hall outside.

"Where's the fire?" Hawkins groused.

"It's Jerrow! Ammit is Dr. Jerrow!" Harry declared.

"You're crazy," Hawkins said. "That nice old lady? A nut case?"

"That nice old lady is a goddamn cosmic mutation," Harry said, pulling the report from his pocket along with Sylvie's list. "Look. It all makes sense. Here's a list of all the Islanders who have been involved in PSI studies. It's a pretty big roster. Ammit is a peeper, but a self-trained peeper. So, he, or she, is someone who's had a peripheral contact with the art form as opposed to formal study. OK. Now, I started by eliminating all these local yokels. Ammit knows about the greenhouse

286

accident. Only the big shots on the hab are privvy to that info. Now the list is considerably smaller, right? A few dozen names."

"So what?" Hawkins said, gnawing his mustache. He was obviously not impressed.

"Give me a minute, will you? I started thinking about Ammit. His laser weapon is a pretty advanced little tool, probably homemade. In order to construct a weapon of that caliber, our friend had to have a pretty good working knowledge of physics. That means that he, or she, had to either have studied in a school for scientific research or have come into pretty close contact with some stellar name in the field "

"Are you near a point?" Hawkins asked.

Harry produced a pencil and began crossing out names. "OK. You took a couple of PSI courses at the Academy. No science. You're out. Dunbar, out, sheer educational stuff. Harper. Out. He couldn't use a screwdriver without a set of instructions. Communications Chief Thorton. Has the technical skill but no PSI contact of an advanced sort. Communications Officer Mullins. No science. Martin Graff . . . a very likely subject. Now deceased. The survivors of the accident: Thomas, Carry, Romano, Abbatiello, Dokey, Chapman, Robin, Marsk, Lohmeyer, Daisy, Metcaff, and Fillion; all logical suspects, all with proper training and all so mentally messed up that they can't even feed themselves. OUT. Who does that leave on my list?"

Hawkins squinted at the paper. "Vallory and Jerrow."

"Right," Harry said. "Now, I just didn't think that Vallory would be schized out enough to turn to murder and then a cover-up, so I zeroed in on Jerrow.

"It made sense from the start, only I was too damned impressed by her professional dedication to notice. Her natural PSI abilities were obviously spawned by the same incident that triggered Graff's . . . the greenhouse accident. Exposed to cosmic radiation, she became a mutation of a sort, her mental abilities increased manifold. What threw me off was her lack of PSI abilities in my presence. I thought, for sure, that an untrained peeper would betray himself mentally and I, being sensitive, would pick up on it. However, I then remembered that Harper had managed to find a way to block out peeper power through sheer practice, through contact with Graff on an almost daily basis. A simple mental exercise for him. So, why couldn't the reversal of that exercise process work for our peeper Jerrow, coming in contact with normal minds everyday, had to hide her power.

"With that thought in mind, I started thinking about the killer's personality and comparing it with Jerrow's. They were both fairly self-righteous, fairly old-fashioned in an almost mystical sense." Harry held up the report. "But here's what cinched it. Jerrow studied at Trotwood. Ring a bell?"

Hawkins frowned, his face furrowing in an attempt at dredging up dim memories. "I feel like I've just run across that name somewhere . . ."

"You have," Harry said. "The place was just destroyed. Gutted. Pulverized by angry locals. It was the world's most ambitious scientific community, sponsored by the U.N. and built in the East. When the local citizens decided to turn on the institute, they did so claiming that the joint had infringed upon their religious beliefs. That, plus some of Jerrow's ravings, set me remembering. Trotwood has always been in trouble with the locals since its opening fifteen years ago. It was a big center for PSI study. It had been open some three years when it had its first encounter with a group of Egyptian citizens. They claimed that the place was attempting to erode their national heritage.

"Actually, what was going on was an almost bizarre re-creation of the ancient religious days of Egypt through peeper study. I don't know what happened, maybe some of the PSI people stayed out in the sun too long but, somehow, their studies dovetailed with the dredging up of ancient Egyptian myths and legends. Now, in olden days, Egyptians considered the world to be a body in a state of permanent unity despite their multitude of gods and cults. The world was watched over by the pharaoh, whose main task it was to establish *ma'at* instead of disorder *Ma'at* stands for *all* order in life. It can be translated as "truth," "order," "justice," that sort of thing. It was a catchall. Now, those who didn't contribute to this order, those folks whose hearts were found lacking were visited by this minor deity, Ammit, who ate out their innards. Twelve years ago, Trotwood has trying to attain *ma'at* through PSI power. It was a fairly powerful neo-Zen movement. Guess who was one of its prime movers according to this report?"

"Nahh," Hawkins protested. "She couldn't have been mixed up in something like that."

"Oh, but she was. Estelle Jerrow, the defender of the old ways, the good ways, the just ways. The eternal nostalgic.

288

And guess what? When she wasn't dabbling with PSI and ancient religions, she studied the use of the advanced solid laser .. for medical use."

Hawkins remained silent. Harry refolded the papers and tucked them back into his pocket. "I'm not saying that Dr. Jerrow wasn't and isn't a dedicated and basically kind individual. I simply think that a massive dose of cosmic radiation gradually drove her to a point where fact and fiction, logic and emotion, reality and fantasy simply collided. Imbued with superhuman strength, mentally and, perhaps, physically, she decided to exact justice for a crime that offended her on every level imaginable. It's my guess that with each passing day, she lost a little more of her self-control, of her civilized nature. Again, it's not so much her natural personality coming through as its mutated alter-ego."

Hawkins took Harry by the arm. "Let's go."

Hawkins's police van sped across the cylinder's land mass with remarkable speed. Harry, hanging on for dear life, read the address aloud from Hawkins's computer dash "Estelle Jerrow: 195 Pace St. Com. II."

"We're only a community away," Hawkins noted. He pressed down on the intercom unit in his cart. "All units. Attention all units. Hawkins here Converge on the address now appearing on your dash. Evacuate any and all residents in the area. Alert the attendant of the building. Isolate apartment 2A. Repeat. Isolate 2A. Stay put until I arrive."

The car reached the end of the first strip of land, Com. I. Twisting the wheel of the cart, Hawkins maneuvered the vehicle onto the cylinder's rim, barreling along its nose until reaching the end of the strip known as Com. II. He swung the cart off the circular roadway and onto the land mass with a jerk of the wheel. Harry closed his eyes.

"You know," he said through clenched teeth. "Even racked with madness, Jerrow was very logical in her plan. She couldn't lose. Either she assassinated all of the officials responsible, directly or indirectly, for the cover-up or she would have attracted enough negative emphasis on the colony to effectively kill it, thus avenging her friends' debilitation. The presence of the Earth delegation set the scene. It was perfect timing. And perfect logic. An eye for an eye. Thirteen victims for thirteen more."

"Damn," Hawkins said for no particular reason. His cart tore up large chunks of grass as it plowed through pedestrian park after pedestrian park, sending hordes of startled citizens scurrying for safety. Hawkins kicked the accelerator to the floor. "I wish these goddamn things could top 40 mph," he muttered. Pounding the dashboard with a closed fist, he sounded the police siren full force. Harry thought his head would burst. At least he couldn't hear the muzak over the din.

The cart slid to a halt outside the Pace Street address, a four-story structure shaped like a pyramid. Hawkins stepped clumsily out of the driver's seat. "You can wait in the cart if you'd like It will be safer."

"And miss the story of the century?"

Both men trotted into the building. Two stern officers stood in front of the doorman's station. "Is everyone in the building safe?" Hawkins asked.

"As safe as possible."

"Good. 2A. Let's take the stairs "

Harry, Hawkins, and the two foot patrolmen huffed up the fire stairs, emerging on the second floor. "Careful," Hawkins cautioned. "Don't get near the door. She may be armed, either with a gun or with that laser sword of hers."

The two men padded silently up to the door, Hawkins motioning the officers to remain in the rear. Harry and Hawkins stood flanking the door. "Now what?" Harry whispered. "Do we kick it in?"

Hawkins sneered at Harry. "Weak ankles."

The police chief reached out and knocked on the door. "Dr. Jerrow?" With his other hand, he clutched a laser pistol. "Dr. Jerrow. Open the door please, It's Chief Hawkins."

Not a sound emerged from the apartment.

"Dr. Jerrow?" Harry called. "It's Harry Porter. Open up. We'd like to talk to you."

No response.

Hawkins took careful aim. With a quick squeeze of the trigger, he sliced the doorknob and lock off the door. Harry nudged the door open with his foot. It swung open unhampered by any resistance from within.

The two men stepped inside the apartment and found a deserted living room. Hawkins motioned for Harry to keep behind his own massive frame. Gun in hand, he surveyed the scene. The apartment was neatly, albeit sparsely furnished; the type of room usually associated with the quintessential spinster. Two chairs. A small TV unit. A casette stereo. A microfilm viewer and library. A few Puritanical holographic sculptures. Two or three Earth magazines scattered on a small table. Bare floors. One throw rug of oriental design. Wall unadorned except for three diplomas or degrees of some sort, framed by dust.

"Look at this," Hawkins muttered.

On the far wall, in a glass-encased cabinet usually associated with old china, sat a collection of Earth weapons. Hand guns spanning the entire twentieth century. "Real museum pieces," Harry said. The glass on the cabinet was broken. The guns inside scattered about.

The two men exited the living room and entered the adjoining bedroom cautiously. Harry heard Hawkins heave a deep sigh. He peeked over the chief's shoulder. There, sprawled across the room's single bed, was the body of Estelle Jerrow.

"Damn," Harry muttered coldly.

"If it makes you feel any better," Hawkins said, replacing his gun in his holster. "You had me convinced that this was our killer."

Harry took one step forward, his foot crunching on broken glass. He stared at the body. It had no face.

10

Vallory refused to look Harry straight in the eye.

Not too good a sign from someone supposedly on the same team, Harry noted to himself. Sitting across from the governor in the confines of Hawkins's office, he allowed himself to collapse into a state of mental exhaustion. He was drained. He was trapped in a maelstrom of events over which he had no power. The more he flailed about, the more he became enmeshed. The more he relied on logic, the worse things got. The more he struggled for survival, the closer destruction seemed to be.

He glanced at Russell Vallory's sunken face. The man was a contradiction in terms; an honor-obsessed hero who wallowed in deceit. Even now, Harry instinctively knew that Vallory was hiding information from him, even though they were working side by side.

There was a strong note of falsehood, for instance, in the governor's version of the greenhouse accident and the subsequent cover-up. It made sense to hush up the accident in order to maintain the habitat's 100% safety record. But why keep the victims under wraps? They could have been shipped back to Earth under a number of pretexts. Injury outside the habitat. Virus. Anything. Those men were kept aboard *Island* for a reason and only Vallory and the killer knew that reason.

Harry certainly didn't, and that irritated the holy hell out of him. He was also getting tired of being manipulated. He had a keen nose for news and a good sense of deductive reasoning. He took secret pleasure in helping people out of difficult situations. Aboard this habitat, however, he was constantly made to feel like a puppet on a string.

Sitting in the office, toying with emotions of anger and helplessness, he reflected on Jerrow's death. She had to have been Ammit. There was no other likely candidate. Everything fit. Although, logically, Harry knew that his entire train of thought could have been wrong, something deep within him, ego perhaps, told him that he had been right.

Hawkins silently entered the room. His face was a portrait of defeat.

"Find out anything interesting?" Harry asked.

Hawkins carried in a small briefcase and placed it on his desk. "Nothing spectacular. She was killed instantly. Full force blast in the head."

"Suicide?" Harry asked.

"Not likely. No weapon around."

"Any prints in the room?"

"None. Professional job. Wiped clean."

"Any sign of a struggle?"

"Aside from the shattered cabinet, none. Jerrow must have known her killer."

"Or of him," Harry said.

Hawkins looked puzzled. Harry attempted an explanation. "It might have been someone she didn't have direct personal contact with, but someone she recognized through title or reputation."

"Oh, yeah, right," Hawkins said, obviously dismissing the thought as lightweight

"How long had she been dead?"

"Four, five hours."

"Damn."

"Yeah," Hawkins sighed. "That takes her out of the Ammit sweepstakes. She was stone cold when those notes were delivered to the meeting room this morning. She'd been dead since dawn."

"Anything left around the apartment?"

"Not really." Hawkins opened the briefcase and removed three clear plastic bags, no more than five inches in width and four inches in height. He spread them out on the desk. They contained small fragments of seemingly shattered material.

"Whoever killed Jerrow did a good job of it," Hawkins said. "The place was pretty tidy. Even the garbage had been emptied. Put out in the hall for the super to pick up."

"And by the time we arrived?" Harry asked.

"Disposed of. Trash collection was at eight this morning. Whatever was in that apartment has already been blasted and is on its way to recyclement now."

"Shit."

"Most likely." Hawkins pushed the bags toward Harry. "We found this stuff in various corners of the bedroom. We don't know what it is, junk most likely. I'm going to send it all out for analysis. Thought you might want to look at it first."

Harry leaned over the desk. One bag contained fragments of what appeared to be glass. Another was filled with what looked like plastic. The third contained a wire fragment. "Could be anything," Harry stated, disappointed by the seemingly routine contents. "For all I know, Jerrow could have dropped her dentures."

Harry walked to the office window. Darkness was being contrived outside. "Governor," he said in a tired voice. "If I were you, I'd call off that celebration tomorrow. The speeches. The air show. The works. Declare a state of martial law and keep your citizens off the streets."

The governor remained in his chair. He stared fixedly at nothing in particular. Harry continued to watch the reflected sunlight fade. "I've spent the last ten years covering crime stories but this one has me stumped. Ammit has beaten us. I don't know what he has planned for your anniversary bash but you can bet that a lot of innocent people are going to be hurt or killed as a result of his scheme."

The governor didn't blink. He didn't move. His lips parted in a small sneer. "Martial law?" he repeated. "I won't even consider it."

"You're being unreasonable," Harry said, facing the politician.

"You're just worried about your own life," the governor whispered, raising his eyes toward Harry. "You're a coward. A short-sighted coward. If you realized how important this colony was, you couldn't even consider the thought of martial law."

Harry felt his blood boil. He clenched his fists at his side. He had half a notion to lift this aging astronaut out of his chair and scramble his skull for good. Hawkins must have sensed Harry's first impulse because, at that precise second, he casually stepped from behind his desk and placed himself between the newsman and the governor. He didn't say a word. He didn't have to. The angry look in his eyes told the story. Vallory's dreams were dying. It was only a matter of time until the formal funeral services occurred. Neither Harry nor Hawkins were sure that the populace of the habitat had enough time left to wait for the death knell.

"You shouldn't talk to Porter like that," Hawkins said firmly. "He's been working his ass off to help us out of this mess and he's not even remotely responsible. He has nothing to gain from this."

Harry felt embarrassed hearing such praise. It was not entirely true. In one way, he was operating from an entirely selfish motive. He wanted to save his own life. He wanted to keep his promise to Ernie Seabruck. He wanted to reap whatever rewards there might be for getting off the habitat in one piece. But, perhaps most importantly, he wanted to redeem himself in the eyes of Sylvie Dunbar. While he hadn't exactly walked out on her years ago, he hadn't done much to prolong their relationship. If this habitat was important to her, it was important to him as well. Harry cleared his throat. He felt like a hypocrite.

He looked around the room nervously, sensing the downward slide of the colony. It was like standing in the middle of a movie lot. Surrounded by a city that looked real but was, upon closer examination, a series of plywood fronts. Now, even the fronts were toppling over. Soon only an empty set would be left. A fallen illusion.

The buzzing of Hawkins's desk videocom brought him out

294

of his reverie. Hawkins walked over to the desk and leaned on a green button. "Yeah?"

A pasty-faced woman in her late thirties appeared on the screen. "A call for the governor."

"Who is it?"

"His wife."

Both Hawkins and Vallory reacted as if they had been hit from behind by a bowling ball. Vallory lurched forward in his seat, his eyes darting nervously back and forth, as if they were trying to escape the confines of their sockets.

"I didn't know you were married," Harry said.

"Just recently," the governor said hesitantly. "We didn't think it would be wise for the public to know ... just yet. Problem of safety."

Harry shook his head from side to side sadly. He felt an emotional piledriver heading his way at increasing speed. "I'll take the call outside," Vallory said.

"Nonsense," Harry said, walking over to the videocom. "We're all the same team here, aren't we?" He glanced at Hawkins. "Put the call through."

Hawkins looked at the governor questioningly.

"Put the call through," Harry repeated

"Put it through, Williams," Hawkins said meekly.

The pasty-faced woman disappeared from the screen, her image replaced by that of Sylvie Dunbar. Seeing Sylvie on the screen didn't hit Harry half as hard as he had expected it to. He had sensed something like this for quite some time. The idea had lingered in the back of his mind with an entire group of other deceits. He had fought it, subdued it, and sent it into limbo for a time. But now, like a mistake long forgotten, it showed up again in sixty-point headline type.

Sylvie saw only Hawkins in her receiver. "Hawk? Is Russ there?"

Harry stepped into the screen's range of vision. "We're all here, Mrs. Vallory. Just one big extremely gregarious family."

Sylvie's mouth formed a capital "O."

Harry returned to his position at the window, passing the governor as he did so. "You'd sacrifice anything to save this tub, wouldn't you?"

Vallory got to his feet to take the call. As he did so, Harry cocked his fist back and let fly with a haphazard left. Vallory, caught offbalance, took the blow full on the face. Harry's fist smashed into his lip, skidding along the side of his cheek. The governor reeled back, arms flailing. He hit the chair and tumbled onto his back with a crunch.

Harry, stunned by his own anger, let out a yelp. He gazed at his fist. Damn. He had taken off half the skin on his knuckles. Jesus but Vallory had strong teeth. His fingers were swelling already, stiffening. So much for macho. Vallory climbed to his feet, his upper lip covered with blood, his right nostril emitting a trickle of crimson. He stumbled to the video unit. The punch had drained him of the little energy he had still retained.

"Russ!" Sylvie exclaimed. "What happened?"

"I . . . I fell," he stammered, embarrassed for everyone involved.

"Russ, is Harry still there?"

"Yes."

"May I speak to him?"

"No," Harry called from the window. The colony outside was swathed in blackness now.

Vallory was tired and irritable. "What is it, Sylvie? Why did you call me here?"

"A note was delivered to the house a few moments ago."

"So?"

"It's for you. From Ammit."

Harry left his window view and walked to Hawkins's desk. The two men avoided his gaze. "Tell her to read it," he instructed.

"Read it," Vallory requested half-heartedly.

Sylvie pursed her lips. "Do not try to fight me. You have already lost. Your sins shall be publicly paid for, Vallory. Tonight, your children will die. Tomorrow, your *Island* will die. You cannot save your offspring, but you can save your colony. I will be in touch. Later, this evening, you will receive precise instructions. Ammit."

Harry drummed his fingers on the desk. "Don't tell me you have a secret family, too?"

Vallory's sense of self-esteem was rapidly returning. "Of course not!"

"Then what is this guy talking about?"

"I have no idea!"

"How about the little woman. Does she know?"

Sylvie frowned into her unit. "You don't have to be sarcastic, Harry. I did what I had to do."

"Yeah, I know," Harry smiled. "You were only obeying

296

orders. One side works on his brain, while the other operates on his balls."

"Mr. Porter," Vallory said, droplets of blood caked on his teeth. "You are talking about my wife!"

"Nice of you to remember that," Harry shrugged. "Now, Mrs. Vallory, do you know what kids this geek is talking about?"

"No."

"Fine. Hang up. Stay put and lock your door."

Sylvie glared at Harry. The screen faded to black.

Harry began pacing the room. "Sit down, governor."

"You can't order me . . ."

"Sit down before I lose my temper," Harry advised. "I'm not very athletic but, right now, I'm fairly deranged. We're the worse kinds of assailants you know, just ask the chief here"

Vallory looked at Hawkins. Hawkins nodded affirmatively. The governor picked up his overturned chair and sat. "Things are actually beginning to fall into place," Harry smiled grimly. "Ammit isn't out to avenge any crime. He's out to do you in personally, gov. He's out to destroy everything you believe in. Vendetta time."

"I don't quite understand," Vallory said.

"These last couple of notes from Ammit have been very personal, governor. They've been aimed at you. Is there anyone you know of who really hates you? A political opponent, perhaps?"

"I rule *Island*," Vallory said. "I have no opposition."

"Pity."

Harry leaned on Hawkins's desk with one hand, facing the governor. "Perhaps it's someone you've misled, lied to, cheated . . ."

"I am an honest man!" Vallory exploded. His face was contorted, both in rage and pain. He seemed to totter on the edge of sanity. His eyes were glazed with a thin film of water. "Whatever I have done, I have done for the good of the community. For the good of the entire world!"

Harry was not impressed. "Right. We've heard all that before. Now, why don't you stop feeling personally wounded by the killer's intentions and wise up. You haven't said two honest words to me since I got up here. You say 'good morning' and I look for rain. The two of you have led me on, used me. By all rights, I should walk out right now and let you two, excuse me, you three—I mustn't forget your missus

—grapple with this loon. But he's used me, too. I owe him a good shot. Then, I'll come to your turn."

Hawkins fidgeted behind his desk. "We deserve all this, Porter . . ."

"You deserve a lot more."

"But we haven't got much time left."

Harry walked over to the window, chatting absent-mindedly. "There's something that's itching me in the back of my head. I'm not sure what it is yet. But right now, let's concentrate on the obvious. The key to that last letter is the mention of the *children.* The earlier notes mentioned the children of light. They were the victims of the accident. This letter, however, refers to the governor's offspring. I don't think they're the same people. This letter denotes ownership." He pointed a finger at the governor. "Are you sure you don't have any kids hanging around? Maybe in a back closet?"

Vallory's face clouded. A sudden thought flashed through his mind. "My God! He wouldn't!"

"He would," Harry replied. "But would what?"

"The greenhouse!" the governor cried getting to his feet. "He'll ruin us!"

"You keep your kids in a greenhouse?" Harry asked.

Hawkins bolted from behind his desk. "There's still time to stop him."

The two men ran from the room, Harry at their heels. He swore under his breath as he followed the pair out of the building. "I was in control there for a minute," he muttered. "I wonder what happened?"

11

Hawkins's police cart zipped through the first cylinder and headed for the cablecraft linking the first tube with the second. Aboard the cablecar, he radioed for a second van to meet them at the docking port aboard the agricylinder. When the trio emerged from the car, a police cruiser awaited them. Hawkins wasted no time in putting distance between the docking station and the vehicle.

The three men traveled in total silence. Vallory and Hawkins nervous and determined. Harry totally confused. Within minutes, their destination appeared before them. Harry was taken aback by the vastness of the scene. From the sky, the large greenhouse looked merely large. From the ground, the structure looked like a man-made mountain; a large scale rectangular glass building vast enough to house a herd of elephants on stilts.

The police cart sputtered to a halt in front of the structure. Two guards trotted out from the shadows, guns drawn. Harry gaped at the weapons. Quite a bit of protection for a fruit farm. Hawkins huffed him. "Everything seems secure."

"They haven't hit us yet," Vallory agreed, obviously relieved.

Harry trailed behind the two men. "I don't suppose anyone would want to clue me in as to what the hell is going on?"

Vallory led them to the entranceway. He turned to Harry. The lines in his face were crevicelike now, deep and weary. "Mr. Porter," he announced wearily. "You are about to see something no other non-*Islander* has ever seen. You are about to gaze upon the habitat's biggest blessing ... but also its biggest curse, it would appear."

That's the second time I've heard that one, Harry thought.

"Here is the secret of our proposed financial success." With a hint of melodrama, Vallory swung open the greenhouse's massive door. Harry's jaw dropped to the slackened position usually associated with TV viewing. The interior of the greenhouse was bathed in an eerie purple light, sparked by a series of elongated bulbs draped from the ceiling throughout. Illuminated in the violet glow were rows and rows of plants; plants unlike anything Harry had ever seen.

Each of the plants stood at least fifteen feet tall. Some of them Harry guessed to exceed thirty feet in height. Their green stems were thick enough to be tree trunks, at least three feet in circumference. Large leaves, the size of a tall man's torso, dotted the stem of the plant from its base to its midway point. On the uppermost section of the stalk, large, bulbous pods of some kind, purple in color, hung precariously. The sight of the pods caused Harry's jaw to drop even lower with a crack. Damn that orthodontist.

"What the hell are they?" he gasped.

"Our manna," Vallory said with forced irony. "Food that fell from the heavens themselves."

"Mutations?"

299

"Precisely," Vallory replied. "In a very real sense, they are the children of *Island*, unique to this habitat alone. Inadvertently, these hybrids were created as a direct result of our radiation-shielding accident. Dr. Jerrow, Dr. Graff, the men that you saw in the hospital ward, actually created this species when the roof fell in on them five years ago. Back then, this greenhouse was a lot smaller. Just one of the many on this cylinder. As you know, most of the diet up here is of a vegetarian nature. We grow both our vegetables and fruit in this cylinder. Well, as a promotional gesture to mark our fifth birthday, we had planned a gigantic agricultural exhibition.

"It was to be a gala affair with special greenhouse exhibits, colorfully designed to attract the attention of TV audiences down on Earth. The festivities would be topped by the opening of our newest greenhouse facility. This one. Seeds were to be planted by some of *Island*'s most prestigious citizens, myself included. Since most of the celebrity farmers were not familiar with either the greenhouse or proper procedures for seed planting, we arranged to have a dry run; sort of a practice maneuver allowing them to get used to the agricylinder.

"The men were gathered here, awaiting my arrival, when the tragedy occurred. They were surrounded by large trays of seeds. Seeds of every kind imaginable. Suddenly, their world caved in on them. The men ran for their lives. Walls shattered. Girders snapped. The men and the trays were scattered over a two block area by the impact. The place was a shambles."

Vallory gazed stoically at the greenhouse roof. "It took us six hours to retrieve the men. We had to seal off the cylinder and get our CD squad to get in here with their suits on. We didn't want to take any chances with cosmic radiation."

Vallory led Hawkins and Porter down a path between two rows of the towering mutations. "We thought we had the situation under control. Graff and the others showed no outward effects of the radiation exposure for a few weeks. The greenhouse was also considered unsullied. Then, these strange stalks began to sprout in this area; stalks that grew at a fantastic rate. It baffled all of us. Within seven days we had plants as big as corn stalks. We were quite aware that we had some sort of mutant hybrid on our hands here. The things just kept on growing. Within two weeks, they had apparently completed their growth cycle. They began to blossom. Purple

300

flowers appeared on the upper half of the stems. The flowers bore fruit. Those pods.

"We were stymied, of course. We didn't know what the hell these plants were. Actually, we still haven't come up with a decent classification for them yet."

"Even after five years?" Harry asked.

"Yes. They're a bit out of the ordinary, you see. They have characteristics of both angiosperms and gymnosperms. In other words, we have plants of the same apparent species whose seeds are both enclosed in pods and free of any covering. That, by the way, is seemingly impossible. And, although their 'fruit' seems to be almost citrus in nature, the plants themselves bear a strong resemblance to the Earth plant plantain of the Musaceae family. That confuses us even more because, even on Earth, agriculturists aren't sure what to do with the plantain. Their fruit is green and larger than a banana, but the botanical classification of plantains is so complicated that the plant is variously viewed as a subspecies of the banana and vice versa.

"Up here, however, instead of bananas, we get those large, purple pods. They're very much of a citrus nature. They yield a blue juice that is quite delicious and that juice can be used for an infinite number of functions."

"*That* is the stuff I've been drinking?" Harry said, horrified.

"Yes. It's incredibly good for you, too. We've found the juice to be teeming with most of the B vitamins, C, and quite a bit of protein. These plants, Mr. Porter, are the source of *Island*'s proposed food and soft drink boom. They were to be the deciding factor in the habitat's future. And now, someone is out to destroy them.

"I can't allow that to happen. Unfortunately, I can't reveal the presence of the plants, either. It was necessary to keep this all very, very secret for the past five years. While we worked to develop an easy breeding method which, by the way, proved almost too successful, we tested the juice on the populace. The consumers loved it. They have never seen the source of the juice, however. I did not intend to allow our proposed Earth customers to see the source, either. Can you imagine what the sight of these things would do to a person used to drinking a liquid squeezed from an adorable little orange, or a rosy apple, or some other innocuous little fruit?"

"They *are* pretty vile to look at," Harry admitted.

"Let's not mince words," Vallory said. "They are utterly hideous. No one would be attracted to a soft drink arising from the fruit picked from one of *those* things. We contrived a plan to keep the plants hidden until we had firmed up our commercial ties and were assured that the colony could continue indefinitely with a self-sufficient source of capital. So, the plants, like the radiation victims, were obliterated from all public records. And the lie continued, getting larger and larger with each passing day."

Vallory looked at Harry, his face collapsed in a mask of sincerity. "You see," he chuckled sadly. "We did start out with the very best intentions." He lifted his hands out before him as if in silent supplication. His sentence trailed off into silence. Harry's mind provided the sympathetic punctuation.

"Well, now that we've made sure that our children are tucked in safely," Vallory shrugged, "let's get back to hunting for Ammit. We'll double the guards tonight."

Stepping outside the greenhouse, Vallory stopped to talk with the guard in charge of security operations. Hawkins accompanied Harry back to the cart. The chief seemed deep in thought. "You know, Porter," he said. "No one really wanted to get involved in all of this. But lies are funny creatures, no matter how good the motive behind them. Once one is loose, it spreads around like a cancer."

Harry caught the expression on Hawkins's face. It was one of both embarrassment and sorrow. Hawk was a good cop. An honest cop. He wasn't a politician nor was he an administrator. It seemed to make him uncomfortable to dabble in either area. He didn't like the smell affixed to those territories. Harry was about to reply with an off-handed, yet understanding remark when a quick, humming sound zipped close by. Harry felt the heat slice past his face in a millisecond. A small flash of light exploded in the corner of his left eye. Hawkins's face seemed to scream from within. The chief's chest suddenly opened, his insides pouring forth in an avalanche of flesh and fire.

Harry pulled the wounded cop to the ground. "Laser fire!" he screamed at the guards. "On your right!"

Harry peered into the blackness before him. A small device came sailing toward the greenhouse. The canister struck the corner of the glass structure and burst into flames. Harry cradled Hawkins helplessly in his arms. The chief had already assumed the pallor of a dead man. Harry trembled with rage.

He watched the two guards in the front of the building fire short bursts of laser fire into the bushes. One of them lobbed a flare into the air. With a small "ping," the flare exploded in a brief orgasm of orange light. In the brief glow, Harry made out the figure of a man darting from the underbrush to a small pedal plane some 100 yards in front of the building. Hawkins shuddered in his arms. "It'll be all right, chief," Harry lied.

"Bullshit," the cop hissed angrily. "My guts are splattered all over my goddamn knees. Burns like a sonofabitch."

The fire began to spread around the corner of the greenhouse. A trio of guards and two men in bright yellow fire-suits converged on the spot. The firefighters carried two large foam guns. Within minutes the brush fire was out. Vallory ran to the police car and radioed for an ambulance and back-up units. Harry watched impotently as the small pedal plane took off, the assassin piloting. The guards in front of the greenhouse, taking no notice of the lift-off, continued to fire haphazardly into the empty bushes. "Knock it off," Harry called. "He's gotten away."

The guards were young, fresh-faced kids. The strain of sudden decision showed in their eyes. They located the pedal plane high above their heads and pointed to it lamely.

Harry heard the high whine of a distant ambulance. Its siren was soon joined by other, equally mournful wails. Police. "Light another flare," Harry shouted to the guards. Hawkins moaned and latched onto Harry's arm. Harry could see that the chief was in the most agonizing pain imaginable. More dead than alive, his muscles could only react instinctively to the sudden removal of half of his internal organs. His eyes rolled. Short spurts of white foam oozed from between his parted lips. Hawkins's fingers dug deep into the flesh around Harry's wrists. The pain in Harry's arm caused tears to well in his eyes. It was as if the chief was trying to absorb some of Harry's life force to sustain his own for precious seconds more.

Harry watched the pedal plane soar. Then, suddenly, with deliberate speed, the craft plunged downward, spiraling toward the main walkway below. With remarkable skill, the pilot sent the plane crashing onto the small pathway, leaping from the plane seconds before impact. The assassin tumbled, catlike, into the grass. In the light of the second flare, Harry watched the man scramble to his feet. The killer was shaken, but not seriously hurt. The sirens approached. The assassin

303

stood on the roadside's edge. He glanced nervously to his left and right before running across the walkway and into the darkness.

"Sonofabitch!" Hawkins grunted.

The ambulance and police carts were forced to swerve off the paved area and onto the green hills in order to reach the greenhouse. The little maneuver caused by the plane's debris cost them precious minutes. By the time the ambulance pulled up to the plant fortress, Hawkins was no longer clutching Harry's arm.

12

The room was small, silent, sterile. A rectangular chamber with small metal hinges affixed to its wall. Its floor was devoid of all furniture but two white metal tables. Everything in the room was flesh toned, shiny and antiseptic. The presence of death had been neatly camouflaged.

Dr. David Mason led Vallory and Porter into the morgue. He opened one of the hinged hatches and pulled out a gleaming, pink tray. On the tray was the body of Joshua Hawkins. Dr. Mason, a blond man of about thirty years of age, regarded the body as one would a stick of wood. It was simply an inanimate object. In his mind, it had always been so.

"The autopsy was a mere formality," he said matter-of-factly. "Chief Hawkins was a dead man as soon as he was hit."

Porter fought back his rising nausea and anger. The man had been alive in his arms. Harry had felt the life's blood drain from the body. Hawkins had not been a dead man when hit. He had been alive, aware of each exploding pinprick of pain dotting his system. Alive, damn it. Writhing. Cursing. Bleeding.

Alive.

He stared contemptuously at the doctor and, then, at the governor. Damn Vallory. If he had only been honest. If he had lived up to his lofty ideals, Hawkins might still be alive.

Young might still be alive. The bellboy. Safian. Jerrow. Graff. All of them. Dead now and for what end?

Under his gaze, Vallory seemed to age a century. The creases beneath his eyes were now furrows. His eyes were puffy and blue.

"Any notion about the type of weapon?" Harry asked numbly.

"Laser rifle. Don't see many of them up here."

"Great."

He left the morgue and sat out in the waiting room on a bench affixed to a pale-green wall. No matter how much you scrubbed away, the stench of death lingered in rooms like that, in halls like these. Rooms and halls designed by the living to traffic the dead.

Vallory emerged from the morgue, drained of all color. He sat down next to Harry. "I never thought it would come to this."

Harry refused his sympathy. "Poor planning on your part, eh?"

"I don't know what to do next, Porter."

"You don't have too much of a choice at this point, do you?"

"I can't surrender the colony."

"You can't sacrifice innocent people at those ceremonies tomorrow, either."

"He might be bluffing about that."

"He hasn't bluffed you yet."

"I have no guarantee that he'll keep his word."

"He has no guarantees about your honor, either." Harry regretted his last verbal thrust as soon as he had uttered it. It was no fun to torture an animal already numb from pain.

Harry noticed a steady, crunching noise and realized that the governor was grinding his teeth together in a rapid, violent motion. "I will not surrender the colony," Vallory stated.

"Oh will you come off it? It's over. You've lost. There's no point of honor involved anymore. It's a question of sanity, of human life."

"This villain has no right . . ."

"You have no right to play god, either."

"I've tried to do my best . . ."

"Yeah well, your best just wasn't good enough, was it?"

A young intern walked down the hall. He stopped in front of the two men. "Governor Vallory?"

Vallory looked up, his green-gray eyes nearly transparent. "Yes?"

"This came for you about a half hour ago, sir. It was delivered to your office. It was forwarded here." He handed Vallory an envelope.

Vallory took it. He held it in his hands. He regarded the parcel with an almost spiritual dread. Finally, he sliced it open and held the message tightly within his shaking fingers. He pursed his lips tightly together. The skin around his mouth turned white.

"Is everything all right, sir?" the orderly asked.

"Yes," Vallory said with a wave of his hand. "Thank you."

Harry thrust his hands into his pockets. He didn't bother to look at the letter. "From Ammit?"

"Yes."

"What now?"

"Instructions telling me how to go about surrendering the colony." Vallory smiled sickly. "Quite ingenious. Listen. 'You have refused to heed my warnings. Hawkins's blood is now on your hands. There is still time to save your followers from needless slaughter. Tomorrow you shall:

" '1) Surrender all authority to the president's science advisor Archibald Curtis.

" '2) Agree to meet the demands of the Earth delegations.

" '3) When and if you are ordered to close down the habitat known as *Island One*, you will do so without hesitation.

" '4) You will instruct the United States government to abandon all claim to the colony and order them to cease any and all plans for military intervention in regards to my existence. Should the United States attempt a retaliation against me or any of my followers, I shall destroy the colony completely.

" '5) Once the colony is abandoned, I, under the laws of space salvage, will be allowed to claim the structure. Using your resources, I shall begin a rule of honesty and altruism that will exceed your concept of present day government.

" 'If you do not proceed as directed by 10 AM tomorrow, your celebration will be transformed into a mass funeral.

" 'Ammit.' "

Harry stared at the wall before him. "He's gotten to be quite a writer in the past few days."

"This is not the time for sarcasm," Vallory spat.

"I'm not being sarcastic," Harry snatched the letter from Vallory, his impatience mounting. "Look. *Read* what's in the letter. This guy is giving orders now. Precise orders. For a fellow who started out on an emotional vendetta, our buddy has certainly evolved into quite the well-organized political philosopher, hasn't he?" He handed the letter back to Vallory. "Here. This isn't from Ammit."

The governor eyed Harry suspiciously. "What the hell are you talking about."

Harry got to his feet and walked down the hall. "Let's go over to the police station. What I mean is this: that note is not from THE Ammit."

"You mean this isn't from the killer?"

"I didn't say that. It's from a killer all right, but not from the killer who almost parted my hair at neck level."

"You're not making sense."

"I am, but you're not hearing it. I told Hawkins I thought that Jerrow was our killer. Now, I'm positive of it. Who's the biggest authority on lasers you have up here?"

"Let's see. Larry Ambrose, I guess. Physics man."

"Good. Get on the horn and tell him to meet us at the station house."

"But it's the middle of the night."

"It may be your last night alive. Just call him, all right?"

Two hours later, Vallory and Harry faced the bleary-eyed Dr. Lawrence Ambrose in one of the police station's laboratories. Ambrose, hiding behind a bushy beard and a pair of coke-bottle glasses, stuffed the crushed particles found in Jerrow's room back into the three plastic bags. Dawn began to illuminate the room. "Yes," he yawned at Harry. "You were correct in your assumptions. These particles are from some sort of laser device. An optically pumped solid one, in fact. You have a little bit of the silvered mirror here. A bit of the partially silvered mirror and flash lamp and this opaque particle here is a section of the Q-switch control. Sophisticated material for a home-made model."

Ambrose shook Vallory and Porter's hands and stumbled out of the room. Vallory was dumbfounded. "Jerrow?"

Harry rubbed the sleep out of his eyes. "Looks that way. Just a good guess on my part. Ammit's original notes were written in a state of blind anger. The woman was outraged by an injustice committed. The injustice was, of course, the greenhouse incident and the inhumane treatment of the victims. Jerrow was a victim too, of course, and as her PSI abilities increased, so did her thirst for revenge.

"Drawing on her experience at Trotwood, she both constructed the traditional sword of justice, but with a scientific twist, and conjured up a handy ancient deity to dispense with the retribution. She wanted to bring the whole situation to the attention of the world. She didn't want to kill everybody aboard *Island*, just dispatch the guilty parties, both figuratively and literally. Her crimes would bring everything to the surface and the American public, at that point, would pass sentence.

"At that point, someone must have found out about her plan. For reasons unknown, this person decided to remove the good doctor from the scene and assume the Ammit role. They murdered her and destroyed her sword in the process. The sword shattered, they tried to eliminate all evidence of both its existence and Jerrow's connection with the killings. I should have noticed, at that point, that there was a second killer around. All the signs were there.

"Ammit did keep her word about not harming anyone for a twenty-four-hour period. Following my talk with Jerrow at the ward, she must have decided to give me a chance to square myself. While the real Ammit was in hibernation, the second killer struck for the first time, taking Tony and his cart out of the picture. If I wasn't so caught up in all of our self-inflicted woes, I would have noticed right off that the MO was different with this killing. Tony was killed by an explosive device rigged in his cart. Sure, Ammit claimed responsibility for it and we all readily believed it. But the real Ammit would have taken Tony out much more dramatically, with the laser sword. Safian's mode of death was too modern, too innocuous.

"The same thing with Hawk. A laser rifle snuffed him out, not a sword. Our new Ammit is a contemporary killer. He's out to close down the colony but not, I fear, for any lofty goals."

"But who . . . and why?"

Harry looked out the window. "I don't know. But I have the feeling that we're going to find out soon."

"Why?"

"What time do you have?"

"My God!" Vallory cried. "It's 9:45!"

The two men ran out of the room. "Why didn't you keep me informed of the time?" Vallory fumed.

"Who do I look like, Mickey Mouse?" Harry said, trotting after the governor. "I don't even own a watch that works right."

"Now what will I do?"

"Why not call out every cop you have. Get most of them in plainclothes and have them work the crowd. How long is this ceremony?"

"The aerial ballet lasts about fifteen minutes. Then, there will be speeches."

"Will the aerial ballet be televised?"

"Yes."

"Then that's the time to watch for Ammit. Prime time viewing."

The governor came to an abrupt halt. "Look. I am quite tired of you giving me orders, Mr. Porter. You are not an expert on habitat security."

"You're not exactly copping any prizes either," Harry pointed out.

Vallory flapped his quintessential hero's jaw up and down as if to reply. He turned on his heel and left the police station. Harry stood at the doorway. Well, fuck him, it was his mess anyway.

Harry stepped outside into the morning sun. Jesus, he felt grubby. Stubble on his face. Hair greasy. He ran his tongue along his front teeth. He felt like he could mow his mouth. Jamming his hands in his pockets, he watched *Island*'s citizens begin to gather for the festivities. Nothing he could do now but watch the disaster unravel. The Islanders gathered in small clusters in the pedestrian parks. At least there wouldn't be any massive mob scenes, Harry noted. The aerial ballet would be clearly visible from any park on the habitat's populated cylinder. No need to jostle for *the* best view.

He strolled toward the small hill the gaily colored pedal planes were to be launched from. A group of perhaps twenty vehicles stood on the as yet empty runway. Lined up neatly, they awaited their pilots. They were garrishly decorated in bright colors and boasted streamers of various lengths and hues. Some had even been modified with lightweight plastic so that the finished planes' bodies resembled large insects, dragons, birds, etc.

Harry snuggled into a park bench some 200 feet from the runway. In a brilliant exhibition of atrocious posture, he slid down in the bench so that the small of his back practically touched the edge of the seat. Legs outstretched before him, he stared dumbly at the planes. His mind whirred in several different mental directions at once.

Right now, he imagined, Vallory was giving orders like a deranged martinet. The governor certainly wasn't acting too cool under pressure; still worrying more about principles than practicalities. The hell with him. Let him get his goddamn colony smashed to smithereens.

Harry crossed his ankles. Maybe there was still something that could be done. If only he could think straight. He must have all the pieces. It's just a matter of getting them to fit. Harry blocked out the image of the brightly decorated pedal planes. Ammit had threatened to blow the colony up. That was impossible. It would take tons of explosives to blow this baby apart. So, how would he do it?

How would he blow the colony *up?* Harry snapped his fingers softly. He wouldn't blow the colony *up,* he'd blow the colony *in!* He straightened up in his bench. That was it. Ammit would blow out a section of the shielding. That would send a shower of debris heading in every direction possible. The populace below would panic. People would be hurt, killed as a result of the accident, but many more would die because of the chain reaction of fear set off on ground level.

Harry looked at the paneling above. No one could actually climb up there without being spotted. They'd have to wear those special suits that the repair crews use. Then how would someone actually get an explosive device onto that paneling. Harry refocused his vision on the pedal craft on the runway. Ammit could always drop the bomb onto the shielding. Harry got to his feet. Aerial bombardment? He stood there, amazed by the thought. If that was the plan, one of the pilots in today's display would have to be the killer. And whoever it was last night that had killed Hawkins was an ace flyer.

Harry slowly eased himself back onto the bench. No, that just didn't make any sense. Why would a space colonist go to so much trouble for a political coup? If someone wanted to disgrace Vallory, there were dozens of less involved ways to do so. He closed his eyes and reconstructed Hawkins's murder as best he could.

The pedal plane soared. It plunged downward. The pilot sent the plane crashing across the walkway. The assassin dove from the craft, tumbling into the grass on the side of the path. The sirens approached. The assassin stood on the roadside's edge, glancing quickly to his left before running across the path into the darkness.

Harry stood. He walked toward the plane runway. Only the pedestrian path stood between him and the planes. He paused on the curbside.

And glanced to his left.

His knees nearly buckled as the realization set in. "Sonofabitch," he muttered, returning his gaze to the runway. That's why nothing made any sense. The new killer wasn't an Islander! It was someone from Earth! Damn it. Sylvie had harped at him about the best way to recognize a recent arrival. They all turned left to spot the nonexistent traffic on the streets.

Harry stood transfixed on the curbside. A group of gaily costumed pilots trudged toward the awaiting pedal planes. Harry backed off from the walkway. Some of the pilots wore multicolored jumpsuits. Some wore large, antique space helmets, which hid their faces. Others wore face masks which fit in with certain planes' fantasy motifs. Harry followed them with his eyes as they passed him. The pilots reached the top of the hill and crossed the foot path. Four men were in the vanguard of the group. Three crossed the pedestrian path without hesitation. The fourth, who appeared to walk with a slight limp, lingered on the curbside for a barely imperceptible second.

Harry took a chance. "Hey. Hey you!" he called.

The pilot, dressed in a light-green costume with a dragon face mask, spun around and saw Harry. The dragonman bolted from the group of pilots. He ran down the other side of the hill. Harry hesitated on the curbside, frantically looking for a passing patrolman. Damn. There was never a cop around when you needed one.

Without giving it too much thought, Harry ran after the retreating figure. The pilot had a good fifty-foot start. The dragon had a slight limp, however, and lost ground rapidly. Harry was out of shape. His legs pumped furiously but his pace was erratic. Each time one of his feet slammed into the ground, the jolt made his teeth chatter. His chest ached from the exertion. (He'd have to start those exercises tomorrow.)

Despite his lack of stamina, he closed in on his dragon. The two men ran down the hillside. As they neared the bottom, Harry leaped into the air. He expected to tackle the man shoulder level. Instead, he crashed down around the pilot's feet. A shoe slammed into the side of Harry's mouth. He tasted blood immediately. Either he had just slit his lip or gotten a bad case of jogger's gums.

The runner stumbled, Harry still affixed to his legs. The two rolled into a flower bed, clawing furiously at each other. Harry attempted to bear hug the wiry man into submission but his prey managed to push him off; biting, scratching, and kicking all the while. The man in green, free of Harry, attempted to run back up the hill to the runway. Harry lurched to his knees. He grabbed a broken tree limb and swung wildly at the retreating figure. The branch struck the man in green in the small of the back.

Squealing like a stuck pig, the pilot whirled onto the ground. Harry dove on top of him. Pinning him to the ground more through the grace of God than athletic prowess, Harry tore off the green dragon mask.

Ira Stramm looked up at Harry wide-eyed. He began to laugh, to giggle hysterically.

"My God!" Harry muttered. "You laugh like a girl!"

His face racked with nervous twitches. Stramm suddenly produced an ancient sidearm, a .44-caliber pistol. He swung the butt of the gun into the side of Harry's head. Porter was stunned. He felt his head leave his body, along with most of his strength. He collapsed backward.

In an instant, Stramm slipped from beneath Harry and ran up the hillside to the runway, his hysterical laughter echoing in Harry's ears. He dove onto his dragon plane and managed to leave the airstrip along with the other flyers.

Harry stumbled to his feet just in time to see the airborne armada buzz the hillside. He touched the side of his head. He was bleeding. Straightening himself up with a groan, he jogged up the hillside to the runway. He spotted an unoccupied vehicle. One of the rental models. He mounted the plane and pedaled, stiff legged, toward the end of the runway. "Bonzai," he muttered as his bike glider lost contact with solid ground and spiraled into the air.

On the ground, a nervous Russell Vallory sat in the reviewing stands outside City Hall with the Earth delegation. "Progress report," he whispered into his wrist communicator. "No progress so far," came the voice of an anonymous policeman.

"Anything wrong, governor?" Howard Retson inquired politely.

"No, nothing," Vallory said. "Just checking crowd control."

"Good work," Retson said. "Oh, look, here come your flyers."

Vallory turned his attention to the swarm of pedal planes undulating through the sky. "Is everything all right?" Sylvie whispered into her husband's ear.

"I wish I knew," Vallory replied, biting his lip.

The planes began to loop and swirl in different formations. With each intricate maneuver, the crowd below applauded. The entire scene resembled an underwater ballet performed in the air.

"Marvelous display," Retson commented.

"Indeed," Archibald Curtis admitted, "well-trained athletes, those men."

"I'm proud to call them Americans," Wayne Ferron beamed, momentarily losing sight of his paranoia.

Vallory watched the aerial ballet in silence. The planes formed a massive "T" and began to undulate like a rippling cross-current. Without warning, a single plane, a green-sequined dragon, drifted off from the flock. A murmur arose from the populace. "What's that fellow doing?" Ferron asked. "He's messing everything up!"

Vallory just shrugged.

A second pedal plane appeared from nowhere, a veritable spastic fly in the ointment. It veered crazily from its altitude and dove toward the green plane.

The crowd below applauded.

Vallory strained his eyes. "Hey," he exclaimed, poking Sylvie in her side. "Isn't that your friend Harry up there?"

Sylvie squinted her eyes. "My God . . . you're right!"

"I didn't know he could fly one of those things!"

"He can't!" she cried.

"Ground alert," Vallory whispered into his communicator. "Order all flyers down. Try to herd the populace toward the shelters at a leisurely pace. Make no announcements. Instigate no panic." He turned to Sylvie. "Get the delegation back to the hotel as soon as possible."

"Fine show," Retson applauded. "Fine show."

"Yes indeed," Vallory said hollowly.

Above the crowds, Harry pedaled with all his might. "Stramm," he bellowed. "You'd better land that damned thing right now."

Ira pedaled his plane with maniacal gusto, keeping several lengths ahead of Harry. "Fuck off, Porter. You can't stop me now!"

313

Stramm, his eyes the size of grapefruits, his forehead drenched with sweat, yanked his steering mechanism to the right. His plane floated gracefully down toward Community I.

Harry yanked the joy stick hard, sending his own craft spiraling down toward Ira. He heard the populace gasp from below. They were obviously expecting a tail spin and a crash. He pulled his plane up at the last possible minute, leveling himself off some ten feet to Stramm's left.

The people below cheered.

"You're going to kill yourself, Porter," Ira called.

"Who are you going to kill, Ira?" Harry panted.

The green man pointed a scaly finger at the crowds below. "As many as I can. This little number I'm riding is loaded with plastic explosives."

"Why the hell do you want to do a thing like that for?"

"My secret."

"Stramm," Harry called. "I hate secrets. Ever since I was a kid, I have hated secrets. I'm not going to let you get away with this."

"You can't stop me."

"I can try."

"I can outmaneuver you any day, Porter. I used to hang glide every weekend."

"I played miniature golf!" Harry cried. He cursed under his breath. Goddamn Ira looked like such a wimp. Who would have suspected that he had any strength under those nervous twitches? That was the trouble with this younger generation today . . . they were too unstereotyped. Harry decided that the only way to distract this sniveling maniac was to embark on a series of reckless swoops and climbs. Actually, that seemed to be the way his piloting skills were heading, anyhow.

He tilted his plane toward Ira. The tiny craft zipped by Stramm's green craft, barely missing Ira's head and forcing the dragon to veer sharply to its right.

"What are you trying to do?" Stramm called. "Kill us both?"

"That's my secret," Harry muttered. He yanked the steering mechanism back into his stomach. His plane executed a haphazard loop the loop. He came spiraling down toward Ira's tail. Stramm, turning his head and catching the action behind him, screamed at the top of his lungs and pedaled harder. He sent his craft into a steep climb. Harry thundered

314

past the spot the green dragon had vacated a few seconds before.

The crowd on the ground went wild.

Harry pulled the nose of the plane up and pursued Ira. At least he was forcing the killer away from the more populated areas below. He aimed his craft like a rocket and zoomed upward at the green vehicle. Ira emitted a birdlike yelp and rolled over to his left. Harry shot by the craft's wing like a bullet, tearing off a small section of green plastic dragon scales. He continued to surge upward, getting closer and closer to the cylinder's center sky.

By now, the audience in the pedestrian parks was in a frenzy, applauding and yelling lustily. Harry wondered how people could perform on stage for a living.

Harry saw Stramm glaring at him from below. The skinny assassin's face was beet red, his eyes filled with hatred. Stramm bared his rodentlike teeth. He was obviously tired of playing space tag. Harry saw him raise the .44. Stramm fired before Harry had a chance to react. A bullet went hissing by Harry's cheek.

Harry whistled between his teeth and continued to climb toward the zero g strip above his head. It wasn't that he had a plan, really. It was just that he was attempting a random spurt of logic during a period when his intestinal system was threatening sudden panic. He puffed his way higher and higher. Stramm was on his tail, gaining speed and assurance with every leg stroke.

Another bullet shot through the air, this time smashing into the metal frame supporting Harry's plane's wings. The kid was a good marksman. Harry watched with morbid fascination as a two-inch section of his metal bracing fell apart, sending a small shower of metal slivers spiraling outward from his vehicle. His right wing began to quiver ominously. He continued to pedal. The zero g strip was only seconds away. He recalled his experience of a few days previous and cackled to himself. He was either a genius or a complete fool. He had to plan this maneuver carefully. He had only entered the zero g sector once before and that outing had been disastrous.

He pedaled with all his remaining strength. His life depended on the actions he now took. His life and the lives of those below (and above and to the side of) him. Just before hitting dead center sky, he stopped pedaling. This had

315

to be like swimming, he reasoned. Each body angle counted when one dove into the sea. He tucked his legs backward, gripping the side of his vehicle with his knees. He tilted his torso forward and hugged the nose of the plane. As sleek as an arrow, he dove through zero g. The feeling was, at once, exhilarating and frightening. The power of his acceleration took him floating into and through the thin section of sky. Directly in the center of the sky, he was surrounded by land and protective paneling alike.

It was a fantastically giddy experience. With no outside force affecting his body, his weight was an ethereal, dreamlike attribute. He didn't move his body. His plane sailed ever onward. Within seconds, he felt the pull of gravity once more. He was coming out of it. Carefully placing his feet back on the pedals of his craft, he began pumping furiously once again, before his vehicle had the chance to fall toward the community below.

He swerved his plane and faced the zero g strip behind him. He saw Ira barreling head first toward it, gun drawn. Harry guessed that Stramm would be too emotionally involved in the pursuit to logically calculate his flight pattern. He figured that Ira would hit the center strip with as much clumsy force as he had that afternoon with Sylvie.

He was right.

Stramm plunged into the zero g section of sky like a motor home hitting a tidal wave. His plane lurched gracefully on its side as a result of his impact. Stramm tried to pedal his way to safety. His leg shot downward, missed the pedal, and sent the entire plane into a gentle, tumbling motion. Ira flailed his arms and legs crazily. The craft continued to roll. Exhausted, Stramm ceased all movement. His craft began to slow down, its pilot more off than on his seat. Stramm spotted Harry. His sallow face sported a wicked grin. With elaborate deliberateness, he pointed the gun at Harry.

Harry, pedaling in an easy circle, shook his head sadly and sent his craft into a sudden nosedive. Stramm took this into account and fired the pistol.

The bullet whistled harmlessly past Harry's shoulder. The recoil of the shot, amplified by the lack of resistance in zero g, sent Stramm flying off his seat. The force propelled him through the air like a puppet being yanked off its stage by an unruly string. Stramm released the gun. It floated harmlessly away. The would-be assassin, however, tumbled through the zero g strip, squealing mournfully. Leaving zero gravity, he

316

entered the gravitational pull of the craft. Stramm let out a final, hideous screech as the craft's centrifugal force pulled his body quickly toward the ground below. The audience in Com. II scattered as Ira's body plummeted to the ground like a rock.

On the other side of the zero g strip, still hovering in a circular pattern, Harry watched the entire event in a stupor. From his point of view, Stramm had just fallen straight up to the ground strip on the cylinder's ceiling. "Jesus," he mumbled, "I'd pay to see him do that again."

Exhausted, Harry began to ease his glider down to the ground. Behind him, the explosives-laden pedal plane hung serenely in zero g. On the way down, Harry passed a quartet of policemen pedaling their way upward. He quickly explained the situation to them. The foursome notified a group of demolitions experts who would ease the plane down safely.

Harry landed in a commuter park, sheering off the tops of some sixteen clumps of flowered shrubs.

His chest reverberating with pain, his legs rubbery from the exertion, he tumbled toward a small fountain and collapsed into it. He wanted to lay there forever. The water washed over his face, mingling with the dried blood. Sleep entered his body. He longed for the water to seep into his mouth and his nose and to fill his lungs with its cooling, soothing sensation. He wanted to sleep. To relax. His body was not used to such physical abuse. Every fiber, every nerve ending ached.

He opened his eyes slowly and saw three distorted faces, children's faces, peering down at him through the watery veil. Goddamn it! He was at the bottom of the fountain. He was drowning in a public park. He lurched to his feet yelling wildly. Water filled his mouth. He shot out of the fountain like a rocket, still yelling, choking, and spitting.

The children screamed and ran the other way.

Feeling like the Loch Ness monster, Harry fell onto the grass of the park. He heard sirens in the background. He hoped that they would find him soon. A sudden spasm racked his chest. He vomited a large amount of water. A young cop ran up to him and made a face. "What's the matter," Harry coughed, "My tie on crooked?"

He grabbed the cop around the waist and pulled himself up. "Get me over to Vallory's in a hurry."

"Right, sir," said the cop. "But first we have to get you

317

over to the police station and take down a complete statement."

"Just get me to the governor's," Harry wheezed. "The killer . . ."

"That's what we have to take your statement about," the cop said. "There are forms to be filled out, mere formalities of course."

Harry grabbed the kid by his shirt pockets. "Where are the members of the Earth delegation?"

"Take your hands off me," the cop sputtered. "I'm an officer of the law."

"You're going to be a casualty in two seconds. Where's the delegation?"

"Back at the hotel."

"Anyone with them?"

"Guards, I guess."

"How fast can you get me there."

"First the police station."

"Uh-uh, sweetheart, first the pool." Harry swung the young officer around in a wide arc. The kid went tumbling backward, entering the fountain with a splash. Harry limped toward the cop's cart. "Quick," he called to the kid's partner. "A policeman's been injured. Hurry!"

Harry watched the second patrolman scramble out of the scooter and run into the commuter park. Harry hopped into the abandoned motor vehicle and drove off, oblivious to the shouting behind him. Siren blaring he sped across the cylinder's pedestrian pathways like a maniac. He pulled up in front of his hotel, nearly skidding up the front stairs.

The place looked deserted. He couldn't see a cop anywhere. "Shit," he muttered. They were probably herding the crowds back home. They probably thought that Stramm was *it*. Finito.

"Damn you all," he swore, plodding up the front stairs into the hotel. He walked unsteadily to the elevator and took it to his floor. Falling out of the elevator, he trudged down the hallway, passed his own door, and stopped in front of a room a few doorways down. He pounded on the door with a bruised fist. Howard Retson answered with a slight flourish, a laser pistol nestled firmly in his right hand. He motioned Harry into the room with a slight movement of the gun barrel. "Judging from your battered condition, Parker, you are a much better flyer than you are a lander."

318

"Porter," Harry said, limping into the room.

"A foolish move, sir, coming to my room all alone."

"Who said I didn't tell the police where I was going?" Harry said, easing himself into a plush chair.

"It's not your style, Porker."

"Porter."

Retson nestled himself into a plexiglass chair across from Harry, chuckling. Harry leaned back in the chair and began to bleed from the nose. Retson seemed to relish every drop. "No, my dear sir, you are cursed with an idiotic sense of bravado. As much as you would like to consider yourself otherwise, you are a hopeless romantic; an impulsive individual and, judging from your solitary arrival here, an utterly dense one as well. You no more told the police in advance of your trip here than you did your astounding flight a few moments ago."

Harry glared at the millionaire.

Retson broke into a casual grin, although a slight tug at the corners of his mouth shattered the total complacency of his smile. "Judging from the silence in the air, Mr. Stramm's bomb must not have gone off as planned."

"I don't think it will, either," Harry replied with a small sense of satisfaction.

"Pity," Retson sighed. "It would have really put the capper on that rather lackluster air show. A really splendid finish it would have been, too; lifting the entire affair from a pretty crass Radio City Music Hall type of ambience to an almost grand opera stature. To give credit where credit is due, however, that finale was totally Ira's idea."

"Bravo."

"Yes. Despite his rather frail appearance, Mr. Stramm was a master of weaponry, a veritable aging boy wonder with explosives. He was trained by some of the most respected experts in the United States Army. Indeed, were it not for some of Ira's more blatant eccentricities, he would probably have been a career soldier of some high rank by now. What a talent. Give that boy a toaster and a few firecrackers and he could wipe out a city block. He was quite useful in securing franchises in certain Third World countries."

Retson leaned forward in his chair. "Am I to assume from your lack of comment that Ira is past tense at this moment?"

Harry shrugged. "Depends on his resiliency."

Retson squinted in a small show of sorrow. "Pity." He looked at his wristwatch. "Well, we have a few moments before we leave so, let's chat, shall we?"

"I'm still a little out of breath," Harry said. "Why don't you chat for both of us?"

"Aha. You're sullen. I gather from this taciturn performance that you actually thought your arrival here could stop my plan. How naïve of you, Mr. Pointer."

"Porter."

"What an idealistic boob you are. I have dreamed of our little encounter for quite some time, so please don't disappoint me and sulk. Let me enjoy myself. It was obvious that our paths would cross eventually, wasn't it? Things always end with a classic good versus evil confrontation, don't they? That's the denouement of every popular novel, movie, and video enterprise. Please, don't act so disappointed."

Harry attempted to gauge the extent of Retson's madness. He was too far off the meter for Harry to bother with. Harry folded his hands on his lap. "Why does a man as respected as yourself resort to murder?"

"Excellent," Retson laughed. "Great lead line. Let's play it through. *Villain*: 'Why?' *Villain looks sincerely at hero, perhaps remembering better days.* 'Why not,' *he replies philosophically.*"

Retson began shaking in merriment. "No. No. I mustn't get carried away. I must stop myself before I begin asking you to say things like 'You're mad, Retson, mad.'"

"I'd never say *that*," Harry answered.

"I have the gun."

"I'd say that, sure," Harry replied.

"Let me explain my stance, Mr. Peepers."

"Porter."

"When I arrived here, I didn't at all expect to find myself murdering people. I simply stumbled onto the whole affair."

"How?"

"Actually, I discovered a note for you from Ammit the first night I was up here. I became interested and decided to follow through."

"On behalf of your company."

"I do everything on behalf of my company. Unofficially of course." The man relaxed his body, but not his trigger finger. "I suppose I should explain. You see, when *Island* was first begun a decade ago, several of us at Kingdoms saw a long-term exploitation value up here that was limitless. We

320

immediately bribed a few government officials and arranged to have a few of our own men brought onboard as citizens. Top of the list was dear Harold Mullins, one of the habitat's finest communications experts. With part of our team onboard, we were able to monitor every development that occurred up here. Kingdoms wanted in on the habitat, but we realized that we had to be patient.

"I mean, initially, can you imagine the reaction we would have gotten if we approached the government and asked to have a few hamburger stands tossed onboard their greatest scientific achievement? They would have thrown us out on our ear. So, we waited. We waited until there was a chink in the armor. In that way, we could have nonviolently stepped in and saved the day. That was our plan. Period.

"Then, five years ago, there was that accident. At first it didn't interest us at all. Accidents happen all over. But when our men began to report some of the dandy cover-up activities, well, that interested us quite a bit, I assure you. That gave us extra leverage for our grand entrance."

Harry wiped a trickle of blood from his nose. "You're mad, Retson, mad," he droned.

"Nice try. I'm going to kill you anyway."

"Thought I'd give it a shot."

"And then, a miraculous event occurred. Public opinion on Earth actually turned against the habitat. What a godsend. And then, your Ammit fellow, er, woman, appeared on the scene. It was a perfect set up for Kingdoms. Judging by the expression of total skepticism on your face, you doubt the veracity of my statement, Pinter."

"Porter."

"Let me assure you that Kingdoms didn't plan any of this. Public opinion turned against *Island* on its own. We saw a way to use that wave of displeasure, but we had nothing to do with its origin. A few farthings dropped here and there and, lo and behold, I was included on the President's advisory committee. Then, Ammit enhanced the impact of our arrival by deciding to strike out against the sinners onboard."

"And when you found Ammit's note, you decided to use her as well in your scheme."

"Correct. But we had to know more about our killer."

"Are you the ones who bugged my room?"

"In point of fact, sir, it is still bugged. As I mentioned before, Mr. Stramm used to be employed by the United States military. Those fellows are experts in deceit. Using our micro transmitters we found out everything you knew...as you discovered it. Thrilling to listen to. You were really quite ingenious, Portnoy."

Harry nodded, accepting the compliment lamely.

"Now, at this point, Mr. Stramm and I really thought we had this affair neatly sewn up. We would just let Ammit do the work and we would prey upon the existing paranoia. The way we saw it, Kingdoms would be able to quietly assume control of the habitat and stave off financial ruin."

"Kingdoms is in trouble?"

"Oh, yes. We are in dire financial straits Earthside. That was our reason for attempting to add *Island* to our commercial roster. For decades, we have dominated the soft drink and fast food market. But times are hard on Earth. The economy is tight. People are depressed and bored. Our sales have plummeted. We need a massive rejuvenating shot of positive publicity. An endorsement from *Island* would have done the trick."

Sweat began to form on Retson's brow as he envisioned the near-successful ending of his trip. "We were so close, Mr. Porthole. So near. You saw their faces when I proposed the leasing deal. They were ecstatic. And then, Vallory had to muck it up by introducing that blue juice! We never suspected it was anything more than a substitute for Earth juice, a passable pinch-hitter. We ignored its presence. We let our guard down. That was our first mistake. In business, as in war, you never let your guard down. Vallory was taking my plan and using it against me! His *Island* drink would have wiped out King Kola! We couldn't allow it."

"So you tried to eliminate the competition."

Retson leaned back in the chair, once more assuming his matter-of-fact demeanor. "Look at the situation logically. Our backs were to the wall. We had to fight back. It was now crucial that Ammit force the government's corruption out into the open. That would have given Kingdoms access to the whole ball of wax, blue juice and all. But, at that point, Ammit decided to declare a moratorium. We couldn't allow that. You see, if you weren't such a good mediator, Dr. Jerrow would still be alive today, merrily lopping off the heads of her foes. Luckily for us, we found out Ammit's identity slightly before you did. Mr. Stramm ran across Jerrow leaving the scene of her last crime and tailed her.

"We paid her a visit a day or so later."

"And killed her."

"A necessary move. We couldn't let Ammit fade from view. So when the original Ammit went into retirement, we came up with our own. Unfortunately, during our visit, Jerrow's sword was smashed. The woman was a weapons fanatic. Ira took to her immediately. He was greatly distressed to see such an innovative killing machine destroyed but, ah, the fortunes of war, eh? He hated killing her. I had to drag him out of her apartment. He would have stood there all day fondling her gun collection."

"As it was, he stole one of her weapons."

"Purloined. A memento. Nothing more. He took it during the clean-up operation."

"And it was Ira who killed Safian."

"Correct."

"And Hawkins."

"A quirk of fate. That really wasn't planned. We were out to get the greenhouse. A show of strength. We figured Vallory would cave in a bit more quickly. However, when the chance to add another victim to our list arose, we took it, of course."

Harry clenched his teeth. "Of course." He cursed himself. "I should have caught on earlier. Different MO."

"Don't blame yourself, Poirot. You were emotionally caught up in all of this. You did very well, actually, considering that the entire governmental structure of the community was conspiring against you. A brilliant show of fortitude."

"Now what?"

A frown tugged Retson's smile downward. "Now, Armageddon. Ira's bomb was to have been the *pièce de résistance*. His aerial fire-works were to have been the straw that would have assuredly obliterated the camel's back. With *Island* falling around Vallory's ankles, I'm sure I could have persuaded Curtis and Ferron to hand over the habitat to Kingdoms, Inc. with no trouble. But you've spoiled all of that. Once they find Ira's body, I'm very much afraid that it will be all over for me. Kingdoms, of course, will deny all knowledge of my doings. I will be tried for multiple murder. I can't allow that. I can't allow *Island* to continue to exist, either. Its blue fruit juice poses the ultimate threat to Kingdoms and, Lord knows, I can't watch my comrades be wiped out."

"A company man to the end," Harry said.

Retson showed him his wristwatch. "Twenty-five years and proud of it!"

Harry peered into Retson's eyes. No one was at home, so

to speak. "This Armageddon you talk about, just what is it?"

"Oh, the usual," Retson said cheerfully. "Total destruction. I intend to wipe out this colony. You see, if I allow the habitat to remain intact and the United States abandons it, Kingdoms still has to contend with the menace of the blue fruit juice. By right of space salvage, any country can take over the habitat. Whoever stumbles upon this goldmine can wipe us out."

"So you're going to wipe out the entire colony instead?"

"Precisely."

"That's horrible."

"I surmise from your tone of voice that you are not altogether in favor of my plan." Retson stood, keeping his gun trained on Harry. "Is there any way I can persuade you to voluntarily aid me in my goal?"

"Not really," Harry said, eyeing the gun.

Retson thought hard. "There could be a vice presidency in Kingdoms for you."

"No thanks. I already have one career going."

"Most of our secretaries are young and wear exceedingly tight slacks."

Harry reflected on this latest development. "Sorry."

"Pity," Retson muttered. "I do respect you, Prober. Now, I'm afraid I'll have to force you to help me."

Harry smiled. "And I'm afraid that you'll fail in your endeavor. No way I'm going to help you."

Retson regarded Harry with a good deal of delight. "Of course you won't. I forgot about that. You see, I'm really quite inexperienced at these blatant good versus evil situations. In the business world they are usually a bit more covert. However, I did manage to take a few precautions that I'm sure you will appreciate. If we hadn't gotten so involved in our chat, I would have mentioned them earlier. I must apologize for my lack of priorities but, as I mentioned, I'm a novice at physical violence. Give me a calculator and someone's IRS files, however, and . . ."

"Just what is it you're trying to say, Retson?"

"Oh, er, yes. If you don't help me, Mr. Pointer, the girl dies."

Harry looked at Retson. He looked around the empty room. "What girl?"

Retson glanced about the room as well. "Uh, oh yes. The girl in the front closet, of course."

Harry looked at the double-doored closet near the entrance. It was closed shut. "Judging from the skeptical look on your face, those arched eyebrows are so effective, you don't believe that there's a girl in the closet. Well, go ahead, open it."

Under the gaze of Retson's gun, Harry slowly walked over to the closet and eased open one of the doors. He suppressed a gasp and closed the door.

"Well?" Retson smiled.

"There's a dead man in the closet," Harry whispered.

"Oh damn," Retson exclaimed. "Wrong door. That would be the late Mr. Mullins. Outlived his usefulness I'm afraid. Try the other one."

Harry didn't want to offend the slightly deranged fellow. He swung open the other door. Inside the closet sat Sylvie Dunbar, hog-tied, with a gag in her mouth. "Jesus," Harry gasped, pulling her to her feet as gently as possible. People always knew what his weak spots were. "She could have suffocated in here."

Retson looked genuinely contrite. "It just slipped my mind, Patter."

Harry led Sylvie to the chair and removed the gag from her mouth. "Porter," she said.

"Are you all right?" Harry asked.

"Just great," she smiled weakly. The rope had already begun to dig into her skin and the haphazard looping had nearly cut off the circulation in her hands. Her blouse was torn and her right breast was almost completely exposed. Harry fought the untimely urge to kiss her. "Do you mind if I untie her?" he asked Retson.

"No, no," Retson replied. "I suppose that now that we all understand the seriousness of this situation, ropes will no longer be necessary. I'm sorry, Ms. Dunbar."

Harry undid the knots and allowed the rope to fall slack onto the chair. "I'm sorry for everything, Harry," she said.

"I'm sorry I ever set foot on this crate," he muttered. He addressed Retson. "Now what?"

Retson pursed his lips playfully. "You really should show a bit more respect to a man who has a gun pointed at your head. But that, again as I pointed out, is your juvenile sense of macho. Quaint albeit distasteful. Well, back to the point. You two will now take me off the habitat in one of those delightful little spacetugs."

"We'll do no such thing!" Sylvie cried.

"Then I'm very much afraid I will blast the eyeballs out of the first person who formally refuses my request."

"She withdraws her refusal," Harry answered. "OK. We get you onboard a tug. Then what?"

"You'll appreciate this, Placard. I thought of this on my own. Then, we go to a space shack and we duplicate the shielding accident on a much grander scale."

"You're going to toss a wad of machinery at *Island?*" Harry asked.

"You disappoint me, sir. No, I'm going to send an entire space shack plowing into the habitat."

"But you'll destroy the colony!" Sylvie exclaimed.

Harry and Retson both looked at her in disbelief. Retson waved the gun at her. "Didn't you listen to anything I said when you were in the closet?"

"That's the whole point of his plan," Harry explained.

"Precisely," Retson added. "You two will be my shields until we get to the spaceport. I'll either bribe or force a pilot to take us to the nearest shack. The place will be nearly deserted now, with the crew still onboard the habitat for the celebration. We'll go inside the shack, secure the tie line from the shack to the tug and, full throttle, we'll get our tug to slowly pull the shack toward the colony. We won't need all that much acceleration. Even if the shack crawls into the side of *Island's* shielding, the damage will be beyond repair. The entire colony will slowly suffocate."

"And you, of course, will be spared aboard the tug," Harry smirked.

"The sole survivor," Retson acknowledged. "The pilot will perish in a freak accident shortly before my eventual rescue."

"And what about us?" Sylvie blinked.

"You two will have a bird's-eye view of the entire cataclysmic event. You'll be onboard the shack as it hits!"

Harry turned to Sylvie. "Can he really do that?"

"Sure," she replied. "The shacks have no steering mechanisms. They have small jets that stabilize their position in space but they're just stuck there in orbit. If you send one tumbling, it will tumble. *Island* can't maneuver itself out of the way, either. If you give the shack a good shove in *Island's* direction, it will hit. No doubt about it."

Retson smiled. "All right. Shall we go?"

"Don't you think we're going to look a little conspicuous?"

Harry asked. "She's got rope burns all over her, I look like I've been wrestling with a tractor-trailer and you're carrying a gun!"

"Mr. Poser, right now, people are scurrying about outside like it was the final page of *The Last Days of Pompeii*. Three more oddities are not going to be noticed outside one way or another."

Harry stood quivering before the gunman. "It's Porter!" he yelled.

"I beg your pardon?"

"It's Porter. The name is Harry Porter, not Piker, Piper, Peepers, Pepper, Popper, or Pamper. What's so hard about remembering Porter?"

Retson furrowed his brow. "Well, nothing, I suppose."

"Well remember it! If you're going to kill me, the least you can do is remember my name, goddamn it!"

Retson pushed the gun into Harry's back and pushed him toward the door. "I quite agree. I apologize for all this unprofessionalism. I'm still learning as I go along. Perhaps it would help if we conversed on a first-name basis. You call me Howie and I'll call you Larry."

"It's Harry," Porter muttered, being shoved out the door.

13

"What the hell happened to you folks?" the attendant at the spaceport asked. A bald man whose body showed signs of corroding physical prowess, he eyed Harry and Sylvie with obvious amazement.

"We were all caught in the viewing stands during the pedal plane crash," Retson said glumly. "There was a small stampede, I'm afraid."

The man behind the clear plastic desk puckered his lips and let out a soft whistle. "Heard about that mess. Didn't get down there myself. Someone had to be here to keep an eye on things." He pointed a thumb at his chest. "Got the short straw."

Retson began to shuffle about nervously. This sudden action prompted the attendant to lapse into a businesslike conversational tone. "Now, what can I do for you?"

"My name is Howard Retson," the capitalist explained. "This is Harry Palmer and Ms. Sylvie Dunbar. Palmer and myself are with the Earth delegation and Ms. Dunbar has promised us a tour of your nearest space shack."

The bald man nodded gravely. "Right. I hear things aren't going too well in those meetings you folks are conducting. Will you really close us down?"

Retson lapsed into a crocodile smile. "My dear man, I can see from the sparkle in your eyes that you are an intelligent man. Do we look like the enemy? *Au contraire*, it is Mr. Portle and myself who are spearheading a campaign to save this magnificent structure."

The attendant looked at Harry. "I thought your name was Palmer?"

"It's Porter, actually. Mr. Retson has trouble with names," Harry shrugged.

"Yeah, I had a sister like that," the bald man acknowledged. "Used to get the names of fruit mixed up. You never knew what the hell you were going to get at her house when you asked for Peach melba."

Sirens sounded in the distance.

"Sir . . ." Retson interrupted.

"And forget about her apple grunt!" the attendant continued.

The sirens seemed to grow in volume.

"Sir," Retson continued. "If we are to save your colony, we must get ourselves onto that space shack immediately!"

The attendant stroked his chin with the bony fingers of his left hand. "Well, I'd truly like to help you, but I can't."

"You can't!" Retson said, wild eyed. "You'd refuse members of the Earth delegation passage into space when the fate of your own beloved ecosystem is at stake?"

The man behind the desk screwed up his face into a sour expression. He was obviously beginning to see the chinks in Retson's pompous facade. "It's not exactly all that 'beloved' to me, pal. But, look, I'm not actually refusing you. I have no spacetugs that are operable."

"What do you mean by that?"

"What I mean by that is that most of our tugs are being reserviced right now. There are only two in operating condition and I have no pilots for those. Everyone's in Coms I and II celebrating."

Harry grabbed Sylvie by the arm and sighed in relief. Retson's mind, however, was already several steps down the road. Reaching into his tunic, he pulled out his billfold. He tossed it onto the desk. "There's $6,000 in there. It will go to the first pilot available."

The attendant stared blankly at the billfold and, then, equally as complacent as Retson. "Like I told you, there are no pilots available, mister."

Retson glared at the fellow. "What's your name, sir?"

"Lowell. George Lowell."

"Have you ever piloted a tug, George?"

"Used to. Now I do desk work. High blood pressure."

"Could you be persuaded to board one of those two tugs and take us out of here?"

"Probably not."

"Not for $6,000."

"Definitely not for $6,000. This little trip you're planning could cost me my career in space service."

Retson pulled the laser pistol from beneath the folds of his tunic. "It could also cost you your life."

George gaped at the gun. "I'm not sure I follow all this."

"Your kind never does," Retson remarked sadly. He took the billfold from the desk and repocketed it. "I can remember a time when money talked. Now people are just too lazy to earn their money. They don't care about the pride of possession, the power of high finance. It's that nationalistic move toward welfare that's spread like a cancer down below. Come on, now. Let's hurry. As you can assume from the nervous timbre in my voice, I am quite uncomfortable standing here holding this gun. It could go off at any moment so, if you would be so kind to take us to your ship immediately . . ."

George's eyes whirled around in their sockets. Harry half expected his face to explode. "Yes, sir. Right away, sir. Just stay calm, sir. We wouldn't want any accidents to happen, would we, sir?"

"Kindly desist in your litany of trepidation," Retson advised. "To the ship."

Harry Porter, Sylvie Dunbar, and George Lowell walked nervously through the spaceport. A dapper Howard Retson, gun tucked safely beneath his tunic, strolled several steps behind them.

"What's this old bird want with a spacetug, anyhow?" George hissed in Harry's ear. Harry told him the entire plan, in abbreviated form. George was aghast. "He can't do that!"

"He's doing it," Sylvie replied.

"Are we almost there?" Retson asked, carefully listening to the ever-approaching wail of sirens.

"We just hang a quick right up here," George said. "It's about thirty yards behind the exit door."

The quartet approached the door. A sign reading, "Restricted. Personnel Only" blinked on and off above the door. George swallowed hard and pushed the door open.

A voice cut through the silence. "Hey, what are you doing over there?"

"Jesus," George coughed. "Security."

The foursome turned and watched an elderly security officer jog toward them. "Can't you folks read?" the old man carped. "Let's see your ID cards."

Before he could begin another sentence, Retson calmly removed the pistol from his cloak and fired a charge directly at the running guard. The blast caught him in the neck. A hissing, gurgling noise erupted from the lower half of the old man's face as the skin sizzled under the force of the firepower. The guard raised his hand as if to wrestle the pain away from his face. By the time his hands reached his chin, he was dead. The momentum he had begun before the shot was fired allowed his body to stumble several more steps before it tumbled onto the ground. The steaming corpse rolled to a stop not four feet away from Howard Retson. He turned to his three hostages. "The best years of his life were already behind him," he rationalized.

Sylvie stifled a sob. Harry held her hand tightly and, approaching the boarding ramp, led her toward the ship. George walked silently at Harry's side. Retson brought up the rear. "Prepare to cast off," Retson bellowed joyfully. *Island One* is about to become one with the cosmos!"

He closed the tug's hatch on both the habitat and the sirens, now screaming very close by.

14

George eased the spacetug into the docking slot of the space shack. "Now, ease in the tie line," Retson ordered.

George sat at the small bridge of the ship, a mass of dials and levers not unlike those found on an Earth airliner. He reached over and pulled down a small handle. A red light began flashing on the console. As time passed, the flashes grew more and more leisurely. Soon, they ceased altogether. "Done," George said.

"Fine," Retson smiled. "Now, Parker. Tie Mr. Lowell to his seat, if you will. Use the wire in the corner."

Harry looked at Retson. He looked at Retson's handgun. He did as he was told. "Wonderful. Now, if you and Ms. Dunbar will be so kind as to accompany me inside the shack, I will connect the tie line and bid you bon voyage."

Harry clenched his fists at his side. Retson took note of the movement. He laughed softly to himself and waved the gun. Sylvie made a sudden movement in Retson's direction. She rushed across the cabin so swiftly that her attack caught both Harry and Retson off guard. "I won't go," she shrieked.

Her lunge for the gunman proved ill-timed. Catching her by her hair, Retson halted her motion. He pulled her face toward his. It appeared as if he was going to kiss the girl. Instead, he held her head immobile and raised the gun with his other hand. He placed the gun in her mouth and smiled. He removed the gun, bringing it smashing down onto the side of her head. Sylvie whimpered like a small child. Her temple began to swell immediately. She slid down onto the floor, still sobbing. Harry's insides tensed. He fought to remain sane. He merely glared at Retson. He knew, at that moment, that he would either kill this man or die trying.

"Enough nonsense," Retson said, staring at the girl. "Get on your feet. Mr. Portage, carry her onboard if you have to, but get her out of my sight."

Harry helped Sylvie stand. Gun to his back, he led her off the tug and into the winding corridors of the space shack.

331

Retson barked directions from behind. Harry stared at the dimly lit corridors. He couldn't be sure, but he thought that this was the same shack he had visited a few days earlier. He would have asked Sylvie for confirmation, but she was in no condition to speak.

Retson led the pair to the inner core. On the observation scaffold he gazed down at the construction area. Below, the tie line stood outstretched, its metallic claw begging for the gift of prey. Retson giggled like a schoolboy. "I've done it. My goodness, I've done it."

He faced Harry and Sylvie. "But now, I must fulfill my promise to you both. I did guarantee you orchestra seats for my little performance, did I not? Well, let's see. Hmmmm. Into this room with you. Come on, the both of you."

Harry found himself being forced into a room with a large window facing the construction pit. Sylvie was pushed in directly behind them. Retson motioned them to move toward the wall furthest from the doorway. "Just stay put for a moment, dear hearts. I wouldn't want you to injure yourselves prematurely. This will only take a minute. I'm about to lock your portal, permanently."

Retson slammed the metal door shut. Harry shielded his eyes with one hand and Sylvie's with the other as Retson fired a blast at the door's lock from the outside. He welded the lock solid. Retson peeked into the window and waved farewell to his hostages. Sylvie dropped to her knees and began to sob. Harry watched her emotionlessly. He took out a handkerchief and stuffed it into her hand. "Here," he barked. "Wipe your face."

Sylvie blinked and did as she was told. Harry walked around the room frantically. "Now, look. We're going to get off this thing one way or another. So just stop crying and pay attention."

Harry took off his shoe. "I never carry more than I can afford to lose." He produced the vibrating lock pick he had used so well in his attempts at breaking into Anson Young's apartment building. "I could have tried opening this lock here but Einstein has fused it shut."

He stared at the lock pick. "Did you know that the guy who developed this was a physicist? Yeah. No shit. A real egghead. I'm still not sure how this works. Speed of the vibration and the angle. This thing gets pretty hot if you use it for an extended period of time."

He walked up to the door. "One time we had to use these

332

things to get out of a cargo hold of an airplane. During the war. Four of us locked in. We had to get out the emergency hatch. The plane was pretty banged up. Artillery had jammed the door handle. Had to go after the hinges. Burned the shit out of my hand. Yes indeed. Burned the holy hell out of my hand."

Harry began to chatter. He knelt next to the metal door-frame and began to angle the pick into the small crack near the two massive hinges. "Now, if this works, we're going to have to pull a dangerous stunt, kiddo. You're going to have to be quick."

The small room filled with the odor of burning flesh and hot metal. "I'm going to try to push this door out. I'll dive through and run to the right. You follow me and run to the left. Hopefully, hawkeye will follow me. The first room you get to, lock yourself in. Don't open the door for anybody. I don't care if the Pope knocks on the door and says he's looking for lost sinners. Tell him to try another door."

"Do you know what you're doing, Harry?" Sylvie asked, dabbing her eyes. "I mean, do you really think we're going to be all right?"

"Sure," Harry said. "I wouldn't be burning my hand off otherwise. I had the whole boat ride over to plan this. You're lucky I have a good memory. Not only will we get out of here in one piece but so will your precious habitat."

Sylvie crawled over to Harry. Harry watched his hand burn from the heat generated by the pick. "Oh, Harry," she said, putting a hand on his cheek.

He looked up at her, an expression of total pain flashing across his features for a brief second. "Just stay put. I'm not doing this for you. This is business."

"But . . ."

He concentrated on the door. "Let's get one thing straight. I never did anything to hurt you. I never lied to you. I was always straight. You were never honest with me. You were never straight. I didn't deserve what I got. That's how things stand."

She began to sob.

Harry pulled the pick from the second hinge. "And cut out the crying."

Harry moved to the far side of the room. He pulled out a chair with coasters on its legs from beneath a cumbersome console. "Help me with this," he muttered. Harry pulled a large desk from a wall. The two captives lifted the desk onto

333

the chair. The chair squeaked from the excess weight. "Let's hope this is strong enough," he said.

"Stand behind me and get ready to either run or catch me when I bounce." Harry aimed the desk at the door. Bracing himself against the back wall, he prepared to launch the battering ram. He pushed himself free and ran crazily toward the hatch, pushing the desk before him. The desk smashed into the metal doorframe. Harry was stopped cold from the impact. The desk had rebounded into his stomach, knocking the wind out of him.

He stared at the door, tears welling in his eyes. The door creaked softly. It flopped open with a resounding crash. They were free.

"Run your ass off," Harry said, jumping through the hatch. He grabbed Sylvie by the hand and pulled her out after him. The two stood on the catwalk outside. He pushed her away from him. "Don't look back."

Harry saw a small slice of wall some two feet to his right turn white hot. He glanced quickly at the factory floor below. Retson had spotted Harry and was aiming his gun a second time. "Portent!" he cried. "I'll kill you for this!"

Harry ran across the catwalk. "Don't put book on it yet, sport."

Retson fired another round at Harry. Harry had already run halfway around the circular catwalk. He recalled his panicked flight during his first visit and now was putting his memory to the test. A shot zipped by his shoulder, burning a neat hole in the wall behind him. Harry hung a quick right down a hallway. It looked familiar. Then again, all these hallways looked alike. The laser barrage ceased. Harry surmised that Retson had tucked the gun away for the time being and had begun the momentous trudge back up the stairs leading from the factory pit to the observation deck. That gave Harry approximately ninety seconds to do what had to be done. He counted to himself. Eighty seconds.

He ran frantically down a corridor. Sixty seconds. It had to be one of the doors nearest the catwalk. He tried one door. It was locked. He could have sworn that *that* was the one. Panic welled within him. Perhaps he was wrong even to consider this plan. Fifty seconds. He ran to the end of a corridor. Was this where he had eluded the security guard the first time aboard? Forty seconds. Retson would almost be up those stairs by now. Thank God the old duffer was out of shape.

He tried another door. An empty room greeted him. Damn it. Thirty seconds. That door had to be around here somewhere. Twenty seconds. He only had time for one last effort. He ran down a hallway and came to a fork. He ran to the right. The corridor sparked a memory. He ran for a familiar looking door. He pushed it open and darted inside. Five seconds.

He shut the door behind him and locked it. Three seconds. He had done it. He was in the control room. He ran to the panel nearest the wall-sized window. Outside on the opposite side of the circular catwalk, he saw Retson reach the top of the stairway, breathing heavily. Some thirty yards across the rim, the businessman waved his gun in the air and shouted for Harry. Harry clenched his jaw. He remembered the expression on Hawkins's face at the moment of impact, the thunderous demise of Safian, the surprised look on the elderly guard's face, the bellboy's eternally open eyes, the sound of the gun hitting Sylvie's forehead. Harry ignored Retson and concentrated on the control room panel before him.

"SEPARATION."

Ignoring all the gradual stages leading up to that single control, he lunged for it. He pulled down a small lever and pounded on an adjacent button. Sirens exploded. Red lights flashed hysterically all around the control room. Retson ran along the catwalk, frantically. Sweat poured from his face. "Potent! You bastard!" he bellowed. "You can't do this to me. I'm too close. I'll kill you. I'll destroy you and your colony."

Retson froze. The very fiber of the station seemed to come to life. A thunderous creaking sound sliced through the air. Retson's face turned white. The station began to rumble. Retson looked up and spotted Harry in the control room. He drew his gun and ran for the glass panel. Harry backed away from the window.

If Retson managed to squeeze off a shot, Harry would surely die as the shack halved itself. Retson ran up to the window cackling wildly. His gray hair was disheveled. He bit his lips until they bled. He took aim. Harry gaped at the gun. Sirens blared. Lights flashed. Retson laughed.

He didn't fire.

The space shack began to separate. At first, a small black crack appeared behind Retson's head on the opposite wall. A black fissure studded with stars. Retson howled in horror.

With an olympian roar, the air inside the shack was sucked out into the vacuum of space. In the midst of the man-made maelstrom outside the control room, Retson hung desperately onto the catwalk directly in front of Harry's window. Within seconds, the fissure had become colossal. Retson inhaled whatever air he could. Still affixed to the catwalk, he hung alone in space.

His eyes were focused on Harry. A glimmer of sunlight appeared in the open section of the shack. The sun focused on Retson. As the raw heat bathed the killer in its glow, the clothing began to disintegrate in small sections. Small bubbles appeared on the man's skin and arms. Harry watched in horror as the air bubbles burst. The body outside the window took on almost surreal proportions, ever changing, ever corroding. The pressure within Retson's form being greater than the pressure without caused the rupturing of several internal organs. The body began to ooze fleshy debris. Harry backed away from the window. He pushed the lever forward. Sirens sounded. Lights flashed. Slowly the space shack reclosed. The interior sector was repressurized slowly. The wailing and the strobe effects ceased.

Harry slid onto a plush seat and closed his eyes.

He knew that Retson would always be there.

15

Harry sat in the communications center. On the viewscreen before him, the face of Leonard Golden nodded appreciatively. "A fine job, Harry. I couldn't have done better myself . . . well, not *much* better anyway."

"Thanks, Lennie," Harry replied. "The whole thing wasn't too melodramatic for you?"

"Not a bit," Golden said, actually grinning. "And the tremendous irony involved has really hit the intelligensia down here. After all that trouble involved in catching the killer and saving the habitat to have the government close down *Island One* anyhow. It's caused quiet an uproar."

"Well," Harry sighed. "The president didn't have too much

of a choice. This place did look like Dodge City there for a while. Not exactly great publicity for a reelection year."

"Yeah, well, our subscriptions have quadrupled during the past four weeks. Your day-to-day account on the closing of the colony has made you a star. Harry, my boy, people are talking movies, video series, the works. Why, there are even a few TV networks down here who'd like to see your homely face in front of their cameras as an anchorman."

"Remind me to buy sunglasses when I get home," Harry said, scratching his nose with a bandaged hand.

"Seriously, Harry, we're all proud of you. How are things going up there?"

Harry offered a noncommital expression. "Well, my bags are all packed. The last shuttle leaves today. Only a handful of people still onboard. Mostly maintenance and a few die-hards. Vallory is still up here."

"How's your lady friend?"

Harry stiffened slightly. "I wouldn't know. I haven't seen her since the space shack."

Golden nodded. "Sorry, Harry."

"Those things happen." He looked out the window of the communications center. The vast strips of land before him glistened in the reflected sunlight. "You know, despite everything that's happened up here, I think it's a mistake to shut this place down. It just doesn't *look* right deserted. This habitat was built by people *for* people. Its job is to work for people. They shouldn't kill it just because of one or two . . ."

"You running for governor of the habitat or something?"

Harry laughed softly. "Not me. It's a thankless job."

"If it makes you feel any better," Golden said, "it looks like the colony's closing may have backfired on our presidential hopeful. NASA's stirred up holy hell because of it. And your stories actually helped their cause. You made the place sound real. You showed how the people worked to keep it going. And, to a nation of Monday morning quarterbacks weaned on silicone stories, that was a welcome jolt of electricity. That NASA guy onboard, whatshisname, Frantz?"

"Yeah."

"He's scored quite a few points. He thinks that, in a year or two, maybe with another president, the habitat can be resurrected."

"But in the interim, a lot of work will die up here, Lenny. Some systems may be damaged beyond repair."

"Like you said, Harry. Things happen. Well, my phone bill

is getting as high as your colony. Have a safe trip back and ring me when you're rested."

Harry hung up the phone and returned to his hotel. For a hero, he felt pretty awful. He phoned the front desk for a bellhop. A few minutes later, he was in an electric cart and heading for the spaceport. He took one last look at the perfectly designed homes and parks of this city in space. He thought of what he was going home to. Yellow air and swearing taxi drivers and a wise-ass home computer unit. He'd have to buy himself a dog when he got back.

Maybe two.

The cart pulled up to the spaceport. Harry loaded his luggage onto a handcart and pushed the cart through the nearly deserted terminal. A familiar figure came puffing into view. Much to his delight, Harry ran, almost literally, into the wheezing figure of Dr. Paul Harper. As Harry's handcart clunked into the tiny scientist's, he let out a small groan. "Sorry."

"My fault entirely," Harper said, quickly backing his cart away. "I was daydreaming. I never was very good at handling these things. I never owned a bicycle on Earth, either."

Harry walked alongside the man. "I think we're headed toward the same gate."

"Logical deduction," Harper smiled.

"Are you sorry to leave?"

"I don't know," Harper said. "I suppose I have very mixed feelings. In one sense, I am returning home. In another sense, I am heading for an alien landscape, away from my home. I certainly wish I could decide how I feel about this place. It would make sleeping at night much easier."

Harry nodded. The two men approached the ramp leading to the final shuttle. "Go ahead onboard," Harry said. "I'll load your luggage on the conveyor belt."

"I'll save you a seat."

"Fine." Harry placed the luggage on the moving sidewalk leading into the bowel of the ship. He watched the bags disappear into the metal hull. He turned and gazed through the terminal's glass walls at the topsy-turvy landscape outside. A pang of loneliness shot through him like an arrow. He would have liked to have stayed a little longer. He regretted leaving, but his regret was not a solid one. It was one of those ambiguous sensations that wrestled a man's spirit to the ground every so often. It was a sense of missing things you had never seen, places you had yet to visit. It was longing

338

for people you had never met. It was a regret that fantasy had never superseded reality. It was a fear of the quiet desperation of approaching middle age.

A soft touch on his elbow brought him back into the terminal. "Harry?"

He turned to find Sylvie at his side. "Uh, hello," he said, faltering.

She wore a small bandage on her forehead. "Thank you for the flowers," she smiled.

"It was nothing."

"Nothing? Flowers every day for two weeks? Three of my nurses came down with hay fever."

"Yeah, well," Harry said, smirking, "I was a little bit hard on you that day in the shack."

"I deserved it."

"That's true," Harry shrugged. "Are you on this shuttle?"

Sylvie shook her head. "No. We're staying."

Harry looked at her, not comprehending. "Come again?"

"A few of us are staying."

"That's illegal."

"Since when have you ever worried about breaking the law?" she laughed. "Russ and I and a dozen or so others are going to keep the place running until the government comes to its senses. We should be able to do it. Keep the plants alive, the agricylinder going, things like that."

She took Harry by the hand. He looked into her eyes. "So," she said, "I just wanted to say good-bye and thank you. We were wrong to use you the way we did."

Harry bent forward and kissed her on the forehead. "It was a pleasure being used . . . now beat it. Your husband is probably worried that you'll run off with me." He peered down her blouse. "Or does he have you bugged."

Sylvie pushed him away. "Bastard," she laughed.

"Bitch," he replied.

He watched her turn and walk away. Before walking out of the terminal, she turned and waved one last time. He gave her a mock salute. He memorized every detail, every movement as she departed. He realized he'd never set eyes on her again. He walked onboard the spaceship feeling as solid as a drum.

He sat down next to Harper. The old man stared straight ahead as the ship left the colony behind. "I suppose we're both leaving a good deal of ourselves aboard the colony, eh?"

"I suppose so," Harry said. "What a waste." As the shuttlecraft made its way to the half-way station, he tried to convince himself that *Island*'s closing was only a temporary set-back. After all, it had been founded on a lie. Maybe next time, with a more honest approach . . .

Harper seemed to sense Harry's inner turmoil. "You'll go back one day," he said casually.

Harry shook his head back and forth. "I don't think so."

"No, you're young enough. People will return to that colony someday. The craft will be repopulated and its work will continue. The people of Earth will demand it."

"Yeah," Harry agreed. "You can take just so much chewable Earth air."

Harper turned to gaze out the porthole to his right. He emitted a small chuckle. "My goodness. I am getting quite good at prognostication."

"Say what?"

"People will return to *Island* and it will be quite a bit sooner than I had anticipated."

"What's out there?" Harry asked.

"Why don't you look yourself?" Harper said. He struggled away from the porthole and began rummaging through his carry-on bag. Harry gazed out the window. In the distance, a small fleet of spacetugs were heading back toward the colony. "The tugs are coming back? It's only been four weeks since the place was closed."

Harper returned to the window with a small pair of binoculars. "They're not *returning*," he said, peering through the glass. "I've never seen ships like that before."

He handed Harry the glasses. Harry took one look and began laughing. "They're not ours."

Harper joined Harry in his laughter. "I do believe when we reach the way station, I shall ask for a return ticket immediately."

Harry held the glasses to his eyes once again, giggling giddily. The dream was not dead. The habitat would continue. As Vallory had once said, it was beyond the whims of one government. "Well, before you go back," he advised the elderly man at his side. "I'll find out how to say 'think tank' in Chinese."

"I'll do the best I can," Harper said, nestling comfortably back into his seat.

Harry held the binoculars in his hands for the rest of the trip home.

ABOUT THE AUTHOR

ED NAHA was abandoned by his gypsy parents while still a tot in a deserted Bohack supermarket parking lot in Elizabeth, New Jersey, a town famous for its thugs. Raised by wolves near the frozen-food loading door, young Naha immediately distinguished himself in the literary world by stalking several well-known authors and then gnawing on their legs while his unsuspecting victims attempted to purchase frozen TV dinners. As his creative juices began to flow, Naha found himself arrested and thrown in jail for long periods of time. In New Jersey, it is illegal to do ANYthing with one's creative juices . . . let alone having them flow in public.

Since his release from prison, Naha has gained fame by penning such classic works as *War and Peace, Crime and Punishment, The Greek Way, Mein Kampf* and *The Tell-Tale Heart.* Unfortunately, at present, his fame rests on the fact that, without exception, all of these works were written previously by other authors. This does not faze the budding genius. "Why tamper with a winning formula?" he is often heard to mutter. Today, the genius lives in a small ranch house located in Elizabeth, New Jersey, outside a frozen-food loading door. He is a bachelor, living with his parents, Lobo and Snowball.

But alas, most of this is unfortunately fiction. In truth, Ed Naha is a New Jersey-born writer living in New York City. Currently the senior writer at *Future* and *Starlog* magazines, two publications dealing with both science fiction and science fact, he has also penned both fiction and non-fiction pieces for *Viva, The Village Voice, Rolling Stone, Crawdaddy, New Ingenue, Playboy, Genesis, Swank, Gallery, More* and *Circus.* He is a contributing editor at *Oui* with a by-lined column appearing monthly. He is the author of two books, *Horrors: From Screen to Scream* and *The Rock Encyclopedia.* Formerly employed by CBS as a writer, publicist and A&R representative, he is the producer of the long-playing record *Gene Roddenberry: Inside Star Trek.*

OUT OF THIS WORLD!

That's the only way to describe Bantam's great series of science fiction classics. These space-age thrillers are filled with terror, fancy and adventure and written by America's most renowned writers of science fiction. Welcome to outer space and have a good trip!

☐ 13179	**THE MARTIAN CHRONICLES** by Ray Bradbury	$2.25
☐ 13695	**SOMETHING WICKED THIS WAY COMES** by Ray Bradbury	$2.25
☐ 14323	**STAR TREK: THE NEW VOYAGES** by Culbreath & Marshak	$2.25
☐ 13260	**ALAS BABYLON** by Pat Frank	$2.25
☐ 14124	**A CANTICLE FOR LEIBOWITZ** by Walter Miller, Jr.	$2.50
☐ 11175	**THE FEMALE MAN** by Joanna Russ	$1.75
☐ 13312	**SUNDIVER** by David Brin	$1.95
☐ 12957	**CITY WARS** by Dennis Palumbo	$1.95
☐ 11662	**SONG OF THE PEARL** by Ruth Nichols	$1.75
☐ 13766	**THE FARTHEST SHORE** by Ursula LeGuin	$2.25
☐ 13594	**THE TOMBS OF ATUAN** by Ursula LeGuin	$2.25
☐ 13767	**A WIZARD OF EARTHSEA** by Ursula LeGuin	$2.25
☐ 13563	**20,000 LEAGUES UNDER THE SEA** by Jules Verne	$1.75
☐ 12655	**FANTASTIC VOYAGE** by Isaac Asimov	$1.95

Buy them at your local bookstore or use this handy coupon for ordering:

FANTASY AND SCIENCE FICTION FAVORITES

Bantam brings you the recognized classics as well as the current favorites in fantasy and science fiction. Here you will find the beloved Conan books along with recent titles by the most respected authors in the genre.

Bantam Book Catalog

Here's your up-to-the-minute listing of over 1,400 titles by your favorite authors.

This illustrated, large format catalog gives a description of each title. For your convenience, it is divided into categories in fiction and non-fiction—gothics, science fiction, westerns, mysteries, cookbooks, mysticism and occult, biographies, history, family living, health, psychology, art.

So don't delay—take advantage of this special opportunity to increase your reading pleasure.

Just send us your name and address and 50¢ (to help defray postage and handling costs).

THIS BOOK IS A GOLD MINE!

How to Make Money in Coins Right Now is *the* source for coin collectors, as well as investors. Written by coin authority Scott Travers, seen on ABC's *Good Morning America*, CNN, and CNBC, this book reveals *all* the secrets of coin pricing.

- What to sell today to your advantage
- Tax-slashing strategies
- How to distinguish between legitimate business practices and marketing gimmicks
- Special chapter on "collectible coins" produced by the U.S. Mint
- And much more!

HOUSE OF COLLECTIBLES
SERVING COLLECTORS FOR MORE THAN THIRTY-FIVE YEARS

TURN YOUR PENNIES INTO PROFITS!